Kennedy Stern
Christian Suspense
Books 7-9

Abridged

Secluded

Captivated

Alana Terry

Note: The views of the characters in this novel do not necessarily reflect the views of the author.

The characters in this book are fictional. Any resemblance to real persons is coincidental.

No part of this book may be reproduced in any form (electronic, audio, print, film, etc.) without the author's written consent.

Abridged Copyright © 2017 Alana Terry.

Secluded Copyright © 2017 Alana Terry

Captivated Copyright © 2018 Alana Terry

Abridged

Alana Terry

CHAPTER 1

"HEY, SORRY I'M LATE." Kennedy gave her roommate a quick hug and glanced around the foyer of the church. "How's everything been going here?"

Willow ran her hand through her bleached hair. "Aside from the constant fighting, you mean?"

"Who's fighting? The kids from youth group?" Kennedy glanced around at a few of the teens who were helping set up for the upcoming Truth Warriors conference.

Willow fingered the neon-green tips of her hair. "Pastor Carl's bringing in nearly a thousand men to talk about the definition of *biblical masculinity*. You get one more guess to tell me who's making the loudest fuss about it around here."

"Nick?"

Willow smiled. "I swear if I weren't so in love with that man, I'd have duct taped his mouth shut by now."

"What's he saying? Or do I really want to know?"

"Oh, it's nothing that would surprise you. The typical. How chauvinistic it is to have a conference like this when it's the patriarchal society that's kept women oppressed as sex toys and domestic slaves for millennia." She rolled her eyes, accentuating the green eyeliner that perfectly matched her hair. "The funny thing is I agree with just about everything he's saying. At least on principle. But he's taking it all out on Carl, who might be a little old-school, but everybody knows he's the most kind-hearted, warm, fuzzy, teddy bear of a Christian you'll ever meet. There's not a mean-spirited bone in that man's body." She shook her head again. "Well, you know how worked up Nick gets."

"Yeah. Where is he now?" Kennedy asked.

Willow glanced down the hall. "Just keep your ears open. I'm sure you'll hear him soon enough."

As if on cue, Nick and Carl emerged from the sound room behind the sanctuary.

"And that's something else," Nick was saying. "You've got to open your eyes and see what this is doing to the community. You've got protestors threatening to march, maybe even block the entrances. You've got the police telling the church to tighten security and expecting St. Margaret's to foot the bill. You've even got the college kids around Cambridge so worked up they're writing their op-eds. I mean, even if you did feel strongly that this conference would be a benefit to the men who come, aren't you concerned about the way it's putting the church in such a negative light in the public eye?"

Kennedy and Willow exchanged smiles. Listening to Nick argue theology or politics with Pastor Carl was so common it was hardly more than background noise.

Kennedy glanced around, trying to figure out where she and her roommate might be needed. The girls were juniors now, back on campus after a wonderfully relaxing summer off. Kennedy's course load was the lightest it had ever been, only eighteen credits. In addition to her science classes, Kennedy was taking two English courses, including one in dystopian literature. Her schedule opened up time for her to get more involved in church, like helping with the after-school Good News Club and volunteering at St. Margaret's for special events like this conference.

Her roommate Willow was at the church now even more than Kennedy was, but of course her flourishing romance with the youth pastor had more to do with that than anything else. Still, it was amazing to watch how fast Willow's faith had matured. Kennedy didn't like to admit it, even to herself, but she often had to combat unexpected feelings of envy. Not just because Willow had found Nick. Anybody who spent more than two minutes with them knew they were a perfect match. In spite of the pain Kennedy had experienced in her own love life, it was difficult to begrudge her friend that happiness.

What made her jealous was how real Willow's relationship with Christ had become in just a few short months. Before her conversion, Willow's idea of fun on a Friday night involved multiple parties, multiple partners, and multiple illicit substances, but now she would invite Nick over to their dorm room where he'd sit in Willow's oversized beanbag chair strumming his guitar, and the two would sing worship songs before playing one of Willow's shooter games on her PC and ending the night in prayer.

Kennedy had never seen anyone change so dramatically. Willow was still just as outlandishly dressed, just as free-spirited with her hair and jewelry. She was just as committed to her veganism and yoga and classic rock music as she'd been before her salvation, but there was something else now, too. A depth, a maturity that made her seem at times like an entirely different person. Willow had developed a deep love of the Bible, especially the poetry books of the Old Testament. She spent as much time in Isaiah and Psalms as Kennedy had all semester with her reading list for her lit courses. Kennedy wouldn't be surprised if by Christmas break, she'd be the one asking Willow questions about prayer or worship or witnessing instead of the other way around.

"... not trying to pick a fight here." Carl's booming voice interrupted Kennedy's thoughts. She hadn't followed all of his argument with Nick, but apparently the two were far from any type of resolution. "But you have to realize that what I mean when I say *biblical masculinity* has nothing to do with what feminists talk about when they say *misogyny* or *patriarchy*. Is it true that some men and some entire church movements over the centuries have twisted certain passages of Scripture to keep women subdued? Unfortunately, yes. Does that mean that we throw out the doctrine of the inerrancy of Scripture and cut and paste the verses in the Bible that are acceptable to us in the twenty-first century? Absolutely not."

Nick followed Carl toward the hall, his blond dreadlocks streaking behind him like a bed of undulating snakes. "You're not listening to me. I'm not saying we throw out certain parts of Scripture. I'm just saying that there were undeniable biases in Paul's day that may have colored what he wrote."

"Oh, yeah?" Carl turned around. He'd lost about fifteen pounds since he was diagnosed with diabetes. His wife told Kennedy in confidence that he was "as prone to mood swings as a four-teen-year-old girl" now that he was forced to such a strict diet. When Kennedy noted the annoyance in Carl's generally good-natured tone, she wondered if Sandy was right. "So tell me, Mr. Theologian. Tell me just how it is that you know with so much certainty which verses are God-breathed and inspired and which are simply guidelines meant to be followed in Paul's day but thrown out in ours. Because I'm sure itching to know how the Holy Spirit's revealed all this to you without breathing a hint of it to the rest of us who've spent our lives studying it." Carl brushed past Kennedy and Willow without looking at either of them.

Nick was nearly jogging to keep up his pace. "If the Bible's true for all people and at all times, then why don't you make every single woman who steps foot into St. Margaret's wear a shawl or handkerchief or other kind of head covering?"

"I don't have time for this." Carl waved his hand in the air. "I've got the press hounding me about this stupid protest, and I've got to get the church ready to receive a thousand men this weekend. To top it all off, my sugar levels are all over the map. I took my insulin but haven't had time to eat lunch yet thanks to all your incessant ..." He turned around in the hallway. His shoulders drooped, and Kennedy noticed a hit of gray around his temples she'd never seen before. "Could we just finish this debate another time? I'm asking you as a friend in the Lord. Please?"

Nick sighed. "Ok. I'm sorry. I get so worked up over this kind of stuff."

Carl put his hand on Nick's shoulder. "I know, son. I know. And that's the way God wired you. I can appreciate that. It's just like Ecclesiastes says though, there's a time and place for everything. Understand?"

Nick nodded.

Carl extended his hand. "Brothers?"

"Yeah. Brothers."

Carl excused himself, and Nick turned around and offered Willow a sheepish smile. He walked up to her and pecked her on the cheek. "How's my girl?"

"First of all, I'm nobody's girl." Willow grinned and swept one of his unruly dreadlocks out of his face. "Other than that, I'm fine. But are you sure you want to get Carl so worked up? I mean, he's on blood-sugar medication and heaven knows what else. You need to be careful, or you'll give the poor man a heart attack."

Nick didn't quite meet Willow's gaze. "Who, Carl? He's strong. He can take it. He's been handling me for years."

Willow kissed him on the cheek. "Just remember your manners, all right?"

He took her hand and squeezed it. "Will do." He nodded to Kennedy. "How's it going?"

"Pretty good." Kennedy didn't know why she felt uneasy. Carl and Nick fought all the time. It was one of the great mysteries of St. Margaret's Church how the two of them got along well enough to work together in the first place, although according to Sandy there was a long, complicated back story that allowed each of them to overlook so many of their inherent differences.

"You ready to get to work?" Nick asked.

Kennedy nodded. "That's what we're here for. How's it going so far?"

Nick looked around. "Great. At the current rate, we should be ready for the conference in about six months." He let out a laugh that nobody else shared then cleared his throat. "Ok, how do you both feel about stacking chairs in the sanctuary?"

Kennedy glanced down at her tennis shoes, which were in perfect working condition. "Sounds good."

"All right." Nick gave Willow one more light kiss. "I'm gonna go talk to Carl."

Willow wrapped her arms around him to lock him in place. "Give him some time. He's under a lot of stress, and you can't blame him for that. The media's treating this whole conference like it's some convention for wife beaters or Klan members. And on top of that he's got you to deal with. Let him cool down a little."

Nick nuzzled his face into her hair. "I'm not going over there to argue. I'm going to apologize." He laughed at Willow's incredulous expression. "What? You don't think I'm capable of saying *I'm sorry?*"

"Oh, sure you are." She laughed. "I can hear it right now. *Carl, I'm sorry that I chose such a bad time to bring up the fact that this conference you've spent the past half year planning is actually nothing more than a bunch of misogynists getting together to come up with new ways to keep women subjugated like they've been throughout human history."*

Nick let out a chuckle that didn't sound as convincing as he probably hoped it would be. "No, it'll be a real apology. Promise."

Willow rolled her eyes. "If you say so. Don't let me stand in your way."

After a few more kisses and endearing exchanges, Nick made his way down the hall toward Carl's office.

"Come on." Willow took Kennedy by the elbow and adjusted her long-feathered earrings. "Those chairs aren't going to stack themselves."

CHAPTER 2

"Is this about as high as you think we should go?" Cocking her head to the side, Willow stared at a column of chairs the girls had pushed against the wall. "Dude, I really shouldn't have worn these shoes."

Kennedy glanced down at Willow's open-toed platform sandals. "Think you'd be more comfortable if you just took them off?"

Willow shrugged. "It's all right. My own fault, really, my punishment for being vain." She smiled to show Kennedy she wasn't serious. "Ok, should we start the ones on the other side now?"

Kennedy didn't want to admit how tired she was. Apparently, reading books all day and working in science labs didn't require that much muscle. She wasn't built for pushing, stacking, and moving hundreds of chairs in a single afternoon. Although she appreciated Nick's commitment to gender equality, she wouldn't have complained if he handed this job over to a bunch of the teen boys from his youth group.

She sat in one of the chairs. "I just need a short break."

Willow plopped down beside her even though Kennedy was sure her roommate could keep up this kind of manual work for hours. Who would have thought yoga built up such impressive endurance? Of course, Willow labored all summer around her parents' farm in rural Alaska. Kennedy had spent the first several weeks of her vacation at the Winters', learning how to milk goats, catch unruly piglets, and muck out chicken stalls. It was no wonder Willow was so fit and toned.

Kennedy leaned back in the chair she was sitting in, panting slightly. In a way, it actually felt good to be breathless for a reason other than an imminent panic attack. After her month in Alaska with Willow, Kennedy had flown back to the East Coast where her parents rented a little cottage so they could spend the rest of the summer in Cape Cod. Her mom and dad needed a break from their missionary work and overseas printing business, and Kennedy was thrilled for some time off her grueling academic schedule. While at the Cape, her parents found a psychiatrist who decided to write Kennedy a prescription for her anxiety. The medicine could take quite a while to fully incorporate into her system, and they'd already had to adjust the dose a couple times, but so far Kennedy was hopeful the worst of her PTSD was behind her. What really convinced her parents to take her to the psychiatrist wasn't the panic though, but the depression she'd fallen into after what happened last spring. Kennedy was glad that the medicine allowed her to get out of bed each day. She was thankful the drugs helped her progress past the stage where walking from one room to another was enough to sap all the energy out of her system, but in a way, she wondered if she shouldn't rely on her pills so much. Ironically, Dominic was the only Christian she'd been close to who was against prescription meds for things like anxiety or depression, and it was losing him that dragged her to the point where she had to accept a little psychiatric help.

"Should we go find Nick?" Willow asked.

"Hmm?" Kennedy had been busy brooding and wasn't paying attention.

"I said should we find Nick? See if he has another job for us to tackle for a little while? My feet are killing me. I could use a change of pace, and it looks like you could, too."

Kennedy grinned. "How about I give you my shoes and cheer for you while you finish?"

Willow stood. "Come on. Let's go see what he's up to. If I find out he's goaded Carl into another one of his arguments ..."

"I think Carl's just as guilty as Nick when it comes to that."

Willow shrugged. "I guess you're probably right. Well, let's make sure neither one is misbehaving, then."

They walked down the hallway, and Kennedy noticed Willow limping slightly in her platform sandals. They slowed their pace when they got closer to Carl's office and heard Nick's angry voice on the other side of the closed door.

"... bunch of wife-abusing, fundamentalist pigs."

Kennedy and Willow glanced at each other. Unfortunately, Kennedy couldn't say she was surprised to find the two had resumed their fight.

"You know that's not fair, and you know that's not what we stand for." Carl's voice was steady but just as elevated as Nick's.

"Of course you won't admit that's what you stand for. But what are you doing to change the status quo? What are you doing to elevate the women in our church to their proper place? Do you know how long it's been since you've called on a woman to offer the opening prayer? The opening prayer! It's not like you'd be asking her to preach from the Bible, heaven forbid. Or are you going to tell me that women are barred from praying in church?"

"I never said that."

"No, but you spend so much time focusing on the verses that say women should be silent in church, that they shouldn't teach or hold positions of authority. Have you forgotten all the women Paul addresses at the end of his epistles, women like Priscilla or Lydia who were just as involved in ministry as the most active of men in their day? Or maybe you've forgotten his instructions that when a woman prophesies in church, she should do it with her head covered. You don't seem to care what women do with their hair these days. You're fine saying that was just a cultural suggestion for the people of ancient Corinth, but Paul obviously didn't have a problem with a prophetess addressing the congregation. So she can prophesy, speak the very words of God, but she can't be one of the ushers who stands in the aisle to collect the offering basket?"

Kennedy shifted her weight uneasily. "Maybe we should come back later," she mumbled.

Willow sighed, her disappointment etched clearly in her expression. "I hate when he gets so worked up. I mean, I see what he's doing, but this isn't the way to change anybody's mind." She shook her head.

Kennedy took Willow gently by the arm. "Come on. We've had our break. Let's see how many more chairs we can stack up."

Willow glanced once more at the door to Carl's office. Carl's reply was too low to hear, but Nick's response was even more vehement than before. "You keep Willow out of this."

Both girls stopped and turned around.

Nick's voice was so loud Kennedy was surprised the walls of the hallway weren't vibrating. "This has nothing to do with who I do or don't plan to marry."

"Marry?" Kennedy stared at her roommate.

Willow fingered her feathered earring. "That's not supposed to be common knowledge yet."

Kennedy couldn't believe what she was hearing.

"I told you to keep her out of this," Nick yelled. "This isn't about her."

Kennedy tugged on Willow's arm. "We should go."

Willow nodded but didn't move. Something crashed in Carl's office. Kennedy flinched.

"Get out." Carl's voice was low and steady the first time but escalated when he had to repeat himself. "I told you to get out."

Kennedy would have preferred to run down the hall, but Willow's silly sandals only allowed the two of them to get a couple feet away from the door before Nick barged out, slamming it shut behind him. "That man!" He started when he saw Kennedy and Willow. "Oh, I mean, umm ... what are you guys doing here?"

"Wanted to see where you were." Willow seemed perfectly content to let Nick hear the annoyance in her voice. "And how's good old Pastor Carl doing?" she asked with sarcastic sweetness. "Did he appreciate your little apology?"

Nick shook his head. "Don't ask."

Willow placed her arm on his shoulder. "Come on. You know I'm just giving you a hard time. You wanna talk about it? Would that help make things better?"

He shook his head. "You won't believe that kind of bull-headed arrogance. Makes me so mad."

"Come on." Willow laid her head against his shoulder. "Let's go to the library or something, ok? Kennedy, think you could give us a few minutes?"

"Of course."

"Come on." Willow spoke soothingly. Like a mother comforting a petulant toddler. "Let's find someplace quiet, and we can talk about whatever you want, all right?"

Kennedy watched them turn down the hall, unable to explain the deep level of sadness, an ever-tumultuous sea of emptiness that crashed around her.

CHAPTER 3

WHEN KENNEDY REACHED THE sanctuary, she was more than grateful to find some of the youth group students stacking up the last of the chairs. She walked back to the main entrance looking for someone who might have work for her.

"You here to set up?"

She turned around to see Dawn, Carl's middle-aged secretary.

Kennedy gave a brief smile, which wasn't returned. "Yeah, I was just wondering if there were any jobs for me to do."

Dawn rolled her eyes. "Plenty of jobs, I'm sure. It's figuring out which ones need to get done first that's the big problem."

Kennedy didn't know what to say. She didn't know Dawn all that well, and even though their past exchanges had been cordial, Kennedy never felt perfectly comfortable around her.

"I'm sure Nick will have an idea of how you can help. I've got to meet my husband for lunch." With that, Dawn swept past.

Kennedy looked around at all the half-opened boxes in the foyer. It was strange. She'd never thought before of how much work went into planning one of these big conferences. She remembered her dad attending something like this back when they still lived in the States. It was so long ago she could hardly remember any details. What stood out most in her mind was how after one men's event, her dad had come home, knelt in front of her, and asked her to forgive him for not being the kind of father he should have been. She didn't know if things changed after his emotional speech. She just remembered the way his words had terrified her.

Back when the world was black and white, when there were good guys and bad guys and it was so easy to tell one from the other, she thought that her father's apology put him on the same level as the villains in her Saturday morning cartoons.

What surprised her now was how many people were scandalized at the thought of the Truth Warriors conference. Back as a kid in New York, she recalled several events like this one. Nobody thought much of it, but she remembered listening to announcements year after year, hearing testimonies of men when they returned home from these sorts of conferences and announced before their God, their family, and their church how encouraged they'd been and inspired to embrace their calling as humble, loving, strong leaders. What was controversial about that? When protestors threatened to march in front of the church if Carl didn't cancel the gathering, she initially thought their complaint was that it was a men's-only event, which seemed ironic since who would bother complaining or boycotting a church that put on a weekend women's retreat?

As the controversy escalated, she skimmed enough news headlines to understand there was more to these protestors' grievances than simple gender-based exclusion. They complained against anything patriarchal, especially traditional religious mores. The feminists were afraid that an all-male conference whose stated goal was to encourage men to embrace their God-given roles as the heads of their families would send waves of oppression cascading throughout the church.

At first, Kennedy had stayed on the sidelines of the debate. She knew enough to understand that women's roles in today's society were freer than they'd ever been, at least in the United States. Leaders in the women's movement in the past had suffered and worked hard, and as a result, Kennedy could get a driver's license, register to vote, attend medical school, and become a top-ranking, respected doctor in whatever field she decided to enter. Of course, there were still many parts of the world where girls weren't given these sorts of opportunities, and one of her hopes for her future was to use her position as a doctor to travel to other countries offering health care and educational opportunities to girls and women trapped in these backwards settings. But that was as far as she'd ever considered feminism or the women's rights movement. She wasn't ready to go out and burn her bra or make the world bow down to her because she had two X chromosomes, but she certainly didn't want to take her educational and vocational opportunities for granted either.

As far as a woman's role went, Kennedy had grown up in a traditional family. Her mom kept house, and her dad worked long hours. But Kennedy knew plenty of other godly, Christian couples where both spouses held gainful employment. She figured those sorts of decisions could vary from one family to the next. She certainly didn't want a pastor to tell her the only job she could do was stay home and have babies, but she also didn't feel like she needed a whole army of angry feminists marching or making women feel bad if they chose to focus on their children instead of their careers.

Which is exactly what they'd done to Sandy. Sandy, the most maternal, godly woman Kennedy had ever met. But because she wasn't using her college degree to earn money as a "productive" member of society, the Harvard editorial team had ridiculed her in last week's edition of the student paper. All because she was a stay-at-home mom married to a pastor who dared to host a Truth Warriors conference at his church. Did these students know how many foster children Sandy had saved from a life on the streets? Did they know how much time she devoted every week volunteering for different causes? Just how did these editors define what *productive* meant anyway? Kennedy had never known a harder working woman.

"That you, Kennedy?"

She turned around to see Carl and Sandy's son Woong wandering the St. Margaret halls. "Hey, bud. What are you doing?"

"I'm supposed to be helping set up for the conference thing, except most of the time the jobs are too big for me, so I'm mostly just walking around."

"I'm a little lost myself." Kennedy was amazed at how fast Woong had grown. He'd gained half a foot over the summer alone. This fall, the Lindgrens had decided to pull him out of Medford Academy and teach him at home. Sandy had a feeling he was older than they initially guessed based on his scant orphanage records. She figured that homeschooling would allow him to excel past his assumed level in some areas (like science, where his curiosity had proved to be his most valuable asset) and would allow her to give him individualized attention to catch up on his weaker subjects like math and reading without the stigma of performing beneath a certain grade level.

Woong let out a loud sigh. "Hey, you know if they got any snacks? I'm hungry."

Kennedy shook her head. "Sorry, bud. I haven't seen anything around here. Maybe you should ask your mom."

He frowned. "No, she went into the prayer room with one of the teens. I don't know which one, but she was crying, so that means they'll be in there for hours. But it's ok. Hey, you know what? My dad was in a really big fight. I could hear him yelling all the way from the other side of the church. Did you hear it, too?"

Kennedy smiled at the slight exaggeration. "Yeah, sometimes even grownups get into arguments."

He shook his head. "No, this wasn't just the kind of thing where they talk angry and then lie and tell you they weren't really fighting. I'm talking about a real, actual fight. Like in those Jackie Chan movies. You ever seen him?"

"What do you mean?"

"I mean the old Chinese man who does kung fu and beats up all the bad guys ten at a time and then puts on his glasses and smiles real big."

"I know who Jackie Chan is. I meant why do you think that's the kind of argument your dad was in?"

Woong stretched himself to his full height. "I heard it. You know. Fighting sounds. Like *oof* and *pow* and *ahh* and things like that. And at one point a whole bunch of books fell over. Or something else real heavy and loud, but it sure sounded like books to me even though I couldn't see it on account of the door being shut."

Kennedy still hadn't decided if Woong's imagination had taken over or if there was really any reason to be concerned. She knew that Nick could be quick tempered when he was debating issues of social justice. She also suspected Sandy was at least partially right when she said Carl had been grumpier than normal although Kennedy wasn't certain if that could be blamed on the diet or not. But still, Nick was the most committed pacifist she'd ever met, and even though Carl could be intimidating, she doubted he had actually hurt a living being since his days as a professional NFL linebacker decades earlier. She figured Woong must be exaggerating, and who could blame him — stuck here wandering the church with nothing to do but stay out of people's way?

She felt in her pockets. She still had a few coins from when she'd bought her ticket for the T ride to St. Margaret's. "Hey, want to come with me to the vending machines? I'll find you a snack, and then after we've had something to eat we can look around for a job for the two of us to work on. How's that sound?"

Woong eyed the coins in Kennedy's hand. "How much money you got there, anyway?"

"Enough for you to get one thing."

He let out a melodramatic sigh. "I guess I'll have to be content with that."

When they turned down the hall toward the vending machines, Nick was running toward them and almost knocked Woong over. "Have you seen Sandy?" he blurted without a hint of apology.

Something was wrong. Something wasn't right.

"Sandy," he repeated. "I need to know where she is."

Kennedy's synapses hadn't connected her tongue to her brain quite yet. She stared at Nick's hands.

His wet, blood-stained hands.

"Holy macaroni!" Woong exclaimed.

Nick ran his fingers through his hair. More blood. Smeared all over.

"What happened to you?" Woong asked.

"Go find your mom." Nick wasn't looking at either of them. He was panting. Totally out of breath. "Find your mom, and tell her it's an emergency. Hurry."

Woong shrugged and darted off.

Kennedy kept staring, but at least now she'd found her voice. "What happened?"

Nick doubled over. For a minute, Kennedy thought he was going to be sick. "There's blood everywhere. It's ..." He swayed, and Kennedy had to put her arm under him to keep him from crashing.

She lowered him to the ground. His face was ashen, a grayish pallor. Sweat beaded on his forehead.

He shook his head, smeared with blood. "Everywhere," he repeated in a whisper.

What was it? An accident? Did one of the teens get hurt? Kennedy lowered her face to his, trying to snap his brain to attention. "What is it?"

He held his head in his hands. "I tried to stop the bleeding. I tried to call for help."

"Help with what? Who's hurt?"

Nick let out a sigh. His whole body reeked. She knew people could get nauseated at the sight of blood, but she didn't know they started to smell bad, too.

"Carl." Nick blinked. "He's unconscious."

CHAPTER 4

BY THE TIME KENNEDY left Nick in his puddle of queasy nerves and ran to Carl's office, Sandy was rushing down the hall from the opposite direction. "What is it, honey?" she asked Kennedy, breathless.

"Carl." Kennedy could barely get the word out.

Sandy rushed into the room, and Kennedy followed right after. Nick hadn't exaggerated. Apparently, neither had Woong. One of the bookshelves was toppled over, leaning precariously against the desk. Carl was on the floor at a painfully awkward angle, blood pooling beneath him.

Sandy dropped to her knees and scooped his head into her lap. "Carl? Darling? Can you hear me?" Her eyes were wide, but her voice held no trace of the panic and fear that gripped Kennedy's heart. "Sweetheart? Do we need to call you an ambulance?"

Sandy glanced over and looked at Kennedy. "Do you have your phone on you, dear?"

Kennedy reached into her pocket. Had she been stupid enough to leave it in her backpack at a time like this? No, there it was. Thank God. "I've got it."

She had already started dialing 911 when Sandy said, "Call the paramedics. Let them know he's a diabetic. I wonder if something went wrong with his medicine. He was supposed to eat his lunch, but he's been so busy getting everything ready for this conference, and he's ... oh, my poor, precious darling." She stroked his cheek with the back of her hand. Either she didn't notice or didn't care that her dress was stained. Kennedy tried to figure out where he was bleeding from but couldn't tell from her vantage point. Were there any gloves in the area? Anything sterile?

Sandy kept stroking his cheek, crooning softly.

"Please state the location of the emergency." Thankfully this dispatcher, unlike others she'd been forced to talk to in the past, sounded more like a human than a robot.

"I'm at St. Margaret's Church on Elm Street. We need medical care. Our pastor here's bleeding. We don't know what happened."

"Is the patient conscious?"

"No. He's lying on the floor. There's a big pool of blood, maybe nine inches in diameter. Maybe more."

"Is he breathing?"

Kennedy stopped. Why hadn't she thought to check? She stared at his chest. "Yes, he's breathing." Praise the Lord.

"And the source of the bleeding?" the dispatcher asked.

"Don't forget to tell them about the diabetes," Sandy interrupted. "He took his insulin a full hour and a half ago."

Kennedy had a hard time keeping up two conversations at the same time, especially with her heart racing so fast and her lungs threatening to close in on her.

"I think it's from his head. It's hard to tell." She glanced at Sandy's dress. Was the blood continuing to pool on her lap?

"Don't forget ..." Sandy began.

"He's got diabetes," Kennedy blurted.

"Is he on any medications?" the dispatcher asked.

Kennedy's lips quivered, but thankfully her voice remained steady. "He takes insulin. I don't know what else. But his wife is here. She could tell you." She held out the phone to Sandy. "Do you mind answering a few of their questions?"

"Of course not." She took the phone with a dignified kind of grace. "This is Sandy Lindgren speaking."

Kennedy didn't listen to the rest of the conversation. She tried to remember what other basic first-aid measures she should take while they waited for the ambulance. Slow down the bleeding. That was the first priority. But how? And with what? She didn't even know where he'd been injured. Something Woong said ran through her mind. *A real, actual fight. Like in those Jackie Chan movies.* It couldn't be that though. There had to be another explanation. Nobody would ever hurt Carl. Nobody ...

She shoved those thoughts aside and opened his desk drawers. A devotional by different Puritan authors. Several folders filled with handwritten sermon notes. No first-aid kit anywhere.

"I don't think so." She heard Sandy's voice over the pulse raging in her ears. "His sugar was a little higher than normal this morning, something like 185 when he first woke up if I remember right. Or maybe that was last night. That's right. Last night was 185. This morning was 192. I told him he should take one of his pills, but he said he'd check it again after breakfast, except he always forgets ..."

Kennedy searched through his desk. More journals. More books. Another drawer filled with nothing but photographs of his dozens of kids and grandkids.

"Oh, you know," Sandy went on as if she were chatting with a friend over tea. "The big white horse one. They're for diabetics. You'd recognize it if you saw it. Shaped like a long oval, have a little number on the side ... no, I'm afraid I can't remember the name."

Kennedy wasn't sure if she would scream or pull her hair out. How could Sandy stay so calm in the midst of this madness? Even if Carl weren't hurt, his office was as chaotic as Murphy's Law itself. Books scattered everywhere. His bust of Charles Spurgeon had been knocked to the floor and now resembled an ancient ruin more than the nineteenth- century preacher. She knelt down and rummaged through the mess. At this point, she didn't even know what she was looking for. Medicine bottles so they could tell the paramedics exactly what Carl was taking? Gloves so she could check his injuries without risking infection? A church the size of St. Margaret's would have a first-aid kit somewhere. But wait. What was ...

"The bleeding?" Sandy asked the dispatcher. "Well, let's see. I've got his head on my lap, and it looks like there's some blood on me now, so I wonder if maybe he got dizzy when his blood sugar dropped and fell and hit his head." She paused. "Well, I'm glad to hear that." She pulled the phone away from her ear and whispered to Kennedy, "The ambulance is only a few minutes away."

Kennedy stood frozen over the object she'd found. She didn't dare touch the thing but stared at it with a mix of both horror and incredulity. She tried to find the words to tell Sandy what she'd discovered.

"I'm sorry, what was that, dear?" Sandy asked.

Kennedy pointed to the heavy bookend. The bookend that was partially chipped and had bright red blood streaking across it.

"I said tell them to send the police, too. This might not have been an accident."

CHAPTER 5

SANDY SHOOK HER HEAD while Kennedy helped her to her feet. "I can't believe someone would have done this on purpose."

The paramedics had just managed to get Carl onto the stretcher. Kennedy grimaced when she looked at him lying there. Her pastor was always so strong. Confident. But now he looked weak, and it wasn't because of the extra weight he'd recently lost. One eye was starting to swell. Cuts and scrapes streaked across his face. His hair was matted with dried blood, but at least he wasn't bleeding as much as at first.

"Nobody had any reason to do this," Sandy whispered.

Kennedy wrapped her arm around her shoulders, doing her best to ignore the stains on Sandy's clothes. "Don't worry about that right now. What matters is the ambulance is here, and they're going to get Carl the care he needs."

"He's such a good man." Sandy's voice caught. "Such an honest, godly man. Who would want to hurt him?"

Kennedy wished she could say it was still unclear if somebody had hurt him or not, but that wasn't the case. After taking one look at the scene, the first responder had radioed in to confirm that this was an attack. The police were on their way, and everyone at the church was ordered to remain on the premises. The officers would want to ask questions. Try to figure out what happened, who would have hurt someone as loving as Carl.

"Will you be following us in your car then, ma'am?" a first responder with thick glasses asked. "We're about ready to take your husband to Providence."

Sandy sniffed slightly and tucked her braid over her shoulder. Unruly strands of gray hair hung in sweaty clumps around her forehead. She smoothed out her dress. "I'm not leaving him. I'll go with you."

The paramedic glanced at one of his partners who shrugged. "It's all right with me. She can give us a better medical history on the way."

Sandy tilted up her chin. "Thank you. I just need to find my son."

The paramedic cleared his throat. "I'm sorry, we don't have that kind of room. If you two want to follow us to the hospital in your own vehicle, that would definitely be ..."

"I can drive Woong," Kennedy offered.

"Mom?" The high-pitched voice in the doorway made Kennedy start.

"Oh, my baby." Sandy rushed toward Woong and hugged him while he made a valiant effort to squirm free.

"What's going on?" he asked. "Someone told me Dad got hurt, but I knew he must be lying because Dad wouldn't ..." Woong stopped when Sandy moved him out of the way to make room for the two men transporting the stretcher. "Holy macaroni." Woong's face scrunched up. "What's wrong with Dad?"

"Shh." Sandy buried her cheek against his hair. "It's all right, son. Daddy had a little accident, and these nice folks are going to take him to the hospital so they can make him all better. Would you like to ride with Daddy in the ambulance, son?"

The paramedic cleared his throat. "I'm afraid there won't be room for both of you, but you're welcome to follow us and meet us at the ..."

Sandy shook her head and stared down at him. "That man you're transporting is the father of my son. He's his only living male relative he's got left in this world, at least so far as we know. And so I'm going to tell you again. We are going to ride to the hospital with his father. Together."

He shook his head. "Not gonna work. I'm sorry. We'll need all the space we can get, and if something happens in transit ..."

"Like what?" Sandy interrupted. "What would you expect to happen? What could go wrong now?"

Kennedy was busy studying Woong's scrunched-up face and put her arm around Sandy. "Let me drive you, ok? It's the least I can do to help."

Sandy hadn't taken her eyes off her husband.

"It will be all right," Kennedy whispered, hoping she was speaking the truth. "Come on. You and Woong get your things ready, and I'll meet you at your car. Do you know where the keys are?"

"Carl usually keeps them in his pocket." Sandy's voice trembled.

After a quick explanation and a little help from the paramedics, Sandy took the car keys from Carl's pants and handed them to Kennedy. "I can drive myself, you know. You don't have to do this."

"I know." Kennedy offered what she hoped was a reassuring smile. "But I want to. Just think of it as a thank you for all the ways you've been there for me in the past, all right?"

Sandy frowned. "Ok. I'll meet you at the Honda. It's in the usual spot." She gave Kennedy a quick hug and turned to her son. "Woong, honey, do you have anything you need to take with you? Did you finish that math assignment I gave you earlier?"

Kennedy slipped out while Woong gave an excuse about losing his workbook. She had to find Willow. Had to tell her that she was driving Sandy and Woong to Providence.

Had to tell Willow about Carl's brutal attack.

CHAPTER 6

BY THE TIME SANDY and Woong emerged from the church, Carl's ambulance had already left. Kennedy knew there was no way to keep up with an emergency response vehicle with its sirens on, but she still wanted to get Sandy and Woong to Providence as soon as she safely could. She was glad for the chance to drive the two of them. Not only did it give her something practical to do, a tangible way to help in this horrific crisis, it would also mean she'd get the most recent updates on Carl's condition. She couldn't imagine having to sit and wait at St. Margaret's wondering about Carl.

The paramedics had worked professionally and efficiently to prepare Carl for transfer. Nobody gave Sandy much of a prognosis, at least nothing more than the fact that he was stable enough to transport to the hospital, but Kennedy had picked up on enough nonverbal cues to fear that Carl was going to need more than some stitches and Band-Aids once he got to Providence.

Or maybe she was just being paranoid. It was a bad semester for someone she loved to get a head wound, given the fact that her neuroscience class was basically a crash course in the scariest, most horrifying types of brain injuries and abnormalities known to modern science. If you were a student reading a textbook or listening to your professor's lecture, the subject matter was fascinating. If you were a young woman driving your worried friend and her scared-silent son to the hospital after her husband suffered some kind of traumatic head injury, it was a curse. Kennedy's mind reeled with all the knowledge she'd gained, with all the worst-case scenarios floating around in her memory banks. It was one of those moments when ignorance could easily be compared to bliss.

Carl's favorite local talk show was on the AM radio. The host was yelling angrily about the protests and marches feminists had planned against St. Margaret's if the church didn't cancel the Truth Warriors conference.

"What is it that's so offensive to these feminists with their combat boots and camo pants, huh? What's so threatening about a religious event whose primary goal — in fact, its only stated goal — was to teach men to be more humble, compassionate defenders of the faith? I've got feminist leader Sandra Green in the studio with me, and I know I, as well as many of you, would love to hear her answer to these questions."

"Well, Chris, here's what I have to say to that." Sandra's voice was low and scratchy, like a woman who'd chain-smoked for half a century. "We certainly have no problem encouraging compassion and humility in a Judeo-Christian setting. Even a gathering that intentionally excluded women wouldn't be considered *threatening* as you put it if that was all there was to it. In other words, it's not the stated goals of the conference that are troublesome. It's the undertone, the subtext. The Truth Warriors movement assumes that anyone on this planet who presents as male has some type of divine right, some manifest destiny to subdue and subjugate anyone and everyone who presents as female. That's what we find so disturbing. That's why we urge anyone who ..."

Kennedy turned the radio off. When she stopped at a red light, she glanced over at Sandy. "Are you doing ok?"

Sandy nodded but her lip was trembling. She turned around to look at her son. "How about you, darling? Are you still my big, brave baby?"

In the rearview mirror, Kennedy saw Woong scowl and cross his arms. "I'm not a baby," he mumbled, "and I've never been scared a day in my life."

Kennedy tried to think of something to say. Sandy was always so good in situations like these. Always had the right words, the right encouragement. But now, Kennedy felt about as lost as all those boys in *Lord of the Flies* right after they crash-landed on their deserted island.

"Well, honey, have you been praying for your daddy?" Sandy asked Woong.

"Yes," he grumbled from the backseat.

"Let's do it out loud this time. It'll make Daddy happy to know that we've been talking to God about him, and if the injuries are real serious ..." Her voice caught, and she coughed quietly.

"If the injuries are serious," Kennedy finished for her, "our prayers can help him recover faster."

"Yeah, whatever," Woong mumbled.

Kennedy figured it was time to jump in instead of passively wait for Sandy to have a teaching moment with her son. "You shouldn't talk about prayer that way," Kennedy told him. "Don't you remember when you got so sick last spring? It was God who helped you get better, you know."

"No it wasn't. It was the doctors. If it was God who healed me, he woulda done it without having to put that medicine in my arm that burned every time they made it drip into my blood."

Kennedy realized that she probably wasn't in the right emotional state of mind to dive headfirst into a theological landmine with an inquisitive boy like Woong.

"Well," she tried again, "sometimes God uses doctors, and sometimes he uses miracles, but that doesn't mean we shouldn't pray because prayer always makes a difference even if we don't always see what that difference is."

Even as the words came out of her mouth, Kennedy realized they lacked both conviction as well as common sense. Hadn't she learned, hadn't she matured enough to realize that those sorts of pat answers kids hear in Sunday school do nothing to prepare them for the trials and uncertainties of life?

But what else could she say?

Apparently, Woong's brain was working at least as fast as hers and dissecting her haphazard arguments as quickly as she was able to voice them.

"So you're saying God might make my dad get better if I pray, but he might not. And maybe he'll do it by some miracle, or he might just let the doctors do what they're supposed to do anyway. So what's the point of talking to Jesus about anything at all if he's already got his old, stubborn mind made up?"

"Woong," Sandy snapped and turned around in her seat. "You don't ever talk about our Lord and Savior that way, you understand me, child? If your dad were here and he heard you talk about his precious Jesus like that, what do you think he'd ..."

"Well, Dad's not here." Woong answered back with just as much vehemence in his squeaky, little voice. "He can't hear me say things like that because ... because ..." He sniffed loudly and tried to choke down a small sob.

Sandy let out her breath. "Oh, my sweet baby, it's ok to be sad. It's ok to be worried about Daddy. I'm worried too, son."

Woong was crying softly with his fists balled up against his eyes.

"It's ok, little pumpkin," Sandy crooned and then began to pray. "Oh, dear sweet Jesus, comfort to all who mourn, protector of all the weak, the one who grants peace and courage to the scared and helpless, you are my King. You are my shield and my fortress and my salvation. You are the stronghold of my life. But I confess that even though I know these things about you, I don't worship you the way I should. I'm so frail, so easily given to fear. But I will yet praise you, my Savior and my God, feeble though my worship is. I bring it to you, Lord, all of it. The fears, the doubts, the dread. Father, you know just what's going on in my Carl's body. You know exactly what needs to be fixed, and you know exactly how to do it. So go now and heal him, Lord Jesus, please. As much as we might try to be brave, the truth of the matter is that Woong and I just wouldn't know how to live without that man. So go be with him now, Lord. And while you're healing all his wounds, come and fill us up in this car with your presence, too. Fill us up with the joy of your salvation, the joy that comes from knowing that neither death nor life, neither the past nor future, neither angels nor demons can separate any one of us from your perfect, eternal love. We ask this all in Jesus' name, and we give you all the glory and power and praise. Amen."

Sandy reached back and rubbed Woong's knee. Kennedy couldn't tell if he was still crying or not. She didn't hear anything, but she had to keep her eyes on the road as she pulled in front of Providence Hospital.

"Do you want me to drop you off at the entrance and Woong and I can come find you after we park?" Kennedy asked.

Sandy stared out her window. "What's that? Did you say something, sweetie?"

Kennedy repeated herself.

"That sounds like a good idea." Sandy still hadn't answered the question, but Kennedy assumed she meant that she wanted to be dropped off. She pulled the Lindgrens' Honda in front of the emergency room exit.

"Woong and I will be right behind you." Kennedy gave Sandy's hand a squeeze before she got out. "And I'll be praying for you. I'm sure Carl's going to be just fine."

Sandy frowned and said in a whisper only Kennedy could hear, "I wish I could be so sure of that myself. I've got a bad feeling about this."

CHAPTER 7

"WHY DOES EVERYBODY WHO gets sick go to the same hospital?" Woong asked once Kennedy parked.

"What do you mean?" She got out and opened Woong's door so he wouldn't bang it against the cement pillar in the parking garage.

"What I mean is folks at hospitals are getting all kinds of different germs, so why don't they have one hospital for all the broken bones, and one hospital for all them folks with diabetes, and some other spot for the ones having their baby and so on?"

Kennedy locked the doors to the Honda and had to remind herself that Woong was too big to hold her hand. "That's a good question. I guess it's just easier having everything all together, so if the doctors need to give the patients X-rays or something it's all right there."

"Yeah, but I've been thinking, and now what I'm wanting to know is how come when all the bad stuff happens it always starts with folks coming here to the hospital or ending up here?"

"It does seem like that's the case, doesn't it?" Kennedy was glad she found a spot not too far from the entrance. She wasn't sure she had the patience for Woong's version of twenty thousand questions.

"Know what else I'm wondering?" he asked as they made their way to the sky bridge that connected the parking garage to the main building.

"What's that?" Kennedy was prepared for anything from a theological discussion about the possibility of extraterrestrial life to an observation about the mating rituals of the giraffes at the zoo.

"What I've been wanting to know is how come Mom got mad at me in the car? I wasn't trying to be disrespectful to God or stuff and nonsense like that. I really wanted to know."

Kennedy had been so worried about Carl's condition she couldn't remember exactly what Woong had said or done.

"Because I've been thinking," he went on, "and what I'm wondering is how come we're supposed to pray that God's gonna heal my dad, only if he doesn't, we're supposed to just say, *Ok, that must not have been the thing God wanted to do.* Because what I'm saying is if God's gonna do what God's gonna do, then why should we have to pray about it so hard, know what I mean?"

Kennedy was having a difficult time focusing. She still wasn't sure if these occasional bursts of mental fog were one of the side effects from her anxiety meds or just a sign of the anxiety itself. One thing she'd learned over the past two years was that as soon as she felt like she'd gotten the upper hand on one of her PTSD symptoms, another one — just as bad or sometimes even worse — was waiting in line, ready to move to the forefront.

"And here's the other thing," Woong said as they got onto the elevator to the main lobby. "Don't you think it'd make God mad if we ask him to heal a Christian? What I mean is don't all the Bible books and all the pastors say that it's better in heaven than it is on earth? And wouldn't God know that so wouldn't he want a Christian to go to heaven and be happy forever? So when we pray like Mom did for God to heal folks that are saved, what's keeping him from getting angry at us for being selfish-like?"

Kennedy knew that this wasn't a question she could brush off like the others. "First of all, God tells us we can talk to him about anything. And it's not selfish to want to keep from losing somebody we love. Jesus cried when his friend Lazarus died, even though he knew he was going to raise him back to life. But even more important, nobody's talking about your dad going to heaven. Lots of people have to ride in ambulances, but that doesn't mean they're so sick or hurt you have to worry about them dying."

Woong didn't respond. They got off the elevator, and Kennedy led him toward the ER. She'd been to Providence so many times by now there was no need to ask the volunteer behind the welcome desk for directions.

"Come on, bud. Let's find your mom and dad and then you'll see that there's no reason to think about anyone going off to heaven."

Even as she said the words, Kennedy prayed that she was right.

CHAPTER 8

KENNEDY STARED AT HER phone when it rang at her. It was a local number, but it wasn't in her contacts list. "Hello?"

"Hi, I'm calling from the T station. Can you hear me?" The voice was familiar, but she couldn't place it.

"Yeah. Who's this?" She'd only been in the ER waiting room for a short time. Sandy had come to take Woong back with her a few minutes earlier. At that point, there was still no word on Carl's condition.

"It's me. Ian."

"Who?"

"Ian. Ian McAlister."

"Oh." Kennedy pictured the journalist with his shock-red hair. She couldn't remember how long it had been since she'd last spoken with him. Over a year probably. Why would he be calling her?

"Hey, I wanted to talk to you about something. Is now a good time?"

Ian was the kind of journalist who seemed to know every local headline a second or two before it happened. Had he already heard about Carl's attack? Kennedy wouldn't be too surprised to find out he knew even more than she did, although she could never guess who his sources were or how he got his information.

"I've got a couple minutes. Not very long."

"I understand. You getting ready for a class?" Ian's voice was casual, but the familiarity in his tone made Kennedy uneasy.

"No. I'm, well, I'm at the hospital with a friend."

"Oh, I'm sorry to hear that. Nothing too serious, I hope?" He sounded polite without being pushy.

"I hope not, too." Kennedy didn't want to give him any further details.

There was an awkward pause before he went on. "Well, I guess now's probably not the best time to talk then, but I wanted to sit down with you to discuss your article that came out today."

"What article?" Kennedy wondered if he'd called the wrong number. Did he think he was talking to someone else, maybe?

The roar of a passing T car in the background made Ian shout. "The one in the Harvard Voice. Your column on the feminist movement."

"Oh. That." Last week, the staff of the Voice had published an op-ed about the Truth Warriors conference at St. Margaret's. It was the same bandwagon every other liberal news outlet in Cambridge had jumped on. *Let's complain about the pastor who hosts a conference for men to talk about male leadership in the home and church.*

The only reason Kennedy wrote back to the editorial team was because they had personally attacked Sandy. In their editorial, they made her out to be some beaten-down housewife married to this megalomaniacal pastor who wanted to keep her barefoot in the kitchen and a perpetual slave to a never-ending line of children and grandchildren. Kennedy wrote a short email, no more than three or four sentences long, defending her friend and almost immediately received an invitation to print a seven-hundred-word rebuttal in the forum section of the Voice. So much had happened between now and then that she hadn't even realized her article had gone to print.

"It's caused quite a stir on campus from what I can tell. Which maybe is what you had in mind." Was Ian accusing her? His tone was indecipherable.

"No, I just wanted to see them treat Sandy better in the future."

His voice softened. "I can respect that. Their original article did hit a little below the belt if you want my opinion."

Kennedy waited. She still couldn't figure out why the journalist was calling her. Ian had graduated from Harvard years ago. Why did he care what students there did or didn't print in the paper?

"Anyway, I wanted to know if I could ask you a few questions. Maybe get your take on what it's like to be a conservative student on a campus like Harvard. It can't be easy, I'm sure."

Kennedy didn't know what to say. She'd never considered herself all that conservative before, especially not compared to people like Carl or her dad. Up until now, she hadn't even felt like her column for the Voice was taking a political side one way or the other. She just wanted to point out that Sandy did a whole lot more than sit around darning socks for her husband like the Harvard editors insinuated.

Kennedy's phone beeped at her. Willow was calling.

"You know what," she said, "I've got to run. There's a lot going on right now, but maybe we can talk soon."

"Breakfast tomorrow?"

Kennedy was fumbling with her phone, trying to disconnect with Ian before Willow hung up. "Ok, maybe." She ended the call before either of them could say good-bye and hoped that she hadn't missed her roommate. "Willow? Hello? Are you there?"

No response.

"Can you hear me?" she asked.

Was that someone sniffling?

"Willow? What's wrong?"

She let out a small sob.

Kennedy's abs tightened, and the all familiar quivering returned to her gut. "What happened? What's the matter?"

"It's Nick. The detective came to ask him what he knows about Carl's accident." It took a few sniffs and another suppressed sob before she could continue. "They think he's the one who attacked Carl."

CHAPTER 9

KENNEDY HAD TO STAND up. Had to move her legs. She paced back and forth along the far wall of the ER waiting room where she hoped not too many patients and visitors could overhear. "What do you mean they think Nick did it? That's ridiculous." She tested her words, surprised they didn't come out a little more forcefully.

"I know, but everyone heard them fighting. That's the thing. And that dumb detective doesn't know him. He doesn't care. I tried explaining to him that Nick and Carl have fought for years and never once did it turn violent, but he was all like, *I'll question you if I've got any time after I'm finished with your boyfriend*, and he just lifted his little coffee cup in my face and basically told me where to go."

Coffee cup? That sounded familiar. "Is it Drisklay?" Kennedy asked.

"Is what drizzling? Outside? No, it's been perfectly clear all day."

"No, I mean the detective. Is his name Drisklay?"

"I don't know." Willow's voice was agitated, but at least she wasn't crying anymore. "His name could be Tutankhamen for all I care. I just want him to leave Nick out of this. He had nothing to do with any of it. Everyone knows that."

Kennedy believed her, but she also had to admit that with as loudly as Nick had been arguing with Carl, it would be amiss for the detective to fail to at least ask him a few standard questions. She thought about how bloody his hands were when he stumbled down the hallway of St. Margaret's.

"What should we do?" Willow asked softly.

"Just try not to worry for one thing. Drisklay's a pain, but he's not an idiot. He'll question Nick, and he'll do a thorough enough job that it'll be obvious he didn't have anything to do with the accident. And then you can talk to the detective yourself and tell him the same thing. Nick and Carl fight all the time. Everyone who spends more than five minutes at St. Margaret's knows that."

Kennedy was trying to lighten the mood, but Willow didn't laugh.

"I just hate thinking of him in there being treated like some terrorist suspect or something ..."

"That's not what's happening. It's going to be all right. Drisklay's just doing his job. It's not personal, and Nick has absolutely nothing to worry about."

"You sure?" Willow sounded so hopeful. So trusting.

Kennedy took a deep breath. "Yeah. I'm sure. This will all blow over. You'll see."

Willow sighed. "I hope so. What's the news on Carl?"

"No news yet." Kennedy checked the time. It hadn't even been ten minutes since she arrived.

"Well, you know we're all praying for him. We got the whole youth group together. All the teens and the helpers, and we spent our time in the sanctuary praying for Carl. You should have been there. It was really special."

Kennedy's throat was sore. "I bet it was."

"You doing ok? Not feeling too anxious or anything? I mean, of course we're all nervous, but you know what I'm saying."

"No panic attacks," Kennedy told her, deciding to take the direct approach to Willow's question. "Nothing like that." Maybe her pills really were helping. She thought about what she and Woong had talked about, how sometimes God heals people through miracles and sometimes through medicine. It still counted as healing because it still came from God, right?

She shouldn't feel guilty, should she?

"Kennedy!"

She turned at the sound of the voice from the opposite side of the lobby. "I better go," she told Willow. "Sandy's here."

"Let me know what you find out," Willow said. "The worst part is just waiting around like this."

"I know. I'll be sure to call you right back or at least send you a text. Gotta run." Kennedy ended the call, disappointed to find she only had one-and-a-half bars of battery life left. She didn't think she'd been talking that long, but it didn't matter. She hurried over to Sandy and Woong. "What's going on?"

Sandy's face was calm and serene, but her voice trembled. "Well, we've got some good news, and we've got some bad news."

Kennedy braced herself.

Sandy kept Woong pressed against her side, only this time he didn't try to squirm away but rested his cheek against her side, hiding part of his face in the folds of her dress. Sandy cleared her throat. "So, the good news is we got him here so fast, and the ambulance crew did such a good job tending to him on the road. He really couldn't have received any better care."

Sandy's use of the past tense sent Kennedy's whole body into a dizzying spiral.

"I better sit down." Sandy scooped Woong onto her lap and buried him against her shoulder. He didn't pull away.

Kennedy had no recollection of moving but realized she was sitting down now, too.

Sandy stroked Woong's head with one hand and wiped her cheek with the other. "It's harder than I thought it would be to say this."

Kennedy's throat was almost entirely swollen shut or she would have found some way to offer Sandy a word of comfort or encouragement.

Sandy sniffed and continued to caress her son. "By the time the ambulance got him here, Carl had stopped breathing. The man I talked to wasn't sure why. Said it might be from blood loss or maybe something like shock." She cleared her throat again and lowered her voice. "He said it might also be the result of brain injury. They won't know more until they run some tests, but they're getting him hooked up to life support. Or maybe they've finished by now. I didn't ask how long it would take."

"Did you get to see him?" Kennedy asked.

Sandy shook her head. "No, this is all from the paramedic I talked to, one of the ambulance crew. He's the one who let me know about how he stopped breathing on the road. Those folks saved your daddy's life." She spoke into Woong's head of black hair. "We've got to remember to thank God for them every single day. You listening to me?"

Woong nodded but kept his face hidden.

Kennedy reached out and touched Sandy's arm. "What can I do?" she asked. She couldn't remember any time all year when she'd felt so helpless.

Sandy grabbed hold of her hand. "You can pray with me. And we've got to pray hard."

CHAPTER 10

KENNEDY HAD NEVER SPENT so long praying for one person before. She'd always had a nagging suspicion that interceding for others was a lot harder than certain pastors and Bible study leaders made it out to be. Even so, she never guessed how exhausting it was to spend that much time in focused, fervent prayer. Kennedy figured they'd prayed at least forty-five minutes and maybe a whole hour, interrupted only a few short times when the nurse popped out to let Sandy know what was happening. Carl's condition hadn't changed. Once he got stabilized on the ventilator, the doctor wanted to monitor him for a little while longer in the ER and then send him to the ICU. Sandy took the news with her typical grace, but Kennedy wanted to jump up and scream to the entire hospital that it wasn't fair.

Carl shouldn't be here. He shouldn't be on a ventilator. He couldn't be. He was so strong. It wasn't as bad as the nurse made it out to be. It just wasn't possible.

And each time the nurse left, Sandy would invite Kennedy again to pray. Woong had gotten past his clingy stage and was antsy, so Kennedy showed him how to play Scrabble on her phone. The battery died just a minute before they ended their prayer. If it hadn't, she had a feeling Sandy could have gone on for another full hour of devoted intercession. As it was, the fact that her phone battery held its charge for even that long was some small miracle, or at the very least an unusual and unexpected blessing.

Sandy stroked Kennedy's arm and smiled gently at her. "Thank you for praying with me, sweetheart. It did my soul a world of good."

"I'm glad to hear that." Kennedy was trying to guess if the softness in Sandy's features was just her regular, warm expression, or if she really did look different after their time in prayer together.

Sandy stood up with a quiet groan. "I guess I'd better go ask the nurse if there's any news. Maybe we can go back and see him soon."

Kennedy was afraid Sandy would ask her to come, too. Of course, she'd go if that's what Sandy wanted, but the thought of seeing Carl so weak, laying there paralyzed with a machine doing all his breathing for him, made Kennedy feel like she was about to suffocate.

Brain damage? Not someone like Carl. God wouldn't let something happen that was so senseless. Such a waste. And because of what? Some hoodlum? Who would attack a person like Carl? Who would want to hurt him? All he did was love people. Love people, take strangers into his home, and share the gospel with everyone around him. Not the type of guy you'd expect to be walking around with a target sign on the back of his head reading *attack me.*

Kennedy squeezed her eyes shut. There was no energy left to ask God for anything. She just had to trust that he had heard her prayers earlier. Now all she could do was wait. Wait and try to offer Sandy some moral support. Woong, too. He'd been pouting ever since the phone battery died, but he was too old to play with the little toddler toys, and there was nothing else in the waiting room but magazines and TVs.

While Sandy went to talk to the nurse, something on one of the screens caught her eye. It was a scene from Harvard right outside the student center. She blinked so her contacts wouldn't be so dry and tried to focus on the small words. She'd have to stand up. Just as well. It was time to give her legs a stretch anyway.

"I'll be right back," she told Woong and walked closer to the television.

"Harvard administration is trying to track down the culprits responsible for a slew of graffiti incidents across campus. It seems as if the attack is a backlash to a conservative newspaper article printed in the student paper, the Voice, in which a Harvard junior defends the traditional role of the stay-at-home mother."

Kennedy stared at the screen with the same undivided attention as the fire chief in *Fahrenheit 451* hunting down books to burn.

The camera switched to a shot of the outside of her dorm room, where ugly green graffiti sported a quote Kennedy recognized from her column. She wasn't listening to the news anchor anymore. All she could hear was her pulse pounding in her ears. It was too much. Carl so badly injured, and now the entire campus was angry at her for daring to suggest some women might prefer to raise kids instead of chasing a career?

She pressed her fingers against her temples. She had a throbbing headache. Who cared if the anxiety meds kept her from having so many panic attacks if she had to put up with a migraine whenever she got stressed?

This was too much. Too much for her to focus on. It didn't matter if someone hadn't liked her article. The editor of the forum section had already warned her about that. She wasn't on campus right now. Who cared what people said? It wasn't like they were attacking her personally. They were just attacking her choice of words.

She glanced once more at the screen, thankful to see Channel 2 had moved on to some other bit of news. It didn't matter what it was, as long as it wasn't about her.

Sandy had finished talking to the nurse and was with Woong. Kennedy returned to her seat, glad that her legs could still support her weight. "Any updates?" she asked.

Sandy straightened out the skirt of her dress, careful to avoid the bloody spots. "Well, they hooked him up to the ventilator without any problems. That's a good thing. I was just asking Woong if he wanted to go back and see his daddy. I told him it'd be a little strange. There'll be tubes and things since Daddy's on the machine that's helping him with his breathing."

"I can stay here with Woong," Kennedy suggested. She couldn't picture any scenario in which it'd be beneficial for a young boy like Woong to see his father in such a state, at least not until he had more time to get used to the idea.

Or until it started to look like Carl would be on the ventilator indefinitely.

But no, that wouldn't happen. He was strong. His body was strong. His spirit was strong. Aside from the diabetes and a little extra weight, he was perfectly healthy. The ventilator was just a short-term solution to a problem that would correct itself in a few hours. A day or two max, and Carl would be better.

He had to be.

There was so much more work for the Lord he still had to do.

CHAPTER 11

"I'M BORED," WOONG ANNOUNCED as the afternoon wore on toward evening. "What's there to do?"

Kennedy sighed. "Want to go on a little walk?"

Woong rolled his head back and stared at the ceiling dramatically. "We've been on like ten walks already." The sad part was he probably wasn't exaggerating. He clutched his stomach. "I'm so hungry."

"If it's that bad, we could go get you a snack," Kennedy finally conceded. Woong had asked her at least a dozen times already, but with her phone dead she didn't want to be gone for too long in case Sandy came back out and wondered where they'd gone. The sun was due to set before long, and Kennedy had skipped lunch to catch the T to St. Margaret's earlier. She was just as ready to eat as Woong.

"We're not too far from the cafeteria," she said, "so if you pick something we can carry back here, I don't think it'll be a problem. We just have to hurry, all right?"

Woong beamed. "Do they have hot dogs?"

Kennedy picked up her backpack. "I don't know. Maybe."

"Holy macaroni!" Woong jumped out of his seat. It was refreshing to see his large grin back for a change.

"But remember we'll need to make up our minds really fast. And just one thing, not a whole bunch. I only have a little bit of cash on me."

"What's cash?" he asked.

"Coins and things. Dollar bills."

"Why don't you just use one of them credit cards like everyone else?"

Kennedy let out her breath. If it would keep Woong's mind off his father and his ventilator, she was willing to jump into another round of question and answers. Heaven knew she could use the mental distraction as well.

"Well, because ..." She stopped when she spotted two familiar faces heading toward them.

"Kennedy!" Willow ran up in her sandals and threw her arms around her in a hug that in most cases would have been far too long for comfort. "I'm so glad we found you. I've been wicked anxious. I've been texting you all afternoon."

"I'm sorry. My battery ..."

Willow rolled her eyes. "Don't say any more."

"Well, it wasn't entirely my fault this time."

Woong was suddenly twice as chipper as before. "Hi, Nick! We're about to get some food because I'm hungrier than a refrigerator."

Nick raised his eyebrows questioningly at Kennedy, but she wasn't able to explain the simile, either. Nick rubbed Woong's head. "That's cool. Maybe we'll join you then. Cafeteria's this way?"

Kennedy nodded. "Yeah, Sandy went back to see Carl a little while ago. We still haven't heard any updates or anything."

"He's on a ventilator now?" Willow asked in a low voice. Kennedy glanced at Woong, who was trying to beat Nick in a rock, paper, scissors game. She nodded.

"Dude," Willow exclaimed.

"I know what you mean," Kennedy replied.

"Dude."

"So," Nick interrupted with a smile, "are we getting a snack at the cafeteria or what?"

"Yeah." Willow rubbed Kennedy on the back. "Let's go."

They walked down the corridor, and Kennedy tried not to think about the last time she'd been led down this hall. The last hour she spent with Dominic. The months of painful mourning that followed.

Her Cape Cod vacation had been so good for her. It had been years since she and her parents had been in the States together. But all summer in that tiny little condo, she felt like the children in *Brave New World* paraded on display for everyone to examine. If she didn't sleep well, her mom clucked around and fretted about adjusting her prescription levels. If she didn't have an appetite, her dad would make her sit through an entire differential where he'd roll off several dozen symptoms and side effects he'd read about online. The worst was when her mom wanted to watch her sappy farm romances or historical sagas. If Kennedy couldn't conjure up the expected amount of warm fuzzies, if she gave even the slightest hint that she detested the predictable plots or clichéd dialog, her mom would assume Kennedy's reaction had to do with Dominic and berate herself for not being more sensitive in her choice of movies.

In fact, it seemed like her mom spent the entire summer hoping to make Kennedy forget all about Dominic. Erase him from her memory forever like the political dissidents in *1984*. Purged entirely until it was as if he'd never existed. Never asked Kennedy out on that first date. Never ...

She couldn't set foot in Providence Hospital without thinking about him. There were reminders all around. She couldn't forget even if she wanted to. Which she didn't. The memories were painful, but they were a part of her now, just like the scars on her arm after what she'd gone through last spring. You could only cover yourself up with sweaters and turtlenecks for so long. Eventually you had to accept that the wounds were now just as much a part of you as your own DNA. Two things in life you can't escape — your genes and your past.

Woong ran ahead, chattering with Nick about his latest homeschool science experiment. Willow was still wearing her platform sandals, and she and Kennedy took a more leisurely pace.

"Looks like Nick's ok after the talk with the detective?" Kennedy asked.

"Yeah. I'm glad that got sorted out. For now, at least. The detective guy ... what's his name again? Driscoll? Briskly?"

"Drisklay."

"Yeah, Drisklay. Whatever kind of name that is. He finished his interview with Nick. Didn't seem too bad. Nick wasn't worried.

The detective will let him know if he has any other questions, but I think you were right. It was just a formality he had to go through." She let out a nervous chuckle. "I mean, who could seriously picture someone like Nick going up against a retired football guy like Carl? The boy faints if you just talk about blood. You should have seen how pale he was before we got him cleaned up."

Kennedy did what she could to keep a positive outlook. "Well, it's good news he's off the suspect list. Do you think there are any other leads?"

Willow shrugged. "Drisklay or whatever his name is was already complaining about his coffee wearing off by the time he got to questioning me. I think he wrote me off as a biased witness anyway. I doubt we spent more than two minutes together, and I haven't heard anything else about the case so far. Speaking of cases, now might be a really bad time to mention it, but I don't want you to be caught off guard. Something happened back at the dorm."

"You mean the graffiti?"

Willow fingered the green tips of her hair. "Yeah. How'd you hear?"

"Saw it on Channel 2."

"Dude."

When they reached the cafeteria, Nick was already in line with Woong, who was trying to balance a whole tray of food stacked precariously high. So much for grabbing something quick and hurrying back to the ER to wait for news about Carl.

Willow gave Kennedy a comforting side hug. "I guess right now there's more important things to worry about than what some fools thought of your newspaper article, right?"

Kennedy's throat was parched, but she forced herself to swallow anyway. "Right."

CHAPTER 12

SANDY WAS JUST COMING out of the back rooms when Kennedy and her friends returned to the ER lobby. Woong ran up to her, apparently in a more congenial mood after Nick bought him two hotdogs, a bag of Cheetos, a big fruit salad ("on account of it having lots of good, healthy vitamins"), and a giant soft pretzel with double portions of melted cheese product.

Sandy bent over her son and gave him a hug. "How's my boy? Are you minding Miss Kennedy?"

Woong nodded. "I beat Nick at paper, scissors, rock," he boasted. "Except this is a new version. It's got a lizard and a funny alien guy with pointy ears who makes his fingers all funny." Woong tried to replicate the hand gesture.

Sandy looked clueless, but she brushed the stray hair out of her eyes and tried to offer everyone a smile. "Willow and Nick, it's good to see you both. How are you doing today?"

Nick stepped beside her and gave her a side hug. "What we really want to know is how's Carl? What have the doctors said?"

Sandy sat down and fidgeted with her skirt. It was a little bit wet. Kennedy wondered if she'd tried to wash some of the bloodstains out of it. Once everyone else was seated, Sandy put her arm around Woong and said, "Well, we have so much to thank the good Lord for. So much. Carl looks real peaceful back there." She sniffed and quickly wiped her cheek. "Real comfortable. And the doctors are confident that he's not in any kind of pain." She cleared her throat. "So right now, I'm counting that as a huge blessing. You know Carl and how much he hates hospitals." She let out a little chuckle that faltered unconvincingly at the end.

She paused for a moment and then resumed. "I guess the injury is a little more complicated than we might have hoped, but I'm convinced that through it all ..." She held Woong a little closer, gave a weak smile, and tried again. "I'm convinced that through it all, God's purpose for my husband still stands. They'll be doing some brain scans before too long now, and after that we'll have a clearer picture of what his recovery might look like."

Nobody spoke. How was it possible? A few hours ago, Carl had been engaged in one of his favorite pastimes, debating politics with Nick, and now this? Brain scans, complicated recovery ... what exactly was Sandy telling them?

Did Kennedy really want to know?

Willow was sitting across from Sandy and rested her hand on her knee. "You know Carl wouldn't want you to worry right now, don't you?"

Sandy nodded and wiped her cheeks again.

Kennedy watched her roommate's face for any sign of breaking. If Willow started to cry, then Kennedy would start to cry, and pretty soon they'd all be making a scene as loud and boisterous as the choir boys in *Lord of the Flies*.

Willow sniffed. It was going to happen. Kennedy couldn't stand the thought.

"Come on, guys." She infused artificial cheer into her voice. "Willow is right that this isn't how Carl would want us to react." Nods all around gave Kennedy encouragement. "He's always said that ... He's never been afraid of anything, know what I mean? I don't think he'd want us to be afraid either." She forced a small chuckle. "In fact, we all can guess what Carl would be doing if one of us was on a ventilator and he was out here waiting for answers."

Woong sat up in his seat. "I know. He'd start praying, and he do it real loud-like on account of him being one of them sorts of Christians who don't care if other people laugh at them for talking to God in someplace besides church."

Instead of lightening the mood, Woong's words clawed and slashed at Kennedy's soul. *Why, God? Why would you put this family that loves you so much and has served you so faithfully through this kind of nightmare?* She looked over at Sandy, at the tears her friend was trying so hard to hide. Sandy had been there for dozens, no hundreds of hurting people over the years. Had rescued foster kids from lives of addiction and abuse, had prayed with the hurting, cried with the distraught. She was a pillar of strength, and an unshakable beacon of hope that so many had turned to during the storms in their lives.

And now it was time for somebody to offer her that same encouragement and love.

Kennedy couldn't remember if it was Willow or maybe Nick who suggested that they pray, or if they all just sensed the movement of the Holy Spirit and entered into God's throne room together out of some silent agreement. Even Woong sat perfectly still while prayers for Carl's healing and recovery were lifted up to the one who comforts the brokenhearted and binds up all their wounds.

CHAPTER 13

"SO YOU'LL CALL ME if you hear anything about Carl, right?" Nick asked when he dropped Kennedy and Willow off on campus.

"Yeah. And you do the same if you get an update first." Willow gave him a light kiss and got out of his VW bus.

"You doing all right?" she asked Kennedy as they made their way toward their dorm.

Kennedy didn't know how to respond. How did you define *all right*? Was Willow talking about the panic attacks? In that case, yes, she felt fine. If anything, it seemed like she should be experiencing more inner turmoil than she was. Or maybe that was just the exhaustion. She and Willow had stayed at the hospital for several hours. Sandy made arrangements for Woong to spend the night with a friend from his former school, so after a quick dinner in the cafeteria, they'd gone with Nick to drop Woong off at the Linklaters' and had just now gotten back to Harvard.

Kennedy couldn't remember if she had any assignments she'd have to work on before bed. Her first class wasn't until noon tomorrow, so maybe she should wait until morning. Was she ready for the next day's lab? Kennedy's former chemistry professor had hired her to TA the introductory chemistry lab, an honor for any undergrad, especially a junior. It was a little weird teaching students who were only two years younger than she was, but it was a fun challenge and reminded Kennedy how much she liked general chemistry. In fact, if she ever needed a fallback plan from med school, she could see herself going into the research side of things.

As humbled as she was to have been chosen as one of Adell's teaching assistants, right now she had other things to worry about besides the thirteen lab reports she couldn't remember if she'd finished grading or not. Oh, well. Even if she was too exhausted to get to it tonight, she'd have time in the morning. She'd find a way to make it work. She always did.

Willow slowed her pace as soon as their dorm came into view. At first Kennedy thought it was because of those high-heeled sandals, but then she saw the graffiti on the side of the building and remembered everything that happened on campus. The newspaper article. The angry students.

Willow glanced at her awkwardly. "You sure you're all right?"

Kennedy kept her eyes in front of her and refused to look at the graffitied wall. "I'm fine. It's just words. Words never hurt anybody." She didn't raise her eyes to Willow to try to guess if her roommate believed her or not.

Willow opened the door of the building, muttering something about closed-minded ignoramuses. Kennedy followed her into the dorm but stopped when someone behind her shouted her name.

"Kennedy! Hold up. I need to talk to you." The forum editor for the Voice ran up to her. O'Brien slipped inside, slightly out of breath. "I've been texting you all afternoon."

"My battery died."

O'Brien rolled his eyes. "Again?" He offered a small smile. "Well, it's a good thing I found you in time. The editors called together a meeting in five minutes. We need you there."

Kennedy did her best not to groan. "A meeting this late?"

He shoved his hands into his pockets. "Yeah, I know it might not be the most convenient, but this is pretty important."

"What's important," Willow interrupted, "is that you leave her alone. She's in the midst of a personal crisis here, and ..."

"That's why the editors called this meeting," he answered. "It's all because of that column you wrote, and since I'm the section head who signed off your article, we're in this together whether you like it or not."

Willow was about to reply, but Kennedy touched her on the arm. "It's ok. You know there's no way I could sleep now anyway. May as well go distract myself for a little bit. Don't worry about me."

Willow crossed her arms and jutted out her hip. "I am going to worry about you because you're my best friend, and no one should have to be alone on a night like ..."

"I won't be alone." Kennedy conjured up a smile and lowered her voice. "It's all right. Trust me."

"Fine," Willow conceded, "but you give me your phone, and I'll plug it in for you so if Sandy tries to get hold of you, I can pick it up."

"Ok." Kennedy took her phone out of her backpack and passed it to Willow.

"You sure you want to do this?" she whispered.

No, Kennedy wasn't sure, but she didn't have the energy to stand here arguing. She nodded. "Yeah. Like I said, it beats sitting around worrying."

"Take care of yourself, hear?" Willow gave her a quick hug and whispered, "Don't let anything they say get to you. You did the right thing publishing that article, and they have no right to bully you into feeling bad just for sharing an unpopular opinion."

Kennedy smiled, thankful to have a friend who took her well-being so seriously.

O'Brien, who'd been biting his lip and avoiding eye contact during Kennedy and Willow's exchange, held open the door. "So then, you ready?"

Kennedy nodded and adjusted her backpack. "I'm ready. Let's get this over with."

CHAPTER 14

KENNEDY LOOKED BACK ONCE as she and O'Brien headed toward the student union building where the Voice held its offices. Willow was staring at her through the window of their dorm.

"She your bodyguard or something?" O'Brien asked.

"No, just my roommate."

O'Brien's hands were in his pockets, and his shoulders jutted up toward his ears. "I'm sorry I had to interrupt your night like this, especially if you've got other stuff going on." He jerked one ear toward his shoulder, making his neck vertebra crack.

Kennedy winced. "Don't worry about it. So what's this meeting all about?"

He wrenched his head the other way. More pops and creaks. "This is basically where you get chewed out for your antifeminist opinions, and I get slaughtered for allowing you to publish it in my section."

"You're joking, right?" Kennedy glanced at O'Brien, who had taken his hands out of his pockets and was now cracking his knuckles.

"No. Perfectly serious. Happens once or twice a year, although I don't think we've had a case this big since President Reinholtz resigned."

"Who?"

"Reinholtz. The guy here the year before you came. You seriously didn't hear about him?"

Kennedy shook her head.

"Wow, you must have been living your entire college career in the dark. Reinholtz published a book citing all kinds of so-called scientific evidence that showed that male brains are different than female brains."

Kennedy hadn't realized you needed to be the president of an Ivy League school like Harvard to reach a conclusion like that, but by the way O'Brien was looking at her, she assumed he expected her to be shocked by the revelation.

"Then what?" she asked.

"What would you expect? The students, the staff, the media. They all crucified him. He resigned less than a month later. You're lucky you missed it. Things got really ugly."

"Because he said that men and women's brains are different?" Kennedy was still trying to figure out what the controversy was in the first place.

"Yeah. I mean, sure the guy's got a few screws loose to even publish garbage like that, but I guess I'm in the minority by thinking we could have actually heard his side and let him speak for himself instead of getting rid of him so fast. But anyway, all that to say you really touched a nerve with your article. I hate to sound smug, but I did try to warn you."

"I remember." Kennedy kept her voice low.

"So, this meeting, it's probably gonna be a little hostile in there, so I just want you to be prepared. Ok? Any questions?"

Kennedy didn't know where to begin. O'Brien had told her how unpopular her opinion would be when she submitted her column to the Voice, but that still hadn't prepared her for graffiti on her dorm or some kind of midnight inquisition where she'd have to defend herself before an entire panel of thought police.

She mentally rehearsed what she'd written in her column. She'd started off by saying that she knew Sandy Lindgren personally and was upset by the way the staff of the Harvard Voice had painted a woman they hadn't ever met in such a negative light simply because she was a stay-at-home mom and married to the man who had organized the Truth Warriors conference.

I'm not saying every woman has to stay home and take care of her family, Kennedy had written. *As a premed student eager to begin my career in medicine, I'm completely against women being denied a place in any academic or vocational field they feel drawn toward. But as a compassionate human being, I'm also against berating women whose life choices may be different than my own. There is nothing debasing or ignoble about a wife or mother who stays home to take care of her family* if that's what she chooses to do. *And it surprises me that a panel claiming to be as open-minded as the editorial staff of the Harvard Voice would malign an individual they've never met and make such a rash judgement call about her life and choices simply because she does not bring home a monthly paycheck.*

That was probably the most heated it got. Kennedy shook her head. She had more important things to do than explain herself to a bunch of students she didn't even know. Students who had most likely already labeled her a close-minded conservative after reading a simple, seven-hundred-word essay. She heard Carl in her head, voicing one of his go-to complaints: *It's like* 1984 *all over again.*

Maybe he was onto something there.

Thinking about Carl reminded her that she had a lot more serious problems to worry about than what some editors said about her silly piece of writing. She was glad Willow had taken her phone. Maybe by the time this interview was over, she'd get some news about Carl's prognosis. She still couldn't believe it was as serious as the doctors had told Sandy.

Actually, she could believe it, especially after all she'd read so far in her neuroscience class. The difference was this was her pastor, mentor, and friend, not some nameless case study in a text book. She'd known Carl since she was a tiny girl attending his church in Manhattan. She'd been half the size of Woong, or even smaller, when Sandy was her Sunday school teacher, when Carl would dress up as a clown or a cowboy or a zookeeper for each summer's theme-based vacation Bible school. Next to her dad, she loved Carl more than any other man in the world. The fear of having to say good-bye to him ...

No, she couldn't think like that. After all God had dragged her through, losing Dominic and everything else that had happened over the past year or two, this would be too much. The Lord wouldn't ask her to give up Carl, too. She was overreacting. Leave it to her panic-prone imagination to exaggerate the situation. Carl was fine. His injuries were serious, but he'd recover by the grace of God and go back to the life and ministry he'd had before today's accident.

No, not accident. Attack. Why was it so hard to remember that?

The student union came into view, and Kennedy was tempted to feign a headache or concoct some other excuse to retreat. Actually, now that she thought about it, her head still hurt.

O'Brien opened the door, and they walked in. "Try not to take what they say personally, and let me do most of the talking, all right?"

Kennedy didn't answer but followed him up the stairs that led to the Voice office.

O'Brien rolled his shoulders and popped his back. "Ok." He led the way into the editorial room. "Let's do this."

CHAPTER 15

KENNEDY STARED AT THE faces around her, trying to figure out if there was anyone she recognized. She was initially surprised at how many staff members of the Voice were here. When O'Brien said she'd be meeting with the editors, she thought he meant the five section heads and the editor-in-chief, but apparently each section editor had an assistant who was also considered part of the staff, and there were also a few senior editors who no longer ran their own pages but still remained involved in the life and pulse of the Voice. Getting through the initial introductions took at least ten minutes.

Ten minutes Kennedy could have spent in her dorm room worrying about Carl. Or praying for him.

"Ok. Let's get to it." Marty, the editor-in-chief, unfolded that week's copy of the Voice. "I think we all know why we're here."

Kennedy didn't feel like now was the best time to point out Marty's mistake.

O'Brien cleared his throat. "I just want to take a minute to point something out before we begin."

Great. Now was the time when he'd say that he had absolutely nothing to do with Kennedy's column.

Marty nodded at him, and he continued. "What I want to say is that I know the ideas in this column are troubling to a lot of us."

So much for his little *we're in this together* pep talk from earlier. Kennedy vowed to never write for publication again.

"But even if Kennedy's ideas are fairly unorthodox, I thought it would be an asset to the paper to present an opposing point of view. I read her article and found it to be a respectful, concise summary of the conservative viewpoint. That's why I allowed it to go to print."

Marty raised an eyebrow. Kennedy thought she recognized her but couldn't remember from where. One of her roommate's plays, maybe.

"So you're saying you stand by your decision to run this column?"

Kennedy held her breath.

O'Brien nodded. "Yes. That's absolutely what I'm saying."

There were quite a few murmurs around the table before Marty got everyone's attention again.

"All right. Thank you to O'Brien for his confirmation that he was not only involved but also gave full support to the opinions in this article."

O'Brien leaned forward in his chair. "Hold up. I didn't say I supported her opinions. I said I supported her right to make her opinions heard."

An assistant editor shook her head. "There's no difference. By giving her space in the paper, you're stating that you support her beliefs."

"That's not true. I gave her space in the paper because I believe that as open-minded individuals, like we all claim to be, we should give fair treatment to various sides of an issue."

"Not when that issue condones misogyny."

Kennedy's head swarmed while the editors bickered back and forth. There were so many different points being made by so many different people that she couldn't keep any of their arguments straight. It was clear, however, that O'Brien was the only one who thought Kennedy's article should have ever made it to print.

"We're a university that stands for free thought and open mindedness," he argued. "So what's it say about us when we silence anybody who doesn't believe what we do? Is it our job to pre-screen every single student's opinion and only publish what we agree with?"

"Of course," answered the news editor.

O'Brien shook his head. "Do you realize what you sound like? Aren't we supposed to be the open-minded ones in these debates? Aren't we the ones promoting tolerance and co-existence? Instead, we've become a mob eager to lynch anyone who ..."

Marty coughed. "That's a problematic word right there. I'll need to ask you to change your language."

"What?" O'Brien looked around the table. "What'd I say?"

Marty rolled her eyes. "You said the word *lynch*, which for certain students from certain historical backgrounds carries an aggressive and threatening connotation."

Kennedy had kept her gaze low during the entire meeting. She didn't know if the fact that O'Brien was taking the entirety of the Voice staff's ire made her feel more guilty or relieved.

"So I can't say *lynched*, huh? It's yet another one of those words that have become offensive? What next? Are we going to force everyone here to start talking in newspeak?"

Several of the students looked confused, but Kennedy recognized the *1984* reference.

"What's next?" O'Brien continued. "We going to start blacking out words in the dictionary? Take a Sharpie and just smudge over them like they never existed?"

Marty shook her head. "I think we've all gotten a clear understanding of what you have to say. What if we have the writer speak for themself at this time?"

It wasn't until all the faces around the table turned toward her that Kennedy realized who Marty was talking about. "Me?"

"Of course." Marty smiled with false serenity. "It was your column that started this whole mess, and O'Brien's right on one point. It would be wrong for us to do anything here tonight without giving you the chance to defend yourself. So go ahead. Tell us why women are supposed to stay at home and do nothing but raise babies. I'm sure we're all dying to hear your opinion." She shot O'Brien an angry glare.

Kennedy rubbed her sweaty palms against her jeans. "Ok." She cleared her voice and tried to sneak a little confidence into her tone. "So, first of all, I never said that women should be forced to stay at home ..."

"But you defended the pastor's wife at that mega-church," someone interrupted.

"Well, yeah, but I guess I see a difference between standing up for one individual and saying that every single person who happens to be a girl has to follow her example."

"Female," Marty inserted.

Kennedy didn't understand. "What's that?"

"Female," she repeated. "The term *girl* carries a derogatory tone. For example, you would never call someone who presents as male who's over the age of eighteen or twenty a boy, so why would you use the word *girl* when you're referring to an adult?"

Kennedy stared at the shiny boardroom table. "Ok, sorry about that. All I meant to say was when I wrote my piece I was trying to show that some females enjoy being stay-at-home moms, and if that's a choice they make, who are we to tell them it's wrong?"

"We're the progressive ones, that's who we are," Marty answered. "The ones on the right side of truth. Do you really think your little pastor's wife *enjoys* all that cooking she does every day?"

"Well, as a matter of fact ..."

"And do you think," Marty interrupted, "that it's socially responsible to praise members of society who've given up all their own ambitions and dreams and career opportunities just so they can enslave themselves to their husbands and children?" She shook her head. "I read your article, and I see nothing but patriarchal propaganda. What about the case where a husband gets disabled and is unable to fulfill his traditional role as bread-winner? Is little Sally Homemaker supposed to smile and keep on baking him her casseroles and let their home get foreclosed? Or what about non-traditional couples, a trans male for example or two females in a monogamous relationship. Which one of them would be expected to stay home and take care of the babies in your perfect little world?"

Kennedy's palms were so wet she probably could have dried them on a paper towel and wrung it out afterward. "It wasn't my intention to dictate how every woman or female's supposed to behave. I just wanted to ..."

"What I'm curious about," interrupted the editor sitting directly across from her, "is how you can justify investing so much time and energy and finances into a Harvard education just so you can find yourself some spouse and live happily ever after."

Kennedy glanced around the table. Several of the editors had been silent the entire meeting, but not even the quiet ones would raise their eyes to hers with anything but open hostility. She wondered what they would do if she simply announced she had lab reports to grade and got up and left. But what would that mean for O'Brien? He'd been right when he told her they were in this pit together. At the time, however, Kennedy had no idea how deep of a pit it would be.

"I'm not planning to be just a stay-at-home mom myself."

"Oh, really?" Marty grinned. "What other plans do you have? Selling cosmetics online?"

One of her dad's sayings ran through her head. *You shouldn't ever be surprised when a non-Christian fails to behave like a Christian.* Kennedy did her best to keep her voice calm so Marty couldn't sense her growing anger. "Actually, I'm going on to med school. I've already been accepted into Harvard's early admissions program."

Unfortunately, Marty didn't seem at all impressed. "So four years of med school and then what? Have a bunch of kids and babysit to pay off all your student loans?"

O'Brien cleared his throat. "This meeting isn't about Kennedy's future plans, or at least it shouldn't be. It's about her article. I think we'd save a lot of time and headache if we stuck to the original issue."

Marty shrugged. "I'm not so sure the two aren't more related than that. Tell me." She glowered at Kennedy. "What will you do if you find someone you want to marry only he doesn't want you to go to medical school? What then? Or what if you get pregnant before you graduate? Aren't all you conservatives against contraceptives? Then what? You're not going to have an abortion, and you can't strap a baby on your back while you're doing your surgical rounds. So what happens then?"

"What happens then," O'Brien boomed, "is irrelevant. This whole interrogation is pointless, but since we're here, let's focus on the matter at hand. Kennedy wrote an article. You guys don't like it because you disagree with what she had to say. So now what? You either fire her from submitting to the paper in the future, you come up with some opposing editorial, or you decide on something tangible to do. That's why we're here, not to talk about how her views on womanhood might complicate her career choice as a doctor. I personally would be happy to go to a practitioner who put a high priority on family life."

A black-haired girl in glasses smirked. "Yeah, unless she leaves you in the middle of an open-heart surgery because her preschooler's got a ballet recital."

Kennedy tried to clench her jaw shut, but even that wasn't enough to keep the torrent of angry words from spewing out of her mouth. "I don't think it's your right to question what any woman does in her personal life. Or to tell me that since I wrote an article defending a friend that I'm going to be an irresponsible doctor or I'm not going to do anything but sit at home all day and watch my kids." Once the words started coming out, she couldn't stop them. "You claim to be so tolerant, but do you know how judgmental you sound right now? Telling me that I'm going to risk a patient's life for a ballet recital?" She glared at the black-haired girl, who at least had the decency to lower her gaze.

"And you." Kennedy turned to Marty. "When did a progressive editor's job become censoring anyone who didn't agree with your viewpoint? You guys called me in so you could hear what I had to say about my article. I told you. I wrote it because in last week's op-ed, you ripped into my friend. You've never met Sandy Lindgren. You have no idea what kind of woman she is. All you know is that she doesn't work a traditional job, and so you jump to the conclusion that she's some backwards, low-life ditz who's incapable of anything but baking and changing diapers. Do you know how ignorant that makes you all sound?

"You know I'm a Christian, you assume I'm conservative, so you jump to all kinds of conclusions about me. Know what? Christian women work all kinds of jobs. Some in the home, some out. And you know what else? They do that because it's their choice. Isn't that what you stand for? Freedom to choose the life you want to lead?"

"Not if your choices squash the freedom of others." Marty crossed her arms.

"Who's talking about squashing? When did I say anything about squashing? Take Sandy. How in the world can you look at all she does and tell me that she's kept other women from living their lives to the fullest?"

"Well, we all know that her husband's church ..."

"I didn't ask about her husband's church," Kennedy interrupted. "I asked about Sandy herself. How does the fact that she stays at home and takes care of her son and grandkids hurt the other women who know her? What's so wrong with that lifestyle if it's truly her choice to make?"

Marty glanced around at the other editors. "Well, for one thing ..." She hit her pen against the edge of the table a few times. "Her example itself is sending the wrong message. It's telling other females that if they don't stay home like she does, they're doing it wrong."

Kennedy shook her head. "Sandy would never say those things."

Marty shrugged. "I don't know that. All I know is her husband's the one spearheading this conference where a bunch of men are going to get together and talk about how to *keep their women in line* and anti-progressive garbage like that. And so even if your friend isn't actively contributing to that sort of chauvinistic mentality, she's definitely complicit."

Kennedy's heart was racing. Her hands were no longer clammy now but cold. Her jaw ached from being clenched so hard.

Apparently eager to make sure her words were the last, Marty composed herself and addressed the staff. "All right, so now we've heard all sides of the argument. What I'd like to do is have O'Brien and his writer friend step out, and we'll take our vote."

O'Brien stood to his feet. Kennedy did the same.

"Vote?" she asked. "What vote?"

She thought she detected a slight gleam in Marty's eyes. "The vote where we decide how to undo all the damage your little misogynistic column has caused."

CHAPTER 16

KENNEDY FOLLOWED O'BRIEN TO a couch just outside the board-room. "So now we wait?" she asked.

He nodded. "Now we wait."

She wanted to tell him something. Thank him maybe for the way he'd stood up for her, but she wasn't sure how to word it. She'd never really considered herself that articulate of an individual. She got good grades on her papers for her literature classes, but most of that had to do with knowing what kind of style and wording her professors expected from her. She'd never done anything like write a column for the paper before, and after today she was certain she wouldn't repeat the same mistake and try it again.

She glanced at the time and wondered if she should call Willow. Ask if there was any news about Carl. But of course, she didn't have her phone with her and didn't have a single number in her contacts list memorized. If God had made anything good come out of her interrogation meeting with the Voice editors, it was that it had taken her mind off Carl and his injuries. Even so, now she felt guilty that she'd wasted all her energy yelling at the editor-in-chief when she could have been praying for Carl's recovery.

Kennedy couldn't remember the last time she'd spilled her frustrations like that, at least not with someone other than her mom or dad. Guilt heated her core. She thought about Sandy, whom she'd been trying so hard to defend. She was so patient and gentle. In fact, today in the car was the first time Kennedy had heard Sandy actually snap at Woong, and that was only because he'd been disrespectful to the Lord.

Maybe there was a time and place for righteous anger, but Kennedy couldn't shake the feeling that all she'd done was let her temper take over and wasted her words on people who didn't want to hear what she had to say anyway. What was that verse in the Bible about casting your pearls before swine? She glanced at O'Brien, who was sulking next to her.

"It was nice of you to take my side in there," she said softly.

O'Brien looked up, as if he were surprised that she'd spoken. "Point taken, but for the record I'm not on your side. I'm on the side of open debate, and that's all."

Kennedy didn't know what to say. It was understandable if he was mad at her. She was the reason he was in trouble with his friends.

They were silent for several minutes. Through the drawn curtain in the meeting room, Kennedy could make out Marty's silhouette as she stood facing the other editors.

"Any guess how long this will take?" she finally worked up the courage to ask. Apparently, her little tantrum in the meeting room had used up her assertiveness quota for the day. Maybe more like the semester.

O'Brien shrugged. "What, this monkey trial? My guess is we'll get our answer in just another minute or two."

"So what exactly is it that they're voting on?"

He shrugged again. "Your article has already been printed. There's nothing they can do about that. It's just damage control now. Retractions, junk like that. And they're probably voting to see if I should keep my position on the paper or not."

"I'm really sorry you got involved in all this." What more could she say?

He let out his breath. "Oh, don't worry about that. If it wasn't your article, it would've been someone else's. It's ironic. They call my pages the forum section, but by definition the word *forum* means open debate. The free spread of ideas. If I had known when I signed up that all they wanted me to do was parrot back their orthodox party line, I would've never bothered. Or at least I would've had them change the name from *forum* to *propaganda*.

It's much more fitting." He let out a mirthless chuckle. "And you ... you sure played your cards right in there. Even before you walked into that room, they all had you pegged as some little dormouse who wouldn't dare have the guts to stand up for herself. I'm glad you proved them wrong." There was genuine respect in his eyes.

Kennedy returned his smile. "To be honest, that's not what I'm usually like, but they kept putting words in my mouth, twisting what I said."

"Yeah. It's what they do best. That and silence anyone who disagrees with them."

Kennedy rubbed her palm on the top of her pants, trying to figure out the best way to word her question. "Can I ask you something?"

"Sure." Another shrug. "What have we got to lose?"

She ignored his cynicism. "I got the feeling in there that you don't agree with what I had to say in my column," she began.

"Correct." He still didn't meet her eyes.

She licked her lips and continued. "But you defended me in the meeting room."

"Also correct. And you already hit on the difference. I don't agree with your statements. I think a woman is completely free to work whatever job she chooses."

Kennedy didn't bother to point out that she'd said almost the same thing verbatim in the meeting room but let O'Brien continue.

"So no, I don't personally support your opinions, but I support you as a freethinking student who has the right to hold whatever ideas you want to have. That's why I thought the forum section would be such a good fit for me. I see no reason to read only things that support what I already believe. When I pick up a book, for example, I'm not looking for something that's going to spoon-feed me what I already know. When I read something by an author whose opinions on the subject are exactly the same as my own, what do I gain other than a sense of self-righteousness? My idea for the forum section was to make it truly that — a forum where people with different viewpoints could have engaging, lively debates. Respectful debates of course. There's no reason for an ideological argument to be the foundation for a personal attack, which is exactly what happened to you in that meeting room.

You asked why I defended you even though I don't believe in your viewpoint. and that's because you're obviously an intelligent individual, and sometimes what we all need is to be stared in the face by an argument that frightens us. That challenges our rigid and oh-so-precious convictions. You've got a right to be heard just as much as anyone else. And if people find your argument offensive, it's their job to prove you wrong rhetorically, not with personal jabs."

Kennedy hadn't expected such a long answer. She thought about Carl and Nick, about their frequent spats. As heated as their arguments got, at least they never resorted to those kind of base attacks. Speaking of attacks ...

She looked at the time. If Willow hadn't already heard from Sandy by now, she probably wouldn't until morning. Kennedy couldn't picture Sandy sending out prayer chain updates this late at night no matter how serious things got. She glanced again at the drawn curtains of the Voice meeting room.

"You worried about the vote?" O'Brien asked. "No need to be. Since you're not on staff, the worst they can do is ban you from writing for us again."

"It's not that." Kennedy sighed. She really didn't want to go into details about what had happened to Carl, but it was all she was able to think about now and she found herself spelling out the abridged version of his injuries.

"That's messed up," was O'Brien's final assessment.

"Yeah." Kennedy couldn't have said it any better.

"So it was definitely intentional? It wasn't just like some bad accident or anything?"

Kennedy shook her head. "The police are already involved, and we found the bookend the attacker used to knock him out with."

"That's messed up," he repeated.

"Yeah." She wondered if they were doomed to repeat the same two lines indefinitely like characters in a sci-fi book trapped in some sort of time loop.

"Think it has something to do with the that men's conference?"

O'Brien's question surprised her. She was in no mood to play detective. That was Drisklay's job.

"I don't know. I know people are upset about it, but I can't see anybody attacking him like that over it."

For a minute, Kennedy wondered if O'Brien was going to tell her how messed up it all was, but he simply shook his head.

"Wonder what they're taking so long for," he said a few minutes later. "Seems like it should be a pretty open and shut case."

"What do you think's going to happen to you?"

A shrug. "They'll probably vote me off the board."

She couldn't understand how he could sound so casual about it. "I'm really sorry. If I had known ..."

"Don't worry about it," he interrupted. "I knew what I was doing, and I don't regret it. Even if they don't vote me off, I'll probably resign anyway. I've got a few friends who are thinking about working together to start a new paper. One that really does give free voice to the wide range of student opinions represented on campus." He gave her a soft smile. "You'd be welcome to write for us if you ever wanted."

She didn't have the heart to turn him down directly. "I'll keep that in mind."

The door to the conference room opened. Marty leaned out. "You can come in now. We're all finished."

CHAPTER 17

KENNEDY SAT DOWN IN the same chair she'd been in just a little while earlier. O'Brien remained standing.

"All right." Marty didn't look at either of them. "So, here's what's going to happen. O'Brien, you're off the staff. Although I enjoyed working with you and you had a lot of strong articles come out during your time here, tonight made it pretty clear that the Voice isn't a good fit for you."

"I couldn't agree with you more." O'Brien shot her an icy smile. None of the other editors would look him in the face.

Marty turned to Kennedy. "As for you, we expect a rebuttal in our hands by Monday afternoon at the latest. We all agree that the opinions you stated in your original column are problematic and potentially triggering to students who are experiencing gender-identity issues or self-directed misogyny, and that's just not something we can leave unadressed."

Kennedy glanced around the table. "You want me to take back what I already said?"

"That's the basic idea behind a rebuttal, correct?" Marty grinned sarcastically.

"But I already told you what I believe."

"Yeah, but unfortunately that's not the kind of archaic thinking that we at the Voice are able to condone. So what we'll need from you is two or three hundred words. Nothing lengthy."

Kennedy felt like she had as a third-grader being told she had to clean her room. "What happens if I don't submit a rebuttal?"

"Oh, I'm sure any of us here would be happy to write it for you. All you'd need to do is make any last-minute changes in style and voice."

"No, I mean what if I still stand by what I originally said?" Out of the corner of her eye, Kennedy caught O'Brien's wide grin.

Marty stared. "Excuse me?"

"I said I stand by what I wrote in my original article. I don't want to change anything."

Marty cleared her throat. "In that case ..." She glanced around the table. "Well, in that case ..."

"In that case," O'Brien broke in for her, "Kennedy, you're free to go. And since I'm on my way out, too, I don't think anyone will mind if I congratulate you for writing the first original thought this paper has published in years."

O'Brien opened the door to the meeting room, and he and Kennedy exited the Voice office.

CHAPTER 18

O'BRIEN'S DORM WAS IN the opposite direction, so Kennedy wished him good night, thanked him again for his support, and hurried back toward her room. Her limbs were exhausted, her mind heavy. She wanted to sleep but knew it would still be a while before her thoughts would quiet down enough for her to get any rest.

The door to her room was slightly open when she got there. Willow's laughter rang through the hallway. Kennedy wondered if Nick had stopped by for another visit. As much fun as it usually was watching him and Willow interact with each other, she hadn't mentally prepared herself for a guest.

Especially not a guest who was four and a half feet tall.

"Hey, Kennedy!" Woong smiled broadly at her.

"What's going on?" she asked before she could remember any sort of decent etiquette.

"Woong was going to spend the night with his friends, the Linklaters," Willow explained in a voice that was a little louder and slower than necessary, "but then he thought to himself, *Hey, I bet my good friends Kennedy and Willow are having more fun than I am* so he asked to come over here."

Kennedy couldn't understand why her roommate was tilting her head toward Woong and apparently trying to send her some sort of telepathic message. All she could think to say was, "Why?"

"I got bored over there, so I asked Mrs. Linklater if I could call my mom. She's got to stay at the hospital with Dad, but she said she'd ask Nick if I could spend the night with him. Well, he was busy talking to some detective or other ..."

Kennedy thought she saw Willow wince.

"So then my mom called you on account of you sometimes being my babysitter and stuff and nonsense like that, but instead of calling you, she called Willow, and then everything got a little confusing, and here I am."

Kennedy looked to her roommate for translation.

"I just got back from picking him up," Willow explained. "He was having a hard time sleeping." She lowered her voice. "Worried about his dad."

"Was not," Woong insisted with a pout.

Kennedy glanced around the room. "So what happens now? Is he sleeping here?"

"I wasn't sure," Willow told her. "I mean, I think Sandy was picturing you spending the night at their place, but she knew it was a lot to ask, and I wasn't sure how late your meeting would go, so I told her I'd pick up Woong, and then we'd decide what to do."

Woong adjusted himself in Willow's beanbag chair. "Well I figure that maybe I'll just sleep right here."

A college dorm was certainly no place for a little boy to spend the night, but Kennedy wondered what other options there were.

Willow leaned toward her desk mirror and applied some of her goat milk chap stick. "If Nick gets done talking with that Broccoli guy or whoever that detective is, he said he could stop by and take Woong to his place. I think that's plan A, but like I said, we don't know how long he's going to be."

"Why is the detective talking to him this late at night?" Kennedy asked, trying to gauge from Willow's expression how worried she was for her boyfriend.

"Beats me. This has all been by text. I haven't talked to him since he dropped us off earlier."

"Ok." Kennedy looked around the room again as if a third bed and a Woong-sized pair of pajamas might miraculously materialize. She wished she had a little privacy to talk with Willow about everything. Get the full account of Carl's health without having to worry about scaring Woong. Talk about that ridiculous meeting she'd just gotten out of.

Willow had taken one of her Alaska-themed quilts off her bed and threw it on top of Woong. "So you know it's really late, right? And you're probably going to have a busy day tomorrow, so I want you to try to get some sleep."

"What if I fall asleep and then Nick comes to take me to his apartment?"

"I'll tell him to carry you real quiet. Maybe you won't even wake up."

"I bet I will. I always do."

"Ok." Willow leaned over and adjusted the blanket around him. "For now, you just rest, all right? Do you need anything else before bed? Use the bathroom? Anything like that?"

Woong frowned. "My mom usually reads me some."

Kennedy was about to tell Woong that he'd have to sleep tonight without a story, but Willow was already over by Kennedy's desk. "What have you got that's good for a kid?" She ran her finger over a few of the titles.

"Nothing dystopian," Kennedy answered quickly. She thought about her American literature class. "What about *Little Women?*"

"Women?" Woong repeated. "Bleh. Why would I want to read a book about a bunch of girls?"

"There's lots of good books about girls," Willow told him. "Have you ever read *Anne of Green Gables?*"

"Yeah, my teacher read it to us in school last year. I liked the movie better. Especially the part where the old man grabs his arm, and then all of a sudden he's dead, and everyone's sad."

Willow glanced at Kennedy, trying to hide her smile.

"*Little Women*'s a good one," Kennedy interjected. "It's got these four sisters, and at the start of the book, it's the middle of the Civil War."

"Do any of them dress up like boys and run off to battle?" he asked.

"Well, no, but ..."

"Do the soldiers come to their house, and the girls have to chase them off with guns and knives?"

"Not exactly."

"So what's it about then?" he demanded with a dubious pout.

"*Little Women* is a story about four sisters, and they ... they ..." Kennedy stopped. They what? Grow up and find husbands?

"They have lots of fun playing make-believe and putting on plays and writing stories." Willow took the book off Kennedy's shelf. "It's really good. I think you'll like it."

"I don't know." Woong frowned at the cover picture of the four girls in their old-fashioned dresses.

"Why don't you let me read you the first chapter, and then you can let me know what you think?" Willow asked.

"It'll probably put me to sleep," Woong complained.

"That's the general idea," mumbled Willow, but Kennedy doubted he heard.

While Willow started to read, Kennedy got together the things she'd need for a shower. She didn't even have the energy to open her lab book and see which assignments from her students she still had to grade. One day at a time. She could worry about all that other stuff in the morning.

Shortly after moving into her dorm room at the start of the semester, Kennedy had found that the two small wardrobe-style closets could open up and make a perfect changing area that gave her just the amount of privacy she needed. She wrapped up in her bathrobe and grabbed her towel. Willow was at the part where Beth was trying to cheer her sisters up at the prospect of a Christmas with no presents as Kennedy slipped on her waterproof flip-flops, headed into the hallway, and nearly bumped into someone coming around the corner. "I'm sorry," she mumbled without raising her eyes.

"No worries. Where you off to so late?"

She glanced up when she recognized the voice. "Oh, hey, Nick. I didn't realize it was you."

He smiled. "Yeah. I noticed. What's going on?"

She clutched her toiletry caddy against herself and felt her cheeks grow hot. Her long-sleeved bathrobe covered everything but her flip-flops, but she still felt exposed. "I was on my way to take a shower. Willow's in there reading to Woong." She hoped Nick would take the hint and go in, but he just smiled.

"Yeah, I had a lot of different texts from Willow and Sandy, and I couldn't keep everything straight. I thought he'd be here though. I guess I'm supposed to take him home with me, right? It's been such a crazy night. I just finished meeting with that detective."

"Oh." Kennedy reminded herself that her typical jeans and sweaters were far more form-fitting and revealing than an over-sized fluffy bathrobe. She was an adult and quite capable of having a conversation like this even if she wasn't as appropriately attired as she'd like to be. "Did it go all right?"

He nodded. "Yeah. Another hour answering the same questions he asked me this afternoon. You know how it is. Wants me to come up with a list of people who might have had it in for Pastor Carl."

Kennedy still had a hard time accepting that what happened to Carl was real and not some sort of bad hallucination or daydream. "Who would want to hurt him?"

Nick shrugged. "Unfortunately, there's a lot of people fitting that description. That's what I told the detective."

Kennedy still couldn't wrap her mind around it. "Like who?"

"Like Sandra Green, the head of that feminist movement. She's not the biggest fan of Truth Warriors, and I can't say that I blame her."

Kennedy wasn't ready to listen to a political tirade, but she found herself asking all the same, "What's wrong with Truth Warriors?"

"Do you know much about the conferences?" Nick asked.

"No. Just that they're for men, to encourage them to grow in their walk with God, that sort of thing."

"Well, the *encouragement* they receive is questionable to say the least. Those men who signed up for Carl's Truth Warriors conference, they're going to be *encouraged* to lead their wives, and of course all the speakers are going to stand up there and talk about how that leadership needs to be covered in a spirit of gentleness and love. But seriously, how many men are going to listen to that part, and how many are just going to go home and demand blind submission from their spouses? And what about all the male-female relationships that aren't marriages? Hmm? What then? And where does it end? If men are supposed to be the leaders of the home, what does that mean for the mother of teenage boys? What's going to happen to Mr. Joe Christian who goes to Truth Warriors and then decides his privilege as a male, as the God-ordained leader of the world, means that he doesn't have to listen to his female boss?"

Kennedy wasn't ready for this kind of discussion. All she wanted was a shower.

Nick looked at the ground. "Sorry. This has been on my mind a lot. I don't even remember how we got on it."

"You were just talking about Carl and the detective."

He nodded. "Yeah. And you know how much I love Carl. I really do, but he's got these blind sides. He doesn't see the injustices he's perpetuating. So St. Margaret's has no women pastors, right? Because we all know what the Bible has to say about that." He rolled his eyes. "But we can hire a *women's ministry leader*. And what's she do? She pastors the women of the church. She does every single thing Carl and I do, but she's not a pastor. She's not allowed to be part of the elder board. Even though Carl obviously thinks highly enough of her to entrust the spiritual well-being of half his adult congregation to her leadership. And do you think she makes close to the same amount of money as Carl does? Not a chance.

"And don't even get me started on poor Dawn. That woman has been Carl's secretary since the day he started St. Margaret's Church. Any guess what her salary is? Come on. Take a stab at it."

Kennedy didn't know enough about American economics to even have a bad estimate to offer. "Minimum wage?"

He laughed. "She'd be lucky if it were that much. Nope. She gets a monthly stipend of four hundred dollars a month. Four hundred dollars a month, and she's in that office at least thirty hours a week."

This was the first Kennedy had heard about Dawn getting paid at all. "I had the feeling she was a volunteer there."

"She basically is. Which is what I'm saying. You think they'd dare treat a man that way?"

Kennedy didn't know how to answer. "Why doesn't she ask for more money then?"

"Oh, it's not about the money." He waved his hand in the air dismissively. "Her husband's got this crazy Wall Street-type job. She doesn't have to work at all, but she wants to serve the church."

Kennedy didn't see what the problem was then, but Nick kept railing against the injustices inherent in the St. Margaret pay scale.

"It's not the fact that she's not getting paid what she's worth. It's the fact that the elders just assume that since her husband's going to take care of all the bills, they can count on Dawn basically for slave labor."

"She seems content whenever I go in," Kennedy remarked, trying to gauge if she knew the secretary enough to jump to any sort of conclusion.

Nick shrugged. "Yeah, she probably doesn't even know how poorly she's being treated." He shuffled his weight from one foot to the other. "Hey, mind if I ask you a question? It's a little awkward."

Kennedy stared down at her front before she realized the awkwardness had to do with his question and not her appearance. "Sure. Go ahead." Why couldn't he have come just a minute later? Two students walked by, apparently oblivious to the fact that one of their dormmates was having a conversation in the middle of the hallway wearing nothing but her bathrobe.

Nick cleared his throat. "So, I was wondering about Willow, and well, it was really strange having that detective single me out, you know. Because of my fight with Carl earlier. And well, I mean, I know we all know I didn't have anything to do with it, but what's been eating at me all night ... I tried calling Willow several times, and when we grabbed dinner, she seemed a little off, and she hasn't said all that much to me today, and I guess what I'm wondering is if she's said anything to you ... about that sort of stuff, you know, like me and the detective and what happened earlier."

It wasn't until she caught him staring at her so expectantly that Kennedy realized he was waiting for a response. "So you want to know ..." she began, hoping her brain would fill in the pieces she must have missed. Had that rambling run-on sentence contained an actual question?

"Does she think I'm guilty?"

Kennedy nearly laughed but stopped herself when she saw how earnest he looked. "No, of course not." She was surprised that his features still didn't change. "No," she repeated more adamantly. "Nobody really believes that. Even the detective. He's just got to follow up on everything. You know how it is."

Nick fingered one of his dreadlocks. "You sure? She's not even a tiny bit suspicious?"

Kennedy wanted to tell Nick that nobody who knew him could believe he'd have the intestinal fortitude to attack someone as formidable as Carl, but she could tell he needed more assurance than that. "It's ok." She gave him a smile, forgetting for the moment about her silly bathrobe. "Willow adores you more than anything. You could be a serial killer, and she'd be the last person in the world to harbor a single suspicion."

Nick winced.

She cleared her throat. "So, did you find anything out about Carl? I've been tied up all night. I haven't been able to check my phone or even get Willow to fill me in yet. Is there any news?"

Nick was staring over her shoulder. "Not that I've heard. The detective isn't exactly Mr. Chatty if you know what I mean."

"Yeah." Kennedy rolled her eyes. "You've got that right."

"So you're sure ..." Nick began and then stopped himself. "You're sure Willow's ok? With me, I mean?"

"Of course. Go on in there. I'll probably see you in a few minutes, or else have a good night."

"Ok." He took a step past her then stopped. "Hey, Kennedy?"

"What?" She turned around.

He offered a shy smile. "Thanks for talking things through with me. I really appreciate that."

"No problem. We all know you're perfectly innocent."

Nick grimaced and then turned around. Kennedy made her way to the showers, puzzling the entire time over his expression and wondering if she'd said something wrong.

CHAPTER 19

FIFTEEN MINUTES LATER, SHOWERED and a little more relaxed than she'd been after her meeting with the Voice staff, Kennedy made her way back to her room. She could hear Willow and Nick fighting from the opposite side of the hallway. Of course, some of that had to do with her roommate's frustrating habit of never shutting the door entirely, but she couldn't remember the two of them getting so heated in the past.

"Who do you think you are, blaming him for what happened?" Willow shouted.

They both fell silent when Kennedy entered the room. The heat from their argument hung heavy in the air like smog. Neither one acknowledged Kennedy as she made her way to her bedside and began putting away her toiletries.

"I'm not saying he deserved it." Nick's voice was softer when he finally spoke up, but Kennedy could tell from his shaky tone he was working hard to mask his rage. "All I'm saying is that with his old-fashioned views on everything and then this whole mess he got the church into planning the Truth Warriors conference, it's not surprising to me that someone got worked up enough to attack him."

Kennedy debated if she wanted to waste the time and energy to dry her hair. It would drown out a little bit of Willow and Nick's spat, which would be nice, but her entire body longed to sink down into her bed and forget everything that had happened over the past twenty-four hours.

"That's fabulous coming from you," Willow retorted. "The one who's always standing up for the little man, the one with all your progressive philosophy. I suppose victim blaming is fair game now as long as the victim's views don't agree with your own?"

Nick began pacing. "I wasn't victim blaming."

Kennedy plugged in her hairdryer but still couldn't decide if she should use it. Woong was asleep in the purple beanbag chair, and Kennedy hated the thought of waking him up. Then again, if he could sleep through an argument like this, he could probably sleep through the tribulation.

"You know what I don't get?" Willow asked. "I don't get how somebody who's as concerned about issues of social justice as you can be so calloused toward your friend. What if this was some random pastor you read about in the news? What if you had no idea what his political views were or what presidential candidate he voted for? I've seen you cry before, remember that? I've seen you watch a documentary about the way those school kids were being treated in Detroit with all those toxins in their playground and poison in the water, and you sobbed your heart out."

"I was just ..." Nick began, but Willow cut him off.

"I'm not mentioning that to make you feel bad. In fact, that night I came back and told Kennedy I'd found the man I wanted to spend the rest of my life with. Don't look at me like that. Ask her yourself if you don't believe me."

Kennedy was still staring at the hairdryer in her hand, still trying to decide if falling asleep now would be worth the bed head she'd wake up with in the morning.

"You are the most socially responsible, compassionate man I've ever met," Willow continued. "But you're as stubborn as a mule. And a smelly, ugly mule at that. You and Carl have this twisted, quasi-sadistic love-to-hate-him kind of relationship that I don't even pretend to understand, but beneath all those superficial disagreements, the two of you have always come together in the end and reaffirmed your love for each other. And now he's hurt, and maybe even dying for all we know, and when I would expect you to be the most compassionate, the most concerned, you're sitting here rattling off all the reasons why Carl brought it on himself."

Willow yanked her brush through her hair. "And I'm sitting here listening to you berate your friend, and all I'm left to wonder now is what happened to that man I fell in love with, the man who cried during a documentary about kids he's never met in Detroit but apparently doesn't have a single tear to shed for his pastor and mentor who at this moment is on a ventilator struggling to survive."

Kennedy put her hairdryer away, wondering how inconspicuously she could tuck herself into bed and try to shut out Willow's words.

Nick stopped his pacing and sat down beside Willow on her mattress. "I suppose you're right. I was acting like a jerk."

Willow rubbed his back. "Yeah, but you're the jerk I love."

Nick stared at his hands and let out a sigh. "It's just that ..." His dreadlocks fell toward the floor, and he shook his head. "It's just that it's easier to be angry. Know what I mean?"

"No," Willow answered. "What do you mean?"

It took Nick several seconds to respond. "I mean that it's easier to pretend I'm still mad at him. Easier to pretend like this is his fault. Because otherwise all I can do is blame myself. I was there just a few minutes before it happened. Maybe I could have stopped it. Or maybe I'd made Carl so upset with all the debating that he couldn't see who was coming. Couldn't fight them off. That's what I mean when I say it's easier to be angry. You tell me that I've lost my sense of compassion, that I'm as stubborn as a ... well, we all heard what you had to say about that." He smiled faintly and gently nudged Willow's side.

"Yeah, I'll admit it wasn't one of my finer moments."

Nick shrugged. "No, but it wasn't that far from the truth. It's just so hard for me to accept that any of this is really happening. That Carl ... that he's ..." Nick's voice broke, and he buried his face in his hands while Willow murmured reassurances into his ear.

Kennedy plugged in her hairdryer for a second time and let the loud noise drown out Nick's cries.

CHAPTER 20

BLINDING SUNLIGHT STREAMED IN from the window. Kennedy rolled over. What time was it? She squinted at her phone. Ten after nine? She couldn't remember the last time she'd slept in so late. In fact, she didn't even remember falling asleep. She knew something had happened last night. What was it?

"No, I'm sorry. She's not up yet." Was that Willow talking? Why was she whispering?

"We had a meeting scheduled for this morning."

Kennedy recognized the voice but couldn't place it, not until her brain had a little more chance to wake up.

"She didn't say anything about it to me," her roommate snapped. "Does she tell you everything?"

Kennedy sat up in bed. "Who's there?" she asked in a groggy voice.

Willow stepped aside to reveal Ian, the red-haired journalist. Kennedy had talked to him yesterday when she was at the hospital. The hospital ... Memories from Carl's attack crashed and swirled in her mind.

"Good morning." He offered a small smile. "Sorry if I woke you up. I tried texting you to see if we were still on for breakfast, but I never got a reply."

At the word *breakfast*, Willow's entire countenance changed. She let out an airy laugh. "Something you learn about Kennedy real quick is that she's got a moral compulsion against checking her messages or keeping her phone charged. Just one of those little idiosyncrasies you grow to love about her."

Willow flung open Kennedy's small wardrobe, pulled out a pair of jeans and a new blouse they'd bought on an impromptu shopping spree together and tossed them onto Kennedy's bed. "You get up and get ready, sunshine," Willow told her then turned to Ian. "And you wait outside until she's presentable. Don't worry, I won't make you wait too long."

She closed the door in Ian's face and ran to Kennedy. "You didn't tell me you had a date with the ginger."

"It's not a date." Kennedy's temples were throbbing. She wasn't a regular caffeine drinker, but she'd need more than a few sips of coffee this morning to get her brain as alert as it needed to be. What day was it, anyway? She had lit class in a few hours and then lab, right? Wait, lab?

She sat up in bed. "I can't go out. I have all my students' reports to grade."

Willow pulled down Kennedy's blankets. "Of course you have time for breakfast. Especially with that cute journalist. Maybe I shouldn't be saying this, but I've been praying that God would send you somebody after Dominic ... well, you know. And I've only been at this praying thing for a little while, so think what it's doing to my brand-new faith to see you finally starting to date again. So you can't let me down now. And someone like the journalist. Didn't I tell you the very first time I saw him that he's absolutely scrumptious? I mean, Dominic wasn't bad looking if you're into the whole huggable-teddy-bear-with-a-beard sort of feel. But the ginger ... when did you even start talking to him anyway? Last I heard, wasn't he filming in your parents' neck of the woods in China or something?"

Kennedy was behind her closet door and halfway dressed, but even though her body was out of bed, her brain couldn't keep up with all of Willow's questions.

"So where you going?" Willow asked. "Is he taking you someplace fancy?" She let out a sigh. "First dates are so romantic. It's too bad Nick and I will never have another."

"It's not a date." Kennedy emerged from the makeshift dressing room.

Willow rolled her eyes. "Sure it isn't. And I'm a virgin. I mean, ok, so maybe it's a bad example since I'm doing the whole abstinence thing now, but you get my point."

Still droopy with exhaustion and trying to recall if she had officially agreed on a time to meet Ian this morning, Kennedy grabbed a pair of socks from her dresser drawer.

"No," Willow protested. "Look outside. It's a gorgeous sunny day. And what about that cute pedicure I gave you? You can't hide those toes in your old worn-out tennies." She reached under her own bed. "Here, wear my platforms. They'll go perfect with those jeans." After tossing the sandals onto the floor by Kennedy's bare feet, Willow rummaged through her desk. "Want to borrow some earrings? I have these beaded ones you like, but I think the turquoise look more mature. Which is what you're going for, because this ginger, how old is he again?"

Kennedy didn't have time to answer before Willow started brushing her hair for her. "If he weren't waiting right out there, I'd mousse it up for you. But this will have to do." She stepped back and crossed her arms. "There you go. Perfect for a breakfast out." Another loud sigh. "Morning dates are so dreamy."

"It's not a date," Kennedy repeated right before Willow shoved her out their bedroom door.

CHAPTER 21

"Sorry again for waking you up." Ian let out a chuckle as he and Kennedy walked across campus.

"That's all right," Kennedy assured him while simultaneously imagining how she'd get back at Willow for making such a big deal about a simple breakfast out.

They walked in silence for a while. Kennedy wondered what Ian was thinking about. She'd run into him randomly several times so far during her time as an undergrad at Harvard, but they'd never gotten the chance to say more than a few words to each other in any given instance.

Once off-campus, they waited until it was safe to cross the street into Harvard Square. Ian suggested they walk over to L'Aroma Bakery. The thought of a buttery crusted quiche made Kennedy's mouth water so much that she probably couldn't have protested without drooling even if she had reason to. At least by going to L'Aroma, she could eat a quick breakfast and arrive back at her dorm in less than an hour. Plenty of time to finish grading all those lab reports. At least she hoped so, seeing as how she still couldn't remember how many more there were left. She struggled to match Ian's pace while keeping her balance in Willow's platform sandals. Once they made it to the other side of the street, he slowed down and gave her a gentle smile. "Guess it's been a rough week for you, hasn't it?"

Maybe it was because he was a member of the press or maybe because Kennedy didn't know him all that well, but she still wasn't sure how much she should trust someone like Ian. On the one hand, he'd helped out in the past when she'd found herself in difficult situations, but there was so much she didn't know about him. And yet, it always seemed as if he knew everything about her.

"Yeah," she agreed, "I can definitely say I've had easier weeks this semester." She realized she hadn't asked Willow for any updates on Carl's condition. She also realized she'd left her phone back in her room.

"You're a junior now, right?" Ian asked.

"Right."

"Still premed?"

"Yeah." Kennedy already regretted letting her roommate talk her into this. Now that the fresh air and sunshine had revived her, she was able to remember the details of Ian's phone call yesterday and knew with almost a hundred percent certainty that even though he'd mentioned breakfast, they'd never actually made any sort of formal agreement.

Thankfully, L'Aroma Bakery was only a few minutes' walk away. It was crowded as usual, but they found a table in the corner that offered some privacy.

"Order anything you'd like," Ian told her. "Or we can split something. My treat." He smiled at her, and Kennedy noticed a dimple right in the middle of his chin. She tried not to blush when she recalled what a big deal Willow had made about their time out together. If it hadn't been for that, Kennedy could treat this interview just like anything else, something to check off her to-do list before she moved on to her next assignment. But now that Willow had filled her head with all her dramatic sighs and reminiscences about the magic of first dates and romantic breakfasts, Kennedy was jittery even before the waitress came and filled her mug with coffee.

This isn't a date, Kennedy reminded herself as Ian asked about her semester.

This isn't a date, she repeated when the waitress brought a platter full of fruit and a giant omelet, which Ian split before setting one half in front of her.

This isn't a date. She glanced at her nearly empty plate and realized she and Ian had been talking about their respective times in East Asia and at Harvard, but that he hadn't asked her a single question about her article by the time the server came back with the bill.

He reached into his pocket.

"You sure you don't want me to pitch in?" Kennedy asked.

He smiled, revealing that boyish dimple. How had she not noticed it before? "No, thank you. It's one of the perks of being freelance." He pulled out his credit card and set it on top of the receipt.

Kennedy gave him a quizzical look.

"Tax write-off," he explained and then frowned. "Oh, that sounded bad. I'm sorry."

She smiled reassuringly. "No, don't apologize or anything. It's just that when you called yesterday and said you wanted to talk, I was expecting it would be about the article."

"You're right. My bad. I just have a real hard time jumping straight into work, especially before I've had any caffeine." He finished off his second cup of coffee. "Tell you what. The weather is fantastic out there. Care to take a walk around Harvard Square?"

Kennedy wished Willow were here so she could kick her under the table with her stupid high-heeled sandals. She wiped her face with her napkin, still trying to figure out why she felt let-down after such a delicious breakfast and interesting conversation. As it turned out, Ian was as involved in the North Korean refugee crisis in China as her parents were, although in a far more public way. While her parents helped harbor refugees in secret, Ian documented the many human rights abuses on both sides of the Chinese-North Korean border. He traveled to the region nearly every year collecting interviews which would eventually be compiled into a full-length documentary. He'd even gone into North Korea twice to collect illegal footage for his project.

"My magnum opus," he'd called it. "At least my first," he added with a jocular twinkle in his green eyes.

They stepped outside into the fresh air. Fall was in no hurry this year. The leaves on the trees had just started to lose their first hint of chlorophyll, and if all she had to judge by was the chirping of the birds, Kennedy might have guessed it was the middle of May.

Ian's pace was slow, and she tried not to think about those lab reports she still needed to grade. She'd started them last weekend. She knew she'd gotten through at least the first four or five, hadn't she? What time was it, anyway? She hated not having her phone on her. What if Sandy was trying to call? What if there was more news about Carl?

She thought it was strange that the subject of her pastor's accident hadn't come up all morning. She didn't know if it was on the news at this point, but St. Margaret's was one of the largest churches in Cambridge and had already been in the limelight because of the upcoming Truth Warriors conference. The entire state of Massachusetts probably knew more about Carl's condition than she did.

"You ever been in that little coffee shop over there?" Ian pointed across the street.

"No. It looks nice." Had she ever noticed it before? She should come up with a way to tell him she had to get back to campus soon. All those lab reports ...

"There's this coffee place in Tumen, not too far from where your parents live," Ian said. "Run by Canadian missionaries. Nicest people you'd ever meet." His voice trailed off.

Kennedy tried to think of a way to steer the conversation toward her massive to-do list for the day. When had she gotten this tongue-tied? She cleared her throat. "So, listen, about our interview ..."

"Right." Ian's pace sped up the faster he talked. Another twenty minutes like this, and Kennedy's feet might never recover. He looked across the street one more time. "So, any chance you've got room for one more cup of coffee?"

Kennedy wished she could tell him she'd love to, but schoolwork had to come first. And Carl. How could she have gone all morning without trying to find out how he was? How calloused could she be? She took in a deep breath. "I'm sorry. It's been really fun, but I honestly wasn't expecting it to last this long. I've got class before long, and I still have a bunch of reports to grade."

"Really?" His eyes lit up. "Are you a TA? For what? No, you can tell me later. I'm sorry. I should have been paying more attention to the time. Do you really have to go back so soon? I was hoping to ask you a few questions ..."

"I know." She hated feeling like she was letting him down. She glanced at the little beatnik coffee shop across the street. "Maybe we can get that coffee another morning?"

Ian smiled. "Deal. And in the meantime, you'll let me walk you back to campus and ask a few questions about your article on the way, right?"

"Sure."

They turned around when Ian's phone rang. "Oh, I better see who that is. Might be for work." He took his cell out of his pocket and squinted at the screen. "Are you calling me?" he asked.

"What?"

He showed her his phone. "This is your number. At least, that's what caller ID says."

Kennedy shook her head. "I left my cell back at the dorm."

He answered his cell. They were almost back to L'Aroma Bakery where they'd spent their morning talking about nothing. About everything.

Ian frowned. He had such expressive features. "Kennedy? Yeah. She's here. Who's this?"

She didn't realize that Ian had stopped walking until she nearly bumped into him.

"Sure." His eyes softened. Was he worried? Sad? "Ok, here she is." He held out his phone. "It's your roommate. Something about your pastor."

Kennedy held her breath and had to remind herself that a simple piece of electronics couldn't physically hurt her. She took Ian's cell phone, placed it against her ear, and croaked, "Hello?"

Willow's voice on the other line was breathless. "Kennedy. Thank God I got hold of you. Do you know how many searches you get when you google *red-haired journalists in Cambridge*? It took me forever just to track down Ginger's name, and then I had to find him on your phone, and after that ... oh, never mind. Sandy called. It's bad news."

Kennedy steadied herself against a newspaper stand. "How bad?"

"Really bad," Willow answered. "I mean, no, not *that* bad. I mean, he's not ... you know, he isn't ... He's still at the hospital. But they got him stable enough that the doctors wanted to do an MRI, you know, to assess how bad the damage was to his brain."

Kennedy wanted to propel herself through time and get to the part of the call when Willow actually told her what was wrong. "And?"

Willow sniffed. "I couldn't understand all the medical details. Sandy called because she thought maybe you could help explain it to her."

"Explain what?" Kennedy turned so she didn't have to look at Ian, but she could still feel the worry and compassion from his gaze. This wasn't his conversation. He didn't know Carl. Wasn't close to him like Kennedy was.

On the other line, Kennedy heard what sounded like paper rustling. What was Willow doing?

"Ok, here's what Sandy said. The MRI showed several different types of hemorrhaging, and then there was something about swelling, and the bottom line is she says the doctors aren't sure he's ever getting off that ventilator."

CHAPTER 22

KENNEDY WOULD HAVE NEVER guessed she could make it from L'Aroma Bakery to Willow's car in J Lot in just a little over five minutes. Shortly after wishing Ian her very hasty and probably not-so-polite goodbye, she'd taken off the platform sandals and ran the rest of the way barefoot, vowing to never let her roommate talk her out of her comfortable tennis shoes again.

Kennedy reached student parking as Willow headed over from the opposite direction.

"Dude." Willow looked Kennedy up and down. "You're a mess."

"I know." Kennedy threw open the passenger door to her roommate's car. "Let's go."

Willow sat down beside her and offered a sympathetic gaze.

Kennedy was in no mood for compassion right now. "What's happened to Carl?" She mentally calculated down to the minute when they could arrive at Providence Hospital and prayed that the rush-hour congestion would have died down by now.

"I've already told you what I know." Willow pulled out of the parking lot and merged into the oncoming traffic.

Kennedy wished Willow's car had a siren or something so they didn't have to crawl at this snail's pace. "So Sandy called?" She wanted Willow to start over from the beginning. She'd been so worried about getting herself to J Lot that she'd forgotten all the details Willow had told her previously, scant as they were.

"Yeah." Willow was almost shouting to be heard over the sounds of her engine and rock station. "She said they did an MRI this morning, and the damage is more extensive than they expected. Basically, she thinks that the only help for Carl now will be some kind of miracle. That's why she's called a few of us over to pray for him."

"So we'll be meeting others there?"

"Yeah. I don't know who, but I figured you wouldn't want to miss it."

Kennedy glanced at the time. There was no way she'd make it to her lit class, which wouldn't end her college career. She was so far ahead in her reading she could probably write the remainder of her papers and finish the course half a semester early if she really wanted. It wasn't like her to skip out on a class, but this was important. Willow was right. She wouldn't miss Carl's prayer meeting for anything.

But wait, didn't she have some other obligation today?

Oh, no.

"I can't go. I forgot all about my lab this afternoon." Why had she ever let Professor Adell talk her into becoming a TA?

Willow scrunched up her moussed hair. "Actually ..."

Kennedy turned down the music. If her roommate wasn't using hearing aids by the time she was fifty, it would be a miracle in and of itself.

Willow cleared her throat. "Ok, so I didn't want to tell you this right away, but I guess it's best to come out now."

Kennedy didn't know what she was talking about. All she knew was those stupid lab reports were going to keep her from Carl's bedside to pray for him as he lay dying. Whatever Willow had to tell her, she was in no mood for a guessing game. "What is it?"

"Ok, well, you know how some kids on campus got upset about your article, right? Calling it misogynistic and all that junk."

"Yeah." What did any of this have to do with Carl or her lab class?

"So, I had your phone this morning because you forgot it when you and Ginger went out for your little date, which you know I'm dying to hear all about even though now's not the best time. Anyway, you left your phone in the bedroom, but surprise of surprises, it was actually charged. So someone called, and it was a local number without a name, so I thought it might be Sandy at the hospital, and I knew you would want to hear how Carl was doing right away, so I answered it. Only it wasn't her."

"Are you or aren't you going to turn around and take me back so I don't miss my lab?" Kennedy interrupted.

"That's the thing." Willow reached out like she was about to turn up the radio but stopped herself. "So, it wasn't Sandy on the phone. It was your chemistry professor, Adell. And she was all upset that she couldn't get hold of you and said it was *of tantamount importance,* and so to calm her down I told her I could give you a message. So that's what I'm doing. And I'm sorry because I know it's horrible timing with Carl being so bad off, and you having to cut your date with Ginger short, but maybe it's for the best. You know how you're always telling me God works all things together for good, right? Maybe this is one of those times. So don't freak out on me, and remember I'm just the messenger, ok?"

"What is it?" Kennedy didn't mean to snap, but she couldn't help it. "Just tell me," she added in a more conciliatory tone.

Willow took in a deep breath. "Ok, so Adell said there's a student or two in your lab that was offended by your article, and I guess they made a big enough stink about it that they went to Adell's supervisor — this is how she made it out to sound at least — and got the science department head to suspend your teaching privileges while they *look into the allegations* or whatever it is they've got to do. I have no idea if it's just to shut these students up or if they're really serious about getting you in trouble or what, but Adell called to tell you that as of right now, you're out of a teaching job."

"What?" Kennedy would be surprised if she didn't end up with whiplash the way she snapped her head around toward Willow.

"Hey, don't take it out on me. Remember, I'm just passing on the message. And Adell, she didn't come right out and say so, but I got the sense she disagreed with the department head. She told me to tell you she was sorry, at the very least."

"That's ridiculous." What in the world did Kennedy's view on motherhood have to do with her ability to teach chemistry? Besides, she'd never said in her article that all women should do nothing but raise babies and mop floors. She just wanted people to stop treating any stay-at-home mom — especially one as kind and capable as Sandy — like a sub-par human being, like a tragic case of someone who'd never realized her full potential, like a threat to the progressive women's movement.

"Try not to worry about it right now."

"Easy for you to say." Kennedy realized it was senseless to get angry at Willow, but all that pent-up stress needed some sort of an outlet. "And how am I supposed to do that? I defended a friend, and look what happened. I got the only editor who ever stood up for me fired, I got my dorm building vandalized, and now I've lost my job. So remind me again what's not to worry about?"

Willow didn't respond. Kennedy wouldn't blame her if she was mad now. That'd be the perfect way to top off an already horrible morning.

After a few minutes of silence, Willow turned up the radio station just a little. "I'm sorry," she said as the Providence parking structure loomed into view.

Kennedy was too ashamed of herself and her petty little outburst to respond.

CHAPTER 23

ONCE INSIDE PROVIDENCE, KENNEDY followed Willow, wondering what to expect when she got up to Carl's floor. Last she heard, he was in the ICU. Would the hospital staff even let them in to visit?

On the way up in the elevator, Kennedy broke the strained silence. "I'm sorry I got so upset in the car. You know I wasn't mad at you, right?"

Willow rubbed her back. "Of course. Hey, I'm just glad to see you standing up for yourself every once in a while. It's been a long time coming."

Kennedy didn't reply. Willow's phone beeped, and she reached into her purse. "Oh, that's Nick." She stared at her screen. "I guess he can't make the prayer meeting. That's too bad."

"What's going on?" Kennedy asked, hoping it didn't have any more to do with Detective Drisklay or the investigation about Carl's assault.

Willow shrugged. "Didn't say. This has been really hard on him, you know. He thinks of Carl like a dad."

Kennedy figured some adults had that sort of argumentative relationship with their fathers, but she didn't think it sounded all that pleasant. "You know what I've been wondering for a while now?"

Willow was digging around in her purse after she put her phone away. "Hmm?"

"How Carl and Nick managed to work together all these years in the first place. I mean, I guess it's one thing to have a friend who believes so differently from you, but if you're a pastor of a prominent church and you're known for being so conservative ..." She wasn't quite sure how to complete her sentence.

"Then why do you put up with someone like Nick in the first place?" Willow finished for her.

Kennedy smiled. "Yeah."

The girls got out of the elevator and started the long walk down the hallway to the ICU. "It's pretty complicated," Willow began. "I'm surprised Sandy never told you the story."

"What story?"

"You know, why Carl's never fired Nick even with all their political disagreements. Why Nick adores Carl even if he'll hardly ever come right out and say so. Why he's so upset now with Carl being in such bad shape ..." Her voice died down at the sight of over a dozen people standing around the nurses' station.

"What do you suppose that is?" Kennedy asked.

Willow fingered her long beaded earring. "My guess is that's Carl's prayer team."

No wonder the nurse looked panicked. As they got closer, Kennedy could hear her words. "I'm sorry. I can only let immediate family members in."

Sandy was there, standing behind someone who looked like he could be Carl's older, larger brother. She smoothed out her French braid. "All right, friends, we don't want to cause the staff here any problems. There's just too many of us, and Carl's condition is too uncertain right now. It wouldn't be right for us all to go in his room. But we came here to pray, and the charge nurse is graciously allowing us to meet down the hall in the little conference center. We can all pray for Carl there."

Sandy smiled when she came up to Kennedy and Willow. "Good morning, my girls. I'm so thankful you came." She gave them both hugs. "I wish we could go in and pray for Carl by his bedside, but it's just not going to work out today."

Kennedy gave her hand a squeeze. "That's ok. I think it's great you put this all together."

"It was Woong's idea, actually," Sandy admitted.

"Really?"

"Yeah, he's been asking all kinds of questions about faith and prayer since he got so sick last spring. It's hard because I want him to remember that we can trust God for miracles, but I'm just not sure this time that the miracle's coming."

Willow rubbed Sandy on the back. "Don't talk like that. We all know God's going to pull Carl through this, and Woong's going to have an even stronger faith after his dad's healed."

Sandy smiled sadly but didn't reply.

Kennedy tried to redirect the subject. "Where is Woong, by the way?"

"He's reading a Bible joke book to his dad, the one Carl sometimes uses for opening up his sermons. He ..." Sandy sniffed. "Well, he said he thought that's what his dad would like to hear."

"How sweet," Willow cooed.

Sandy looked like she was about to cry. To get her mind off her husband, Kennedy offered lamely, "A lot of people showed up today."

Another tired smile. "Sure did. That man is so well-loved and well-respected. It would be such a tragedy if ... well, never mind me. I didn't sleep well last night, and that always turns me into a grouch."

Kennedy caught Willow's grin and had to smile herself. On a bad day, Sandy was still nicer than just about everyone else on the globe.

Once everyone was crowded around a meeting table designed for a group about half as large, Sandy called for everyone's attention. She had no problem taking charge in the cramped conference room.

"First of all, I can't tell you what a blessing and an honor it is to have all of you come out here to join me in prayer for my Carl. You know that man has touched so many lives, but he's so humble I don't think he realizes the half of it. The fact that all of you showed up here is a testimony to Carl's love for God and his love for others. I know all of us around this table have been touched by his faith and his teaching and his encouragement."

There were nods of general agreement all around, but nobody tried to interrupt Sandy's speech.

"Now, I know the prayer chain's been sending out updates, but I'm still getting lots of questions about what happened, so I figured that before we started to pray, I'd fill you in on everything I know so we're all on the same page. Yesterday afternoon, while he was in his office working, Carl was hit on the head with a heavy bookend. Knocked him out. At first, we were only worried about the blood loss, but on the way to the hospital, he had an incident. They still don't know exactly what. Brain bleed maybe, head trauma, something like that. That's why he's on the ventilator now. Last night we were hopeful that once he got stable and they got the internal bleeding and swelling under control, he'd be just fine. He had a peaceful night. No major scares or anything, but when they turned down the machine to see how he'd do on his own, his brain still wasn't telling his body to breathe like it should. So they did an MRI, and I can't remember all the medical details, but the general impression I got from the meeting with the neurologist is that the injuries Carl sustained, both the initial hit to the head and all the internal wounds that followed, are far more serious than anyone expected."

She paused. Kennedy didn't know if she was done or if there was more to it. Sandy was always so positive, so encouraging. Kennedy felt like everyone around the room was waiting for some word of hope or comfort.

"So, what's the long-term prognosis?" someone asked from the back.

Sandy shook her head. "None at this point. The neurologist told me it can go either way. He said he's seen patients older and frailer than Carl come in with injuries like this and heal up in a matter of days. But he also said there's the chance that we're looking at permanent disability." She glanced around, her eyes shining in the harsh light from the fixture overhead. "And I may as well come out and say it, but we need to all brace ourselves for the fact that Carl might not recover at all."

Murmurs of dissent broke out across the room until Sandy shushed everyone. "Now I'm trying to keep this from Woong. Lord knows that boy's had enough to worry about to last several lifetimes over. He's with his daddy now, and the detective's stopping by soon. Going to ask Woong some questions. There's a chance my boy saw who went into his daddy's office before the attack. But let's remember, we didn't come here to gossip or speculate. I only wanted to share what's been going on so we all know better how to direct our prayers. Now, we're here to talk to God, and that's just what I intend to do. But before we start, I want to say something, and because I know you love and respect my husband, I ask you to listen carefully.

"Carl and me have recognized for years that our days are numbered and that only God himself knows when our time to pass will come. You've heard Carl say so himself, each and every one of you. He's not the least bit scared of dying because he knows that when God calls him home, nothing can stand between him and his eternal reward, not modern medicine or heroic measures or even our steadfast love for each other will hold him back.

"Carl's got a living will. He makes no effort to hide that, and he's made it clear for decades that he doesn't want to just survive indefinitely on life support. Now, don't get yourselves too worked up yet. I've showed the doctor his will, and I've talked with both the social worker and the chaplain here at Providence, and all four of us are in agreement that in this instance, Carl would want us to try to do what we can to save his life. That man's been given a mission from God, a mission he's labored at tirelessly for decades, and I know for a fact that he doesn't consider his work on earth to be finished. But I also know that if it comes down to the brain damage being so severe that he couldn't make it without all kinds of outside measures keeping his body alive, there's no way my husband would wish to postpone his homecoming in that sort of situation.

"I'm not saying this to get anybody upset, and I'm not asking for suggestions or opinions here. Carl's wishes are quite clear, it's all documented and signed, and that's how I'm going to base all my decisions for his care if it comes down to it. We're not talking about pulling the plug. That's not even in the equation at this point. The doctor wants to redo the brain scan in three or four days. Whether or not we see improvement then will determine the next course of action.

"So here's what I'm asking for, friends. I don't pretend to know God's will in this situation. Heaven knows I've asked, but the Holy Spirit's either quiet, or my love for my husband and my desire to see him healed is getting in the way of me hearing clearly from the Lord. First and foremost, I want our prayers to be that God's will be done. Nothing more, nothing less. If God wants to miraculously touch my husband to stop any further injury and to heal the part of his brain that's already been damaged, then come, sweet Jesus, and work your miracles in Carl's mind and body. But if that's not the case, if this really is my husband's invitation to pass into glory, I'd like to ask God to answer my husband's wish and make that so clear that nothing could stop him from rushing into his Savior's arms. On a strictly human level, I'm asking that one way or the other Carl's suffering would not be unnecessarily prolonged, and of course you know that Woong and all our other children and grandchildren are in desperate need of our prayers and our support at this time."

Kennedy glanced around the room. Sandy's words sounded so morbid. The thought of someone as strong and robust as Carl ending up with such severe brain trauma was grotesque, and yet the room filled with an unexpected peace even before the praying began.

Sandy started, but she got choked up before she could even get past her very first "Thy will be done." At that point, someone else took up where she left off, and around the room the prayers rose and fell and were passed on to others like a synchronized dance. Kennedy wasn't comfortable speaking in front of such a large group, but nobody seemed to mind or even notice when some people prayed out loud and others only joined in silent agreement.

Kennedy had never experienced anything like this. She'd encountered people she considered prayer warriors before, like Dominic whose prayer over her had stopped a full-fledged panic attack the very first night they met. Or Grandma Lucy, the bold and faithful stranger Kennedy sat next to in an airplane on the way to her first trip to Alaska. Sandy had interceded over her dozens of times, and Kennedy and Willow tried to end each day with a short time of prayer together. But still nothing she'd encountered in the past came close to this. She'd experienced peace before while she prayed. She'd experienced overwhelming waves of comfort or the certainty of God's love or the glory of his divine presence.

But this prayer meeting in the overstuffed conference room was different. Yes, there was peace. Yes, there was comfort even though at least a third of the people present were crying or had shed tears at some point during the meeting. But there was something else too. A power. An undeniable surge of energy that raced around the room. Kennedy noticed that even though the first few people who prayed asked God humbly for his will to be done, now nearly everybody who spoke was beseeching God for Carl's full and perfect healing. Kennedy found herself surprised by the confidence surging in her own spirit. She'd never felt such a burning fire, such a sincere conviction that she could ask God right now to do the impossible, to heal Carl and grant him a complete recovery, and that he would answer her fully. Her heart raced faster, and she wondered if a nurse was about to enter the room to tell them Carl had woken up from his coma and was breathing perfectly well now on his own.

It could have been forty minutes, it could have been two hours later, but at some point, as if by general consensus, everyone stopped praying. The ones who'd kept their eyes closed now opened them. Bowed heads lifted and looked around the room. Sandy sat in a corner, comforted by at least a dozen loving arms stretching out to embrace her. She smiled at the group and said, "I suppose that's *amen*."

Kennedy glanced at Willow. What now? The prayers had been so sincere. The faith so real. Should they all go check on Carl? Would they see him sitting up in bed sharing corny Bible jokes with his son?

Sandy rose. She looked half a foot taller now and even more stately than normal. "This was such a blessing. It just means the world to me and brings me so much hope and encouragement that you all joined with me. I hate to pray and run, but I really should go check on Woong. I'll update the prayer chain tonight, and I'll do it sooner if Carl's condition changes at all between now and then. Thanks again for praying with me." She glided gracefully out the door.

So that was it?

Willow looked just as surprised. "What now?" she asked.

Kennedy shrugged. Some of the people she'd recently prayed with were already gathering their bags and buttoning their sweaters, while others formed small pockets and began to talk to one another.

Willow grabbed Kennedy by the arm. "Come on. There's something I want to show you before we leave."

CHAPTER 24

KENNEDY HAD NO IDEA why Willow was dragging her down hallway after hallway or why they had to take two different elevators. By the time Willow slowed down to look at a map of the hospital, they were already four towers away from the ICU where they'd prayed for Carl.

"Can you just tell me what we're doing?" Kennedy wasn't in the mood for games. Sandy's words about Carl now sat ominously in her gut like a spoiled dinner. Words like *permanent disability* crashed around her cerebral cortex like the wild, unquenchable flames of *Fahrenheit 451.*

Willow looked back in the direction they'd just come from. Were they lost? She studied the map again. "Ok, it should be right down this hall. Or maybe that one."

"Where are we going?" Kennedy hated to admit how whiney she sounded.

"You'll see when we get there."

Kennedy's feet ached from clunking those awkward heels all around Providence. She struggled to keep up with her roommate, who finally stopped in front of a small plaque hanging up outside a closed door.

"What's this?" Kennedy asked. The room wasn't marked, and there were no windows. It was more likely a janitorial closet than an office. What had Willow planned?

"Look." She pointed at the plaque on the wall. "That's what I wanted you to see."

When Kennedy saw the name and read the inscription, she realized why this hall felt familiar. It was different now, the construction newer, the whole section remodeled since last spring. But here they were. Outside the same room where she'd been trapped the last day she and Dominic had been together.

Willow's hand rested on the doorknob. "Do you want to go in?"

Kennedy shook her head. She wasn't ready. Not for this.

Willow frowned. "I'm sorry. Was this too hard of a surprise? Should I have told you about it first?"

Kennedy blinked and tried to read the inscription again through her blurry field of vision. *Dominic Martinez, Courageous Chaplain, Devoted Servant.* John 15:13 was written across the bottom. *Greater love has no one than this: to lay down one's life for one's friends.*

Willow wrapped an arm around her. "I just thought you'd like to see it. And you know, maybe go in there. It doesn't have to be today. But the two of you never got the chance to say good-bye."

Kennedy swallowed. Her throat felt like it had been prodded with a red-hot fire poker.

"Want me to give you a little time here alone?" Willow asked.

Kennedy shook her head.

"Too much?" Willow whispered.

She nodded.

"Should we go?" Willow held her around the waist and led her back down the hall.

The suffocating constriction in Kennedy's chest widened like a gaping chasm. A black hole whose event horizon kept expanding infinitesimally. There were days when she thought she was doing so well. Days when she was sure she'd trudged her way through the deepest caverns of grief. But after the intense pain came the aching. The missing. The emptiness that sometimes she was certain nothing could fill, the wound without balm. He should have been here today, should have joined in interceding for Carl's healing. Kennedy had never met someone with a prayer life like his.

Would it always be like this? Always good-bye, no matter how much time had passed, time that was promised to heal all wounds? Would she always feel so lost?

But then she could go days on end hardly mourning at all. Good days. Busy days. Filled with schoolwork and reading and lab reports. Should she feel guilty that she was trying to move on? Did the fact that she was still functioning — although now with the help of prescription medicine — somehow diminish the loss she'd suffered? If she and Dominic had been even closer, would her recovery take that much longer?

Was it wrong for her to want to live again? Laugh again? Love again?

Was it even possible?

"Come on." Willow led her toward the elevator. "Now that you know it's here, you can come back any time you want, ok?"

"Ok." Kennedy wasn't sure if she'd ever be ready to face the memories flooding this corridor in Providence again, but when the time came, *if* the time came, she knew she had a friend who would walk with her through the grief.

Who would help her say good-bye.

CHAPTER 25

THE PHONE RANG ALMOST the same instant they stepped outside of Providence Hospital. "Oh." Willow reached into her purse. "I forgot. I've been carrying around your cell all morning." She handed it to Kennedy. "Here you go."

Kennedy didn't recognize the number. "Hello?"

"This is Adell. Are you free to talk?"

Actually, her professor's timing couldn't be worse, but Kennedy didn't say so. "Yeah, this is great." She put her hand over the receiver and whispered to Willow, "It's my chemistry professor."

Adell had never been the type to squander words. "I'm calling to confirm you got my previous message. The one about not coming into lab today."

"Yes." Kennedy wasn't sure how her voice was supposed to sound right now. Hurt? Stoic? Disappointed?

"Well ..." Adell let out a small cough. "I don't mind going on record stating that I'm in complete disagreement with Dr. Faber on this one."

Kennedy wondered what to say. Did Adell want to vent about her colleague? Did she expect Kennedy to join in her complaints against the department head who'd barred Kennedy from her lab?

"Regardless," Adell went on, "it's not to be helped. He's made up his mind, at least for today. I can't promise you your position back, but I did manage to get him to agree to a meeting."

"Meeting?"

Kennedy could almost taste the impatience in her professor's voice. "Yes. A meeting. My office, this afternoon at three. You'll be there." It was far more of a statement than a question.

Kennedy checked the time. It was only a few minutes after noon. "Yeah, I can make it."

"See that you do." Adell ended the call before saying anything else.

Kennedy slipped her phone into her pocket, aware of Willow's quizzical eyes on her. "Problems again with the professor?"

Kennedy shrugged. She didn't want to get into any details. What she really needed was a nap. Who would have thought a prayer meeting could be so exhausting?

Willow unlocked her car, but Kennedy stopped when her phone rang again. Had Adell forgotten to tell her something? She glanced at the screen.

"Hi, Sandy." Kennedy paused with her hand on the car door. Willow stopped too and stared openly.

"Kennedy, thank God I got hold of you." Sandy was breathless. Fear iced over Kennedy's heart when Sandy asked, "Is Woong with you by any chance?"

"No." Kennedy looked around the parking lot as if he were about to jump out from behind one of the cars and shout *surprise*. "No," she repeated. "I haven't seen him all morning."

"Oh, dear. I was afraid of that."

Kennedy had already started walking back toward the hospital. Willow was right behind her.

Sandy mumbled something, but Kennedy couldn't make it out. "What's that?"

"I'm sorry, sweetie," Sandy answered. "I'm here with the detective. You've probably already left the hospital by now, haven't you?"

"No. We're in the parking garage, but we're on our way back in. We'll help you look around for Woong." Kennedy was nearly jogging now, platform shoes or not. "Do you think he wandered or something?"

Sandy sighed on the other line. "I wish it were that simple."

CHAPTER 26

"SO WOONG'S MISSING?" WILLOW had picked up on enough of Kennedy's conversation with Sandy to be worried. The girls sprinted toward the elevator that would take them to the ICU. Kennedy prayed she wouldn't twist an ankle in those heeled sandals.

"Yeah. I don't know what happened." Kennedy stared at every strange face she passed, wondering if Woong would be among them.

Willow rubbed her back when they got on the elevator. "I'm sure he's just fine."

Kennedy wished she could borrow some of her friend's optimism.

When they reached the ICU, Sandy was at the front desk, surrounded by several nurses, security officers, and Detective Drisklay, who raised his Styrofoam cup in expressionless greeting when he saw Kennedy come near.

Sandy rushed toward her and wrapped her up in a hug. "I'm so glad you came back, darling. I declare it's a miracle I'm still standing. That's how rattled my nerves are." She hugged Willow next. "You two are such sweethearts to be here right now. You're not skipping classes or missing anything important, are you?"

Kennedy shook her head and tried not to think of the lab she wasn't teaching this afternoon. "We're fine. What's going on here? What happened to Woong?"

Soft wrinkles furrowed around Sandy's eyes. "Oh, it's terrible, honey. Just terrible."

"Do you think he got lost looking for a snack or something?" Willow asked with an awkward chuckle that was hardly convincing.

"No, nothing like that, love." Sandy walked back up toward the desk. The security officers and nurses spread out in different directions. Only Drisklay remained, sipping his coffee as if he were an actor in some TV commercial for cheap Styrofoam cups.

Sandy put her hands up to her temples. "I think maybe the detective should fill you in on the details. My mind's just spinning and racing, and I can hardly focus on anything right about now."

Drisklay was scowling at them, an expression which Kennedy had figured out years ago simply indicated he was alive and breathing. "Miss Stern," he mumbled without acknowledging Willow right next to her.

"What happened?" her roommate asked.

Drisklay took a noisy sip of coffee. "That's the thousand-dollar question, isn't it?"

"Well, what do you guess happened?" Kennedy tried.

The detective set his Styrofoam cup on the nurses' station. "Here's what we know. This morning the boy mentioned that he saw someone going into his dad's office at the church a few minutes before the attack. Said he looked a little familiar, but he didn't know who it was. His mother called, asked if it was relevant to the case, and I said I'd come right over and we'd try to reconstruct what the suspect looked like. She asked me to wait since you were all doing your little kumbaya prayer thing for the pastor, so I said I'd come at noon.

"In the meantime, while all you folks were busy talking with the unseen Almighty, the boy was sitting by his father's bedside, reading joke books to a coma patient. That's when someone came and told the nurse he was the detective here to talk to the boy. The nurse called the kid out, kid acted like he recognized the man, and the nurse said they could talk in the break room since all you folks were so conveniently taking up the regular meeting room.

"Problem is, whoever that man was, he obviously wasn't me, and now he and the kid are gone. Security's pulling footage right now. Hospital's going on lockdown, but if you ask me, it won't do a gram of good. That man and the kid made their escape a full half hour before you all stopped asking some invisible deity to heal the pastor."

"It's all my fault, I'm afraid," Sandy added. "I came out to check on Woong, and the nurse told me he was already in a meeting with the detective. I should have gone right then to see him, but the doctor stopped by, and I had some questions for him about my husband, and ..." She shook her head. "I should have never left Woong in that room alone for so long."

Willow wrapped her arm around Sandy's shoulder. "You had no way to know something like this would happen."

"No, but he should have been with me. He should have been at that prayer meeting. Might have done his spirit good, too, listening to all them folks loving his father."

Willow shook her head. "Woong wanted to be by his dad. He was doing exactly what he was supposed to be doing, just like you were. This isn't anybody's fault."

"Except, of course, the perpetrator's," Drisklay added in his usual lifeless monotone.

"Ok." Kennedy looked around her. The security officers must be sweeping the whole building or something. She didn't see any of them. "How can we help? Do we start going room to room? Knocking on doors? What?"

Drisklay shook his head. "That kid's as far out of here as a baseball in the Polo Grounds with the Bambino up to bat."

Kennedy tried to decipher what he'd just said while Willow snapped, "A little more positive thinking, maybe?"

Drisklay held up his hand. "Hey, you three want to go back in the conference room and talk to God about it some more, be my guest. Or you could start by listing the names of all the men who came this morning to your little prayer session."

"What would be the point of that?" Willow asked with slightly less edge in her voice.

"The man who came in here wasn't a stranger. The boy knew him. Seems to me a pretty likely guess he started out at your prayer meeting, waited until you were all in your holy huddle and not paying any attention, and he snuck out and kidnapped the kid."

Kennedy wanted to cover Sandy's ears. Who did the detective think he was using language like that? Woong hadn't been kidnapped. He'd been ... he'd been ...

She let out her breath.

Maybe Drisklay had the right idea after all. Maybe they should focus on the people at the prayer meeting. At least it was something proactive they could do. Try to get Woong back.

Kennedy turned to the detective. "Got any paper?"

CHAPTER 27

Fifteen minutes later, they were seated in the small conference room around Drisklay and his list of ten men they could remember being at the morning's prayer meeting. "Now," Drisklay announced, "we figure out who'd want to take the kid."

Willow ran her fingers through her hair. "You know, I've been thinking, and I've got an idea that makes pretty good sense."

Drisklay leaned forward. Kennedy couldn't tell from his expression if he was eager for any sort of lead on this case or if he was surprised that a college girl with neon-green hair could have anything even partially resembling a good idea.

"All right." Willow paused dramatically. "So this morning Woong told his mom he remembered seeing someone go into his dad's office. That's probably the same guy who attacked Carl." She glanced at Drisklay, who remained expressionless. "Ok, and then Sandy told the people in the prayer meeting that Woong was going to meet with the detective. We all heard her say so."

Kennedy nodded, clearly remembering the incident.

"So here's what I'm thinking." Willow got up from her chair and started to pace, pointing her pen in the air. "What if the same guy who attacked Carl was in the prayer meeting this morning? He heard Sandy say Woong was going to meet with the detective, got scared, and came up with this plan to get Woong out of the hospital before he had a chance to tell the police what he knew?" She stopped, smiling broadly and clearly enjoying her dramatic role.

Drisklay raised an eyebrow. Kennedy wasn't sure she'd ever seen him put that much expression into his face before. "You come up with that all on your own?"

Kennedy's cheeks warmed up on her roommate's behalf.

"I think that's a very possible explanation." Sandy reached out and petted Willow on the arm like she was a puppy who'd just learned a new trick. "I think we should move forward with Willow's assumption."

Drisklay muttered something under his breath, but Kennedy could only make out the last half: "... made it all the way into Harvard."

Willow sat down, clearly less sure of herself now but still wanting to help. "So which of these people would have any reason to hurt Carl in the first place?"

Sandy shook her head. "I just don't know. Carl and me decided years ago that when he was having issues with folks at the church, he would talk to me about it, but we used a strict no-names policy. It made it easier for me that way. If Jack cheats on Jill, and they go to Carl about it for counseling, Carl comes home and tells me there's a couple struggling from the consequences of infidelity so I can pray for them. But he doesn't tell me who Jack is, and he doesn't tell me who Jill is. I like it that way because when folks know that's our policy, Jill doesn't feel like she has to tiptoe around me, and Jack doesn't feel like I'm judging him. If folks want to come to me and tell me what's going on, they can do that, or sometimes Carl and I meet with them together, so of course at that point I know who they are." She glanced at the list again. "But I don't think I've met with any of these men."

"By the way, why are we only focusing on the men?" Willow asked. "Isn't it just as possible that a woman could have attacked Carl for some reason? I mean, you hear about churches all the time where the pastor counsels the wife to stay with an abusive husband. What if it was something like that, and she got mad at Carl for putting her and her family in danger?"

"Oh, no, dear." Sandy rested her hand on Willow's arm. "Carl's never been the kind to tell women they just have to roll over and take it in cases like that. He always advocates they get themselves and their children — if there are any children involved — to safety.

He's very adamant about that because he's seen too many woman stay in horrible situations in the name of biblical submission."

Drisklay was staring at Sandy and Willow with wide, unbelieving eyes, but Kennedy suspected she was the only one who noticed. "A much simpler explanation," he offered, "is that the individual masquerading as a police detective was male."

"Oh." Willow stared at her fingernails which she'd recently painted orange in celebration of autumn. "That makes sense."

"Should we make a list of any of the women who were here that we think could pull off an impressive male impersonation, or are we content with the names we've got?" Drisklay asked.

"No, we're good," Willow answered, somewhat sheepishly.

Drisklay's comment reminded Kennedy of a problem she'd been mulling over. "Now that you mention it though, how can we be sure these are all the names here? I mean, it's not like we took roll or anything. And it was so crowded. Some people could have come in late or left early ..." She caught Drisklay's scowl and tried to make her point more concisely. "All I'm saying is we might not have a comprehensive list to work with."

Drisklay gave a brisk nod. "We've got a security team pulling up footage as we speak. It won't be a perfect image, but it might fill in some blanks."

Sandy was shaking her head. "Sweet Jesus, you're really stretching my faith this time, Lord, and I don't mean to sound ungrateful, but I don't know how much more worry my poor soul can bear."

"Excuse my lack of religious fervor, but I'd bet your energy would be better spent talking to your friends here about which of these men would have reason to assault your husband and kidnap your son."

Kennedy kept her eyes low, but Willow stood up from her chair. "Excuse me, Detective Barkley or Berkley or whatever your name is, but while we're talking about gambling, I've got a wager for you. I'm betting that you've never had a spouse on life support, and you've never had a child kidnapped right out from under your nose. So until you've gone through a fraction of what Sandy has, my *bet* is that you'll want to keep your mouth shut about things you know absolutely nothing about."

Nobody spoke. Drisklay cleared his throat and picked up his coffee cup. "I'm going to see about that security footage. I expect some pertinent information about each individual listed by the time I get back."

CHAPTER 28

KENNEDY STARED WHILE DRISKLAY shut the door nosily behind him.

"Good riddance," Willow mumbled.

Sandy took her by the hand. "Now, sweetheart, it was kind of you to stand up for me like that, and I know you did it with kind intentions, but is yelling at that detective the best way to love him into the kingdom of God?"

"I'm not trying to love anyone into anywhere right now," Willow replied, then added more softly, "but I'm sorry if I embarrassed you."

Sandy reached over and hugged her. "It's not me you need to apologize to, dear. But there now. As curmudgeonly as that detective is, he knows what he's doing. I was wrong to allow myself to get so emotional while he was here, but he's right about one thing. We need to focus on these names if we want to figure out who may have wanted to hurt my Carl. It's the best shot we've got at finding Woong. So ..." She put the piece of paper out in front of her. "This is what we've got."

Kennedy looked over the names. She only recognized two or three.

Sandy stared at the list. Kennedy hated to interrupt but finally admitted, "I'm not sure how helpful Willow and I are going to be at this."

"Nonsense." Sandy smoothed out the list again, as if touching the paper itself might give her insight into the motives of the men whose names were written there. "We'll find our answer here.

There's got to be something. Now, let me think. Scott Phillips, he's a dear of a saint. Spent the past ten years on the mission field and now that he's back Stateside we have him over for lunch sometimes after church. He loves the Lord and has his heart set on marrying this young girl he met, and I declare he doesn't have a violent bone in his body. Now." She moved her graceful finger down the page. "John August is a newer member of the church. Got saved just a year ago, I think, but Carl and I know him pretty well. We met him when he served at our table when we went out for our anniversary last year, and we struck up a friendship there. He accepted Christ a few months later, and Carl's been discipling him since then. They meet pretty regularly still, and I have no reason to suspect there's any tension between them. But you know who'd have a better idea for these things than me?" Sandy's eyes lit. "Let's call Dawn, Carl's secretary. She handles all his appointments, knows who he's meeting when. I think if we explained to her why it's so important, she'd be willing to listen to our list of names and go through them with us."

A minute later, the secretary from St. Margaret's Church was on speaker phone. Sandy explained in a rather roundabout way why they needed information about the different men listed, and Dawn seemed willing to help. Two of them Dawn had never met, which made it likely they'd never visited Carl in his office, so for now, the women decided to focus on the other eight.

"All right." Sandy looked at the names again. "What do you know about Simon Golding?"

Dawn paused for a moment. "Let's see. He comes in every so often. He and Carl ..." She hesitated.

"I know this is hard," Sandy said. "You're so discreet, which is why Carl trusts you with everything. I know you hate the thought of gossip, but this information may lead us to my son."

"I know." Dawn cleared her throat. "I know. Ok, so Simon and Carl meet maybe once a month, once every other month. He's having some struggles. I don't know all the details." She lowered her voice. "He and Carl are going through the blue book."

Sandy's eyes widened. "Oh. That. Ok, and you don't hear them fight ever?"

"Not a peep."

"When was the last time he was in?" Sandy asked.

"Let me check." The sound of Dawn's fingers typing on her keyboard carried over through the speaker phone.

Kennedy waited, wondering what this blue book was that Dawn and Sandy seemed so eager to not discuss.

"He hasn't been in since August," Dawn finally answered.

"Ok. Probably not him." Sandy crossed out his name and then pointed to the list with her pen. "Next we've got George Winston."

Dawn took in a deep breath. "His case is pretty basic. Grief counseling after his wife died, and that's about it. Once or twice he's brought the kids in with him, but they're teens, and as far as I can tell they're handling her passing as well as can be expected."

Kennedy didn't know the family they were referring to and wondered if she and Willow would be better off searching for Woong room to room. But, of course, Drisklay was right. If the abductor's goal was to keep Woong from telling the detective what he knew, there's no way the two of them would still be here at Providence.

Sandy and Dawn discussed the personal lives of several other men in the church. As it turns out, one other was going through *the blue book* with Carl, and like before Sandy rushed to finish that conversation as quickly as possible.

"So is that everyone?" Dawn finally asked.

"Well, Jackson stopped by." Sandy let out a little laugh, even though Kennedy didn't know what was funny.

"He did?"

"It must have been his work break or something," Sandy said. "I know how busy the office keeps him. It was nice he got a free minute to sneak away and pray with us. I know his schedule isn't easy for the two of you."

"Yeah," Dawn muttered. "Well, did you ever wonder if maybe it wasn't one of these men at all? Maybe it was a coincidence that what happened took place during the prayer meeting. Or maybe someone was waiting for a distraction."

Sandy frowned. "It's possible, I suppose. I hate to ask you to betray confidences like this, but is there anyone else you can think of who's given Carl trouble lately?"

Dawn was quiet for so long, Kennedy began to wonder if the call had been disconnected.

"I know it's not easy to talk about," Sandy prodded, "but please. This is my son who's missing."

"It's ok," Dawn assured her. "I'm just trying to think of the best way to put this. I don't want to give you one more thing to worry about. You've been through so much."

"Right now, I want to know everything so when the detective comes back, we can give him a full picture of who may or may not have wanted to harm my husband."

Dawn let out a noisy sigh. "All right, then. Well, I hate to bring it up because I know you and Carl have already dealt with a lot because of the Truth Warriors event coming up. But it's more than the media and the college students around town who've gotten upset. I'm not sure Carl told you about it. He didn't want to worry you, but there have been quite a few women from the church pretty outspoken against the conference."

"All this about a men's retreat?" Sandy asked.

Dawn cleared her throat. "It's more than that. Some women feel like St. Margaret's is already too patriarchal in its structure."

Sandy straightened her spine. "You know my husband has the utmost respect for everyone."

"Yes," Dawn replied, "but he also is very conservative in his interpretation of Scripture, and some women worry that he takes certain passages from the Bible too far."

Kennedy could tell that Sandy wanted to reply but was restraining herself.

"I can only imagine how hard it must be as the pastor's wife to know there are people upset with the way things are, but with a church the size of St. Margaret's, there's no way everyone will be happy."

"Just what kind of complaints have you heard?" Sandy asked.

"Actually, I have a list of several grievances that some women wanted Carl to bring up at the next elders' meeting."

"I never knew about a list," Sandy remarked.

"Yeah, well, your husband likes to protect you from church politics as much as he can."

Kennedy thought she heard some sort of hidden barb beneath the words, but she couldn't be exactly sure.

Sandy let out her breath. "So this list, do you think there's any way it has to do with Carl's attack?"

"I really wouldn't know."

Sandy ran her hand across the floral pattern of her skirt. "Well, why don't you tell me a few of the points so I at least have something of an idea of what to share with the detective. I honestly can't believe how anyone from St. Margaret's could accuse my husband of treating the women of our church unfairly."

"You sure this will be helpful?" Dawn asked doubtfully.

"I have no clue. But you know more about it than I do, so it's hard for me to make any judgment at this point in time."

Kennedy glanced at Willow and wondered if her roommate was also picking up on a hint of animosity between the two women.

"All right." Dawn sighed. "First of all, there have been some complaints about the way the elder board handled the Gordons. You remember the missionaries who came to speak last month."

"Yes, I remember."

"The couple made it clear when we invited them that Mrs. Gordon was the one involved in the direct, day-to-day ministry, and her husband was the one who oversaw the behind-the-scenes details of their work."

"I fail to see what objections an advocate of women's rights would raise to a situation like that," Sandy stated.

"They didn't object to their situation. What upset them was that it was only Mr. Gordon who presented in church, even though his wife was obviously the one with the greater field experience and knowledge of the region. But unless you went to the separate event just for women Tuesday morning, you wouldn't have been able to hear a word she had to say about her ministry overseas."

"So the women of St. Margaret's are so offended by that they're taking their complaints to the elder board?" There was a tremor in Sandy's voice.

"It's not just that, but since you asked, there's quite a large list of things like this. Some might sound petty, like how it's only men who read the opening Scripture passages on Sunday mornings, but they add up. One woman sent me an email to pass on anonymously that she's afraid to say anything in Carl's Sunday school class because she feels like women aren't supposed to talk in church."

"That's ridiculous. Carl would never preach something like that."

"No, but where does the line get drawn? If a woman can't teach an adult Sunday School class, can she raise an objection or offer a differing viewpoint, or will some people feel threatened because she's assumed a teaching position even for those few minutes? If ninety percent of the people the pastor asks to open the service in prayer are men, might that send the message to women that their prayers are somehow less important?"

"Carl has a Scriptural reason behind every decision he's made for our church." Sandy's voice was defensive. Kennedy wondered if it would be best for her and Willow to head out. It didn't sound like this conversation would lead them to Woong's abductor or Carl's attacker anytime soon.

"Well, you'd have to have Carl show me the chapter and verse that says women shouldn't pass around an offering plate. I'm not here to argue the Bible with you, Sandy. I'm really not. But I've heard these women's concerns, and I've talked with several of them firsthand, and some are deeply wounded."

"I'm very sorry to hear that. Carl never mentioned any complaints like this to me."

"Yeah, well, we both know how he likes to shield you from church politics as much as possible. And I'm sorry for burdening you with all of this. You know how much I enjoy working with your husband. I personally have no complaints."

"Well, I'm glad to hear that, and I understand that you're only the messenger here. I'm so deeply indebted to you for the way you serve our congregation and encourage my husband. You and I know better than anyone else at St. Margaret's how that man needs full-time help to stay organized and on task, and I thank God nearly every day that he raised you up for that purpose, and I'm grateful to you for all the time and energy you sacrifice."

The conversation probably would have turned mushy if Detective Drisklay hadn't chosen that moment to bang the doors open and stride in.

Oblivious to Sandy's phone call, he tossed a folder onto the table in front of them. "Well, looks like security found our perp."

CHAPTER 29

KENNEDY STARED AT THE image of a tall man walking beside Woong out the hospital exit.

"Who's he?" Willow asked the question Kennedy was eager to have answered.

Sandy stared at the image. "That's Jackson Phelps," she answered in a lifeless voice. "Dawn's husband." She shook her head. "Dawn's the church secretary," she told the detective.

"Volunteer secretary, from what I gather," he inserted.

Sandy hadn't stopped shaking her head.

Drisklay took a sip of coffee. "Now that we know who we're looking for, our chances of finding the kid just went from basically impossible to likely. If we get even more information, if for example we're able to go over to St. Margaret's and ask his wife where her husband might be, if we can coerce her to tell us what she ..."

"Coercing will be unnecessary, officer." The tinny voice from Sandy's cell phone made Kennedy jump. Willow raised her penciled eyebrows and let out a low, whispered, "Dude," and Sandy gasped aloud. Drisklay was the only one who didn't seem fazed by the unexpected interruption. "This is Mrs. Phelps I presume?"

"Yes." Dawn's voice from Sandy's speaker was strong and somewhat stoic. "And whom am I addressing?"

"Detective Drisklay. I take it you overheard our conversation about your husband?"

"Yes, sir."

"Do you have anything helpful that you'd like to add?"

There was a pause on the other end.

Kennedy hoped that Dawn would cooperate. "It'd be easier to talk this through in person," she finally said.

Drisklay scowled. "No time. You do realize that your husband has just kidnapped a child, don't you?"

"You have actual pictures to prove it?"

"We do," Drisklay answered.

Dawn's voice was hopeful when she asked quietly, "Sandy?"

Sandy nodded her head at her cell phone. "I'm afraid so. The pictures couldn't be much clearer. That's Jackson, and he and Woong ..." She didn't finish her sentence.

"All right." Drisklay took a slow sip from his Styrofoam cup. "It's time for you to tell us everything you know. Starting with where your husband might be taking the kid."

CHAPTER 30

"YOU WANT TO KNOW where my husband is, you show me those pictures yourself." Dawn's voice was as resolute as Woong's whenever he was preparing to throw a full-fledged temper tantrum. It got softer for just a minute when she added, "It's not you I don't trust, Sandy. It's the whole system. If that detective wants information, he's got to show me those photographs, and then I'll tell him anything he wants to know."

The vein in Drisklay's forearm bulged slightly as he picked up his cup. "No good. Every minute lost puts that kid at even more risk."

"Sir, I don't know you, and you sure as anything don't know me, and that means we've got to trust each other. Trust goes both ways, see. My husband for all his faults is not a dangerous man. Not in the least. You ask Sandy, and she'll tell you the exact same thing."

Drisklay's tone never changed. "I don't know what dictionary you use over there at that church you work at, but in the one I use, a *dangerous* man is someone who lies and kidnaps a child. You talk about trust. Well I can talk about trust, too. For example, I want to trust that you're not complicit in your husband's crimes, but unless I get some evidence toward that end, well, we've got ourselves a problem."

Sandy leaned toward the phone. "Dawn, love, do you have any idea where your husband might be fixing to take my son? I'm asking you mother to mother now, and I hope I might say friend to friend. Do you know where they might be going?" Sandy ignored Drisklay's well-rehearsed glare of death.

"Yes, I do," Dawn answered. "As soon as I overheard that detective — you'll pardon me, sir, if I forget your name for the moment — but as soon as I heard him saying it was my Jackson in the photo, I knew where he was off to. I'm home now and just confirmed it." Dawn ended as if that was all there was to say about it. Kennedy leaned forward, waiting to hear more.

Drisklay glowered at the phone for a silent moment before finally asking, "Well, care to enlighten the rest of us with that little bit of information?" Sandy clasped her hands in front of her and started to whisper a prayer. All Kennedy could make out was, "Please, sweet Jesus."

On the other end of the line, Dawn let out a heavy sigh. "His cousin owns a place near Salisbury. A little cabin, way out in the woods. Lets us use it anytime we want. We've even got our own key. When you said you'd identified Jackson on the security cameras, I checked to see if my suspicions were right. The key's gone. Now, I can't promise you it was in its usual spot this morning when I woke up, but I'd say it's a pretty reasonable guess that Jackson's on his way there. I'm so sorry, Sandy. I never thought he'd do anything like this. I would have stopped him. God is my witness, I would have done anything to keep him from acting out like this if I had the smallest inkling of suspicion. And I will do everything in my power to help you get your son back safe and sound."

Sandy nodded and wiped a tear off her cheek but didn't say anything.

Drisklay cleared his throat. "I'm glad to see you've finally come to your senses and decided to cooperate. Where in Salisbury is this cabin you mentioned? How far away? How do we get there?"

Dawn sniffed loudly enough for it to carry over the speakerphone. Drisklay grimaced.

"It's a little over an hour from here. I can meet you at the church and show you where to go."

"No." Drisklay pulled out his notebook with a scowl. "You tell me now, so I can relay directions to my men. Then you come with us in case we need you to talk some sense into that spouse of yours."

He straightened his shirt and tossed his cup into the trash. "Let's get this woman her son back."

CHAPTER 31

"YOU'RE SURE YOU'RE GOING to be ok?" Willow asked as Kennedy lowered herself into the passenger seat of Sandy's Honda.

"Yeah." She offered her roommate what she hoped was a reassuring smile. "Remember, I don't have to go to my lab class today. I'm as free as a bird."

The tender concern didn't leave Willow's face. "You know that's not what I'm talking about. I mean Woong, Carl, everything with Dominic earlier. You sure you want to go? Nobody would blame you for sitting back and praying from the sidelines this time."

Kennedy shook her head. "I've got to do this." It was hard to explain. It wasn't just that Kennedy wanted to be there as a support and comfort to Sandy. Of course that was a large part of it, but there was more to it than that. For starters, Woong was something between a cousin and a little brother to her. Kennedy had grown up as an only child in a family without even distant relatives close to her age. She'd had friends at school but never that kind of intimacy and togetherness she always imagined would come from a larger family. Besides, she knew what it was like to be abducted. She knew how scared Woong must be. Even if all she did was sit next to Sandy and pray with her for Woong's safe return, she had to be doing something.

Willow leaned down and gave her a noisy peck right next to her cheek in classic New England style. "I'll be praying for you," she whispered.

"You want to come?" Kennedy asked, trying not to sound too pushy.

Willow shook her head. "I'm actually kind of worried about Nick. I haven't heard from him all day. He's taking this whole thing harder than he wants any of us to guess. I'm not sure he even knows about Woong yet. I've been leaving him messages, but he's not returning my texts."

"Well, try not to worry." Kennedy offered one last smile as her roommate shut the door.

Sandy sat down next to her. "You sure you want to come along?" she asked. "God knows I'm happy for the company, but with all you've been through ..."

Kennedy didn't want to rehash the same conversation she'd just had with Willow. "I'm sure."

Sandy turned the car key with one hand and wiped her cheek with the other. It pained Kennedy to see her friend and mentor suffering so greatly.

"Want me to drive?" Kennedy asked.

Sandy shook her head. "No, dear. This will be good for me, give me something to focus on. And I'm sorry, but that detective talks in such a monotone, and I'm so worried over poor little Woong that I'm afraid I only caught every other word he said. Is Dawn going with him, or do we pick her up at her house?"

"No." Kennedy was glad she'd decided to come along. She'd never seen Sandy so frail before. "Dawn will meet us at the church since it's on the way. Drisklay and his men are already headed to the cabin."

"Think it's going to be dangerous?" Sandy asked as she pulled out of Providence parking lot.

Kennedy tried not to recall the details of her own kidnapping her first year at Harvard. "I'm sure it's going to work out just fine."

Sandy was halfway to St. Margaret's Church before she turned off her praise and worship music. "Sometimes the newer songs are just too upbeat for me. Do you ever find that yourself?"

Kennedy hadn't been listening to the album. She'd been too busy worrying about Woong. Wondering what would go through the head of a child that young. He must be terrified. And after all he'd suffered growing up on the streets in Korea. Why did some people seem to be cursed with all the bad luck?

Sandy pointed to a small collection of CDs in the center console. "Somewhere in here I've got one called *Hymns of the Faith*. Do you see that one, darling?"

Kennedy thumbed through the albums until she found it. Once she put it in, she realized that Sandy was right. The bright, chipper choruses from the first CD had been entirely inappropriate for a day like this.

When peace like a river attendeth my way ...

Kennedy thought back to the times she'd spent with Sandy. The Lindgren home was always such a respite, such a comfort to her. There was some kind of special blessing, an anointing on the house itself. Kennedy was sure of it. She'd never spent time at the Lindgrens' and failed to come away more relaxed than before. Only this time, it was Sandy who needed that peace and comfort.

When sorrows like sea billows roll.

Kennedy would have never understood what that phrase meant before last spring. Losing Dominic had been one of the most intense trials she'd ever suffered. And yet God was bringing her through it. Just like God would bring Sandy through the tempest raging around her today. The difference was that everything with Dominic happened so fast. Completely unexpected, which came with its own sort of emotional trauma, but there had been no pins-and-needles wait at the end. No uncertainty.

Poor Sandy was surrounded by nothing but uncertainty. Uncertainty regarding her husband as well as her son. Where was Woong? Kennedy hoped the detective was on the right track now. What if Dawn was wrong? What if her husband had no intention of taking Woong to that cabin? What if Woong was already ...

No, she couldn't think like that. Especially now when Sandy needed her the most.

Whatever my lot, thou hast taught me to say, "It is well, it is well with my soul."

Sandy hummed along so quietly Kennedy wasn't entirely sure she could hear it. During the first instrumental break, Sandy whispered, "Thank you, sweet Jesus." Kennedy wondered if she would be like that someday. Serene in the face of fear. Calm in the midst of the storm.

When Kennedy first met her, Sandy appeared immune to sadness. But now Kennedy could discern the underlying heaviness, the body of grief that weighed down Sandy's spirit. And yet still she could hum softly along with her hymns or lift up her voice, quiet and weak though it was, to praise her Savior.

Kennedy had never met anyone else like her.

"I'm sorry I'm being such poor company," Sandy said when the song ended.

Kennedy smiled. "I was actually about to say the same thing myself, but I didn't want to interrupt your time of worship."

Sandy turned down her music. "It's a sweet gift to be able to wrap myself up in the love and peace of my heavenly Father. I don't know what I'd do without that comfort." She hummed along a little more when the next song started. "You know, I read an interesting devotional once on grief. Sent it to a foster daughter of mine whose baby stopped breathing right after birth and suffered some real bad brain damage. This article, it had a lot of good points, but the one that stood out to me most is how in heaven, we're all going to worship Jesus, and there won't be any trials to burden us or distract us from our goal. It's only here on earth that we're given the opportunity to praise our Savior during times of sorrow and fear. That's why it's called a sacrifice of praise, I suppose.

"I don't pretend to know what God has in store for my family. There are so many things to worry about. But I know that no matter how bad it gets, once I get to heaven, he'll take that sorrow away. Heal it completely, even if I never find complete comfort here on earth. So what I tell myself when it gets real hard, what I tell myself when I wonder how I can ever possibly thank Jesus for anything when life is so difficult right now — I remind myself that by the time I get to heaven, that sorrow will find perfect healing, and I'll praise my Savior with so much joy and gratitude. And I don't want to be ashamed on that day. I don't want to look back on my life and say, *I wish I'd just trusted God even when things were hard*, or *I wish I'd learned how to praise God during the sorrowful times when I still had the chance*. I take comfort in the reminder that my God never changes, so why should I only praise him when life is going my way?"

Kennedy didn't answer. She was too busy thinking about what happened to Dominic last spring, about the tearful nights that followed, about the dull ache that resurfaced at the most inopportune times.

Sandy let out a little chuckle. "Here I am gabbing away, and I haven't even asked how you're doing. Is everything ok? You hanging in there?"

Kennedy wasn't about to burden Sandy with her own sorrows and uncertainties. Not when Sandy had so many of her own to confront. "I'm all right."

Sandy stole a quick glance at her, enough to show Kennedy she wasn't satisfied with her answer. "Tell me about what's going on in your world. It's been a few weeks since we've had a good sit-down together to talk."

Kennedy tried to think back over the first half of her semester but couldn't even remember what she'd done yesterday morning. "Classes are going well."

Sandy shook her head. "I want to hear about you, sweetheart, not school."

Kennedy should have known from previous experience that she wouldn't get out of this conversation easily.

"And don't be thinking to yourself that I've got too much to worry over to have a good heart-to-heart with you," Sandy added. "Heaven knows I could use some conversation to distract my mind right now."

"In that case," Kennedy began and found herself talking with Sandy about her class schedule, her relationship with Willow, her TA job. She didn't mention the newspaper column she'd written. She didn't even think Sandy realized the editors of the Voice attacked her in last week's article, so she didn't want to bring up how she'd defended her. It all seemed so trivial now compared to what Woong and Carl were suffering.

"And how's your anxiety been?" Sandy asked. "I was happy when you told me you'd gotten that prescription. Do you think it's helping?"

Kennedy had already wrestled with a lot of guilt for not being able to pray her way out of her PTSD. She doubted Sandy would ever know what a comfort it was for her mentor to affirm her decision like that.

"I think things are getting better," she answered. "I don't worry about having panic attacks out of the blue now. So in that sense I think it really has helped. But then sometimes ..." Her voice trailed off, and she wondered how to best express herself.

"Sometimes what, dear?"

Kennedy sighed. "Sometimes I wonder if I took the easy way out. I mean, not with the anxiety and panic so much, but with Dominic. I was really grieving this summer. I think that's when it finally got my parents concerned enough that they made those appointments. And sometimes I feel like ..." She didn't know how to finish.

"You feel like taking medicine to take the edge off your grief is dishonoring Dominic's memory?"

Kennedy nodded. "Yeah, something like that. He didn't like the idea of antidepressants or things, at least not in anything but the most extreme cases. And I mean, I know it was pretty bad for me, but I was still functioning all right."

"That's a hard call," Sandy agreed, "but something to bear in mind is that Dominic was never your authority. You're young. You're living on your own now, but in a lot of ways your parents are still the tool God uses to lead you and guide you. The fact that they know you so well that they saw the medicine was at least an option worth exploring says a lot to me. And that you're not having the panic attacks anymore. I know you still grieve for Dominic. Even if the medicine helps you process through that grief more effectively, it doesn't mean you don't feel the pain."

Sandy was right about that. Still, Kennedy hated talking about her own problems. "So how well do you know Dawn's husband?"

Sandy sighed. "Well, Dawn's been working for Carl from the time he came to St. Margaret's. I guess some people are raising a fuss because she only gets paid a part-time stipend — and a very small one at that — even though she does close to full-time work. But that's her choice more than anything else. When we were advertising for the position, it was a paid, hourly wage. She came and interviewed, and once she got the job, she said she didn't need that much money. Her husband works in some kind of financial department. I wouldn't know the details, but he has clients all over the world, takes care of important bank accounts and investments, things like that. I don't know how much he makes, but they have a home out in Newton, so that tells you a lot right there. So once she got the job, Dawn said she didn't need an hourly wage. She'd just take a little stipend to cover gas expenses and stopping for her fancy coffee every morning before work, things like that. The elders were all in agreement that they'd take that extra money just as if they were paying Dawn what any other person would be making, and they'd devote that to missions above the regular budget for giving overseas. It's very generous of Dawn and her husband, really. St. Margaret's has been able to do a lot of good for the kingdom that we otherwise might not have had the resources for."

Kennedy wondered if during her complimentary speech, Sandy had forgotten they were talking about the man accused of kidnapping her son. She replayed the conversation between Sandy and Dawn on the phone. She'd detected a hint of animosity, and she thought Willow had too. Maybe it was because Dawn was married to the man who'd abducted Woong from the hospital. But maybe there was more to it. Dawn had seemed pretty willing to cooperate with the detective. Unless she was sending everybody in the exact opposite direction from where she knew Jackson had taken Woong. But Kennedy had no reason to doubt Dawn's character. She was a little brusque at times, but for a congregation the size of St. Margaret's, a certain level of discretion would definitely be an asset to someone in her position. Still, she didn't meet the stereotype of a chatty church secretary. In fact, Kennedy could see Sandy filling in that role perfectly.

"Did you ever think of doing office work for Carl?" she asked.

Sandy chuckled. "My goodness, no. Carl and I tried that once back at the church plant in New York. It was a disaster."

"Really?"

"Most definitely. After about two hours working together, we realized that it would never do to have one of us bossing the other around. I mean, don't get me wrong, I completely agree with the Bible that a wife should show her husband respect in all things. But the marriage relationship is worlds different than an employee relationship. Carl didn't like giving me orders, and frankly I didn't like taking them. I'm sure there are some marriages where that kind of arrangement would work out just fine, but Carl and me knew it wouldn't work for us. When it comes to the Bible, then absolutely yes, he's the head of our home. But when it comes to our day-to-day lives, we're happy to fuss and fret and come to decisions together. Sometimes he gives in to me, sometimes I give in to him. I know other happy, godly marriages that take a more structural view on the husband's role as head of the wife, but in our marriage, that's never what we've chosen to emphasize."

Kennedy didn't have time to ask any more questions once Sandy pulled into the St. Margaret's parking lot.

"All right. Let's go in and find Dawn."

CHAPTER 32

KENNEDY FOLLOWED SANDY INTO the foyer. Tables were stacked against all the walls. Boxes of fliers and books were haphazardly strewn about, and there was nobody in sight. Kennedy wondered if all the volunteers had stopped in the middle of their work when they heard what happened to Carl. With his condition being so questionable, would they even hold the conference this weekend?

"Dawn?" Sandy's voice echoed throughout the empty building.

"I'm back here," came the somewhat muffled reply.

Sandy made her way down the hall. Kennedy wondered if maybe they should just wait for Dawn to come to them. Dawn knew what kind of a rush they'd be in, didn't she? Wouldn't she realize how urgent this was?

Sandy stopped outside her husband's office. Kennedy glanced in at Dawn, who was on her knees sweeping up the shattered pieces from the broken bust of Charles Spurgeon. "Such a shame," she muttered without a word of greeting. "He loved looking at that old fat man with his ridiculous beard."

Sandy helped Dawn up. "I'm so glad you've agreed to come with us and help."

Dawn sniffed. "Least I could do. I don't suppose I need to tell you how truly sorry I am."

"You're not responsible for your husband's actions," Sandy told her. "There's no way you could have known this was what he'd do."

"Well, maybe you're right, but I should have had my eyes open wider. And I shouldn't have been snarky with that detective. It just threw me off guard, you know. I certainly wasn't trying to keep you from your son."

"Of course you weren't. The thought never even crossed my mind." Sandy gave her a hug, which made Dawn bristle.

After their somewhat awkward reconciliation, Dawn brushed her hands off on her pants. "I guess we can clean up the rest of his office once we've got Woong home safe and sound, don't you think?"

"Yes, of course," Sandy replied, and together they all headed out of St. Margaret's and back to Sandy's Honda. Kennedy sat in the back. Sandy and Dawn didn't have much to say to one another other than a few brief directions on where to turn.

"Oh rats," Sandy exclaimed when they were about ten minutes away from the church. "I wanted to pick up another one of Carl's joke books. Now that Woong's learned more of the Bible stories, he can find the humor in a lot of them."

Dawn rolled her eyes. "Your husband must have taken a bad joke class in seminary. He did, didn't he?"

Sandy smiled. "Well, he's been starting his sermons off with a funny story or a riddle or a bad pun for as long as he's been preaching. I'm not sure he picked that up at seminary though."

The women were quiet for a while longer. Kennedy pulled out her phone and checked her email messages. She was surprised to find her inbox so full. A quick browsing of the first few lines explained what it was all about. "Kennedy, I don't know you, but after I read your column in the Voice, I'm glad for that." Or the next one: "As a transgender man, I'm appalled that anyone in this century would think to tell me that my life choices are ordained by the absence or presence of one small piece of anatomy."

Kennedy didn't have the energy for any of this. She'd never asked to become a lightning rod or a target. She skimmed the rest of her inbox. Other than an interview request from some guy who ran a website that focused on issues of censorship and free speech on college campuses, everything else appeared to be an incendiary reaction against her article from yesterday's paper.

She even got an angry message from the parent of one of her lab students. "When Clarisse got a C- on her chemistry midterm, I

thought it was because she wasn't studying hard enough. Now that
I've seen the sort of drivel her teaching assistant believes, it's no
small wonder my child is struggling under your so-called tutelage.
I'm actually surprised that your pastor allows you, a young woman,
to hold a teaching position at a coed institution."

Kennedy didn't read the rest. Once things calmed down, once
Woong was home safe with his mom and Carl was recovered from
his injuries, Willow would help her sift through these piles of
cyber junk. Her counselor on campus had talked with her several
times about her propensity to avoid difficult issues instead of
dealing with them straight on, but in this case there was no other
option but to ignore the hate.

"We're about forty-five minutes away," Dawn said as she directed Sandy out of the city. Kennedy didn't know where they
were going. Couldn't remember if she'd been this way before.
She had never been too astute when it came to observing her
surroundings, and her sense of direction was almost as deplorable
as some of her lab students' sense of entitlement.

"I should call the detective again." Dawn pulled her cell phone
out of her designer purse. "Do you think he and his men have
made it to the cabin by now?" She glanced at her diamond-stud-
ded watch. "I should have paid more attention to the time." She
held the phone to her ear and eventually sighed. "No answer.
Coverage out that way is spotty at best."

Sandy wasn't very talkative. Kennedy could only imagine what
darkness and fear must be swarming around in her spirit. Kennedy
had tried so hard to remain hopeful, to imagine that they were
simply driving to this cabin to pick up Woong and reunite him
with his mother. But what if that's not what happened? What if
Dawn's husband panicked? What if he hurt Woong? What if the
two of them weren't there at all?

Kennedy's phone beeped with an incoming text. It was from
Willow.

*Heard anything from Nick? Still haven't been able to reach him.
Starting to worry.*

Kennedy typed back her response, trying to be as gentle as she
could. As much as she cared for her roommate, as happy as she
was about her whirlwind, made-in-heaven romance, she didn't

have the mental energy to worry about Nick right now. He was an adult and quite capable of taking care of himself.

"I'm still so sorry this happened," Dawn muttered.

Sandy clucked her tongue. "Shh. You don't need to feel guilty at all. Your husband is his own man and responsible for his own actions."

"But I should have known he was planning something." Dawn shook her head and quickly added, "I mean, maybe not something this drastic, but I knew the stress was building up and looking for an outlet."

"So work's been real hard for him lately?" Sandy asked.

"I wish." Dawn laughed mirthlessly. "He was fired, Sandy. He's been out of a job for four months now."

"I'm sorry, dear. I had no idea."

"Yeah, that's the way Jackson wanted it. Wouldn't allow me to tell anybody. Not you, not Carl. It's a big sore spot for him. I thought I was doing the right thing by keeping it quiet like he wanted, but obviously I was wrong."

"How did he lose his job? Did the company downsize?"

"No. I wish to heaven it would have been something that simple. I don't even have all the details, but I can read between the lines well enough. He was forced to resign. Something to do with the way he was handling a client's money. You know I've never been good with numbers and figures. No thanks to Jackson. He never talks to me about work. Doesn't want to worry my pretty little head about it. Sort of like Carl not coming home and dumping all his church worries on you, I suppose."

Sandy didn't respond, but her lips tightened.

"Anyway," Dawn went on, "at first he just planned to find another line of work. He'd thought about going into consulting before. He was only three years away from getting fully vested in the firm. After that point, he had planned to phase out and start his own business, so at first we figured this was just God's way of speeding up our original plan. But he ran into far more obstacles than he'd expected. He won't come out and say so, but his reputation's basically shot in the finance community. He'd be better off assuming a new name and starting as an hourly bank teller at this point."

"You should have told us, darling. If the two of you have been worried about money ..."

"The money's not a problem. Jackson could retire today, and we'd still be set for life, just perhaps without the extra traveling we'd planned on. That's not what's been stressing him out. It's that his whole identity is wrapped up in his job. I thought I had it bad when I became an empty nester, but that was nothing like the identity crisis Jackson's been going through. And I hate to rub on an already sore spot, but this Truth Warriors conference coming up hasn't helped matters either."

"How so?"

"Well, Carl asked Jackson to lead a breakout session. Thought it would be neat for a businessman as successful as my husband to talk about maintaining godly ethics in the workplace. This was planned months before Jackson had to resign, but I know it's been eating him up. And honestly, I can't say that I blame him in this particular instance. I read some of Carl's books from the Truth Warriors movements, or at least I browsed through some of them when things at the office were slow. And if I were a man who'd recently lost his job and felt like his whole life was imploding in around him, I'm not sure how encouraged I'd feel spending the whole weekend being reminded that one of a godly man's primary responsibilities is to provide for his family."

Sandy's jaw was still tense, but there was softness in her voice again. "I'm sure it's been a very difficult time for both of you."

"I had no idea my husband would take it out on Carl like that. I'll testify on oath before every single court in the nation."

"Is it possible we're following the wrong trail?" Sandy wiped a wisp of hair off her forehead and tucked it back into her French braid. "I mean, we've seen the footage of Jackson leaving the hospital with Woong, at least Kennedy and I have. But that doesn't necessarily mean your husband is the one who attacked Carl. You say he was under a lot of stress, that he didn't want to lead a session at the conference this weekend, but that still doesn't explain such a violent ..." Sandy didn't finish her thought.

Dawn strummed her manicured fingers against her purse. "I appreciate the good faith you're showing my husband at the moment, but I'm afraid he doesn't deserve it. It wouldn't surprise me in the least to learn that Jackson's responsible for Carl's attack as well as your son's kidnapping."

CHAPTER 33

KENNEDY LEANED FORWARD SLIGHTLY in the backseat. She didn't want to miss anything Dawn was going to say.

"Jackson's having a hard time with being between jobs right now. That's only natural. But there's more to it than just that. His issues aren't with Carl specifically, more with conservative Christianity in general, but Carl's the face of that in Jackson's mind. And all this media hype about the Truth Warriors conference has done nothing but rub salt in old wounds.

"Jackson's sister died. It was about ten years ago now, back when we were still living out in Washington. Her husband was no good. She went and talked to her family pastor, and he told her what so many conservative ministers tell their congregants in cases like that. Be more respectful. Be more submissive. Pray for God to change his heart. And unless you've got verifiable proof he's having an affair, you've got no Scriptural basis for divorce.

"Well, she was a devout believer, his sister was. Took everything that pastor said to heart. Submitted to her husband, prayed for God to change him all the way up to the day he murdered her and their eight-year-old twins with a crowbar."

Kennedy winced and wondered how anyone could get through telling a story like that without the least trace of expression in their voice.

"Jackson was really close to his sister. Had been telling her for years to get out of her marriage. But she was convinced that to leave her husband would be a grave sin, and she took that pastor's advice and sat around waiting for God to change him. Except he never did.

"Like I said, this was years ago, but Jackson's still sore. Still mistrusts any pastor who even hints at wives submitting to their husbands because of what he saw it do to his sister. He'd been handling his grief well for a while, but then the media came and started stirring the pot with their mayhem about the Truth Warriors conference, and I already told you he was feeling insecure about that after losing his job." Dawn shook her head. "I don't want you to think I'm blaming Carl, you know. That man is a treasure of a boss and a joy to work for. But that's the other thing. When these journalists started looking for muck to rake about St. Margaret's, they had a heyday when they found out that the church was paying me so little. They made it out like since I wasn't the one responsible for supporting our family that Carl and the elders chained me to a wall and forced me to take dictation for pennies. Jackson was really scared that it would be one of these sensationalist reporters who found out that he lost his job. You know how these writers can be like sharks. The smallest whiff of blood, a scandal, and they're all right there.

"He wanted me to resign, you know. I fought with him about it. Most of all because I know that if he's sitting around the house moping all day without anything to do, it's only going to make things worse if I'm there bored out of my mind. Jackson kept threatening to go to Carl himself and tell him I was quitting my job. I don't know what Carl would have said about that, but I wonder if that's what happened yesterday afternoon." She shook her head.

Sandy reached over and squeezed her hand. "Whatever his reasons, hon, I don't blame you for them and I don't want you to keep on blaming yourself. Remember Ananias and Saphira in the book of Acts? Each one of them was found guilty before God. Each one had the opportunity to repent independent of each other. God's not looking down at you and holding you accountable for your husband's sins."

Dawn clasped Sandy's hand in hers. "You're an honorable woman. And I'm sorry for not being a better friend to you. I know it's hard being a pastor's wife, up there on that pedestal you wish nobody would set you up on. I've thought plenty of times you must get lonely up there all by yourself, and every so often I made up my mind to do something about it. Invite you over for some girl time, treat you to a spa day, but I never did. In all honesty, I felt a little intimidated by you. You're like this stay-at-home grandma ninja with the spirit of one of the old-school missionaries and the energy level of a twenty-year-old. And you do it all without pay. Small as my stipend is, I think of myself as a working woman. I put on my business casual, I show up at the office the same time every day, I go home, and at the end of each month I take my little paycheck to the bank and enjoy some spending money. But you, you're raising Woong, you're homeschooling him now on top of all the days you've been watching your grandkids. You oversee the children's ministry and are active in the pregnancy center, and you still manage to make those healthy, delicious home-cooked lunches Carl brings to the office. I guess it's my fault for not taking the time to get to know you better, but part of me assumed that you'd look down at someone like me, a woman who's in the office all day instead of keeping up home or running around town doing good."

Sandy drove with one hand on the steering wheel and one hand still holding Dawn's. "It's such a shame, isn't it, the way we women label each other," Sandy began. "Who's a stay-at-home mom, who's a working woman, who homeschools, who doesn't. The Christian life gives believers so much freedom, but even when we're not judging others for being different than we are, we get the feeling like someone else is judging us. I had no idea what a stigma there was against public school in the homeschool community until I pulled Woong out of Medford Academy. And let me tell you, it's an ugly thing. Whenever a woman's told *you must raise your children exactly this way* or *all wives must behave exactly like this*, you've lost sight of grace. Am I glad I homeschool Woong? Sure am. Turns out it's a great time for us to bond, and I declare I'm learning nearly as much as he is, things I either never studied or have forgotten since I was his age. Does that mean I'll go on homeschooling him until he graduates? Probably not. And it doesn't mean I'm about to vilify every parent who sends their child to public school or private school or makes a choice that's different than mine.

"I think the devil delights in splitting us up. You know, we women have gone through our fair share of trials to get to where we are now. To get to the point where you can work in an office and not have to worry about being harassed on the job. Where I can be involved in the start-up of a new pregnancy center and still not feel like I'm neglecting my duties at home.

"I've met such wonderful moms in the homeschool co-op Woong and I joined. A lot of them are running their own businesses. The mom who's teaching Woong's nutrition class for his science elective, she's got an online coaching business about healthy eating. Another woman, she and her husband write and publish their own homeschool materials. Next spring, they're taking their kids on a nine-month long book tour across the states in their camper. What I'm saying is that there are so many opportunities today that it should be a great time to be a woman. We should celebrate our accomplishments, spur one another on and fan our dreams into flame. Not sit around and bicker like old hens about who buys their kids goldfish crackers from the store and who's cooking gluten-free snacks from scratch. Or who works an outside job and who stays home keeping a picture-perfect house.

"We're so divided, and I think the devil's planned it that way because he knows how important female friendships are, and he's scared of what can happen if we truly do join together in unity and celebrate not only the characteristics that make us women, but the differences that make us unique daughters of our King."

Dawn was quiet for a minute before finally stating, "You should become a motivational speaker or something. I mean it."

Sandy chuckled. "Well, it's kind of you to say so, but I am very content with the role God's given me at this stage of my life. I wouldn't ask for anything more, and I certainly wouldn't ask for anything less."

Kennedy wished Marty and the other editors of the Voice could listen to Sandy. To realize that just because one woman chooses a certain lifestyle it doesn't mean she's making a statement and telling the world it's the only way to live. Why couldn't more people understand that?

They drove for a while without talking, with the soft music from Sandy's hymns playing in the background. When they turned into a wooded area, Kennedy wondered if they were getting closer to the cabin. Just how remote was it?

She tried to channel the fear she was feeling into prayer, but images of Woong alone and scared ran unchecked through her mind. At last, Dawn pointed her finger. "Turn down here. The cabin's about three quarters of a mile away. It's really bumpy, so you want to go slow."

CHAPTER 34

"SO DO WE PULL all the way up?" Sandy asked. "Should we call the detective and ask him where to park?"

Dawn shook her head. "You won't get any coverage out here. That's both the blessing and the curse of this place. We used to come out here to relax, get away from the rat race, but the last few years Jackson's been so tied to his phone that he hasn't wanted to unplug for even one night."

Sandy followed a curve in the road and had to stop behind a police car that was blocking the way. She rolled down the window to talk to the officer standing outside.

"I'm Woong's mother. Is my son ok? Have you found him yet?"

Kennedy rolled down her window as well, refusing to miss the officer's words.

The policeman pushed a button and spoke into his radio. "I've got the mother here. Should I send her through?"

Kennedy couldn't make out the reply, but the officer stepped back and told Sandy, "Go on ahead. They're just down the drive about another quarter of a mile."

"What about my son?" Sandy asked with a catch in her voice. "Do they know where my son is?"

The officer's radio hummed to life. "Mom? Is that you?" Woong's voice, though somewhat garbled by static, was unmistakable.

"Oh, thank you, sweet Jesus!" Sandy exclaimed. "Woong? Woong, honey, can you hear me?" She looked up at the officer. "Can he hear me on that thing?"

He smiled. "You want to talk to your son on my radio, or do you want to roll on by and see him for yourself?"

"Myself," Sandy answered breathlessly. "I'll go see him myself, Officer. Thank you so much. Oh, thank you, precious Savior. So he's ok, right?" she asked out her window as she started to roll the Honda forward.

The officer's grin spread wide. "Happy and safe and unharmed. But go see him for yourself. You don't want to take my word for it."

Sandy was laughing while tears streamed down her cheeks. She chuckled away a happy sob. "No, I don't want to take your word for it. Thank you, sir."

Kennedy didn't say anything. Neither did Dawn. Sandy acted as if she had forgotten there was anyone else in the car with her except for Jesus, and she poured out her profuse praises through her tears.

The Honda slowed to a halt when the cabin came into view, surrounded by at least half a dozen police cars.

"Mom?" The familiar voice carried over the top of Sandy's grateful prayers, and she opened her car door and managed to kneel down in the dirt before Woong ran into her open arms.

"That was wicked awesome!" he shouted. "Mr. Jackson told me he had a present for Dad, and I needed to come with him to the parking lot to help him carry it up, only when we got to the car, he said he musta left it at his house. So we started driving, and I've already talked with the police officer, Mom, so I know I didn't do the right thing just then, but he was an adult and wasn't a stranger, so I thought I had to obey him. So I hope you'll forgive me that part, because I really wasn't trying to be naughty or stuff and nonsense like that. But then we started driving, and we kept driving and driving and driving, and I could tell by the signs we weren't in Cambridge no more, and from the looks of all the trees in the woods it was like we weren't anywhere no more, so I asked Mr. Jackson about it, and he said that the present was a real bearskin rug that he shot on this island way up in Alaska. And I never seen a rug like that, so I got real curious, and then he took me to this cabin and it wasn't just the rug, but there was a whole stuffed deer. I'm not talking about the kind of baby toy you get in the store, neither, but a real live deer, except it weren't alive no more on account of Mr. Jackson shooting it. Right in the head, too, and you can see the part between its eyes where the taxi man — that's the one who stuffed the deer to begin with — had to use some fake hair on account of not wanting there to be a bullet hole right there on his face. So anyway, I knew enough by then to figure you'd be pretty worried about me, only Mr. Jackson said that cell phones don't work all the way out here, but that he'd left you a message so you'd come and meet us, and then we'd all go camping. Well, it sounded a little fishy to me on account of you liking the kinds of vacations with nice houses that serve you big fancy breakfasts in the morning, only you never said anything before about enjoying camping, and even though Mr. Jackson said that we could go hunting, I couldn't picture you holding one of them big guns and blowing the brains out of a cute little deer or stuff and nonsense like that.

"So that's when I figured I'd been kidnapped, only I couldn't let Mr. Jackson know that I'd caught on, so I just had to go along with it. I had it all planned out, too. I was gonna wait until he was asleep, and then I found some fishing poles and whatnot in this little shed, kinda like a garage only there were no cars parked in there on account of it being too little, but it was messy like a garage, and there were these fishing poles, so what I decided I'd do was wait until Mr. Jackson was asleep, and then I'd come get the string and tie him up real good with it. Because that time Dad took me fishing, I remember how the string looks real thin, only it's strong enough to cut your finger, so I figured that since I couldn't find no rope, it would do to tie up Mr. Jackson and then escape. Except that's not what happened. Turns out I didn't have to tie anybody up after all. Mr. Jackson said I could pick out a movie, so I chose one of the Pixar ones. He had the Avengers, too, and I hafta admit I got a little tempted to watch that even though I know you think it's too violent for me. But I figured that once I escaped you'd want me to tell you exactly what happened, and I didn't wanna make you sad, so I chose one of the Toy Story movies I hadn't seen yet, and it was pretty good, only I didn't get to finish it because I was sitting there watching, and Mr. Jackson, he was working at this desk in the kitchen doing something on his computer way over in the other room, and all of a sudden there was a loud *pow*! And the door just broke right in two, and the next thing I knew this big old policeman had picked me up and carried me outside, and they told me I was safe, and that you were coming to get me. Which is exactly what happened."

Sandy had started crying about halfway into Woong's story, but he was so engrossed in the retelling that he didn't notice until he was done. "Aww, Mom," he whined and submitted himself to his mother's tearful hugs and smothering kisses for a few seconds before wiggling himself free.

Peering into the backseat, Woong gave a giant smile. "Hi, Kennedy. Did Willow and Nick come, too? I can't wait to tell Willow that I met a bear all the way from Alaska. Do you think maybe she saw that very same bear one day before Mr. Jackson shot it?"

Kennedy was too relieved to find Woong talkative and unharmed to worry about something like a geography lesson about how big the state of Alaska really is. "You'll have to ask her when you see her."

"Yeah, I'm ready to go back to Cambridge now. I'm awfully hungry. I told Mr. Jackson it was past my lunch time, but all he did was heat up one little can of ratiolis or whatever that kind of pasta it is with the cheese on the inside and covered in spaghetti sauce."

Sandy gave him one more hug as Detective Drisklay walked up. For the first time that Kennedy could remember, both his hands were empty.

"Doesn't look like he's been hurt at all," he declared flatly.

"Thank you, Jesus," Sandy breathed.

Drisklay frowned. "Well, we got Jackson. Not that he put up much of a fight. He's on his way to the police department now, but I thought you might want to know that in addition to kidnapping your son, he also confessed to attacking your husband. Something about wanting his wife to quit her job at the church only she wouldn't listen. Of course, nothing is admissible yet, and his lawyer may try to get him to rescind his original statement, so I can't tell you the case is closed, but unofficially, I thought it might put your mind at ease to know that we got the right man."

"I appreciate that, detective," Sandy replied. "Words can't tell you how relieved I am to have my son back safe and sound." She glanced at Dawn who was still in the passenger seat. "Can you let us know what's going to happen now to Jackson?"

Drisklay peered into the window and frowned at Dawn. "You the wife?" he asked flatly.

Dawn nodded her head, her expression as stoic as the detective's.

"I got a message for you from your husband." Drisklay coughed. His voice was hoarse. "Since he cooperated with us during the arrest, and since you're the one who led us here, I told him I'd pass his words on to you. If you want to hear them, that is."

Dawn sat up a little taller in her seat. "I'm ready whenever you are."

Drisklay gave her a small tilt of the head. If Kennedy didn't know the detective better, it would have looked like a nod of respect.

"Your husband wanted me to tell you that he's very, very sorry."

CHAPTER 35

THE DRIVE BACK TO Cambridge was partly like an impromptu worship session, with Sandy regularly breaking out into prayer or song, and partly like a children's slumber party, with Woong talking so fast he was the equivalent of four or five different kids rolled into one. Kennedy was glad he was unharmed. She didn't know if under the surface he'd been more scared than he cared to publicly admit, but right now he seemed to relish the extra attention, and each time he told the story of his capture and rescue it grew more and more embellished. She wouldn't be surprised if by tomorrow Woong was telling everyone that he fought Jackson off with his bare hands.

Dawn was quiet, and Kennedy was conscious of the awkward situation she and Sandy found themselves in, but she didn't know how to ease any of that tension. Her phone beeped almost immediately after they got back on the main highway headed back to Cambridge. She'd missed a call. Praying it wasn't another hate message, she listened to her voicemail.

"This is Devorah Adell attempting to reach Kennedy Stern. Kennedy, I have to confess that I'm disappointed in you. When Dr. Faber threatened to fire you from my lab, I told him you were a model student, the epitome of responsibility and respectability. I hate to inform you that there's nothing respectable about missing a meeting your professor and perhaps your most vocal advocate has gone through the efforts of setting up for you. Seeing as how it's already ten minutes to four, I have no choice but to leave your future as a TA in my class up to Dr. Faber's judgment. If you'd like to try to reach him before his office hours end at 5:30, you're more than welcome to try. Good day."

Kennedy looked at the time. How could she have forgotten?

"What is it, dear?" Sandy asked, glancing at Kennedy in the rearview mirror.

"I missed a meeting this afternoon. A pretty important one." How could she be so stupid? How hard would it have been to call and cancel before driving with Sandy all around Massachusetts? Her professor was right. Adell might be her only supporter right now. How could she have forgotten something so serious?

"Could you reschedule?" Sandy asked.

Kennedy did the math. If Sandy dropped her off at the T station, she could probably make it back to campus to meet Dr. Faber in his office. The bigger question was did she really want to? Why should she keep on working in a department that was so quick to profile her after reading one single article she wrote? But if she didn't show up, if she didn't humble herself before Faber and beg to get her job back, wouldn't that reflect poorly on Adell who'd stood up for her?

No, she had to make that appointment, or at least she had to try.

"I know you want to get back to be with Carl as soon as possible," Kennedy said, "but do you think you could drop me off by the Red Line?"

"I'll take you back to campus myself, sweetie. It's only a few minutes out of the way. I don't mind."

"No, I want you to be with Carl. I know it's been hard for you being gone from him for so long. I think if you take me to the T station, I'll still be able to meet with the professor before he goes home for the day."

"If you're sure, honey."

Kennedy nodded. "I'm sure."

"What's the meeting about?"

She shut her eyes, trying to escape from the guilt and stress that pounded down on her. "Just about the lab I teach. Nothing all that interesting."

CHAPTER 36

"So you're the infamous Kennedy Stern." Dr. Faber leaned back in his chair and studied her over the top of his glasses. "Have we met before?"

"You were on the panel when I interviewed for the med school early acceptance program."

Faber nodded. "I see. Did I let you in?"

She nodded.

He cleared his throat. "Well, since you're here, may as well ask you to sit down."

"I'm really sorry I missed our appointment earlier," she began.

He shrugged. "No need to apologize to me. It's Dr. Adell who scheduled that meeting to begin with."

"Well, it was wrong for me to miss it. I feel terrible. We had something of an emergency with some friends ..."

"Your pastor?" he interrupted.

She stared.

"He's been on the news. I'm not so calloused that I don't care if someone's been attacked and left in a coma."

Kennedy didn't reply.

Faber stared at her. She couldn't tell if his expression was his version of a smile or a scowl. "So, tell me what I can do for you today."

Kennedy wasn't prepared for his question. She'd been expecting a lecture.

"I'd like to keep working as a TA," she stammered.

Faber leaned back in his chair. "Yes, Adell tells me you're quite gifted for an undergrad student."

Kennedy couldn't figure out if he was being condescending or not. Mustering up her sense of confidence, she continued, "I know my article got some people upset, but first of all, my opinion on things like politics or religion really has nothing to do with how well I can teach a lab class. Second of all, I think a lot of people are misinterpreting what I wrote in the first place. I never said that all women should stay at home and take care of the kids. I just said that we should have more respect for those who do."

Faber's expression didn't change. "So tell me, Miss Stern, what were your thoughts when you were admitted into the early acceptance program at Harvard?"

Kennedy didn't know what an application that she sent in nearly four years ago had to do with her article on women's rights and roles, but she didn't want to antagonize Dr. Faber, especially since he'd been on the committee that accepted her into the prestigious program. "I was very honored. I don't think words can express how excited I was."

"And is that because in the household and religious structure in which you were raised, women weren't expected to receive higher educational opportunities?"

Kennedy blinked. "No. It was because I worked really hard in high school so that I could one day become a doctor."

"And was it concerning to you or to your family that you might start out your time in college, fall in love, and get married? What if you have kids? Do you just plan to tell the admissions committee of Harvard Medical School that everything they invested in your education was for nothing because you're going to drop out and become a stay-at-home mom?"

Kennedy wondered if Dr. Faber, brilliant as he must be to head the science department at Harvard University, had even read her article. "I thought this discussion was about whether or not I could continue teaching in the lab."

"All right then." Faber interlaced his fingers and set them in front of him on his desk. "Let's talk about your lab. I received two phone calls today from parents very distraught that their children are being subjected to misogynistic biases."

Misogynistic biases? "Just what do you think I'm teaching these students?"

"I'm sure I don't know," Faber replied, "which is why it would have been convenient if you had kept our original appointment with Adell, who apparently is ready to stick her academic reputation on the line for someone who doesn't even have the decency to reschedule a meeting that her professor has worked quite hard to set up."

Kennedy was about to mention Woong's kidnapping, but Faber went on without pause.

"Furthermore, as a student who's been invited into the early admissions medical program at our school, you represent our science department specifically and Harvard University in general whether you feel up to the task or not. And frankly, your column defending dangerous and oppressive patriarchal ideology is simply not the image that we want associated with Harvard University, its science department, or its medical school."

"What are you saying exactly?" Kennedy asked and braced herself for Faber's answer.

"I'm saying that unless I see a printed retraction of your views in the Voice, I not only will have to terminate your privileges as a teaching assistant in the science department, I'll have to take a long and serious look at your provisional admittance to the medical school, an admittance I'd like to remind you that is contingent on your keeping up your grades and your conduct in a manner befitting a student at our university."

CHAPTER 37

Twenty minutes later Kennedy had returned to her dorm room and told her roommate everything about Woong's rescue and her meeting with the head of the science department.

"Dude," Willow exclaimed after Kennedy mentioned Dr. Faber's ultimatum. "So what are you going to do?"

"I still haven't decided yet. I'm going to call my dad this evening. It's too early now. Besides, it's been such a stressful two days anyway that I didn't want to make any rash decisions."

"I would have told that hoity-toity professor exactly where to take his threats, and I would have walked right out of there."

"I guess maybe if it was just getting fired as a TA. But this isn't just a four-hour-a-week job we're talking about anymore. This is my whole career."

Willow applied some of her eye shadow. "Dude," she repeated.

"What about you?" Kennedy asked. "Are you doing ok? Have you heard from Nick yet?"

"Yeah, I got a quick text. Said he was going out for a drive and not to worry. He does that every once in a while. Turns off his phone and just takes off. I think it helps him unwind. I know the situation with Carl has gotten him really upset. I shouldn't worry about him so much, but I can't help it."

"That's because you love him."

Willow focused on filing her nail. "I really do. It's funny. I've had more boyfriends than I'd ever want to try to count, so you'd think I might have already been jaded by love or whatnot. But I've never experienced anything like what I have with Nick before. I used to think about marriage, about how unnatural it was to choose one mate and stick with them for the rest of your life. I used to think it was the epitome of hubris to assume that you knew yourself well enough, let alone your partner, to be able to decide if you should commit to a lifetime together. But with Nick ..." Willow paused to study herself in the mirror.

"Anyway, I just hope you find the same thing one day. I know you and Dominic were taking things slow, and who knows what might have happened if you'd had more time together, but believe it or not, it's actually something I started praying about for you."

Kennedy couldn't help laughing. "You're praying that God will send me someone to marry?"

Willow looked hurt. "I'm being serious now. I sometimes feel bad because Nick and I have this really special thing going on. I know you're still getting over what happened with Dominic. But what I'd love more than anything is if God were to send somebody your way so we could share our special relationships together. Sandy told me something a few weeks ago, and I've been thinking about it a lot. I was telling her it's wicked hard to think of staying totally abstinent until Nick and I get married, and I joked and said something like we should just go elope one weekend and get it over with. But she told me not to rush these days. Said that as much as she loves Carl and as close as they've grown over the years, there was something really special about the time they were together right before he proposed and then before they got married. You think I'm a big dork, don't you?"

"No, of course I don't."

"Yes, you do. I can see it in your eyes. Well, you just remember. One day, you and I are going to be little old ladies, twice as old as Sandy, and we'll be sitting in rocking chairs knitting little booties for our great-grandbabies and reminiscing about the good old days, and you'll say, *remember when I was so sad because I missed my old boyfriend so much? And we had that talk about you and Nick and how no matter how close you grow to your spouse over the years, there's nothing quite like those months leading up to the wedding, hard as they may be and impatient as your horny little body might get? You remember that? Well, Willow, you were absolutely right. And Mr. Wonderful and I, we've had the most incredible marriage anyone could imagine, visiting no less than two hundred different countries on our medical mission trips and raising those ten delightful kids of ours and welcoming our ninety delightful grandbabies into the world, but there's nothing like falling in love for the very first time. You were absolutely right about that."*

Kennedy finally gave in to a chuckle.

"There's a smile," Willow exclaimed, and then her face grew serious. "If it's too soon for you to be thinking this way, just tell me. I'm not trying to make things harder on you."

"I know that."

"So we're ok?" Willow asked hopefully.

"Yeah, we're ok."

Willow grinned and jumped over to slide in next to Kennedy on her bed. "Good. Because I've been dying to ask about your breakfast this morning."

Kennedy couldn't remember what she had to eat. "What breakfast?"

Willow rolled her eyes, revealing glittery purple eyeshadow. "Your breakfast," she repeated with significance. "With Ginger?"

"You mean Ian?"

Willow shrugged. "Ginger, Ian, what's the difference when he's that hot?" She scooted closer. "So, how'd it go? Did you have a good time? What did you talk about? Did he interview you for a story? Will it be in the paper? You haven't told me anything."

Kennedy sank back against her pillow. "It was just breakfast."

"Sure it was." Willow pulled Kennedy's pillow out from behind her and swatted her playfully with it. "Come on. There's got to be more to it than that. Did you enjoy yourself? Did you run out of things to talk about? Did he pay? Did you go Dutch? Tell me something. This has been like the longest day of my entire life. The least you can do is get my mind off all my worries and spare at least one or two juicy details."

"No juicy details." Kennedy was glad the pillow was still covering half her face so Willow couldn't catch her trying to hide her grin.

"What do you mean no juicy details? You were out for almost two hours before I had to track you down. Don't tell me you spent that whole time on the interview and nothing else."

Kennedy grabbed the pillow when her roommate tried to lift it off her face. "No juicy details," she protested again, but her voice betrayed her by a laugh.

Willow smacked her once more. "I knew it. So come on. Tell me. What all did you talk about? Do you like him? Is he a Christian? Are you going to see him again?"

Kennedy stopped giggling when her cell rang. Willow reached over and picked it up from the desk. "It's Sandy calling." She handed the phone to Kennedy.

"Hello?" She tried to make her voice sound serious, worrying it might hurt Sandy's feelings to know she had found anything to laugh about on a day like this.

Sandy sounded flushed. "Kennedy?" That one single word made Kennedy's heart swell with hope.

"Yeah?" Her own tone matched Sandy's excited one. Even Willow must have picked up on the change because she leaned forward, trying to get her ear as close to Kennedy's phone as possible.

"Glorious news, dear. Carl still hasn't woken up, but the brain swelling went down so dramatically after the prayer meeting that they decided to test him one more time without the ventilator. He's doing just fine. If we keep seeing this kind of steady progress, they'll take him off the machine this evening."

CHAPTER 38

KENNEDY HAD NEVER SEEN Willow drive as fast as she did that night on the way to Providence Hospital. She thought about an old adage her mom used to say: *Trials and blessings always come in threes.* With Carl on the ventilator, Woong kidnapped, and Kennedy about to lose her job as a TA, the first half of the proverb had certainly appeared true. Kennedy was grateful to receive some good news for a change.

They got stuck in rush hour traffic and got to Carl's room in the ICU right after they took out his breathing tube. Technically, visiting rights were reserved for immediate family members only, but Sandy talked the sympathetic nurse into letting Kennedy and Willow come in if they promised not to stay long.

Woong was in a corner with one of his dad's Bible joke books, occasionally breaking out into a smile and looking no worse off after being kidnapped and rescued. Sandy was flushed. Nearly half her hair had fallen out of her braid, but there was a radiance that shined around her and filled the room with so much joy Kennedy couldn't have felt sad even if she wanted to.

"The Lord is so good. The Lord is so good," Sandy repeated over and over as she related to the girls what had happened that afternoon.

When they first got back to Providence after saving Woong, Carl's condition was basically unchanged. "And I wasn't too disappointed," Sandy remarked. "If he had gotten a lot better or a lot worse while I wasn't here to look after him, I would have felt terribly guilty."

Drisklay had questions for Woong, so he and Sandy met with the detective in the ICU conference room. Dawn waited in the lobby for the detective to take her to the police department so she could speak with her husband.

Sandy clucked her tongue. "I know the poor woman feels awful about what happened. I just pray that Jesus shows her his truth so she doesn't keep beating herself up for her husband's crimes."

After Drisklay left, Sandy and Woong went back to Carl's bedside. "It was Woong who noticed the change first. Something different about Carl's face. He wasn't so pale, and he stopped looking like he was in a coma and more like he was just in a deep sleep. I didn't want to call the nurse in right away. I didn't want to find out it was just wishful thinking or something like that. But when she came in to check his vitals, she noticed it, too, and said his numbers were the best they'd been all day. The doctor asked me if I wanted to turn off the machine just for a short time. Nothing dangerous at all. It would just tell them if Carl could breathe on his own or not. Well, I felt so encouraged by how much stronger he looked, so I said, 'Ok, let's do it.'

"I was so scared I was shaking because the whole time I'd been talking with the doctors there was this little voice in the back my head that told me I was making it all up. There weren't any improvements, and there wouldn't be any improvements. But then they turned the machine off, and we all waited, and Carl just kept on breathing peacefully like he was taking one of his Sunday afternoon naps. Well, he was still working a little harder than he should have to keep his numbers up, so the doctor wanted to keep the machine running as backup, but then they tried it again this evening, and praise the Lord, he's holding perfectly steady."

"That's great news." Willow gave Sandy a hug and then let out a surprised, "Oh," as if she'd been startled. Kennedy turned to see Nick in the doorway with his head hung low, his dreads trailing behind him like the tail of a lost little puppy.

CHAPTER 39

"NICK!" WILLOW RAN TOWARD him but stopped halfway to the door. "What is it? What's wrong?"

Nick's face was pale. He appeared almost clammy. Willow took him by the arm and sat him down on the doctor's swivel chair.

"You know," she began, "I should be wicked mad at you for deserting me like you did today, except you look like you got hit by a truck. What happened?" Her voice was full of tenderness.

Nick shook his head. His dreadlocks, usually so animated, hung limp past his shoulders. "I'm a terrible, horrible person."

Willow stood behind him, rubbing his back. "Don't talk like that. You had a bad day, that's all. So tell me what the matter is. I'm done lecturing you. Now I just want to help you feel better."

"There are some things I've got to get off my chest first." Nick turned to Sandy and took both her hands in his. "Sandy, I am so sorry for taking advantage of you and Carl's friendship for so long. We'd gotten so close, close as family, and like family, I began to grow resentful." He sniffed. "I should have never treated your husband the way I did. All those fights, the accusations. I think what got me so worked up — aside from seeing Carl on the ventilator which is bad enough — was realizing that I'm no better than whatever thug did this to him. I've got just as many anger issues, just as much hatred in my heart. So I came here to apologize."

He let go of Sandy's hands. Clutching the side of the bed, he lowered himself to his knees and rested his forehead near Carl's pillow.

"Pastor Carl," he began in a shaky voice. "Friend. Brother. You've been more of a father to me than anyone else in the past decade. And like the prodigal son, I've made a fool of myself. Let our disagreements get in the way of our friendship. I hate to confess it, but I have to. Over the last several months in particular, I've allowed so much hardness and resentment to creep into my heart. Tarnish my opinion of you. I haven't shown you the respect you deserve as my pastor, my employer, and my mentor.

"We've always had our disagreements, but things got really bad when you began planning that Truth Warriors conference. And there are still a lot of things about it that I don't agree with, but that certainly doesn't mean that you're the misogynistic monster the media has made you out to be. You love and honor your wife in a way that is truly selfless. I can only hope to be half the man you are one day. You speak out openly against how degrading and demeaning pornography is to women, and I know God has used you and that little blue book of yours to lead dozens of men out of their addictions. The more I wanted to side with the media against you, the more I realized that even though we might have different views on exactly how to love our brothers and sisters in Christ, nobody with two eyes in their head could accuse you of being anything but the epitome of sacrificial, godly love. The more I thought about it, the more I realized how far I have to go in my own walk with Christ before I can learn to love and serve as selflessly as you do.

"When I found you knocked out in your office, I was so scared. Scared of losing you. Scared that I would never be able to tell you how sorry I am that I've allowed this wall of resentment to grow up between us. You more than anyone else have taught me that it's possible for two believers to share their deep fellowship even when they disagree. Forgive me, brother. Forgive me for forgetting that when you found me and took me in, I was so broken and beat up by the world, floundering in my faith and about to give up all hope in the Lord. But you picked me up. Dragged me up is more like it, out of that mud and showed me the solid rock I could stand on. If it hadn't been for you, I probably would have given up on God years ago. But you didn't let that happen. And I never thanked you for that, and now I'm so scared that you won't ever wake up. That I'll never get the chance to tell you how much I love you."

By the time Nick was finished talking, Carl and Woong were the only two in the room with dry eyes. Kennedy, sensing how inappropriate it was for her to be here witnessing a scene so intimate, focused on Woong, who smiled to himself as he turned the pages in his father's joke book.

"That was beautiful," Sandy breathed and tried to help Nick back up on his feet.

"Not so fast," he said. Still on his knees, he reached out to Willow and made her stand in front of him.

"What are you doing?" she whispered.

"Oh, just about the most terrifying thing I've ever done in my life, that's all." He let out a nervous chuckle. "Willow Winters, for years I've been asking God to send me a partner. Someone who shares my love for the Lord, my desire to see justice reign on the earth, my passion for ministry. On the day I met you, I knew that you were the one that God had planned for me to meet, fall passionately in love with, and spend the rest of my life with."

Willow tried to pull him off the ground, but Nick took hold of both her hands again and made her face him. "At the risk of sounding ridiculously mushy, I have never met anyone who's made me feel so excited about life. So eager to serve the Lord. So expectant about the future God has planned for us. Last summer, I asked you to pray and seek God's heart to discern if this romance was truly destined to blossom into something permanent. I've been praying, too, and I know beyond any doubt that if you stand here in agreement with me, nothing would bring me more joy than to spend the rest my life worshiping and serving God side by side with you as my partner, my soulmate, and my spouse."

He searched several of his pants pockets before he pulled out a small box. "I know it was a bad day to leave you alone, and I'm sorry for that, but I needed to think and make sure that now was the right time. I also needed to look for this." He opened the box and stared up at Willow with joyful, shining eyes. "Willow Winters, will you marry me?"

"Yes, you silly thing, now get off the floor before you hurt your knees." Willow lifted him to his feet once he slipped on the ring. "This is beautiful. Where did you find it?"

"I knew how you felt about blood diamonds, so I went to the free trade store to see what kind of jewelry they had there. This particular ring was made by girls and women living in a safe house in Vietnam who have been rescued from a life of sex slavery. I chose it as a symbol of the way I believe God will use our union and our ministry together to stand up for the rights of the oppressed and to make the world a more just, beautiful, glorious place."

Willow showed off the beaded ring to Kennedy and then to Sandy who sat in a corner dabbing her eyes with a tissue.

"I am so happy for you two," she exclaimed.

"Yes, of course, we're all happy." Carl's voice from the hospital bed made everyone turn.

Sandy gasped and rushed to her husband's side.

He smiled faintly and tried to raise himself from his pillow. "Now, Nick, don't you think it's about time to kiss your fiancée?"

CHAPTER 40

KENNEDY COULDN'T REMEMBER A twenty-four-hour period filled with so much of both heartache and joy. By the time she and Willow returned back to campus, she was exhausted.

"What a day," Willow sighed.

Kennedy's thoughts exactly.

They were quiet on the walk to their dorm. They'd stayed far past the typical ICU visiting hours, but Carl had shown so much improvement once he woke up that the nurse didn't have the heart to send anyone away.

Kennedy still couldn't believe her roommate was engaged. She figured Nick would end up proposing one day, but she'd been sure they'd wait until Willow was at least a senior to make things official. Kennedy didn't have the heart to ask Willow how soon they'd plan the wedding. Would she need to find herself a new roommate before graduation?

Carl had surprised them all when he woke up from his coma in the middle of Nick's proposal. It took several minutes before Nick mustered the courage to ask if he'd been awake during his apology and confession as well. Carl said he slept right through it but asked Nick to give a repeat (albeit abridged) performance.

Woong had been so excited when his dad woke up. He wanted to tell Carl all about getting kidnapped and rescued, but his mom shushed him and told him she'd tell him about it a little later once he had a chance to recover some of his strength. So instead,

Woong asked if Carl heard any of the jokes from the book he'd been reading to him.

"Jokes?" Carl frowned. "Well, let me think. I don't remember hearing any jokes, but I've got a new one for you. Do you know why there are no potholes on the way to heaven?"

After asking what a pothole was, Woong said he was stumped.

His dad smiled. "Because Jesus paved it all."

Any concerns about Carl's long-term recovery were put to rest in that one evening. The doctors would still monitor him in the hospital, but it was clear to everyone that they bore witness to some sort of miracle, whether medical or divine or both.

Kennedy's heart was full in spite of how exhausted she felt. It was past nine when they walked up to their dorm. The graffiti on the wall had already been painted over.

"Well, look who that is."

Kennedy turned at the familiar voice. Ian was sitting on a bench beneath a security light, an open book on his lap. "I was wondering if I'd catch you tonight."

Willow made a dramatic show of digging through her purse. "Oh, I completely forgot, I need to call Nick and talk to him about that thing we were supposed to talk about tonight when I called. Sorry to be rude and run off, but I don't want to keep him waiting." She scurried into the dorm, leaving Kennedy outside with Ian.

He smiled. "Hey."

"Hey."

"Long day?"

"You could say that."

Ian stood up and stretched. "Care to take a walk and tell me about it?"

Kennedy thought about her nine o'clock class the next morning. About the decision she'd have to make to write that redaction and keep her guaranteed admission to medical school or not. About all the talking and giggling and wedding planning Willow would be sure to want her to join in over the next months.

She found it easy to return Ian's smile. "Sure."

Forty-five minutes later, seated in front of his empty plate at L'Aroma Bakery, Ian let out a sigh. "So have you decided what you're going to do about the medical school thing?"

"I don't know. I want to talk it over with my dad before I make any big decisions." Why did she say that? Was she twelve years old all over again?

There was something in Ian's eyes, but she couldn't tell what it was. Amusement? Respect? "Well, if you want to make a big fuss about it, let me know. I've got a few friends very interested in cases of free speech on college campuses."

"Thanks. I've already gotten a few emails from people like that."

"Just be careful who you talk to. You're welcome to run the names by me, and I can tell you who's legit and who's just looking for a pretty face for their clickbait articles."

Kennedy was glad the lights at L'Aroma were dim so he couldn't see her blush. Maybe it was just because of Willow's good news and Carl's miraculous recovery, but she didn't think she'd enjoyed herself so much in one evening before.

Ian closed the little book he'd used to jot down a few notes while they talked about Kennedy's article in the Voice and about the drama the Lindgrens had lived through that day. He was such a good listener Kennedy couldn't even tell what his own opinions were on certain matters, but he knew how to ask the right kinds of questions that helped her process the thoughts and half-conceived ideas that had been swirling around in her brain.

Ian looked at the time. "Well, it's getting late. You probably have class tomorrow, don't you?"

"First thing in the morning," Kennedy answered.

"Can I walk you back to campus?"

"Sure." She heard Willow's voice in the back of her head. *First dates are so romantic.* She couldn't turn the recording off, not that she was sure she wanted to.

She gave Ian a smile and let him hold the door open for her as they walked out of L'Aroma Bakery into the clear night. Stars twinkled overhead, stars that whispered to Kennedy promises of hope and joys to come.

Secluded

Alana Terry

CHAPTER 1

11:48 PM, THE DAY before the Winter Solstice

"I can't believe Nick and I are actually getting married!" Willow squealed.

Kennedy listened to her roommate through a thick fog of jet lag-induced exhaustion. Driving five hours in the dark wasn't how she'd planned to spend her first night of Christmas vacation in Alaska. She took a sip of what had once been hot cocoa and was now a grainier version of chocolate milk.

"I'm really excited for you." Kennedy hoped her voice held the right amount of enthusiasm. If she thought Willow and Nick's engagement came suddenly, it was nothing compared to how fast they'd set the date.

The day after tomorrow, just a few days before Christmas, Willow and Nick would exchange their vows in the little country church near Willow's childhood home in Copper Lake, a small homestead community about forty-five minutes beyond Glennallen and the edge of the Glenn Highway.

Willow drummed her mittens on the steering wheel to keep time with her classic rock music. "I'm so glad you're here. I couldn't ask for a better maid of honor."

Kennedy had never been in a wedding before and could only guess what she was expected to do. Her roommate assured her the ceremony would be a casual event and she had nothing to worry about, but Willow obviously didn't understand the way Kennedy's brain worked.

There was always something to worry about.

Like the way her friend Ian had asked her out on several break-fast dates before his business trip to Asia and hadn't called or emailed or texted her since.

Or like the way she'd been fired from her TA job last semester because she refused to take back what she'd written for a column in the school paper. The details regarding how she'd been treated after publishing her piece in the Harvard Forum had made little waves in pro First Amendment blogs and news outlets, but the publicity was finally starting to die down, thank God.

"Oh!" Willow exclaimed. "I almost forgot. You were going to answer some of those questions I had about Revelations, remember?"

Kennedy remembered, but she was exhausted after three different flights and two drawn-out layovers, not to mention all the strange events that had happened since she landed in Alaska. There was no way she could muster up the energy it'd take to field all of Willow's questions about the end times. She should be asleep in a nice Anchorage hotel right now like she'd originally planned, not making the five-hour drive to Copper Lake this late at night.

Willow turned her music down. "All right. First question is about the rapture. I basically know what it means, at least I think I do. It's when Jesus comes back and takes all the believers up to heaven, right?"

Kennedy was pining away for a soft pillow and layer upon layer of blankets. Even with the heat running in Willow's car, she hadn't been able to shake her chill since arriving in Alaska. The outside temperature had dropped below negative twenty once they approached the mountain pass on the Glenn Highway. Kennedy had decided that all the handmade quilts Willow's family owned still wouldn't be enough to warm her entirely.

Or help her forget her fears from that night.

"... why some people argue that the rapture's got to happen first but others say it won't come until later, and when I went to study it for myself, the word *rapture* wasn't even in the New Testament, so that's my first question."

Kennedy tried to figure out what she'd missed. The rapture? She didn't know how to respond. She'd read through Revelation once or maybe twice before, but she always stepped into it assuming it would be too hard to grasp, a prediction that turned into a self-fulfilling prophecy. She liked the last couple chapters that talked about having no more death or crying or pain in heaven, and she figured that the letters to the churches at the beginning of the book had some good advice for believers today, but all the stuff in the middle was so wrapped up in convoluted symbolism that she never bothered trying to make sense out of it.

If experts who'd been studying theology for hundreds of years couldn't agree, how could Kennedy presume to understand? Jesus would come back, and all believers would end up in heaven. The rest of the details were best left for pastors and seminary professors to discuss and debate.

Still, she owed Willow some sort of response, but unfortunately her brain had already shut down for the night. Her roommate had been growing so fast in her faith, Kennedy was scrambling to catch up.

"And then there's the tribulation," Willow went on. Maybe if she talked long enough, she would eventually land on a question Kennedy felt qualified to answer. "I read one commentator who said the tribulation's just this sort of symbolic idea that Christians are going to suffer before Jesus returns, but then Pastor Carl was talking in his sermon about how it's this literal seven-year period, and either way you look at it is pretty depressing."

Kennedy muttered some sort of response about how that was a good point and wondered what else she could contribute to the conversation.

Willow moved on to the millennium, but Kennedy was only half listening. After everything she'd experienced in Anchorage that night, it was understandable for her to feel more than a little edgy. The sun had already set by the time her plane touched down that afternoon, and now it was even darker. No street lamps, no light pollution because they were on that stretch of the Glenn Highway where you could travel fifty or sixty miles between towns.

She shouldn't be worried about the dark. That was just her anxiety kicking in. She'd picked the second shortest day of the year to land in Alaska, and the entire state felt on the verge of panic. Of course, the increasingly vocal number of wackos claiming that the winter solstice would mark the beginning of some sort of

Armageddon-like end-of-days scenario did nothing to settle her nerves, not to mention the recent events that seemed to verify their predictions.

She wouldn't think about that. If she knew anything about what the Bible said, it was that nobody could guess the time or the day of Christ's return. Everyone claiming something contrary was making stuff up, even the ones who seemed to forecast with uncanny accuracy the meteorological events that had been popping up worldwide.

An F-4 tornado in the Midwest in December. An unseasonably late typhoon hitting the Philippines that same week, and that was on top of everything going on in Alaska.

Her dad had warned her, hadn't he? Said that even if the geological predictions weren't accurate, the civil unrest that could ensue from such wild claims would make the state volatile. Dangerous.

He hadn't told her not to go. She was too old to be ordered around like that, and he knew how much it meant to her to be the maid of honor at her roommate's wedding. But he'd asked her several times to reconsider.

When she came here with Willow in the past, Alaska felt so quiet, so safe. Should she have listened to her dad? Well, it was too late now. All the planes were grounded, so it's not like she could change her mind even if she wanted to.

At least Copper Lake was far enough removed from the chaos. Hopefully.

No, she shouldn't think like that. She had to be more positive.

"So I'm leaning towards what Sproul says when it comes to the millennium, but I'm still planning to read up a little more on it. What do you think?"

Kennedy frantically tried to replay the last few lines of conversation.

"You weren't listening were you?" Willow accused.

"I was listening," Kennedy protested. "I heard what you were saying, I just didn't ..." She tried to find the right words.

"Didn't pay attention?" Willow let out a good-natured chuckle.

Kennedy stared at her lap. "Sorry."

"It's ok. It's been a wicked long day for you, hasn't it?"

"That's one way of putting it." Kennedy had been looking forward to spending Christmas break in Alaska, not just because she was excited to share in all the wedding plans but because Copper Lake was so peaceful. Maybe spending a week or two with the Winters each year was the cure for her anxiety that she'd been hunting for. But now, after everything that had happened in one short evening ...

"Well, we can discuss Revelations later, all right?" Willow turned off her classic rock music. "Let's talk about something else. Like what did you think of the movie? At least the parts we got to see."

Kennedy didn't want to admit she'd been too tired to pay attention when they were at the theater earlier. The end-times flick Willow had dragged her to was horribly canned. "It was all right."

Willow turned the music off. "Do you think it really could happen like that, with them rounding up the Christians and taking away all the Bibles?"

At least this was a question Kennedy felt somewhat qualified to answer after the ten years she spent with her parents in China. "It's like that already in some parts of the world. I told you the story about that Bible smuggler from North Korea, right?"

"Yeah. So I guess we just need to be prepared to die for our faith one day?"

The question surprised Kennedy. "I suppose so. At least theoretically."

"And what about people like that mother in the movie, the one who pretended to go along with them and got that chip in her hand and said she didn't believe in Jesus? It wasn't like she meant it. She just told them that so they wouldn't take her baby away from her. God wouldn't send her to hell over something like that, right?"

Now they had officially crossed into territory in which Kennedy was too tired and too inexperienced to offer any kind of reasonable answer. "I really don't think it's a question of heaven or hell. It's just doing what God thinks you should do and knowing that despite everything he's watching you and he'll be with you."

Apparently, Willow wasn't satisfied with Kennedy's rambling response. "Ok, let me put it another way. Let's say that she stood up for her beliefs, that she didn't let them put in that chip and she didn't deny Christ, so then she gets thrown in jail and her daughter gets handed over to the atheist family. What then? Does God promise that at some point he'll make sure the little girl will grow up and learn the truth? Because otherwise, if you're asking a mother to either lie about her own faith or surrender her kid to hell ..."

Kennedy was glad Willow's voice trailed off. Glad there wasn't an actual question she was expected to answer. As a result of her parents' work with underground Christians, Kennedy had heard harrowing stories of the suffering believers endured, but she did her best to compartmentalize them as things that happened on the other side of the world to people who looked and spoke and lived entirely differently than she did.

"Anyway," Willow added, "I thought the policeman was wicked hot. And I've seen him in something else, but I can't remember what. Maybe that hospital drama on HBO? Was he on there?"

Kennedy was relieved at the conversational turn. While Willow rambled on about different TV shows, Kennedy could stare out the window at the blinding darkness without having to think.

"... she's the one in that super cute detective series. You know which one I mean?"

Kennedy snapped her head around. "Huh?"

Willow sighed. "How about you pick something to talk about? I'm out of ideas."

Kennedy's hands grew sweaty even though her core was chilled. What should she say? That after everything that had happened since she arrived in Alaska, it was taking every bit of her mental energy to keep from panicking? That she was starting to wonder if she should have listened to her dad even if it meant missing out on Willow's big day. That knowing all the flights in and out of Anchorage were grounded made her feel claustrophobic in spite of how large this state was, and driving in the pitch dark in the snow in sub-zero temperatures was one of the creepiest things she'd done all year.

No, she couldn't focus on her fear. Even if she was stuck here in Alaska, even if the dire predictions made by these end-of-the-worlders with their picket signs came true, it's not like she could turn around now, hop on a plane, and fly back East. There was nothing to do but make the best of her situation and focus on positive things.

Like Willow getting ready to marry the love of her life.

"How are things going back home?" she asked. "What do your parents think of Nick?"

"Oh, they love him to pieces." Willow ran her fingers through her hair, which she'd reverted back to its natural color for the wedding. Up until now Kennedy thought it was those outrageous dye jobs that made Willow stand out in a crowd, but now she realized her roommate would look stunning no matter what she did with her hair. "You should have heard Nick and my dad last night. They were talking about everything that's been happening, then got onto global warming and carbon footprints and climate change. I swear if I weren't going to marry him, my dad would do it for me."

"Do they have any problems with him being a Christian?"

Willow shook her feathery head of hair. "Not at all. My mom thinks those goofy shirts of his are adorable, and he and my parents are always having really deep discussions about faith and politics — you know, all those things that Nick hates talking about," she added with a sarcastic grin.

Kennedy hoped her chuckle sounded convincing. "Well, I'm glad he's fitting in so well."

"Me too. I think my only real complaint is that my parents don't see the difference between me being a Christian and me falling in love with Nick. The way they look at it, they assume I converted because of him."

"But you got saved before you and Nick met."

Willow shrugged. "Yeah, I know, but in their minds it's all one big life event. But it's not that bad. They're really happy for me. They know I've been taking my faith seriously, and I think it's been good for them to meet Nick, who's so different from the typical Christian you see in sitcoms or read about in the news, you know?" She laughed. "I'm just glad that they're so comfortable with him. I swear they act like he's their long-lost son or something."

"What about Nick's family?" Kennedy asked. "Are many of them coming up for the wedding? Did anybody get stuck before they could fly in?"

"No, it's so cold up here we didn't want to make everyone fly out. We'll head to Washington right after Christmas, assuming the planes are up and running by then."

Kennedy calmed the quivering in her core. Tried to forget everything that had happened to spook her once she'd arrived in Alaska. Did her best to convince herself that Copper Lake was far enough from Anchorage that she'd be perfectly fine. By the time she was ready to fly back East to spend Christmas with her pastor's family, everything would be back to normal again.

She hoped.

"What about you?" Willow asked.

"Me what?"

"I don't know. Tell me about your finals or about your premed stuff or about Mr. Redhead who's taken you out to breakfast like five times this semester. I've been doing nothing but listen to Nick and my dad talk politics for the past week. I need some kind of distraction."

Kennedy tried to think of something interesting to tell her roommate that she didn't already know. She had spent most of the past semester wondering about her relationship with Ian and stressing out about med school. Her provisional acceptance to Harvard's program had been revoked after she wrote a newspaper article that turned out to be far more controversial than she'd expected. It had taken both her dad and her reporter friend Ian several different phone calls to several different news outlets to convince the university to change their minds. Thanks to their concerted effort, she had a guaranteed spot in Harvard Med School once she graduated, but did she want to go anymore? Why should she come crawling back to the administration that slammed their doors in her face for doing nothing but stating her opinion?

The question had reverberated in the back of her head all semester. Unfortunately, it was a decision she couldn't postpone indefinitely. By summer at the latest, she'd have to decide. It wasn't like her to be without a solid, definitive course of action. As much as she trusted God's guidance, she needed a plan, a plan that preferably laid out the next five to ten years in a neat, tidy package.

As for Ian ...

"You can start that conversation any time, you know."

Kennedy snapped back to the present. "What were we talking about?"

"That's what you were supposed to decide, remember?"

"Oh, yeah. Umm ..." Kennedy stared at the snowflakes illuminated in Willow's headlights. "Let's see ... Is everything ready for the big day?"

Willow laughed. "I'm going to be so sick of planning weddings when this is all over. I can guarantee you that. Sandy called me a few nights ago to see how things were coming along. It was really sweet of her. I joked and told her if I'd known how stressful it was to plan even a simple wedding like ours, Nick and I would have eloped months ago. But she reminded me how special it is to be engaged, and something about that gave me more perspective, I guess. I mean, every single day that we have to keep ourselves pure is a new adventure in self-control, but here we are, and in two days we'll be husband and wife, so it's not like waiting was the end of the world.

"Oh, speaking of the end of the world, that was another question I wanted to ask you. The mark of the beast. Is the number 666 some really crazy dangerous thing like some people say? I mean, I saw it mentioned there in Revelations and they talked about it a lot in that movie, but I wasn't sure if it was the number itself that was so evil or if it's more symbolic or whatnot."

Kennedy wished she could transport herself through time and space and end up at the Winters' homestead in Copper Lake, hopefully beneath ten or twelve quilts. "I don't know."

Willow glanced over at her, clearly expecting more.

"I don't know," she repeated. "I seriously have no idea."

Willow frowned and finally shrugged. "Fair enough." She sighed. "I kind of want to call Nick and see how he's doing, but we won't have cell coverage for quite a while." She pointed at the time. "Hey, look. We made it to midnight." She cracked a huge grin. "Happy solstice."

Kennedy wasn't sure if the greeting was an Alaskan tradition or something her roommate came up with. "You too," she replied tentatively.

Willow let out a carefree laugh. "Looks like the end-of-the-worlders were wrong again. I'm still here. Are you?"

"Yeah." Kennedy tried to sound amused, but she was still thinking about how worried her dad had been about her traveling to Alaska in the first place.

Willow started to hum under her breath, and Kennedy chuckled when she recognized the tune.

"Don't tease me," Willow protested. "Can't I be excited without you making fun of me?"

Kennedy giggled. It felt nice to stop focusing on Alaskan crises and apocalyptic predictions and bizarre meteorological phenomena. Willow was getting married in two days, and Kennedy was going to toss aside her worries long enough to give her roommate the celebration she deserved.

Willow increased her volume, and Kennedy started singing with her.

Because we're going to the chapel ...

Before long, they were both belting as loudly as they could, making up in enthusiasm what they lacked in musical ability.

And we're gonna get married.

Their singing was terrible, but the stress of the day coupled with her exhaustion made it seem that much funnier. Kennedy couldn't hold in her laugh.

That's when she heard Willow scream.

Saw the massive animal directly in front of them.

Felt the seatbelt yank against her chest as the car plowed into a moose.

CHAPTER 2

3:48 PM, SEVEN HOURS earlier

For Alaska's biggest city, Anchorage looked tiny from this high up. Kennedy leaned toward the window of the plane. A full day of traveling, and she was ready to be on land.

Her junior year of college was whizzing by. Wasn't it only a few months ago she'd flown into Boston for the first time, a scared little eighteen-year-old girl who could have never been prepared for all the excitement, adventure, heartache and growth she was about to experience at Harvard?

Her course load was easier now than it had ever been, especially after losing her job as a teaching assistant. She devoted her extra free time to volunteering for the afterschool club for students at Medford Academy, trying to get more involved at St. Margaret's Church, and daydreaming with Willow about her wedding.

She couldn't believe how fast the big day was approaching. She thought about the phone call she'd had with her dad this morning while she waited for her first flight to take off from Logan Airport.

"You still think it's going to be safe over there, Kensie girl?" he asked.

Kennedy was certain that even from China he could see her roll her eyes. "It's going to be fine. They've been talking about this volcano for weeks now. It's not that big of a deal. And it's nowhere near Copper Lake."

"No," he replied, "but it's near Anchorage. When that mountain blows, the ash will cover the city in an hour, two at most."

"It's just a little dust, Dad." What did he think? That a volcano a hundred miles away would rain lava down on them?

"It's dust that's going to clog up car engines, ground planes, and potentially cause a major panic. Anchorage isn't Yanji or Boston, but it's still a big city, Kensie girl. And worst case scenario, if something does happen there, even if you're with the Winters already, that means no food trucks, no supplies being brought into the rural areas."

"I can't miss Willow's wedding."

He sighed. "Well, I won't tell you what to do, but if you go, you've got to be extra careful. Like I said, if that volcano blows, you need to get out of Anchorage right away. Promise me that much, at least."

"Yeah, I promise."

"Good. So your plane lands around four, and then you're driving with Willow to her home?"

Now it was Kennedy's turn to let out a massive sigh. Did her dad expect her to recite every single calorie she planned on eating in Alaska too? "We're spending the night in Anchorage. It's already going to be dark by the time I land, and Willow has some shopping to do in town anyway."

"I don't like that plan," her dad announced, as if that simple statement should be enough to change her mind.

"I already told you, if the volcano erupts, we'll get on the road before the ash falls."

"What if you're asleep?" he demanded.

Then I'm sure you'll find a way to call or text or wake me up, she thought to herself but instead just answered, "We'll be fine."

"It's not only the volcano I'm worried about, you know. Those winter solstice guys, they're all convinced that the end of the world's going to start tomorrow."

"They're just a bunch of weirdos," Kennedy protested. Her dad might be paranoid, but he certainly wasn't so removed from reality that he gave credence to their ideas, did he?

"I know that, and you know that, but what about all the people they've got so freaked out? What's going to happen when that volcano erupts and these internet junkies use it to fuel all the fear and chaos they've been creating? I just don't want to see you in harm's way."

"Yeah, ok." What else was there she could say?
"Yeah ok what?" he asked.
"I'll be careful."
"That's all I can ask," he replied with an air of defeat.

CHAPTER 3

PAST MIDNIGHT, WINTER SOLSTICE

"You all right in there? Hey, you all right?"

Cold. Kennedy had never been so cold in her life.

"You ok?" There was a pounding on the car window, a flashlight beam blinding her eyes.

She reached her hand to the side and croaked weakly, "Willow?"

"I'm here."

A small breath of warmth when her fingertips brushed her roommate's shoulder.

"We're ok?" Kennedy asked.

"Yeah, we're ok. We hit a moose."

"I know. I saw it."

"Me, too. Just too late."

More tapping on the window. "Can you hear me? Do you need help?"

"Someone's here," Kennedy announced. Feeling was returning to her limbs. Limbs that ached as if frost had seeped into each individual nerve bundle. How long had she and Willow been lying here? She tried her door and did her best to rouse up her energy. There was a fierce pain in her neck and shoulder, but she didn't think anything was broken. Her leg was pinned beneath the crumpled dashboard, but it didn't hurt. Just felt cold.

Terribly cold.

"Unlock the door!" The shout was muffled. He had to repeat himself several times before Kennedy fully understood.

She undid the locks, and the man opened the driver's side. The cold burst in through the open door and settled in her bone marrow.

"You hurt?" He shined his flashlight into the car, studying both girls' faces, then checked the backseat. "Just the two of you? Are you all right?"

"My leg's stuck," Kennedy told him.

"What about you?" He turned to Willow.

"Yeah. I'm ok. Just a little ..." She shook her head slightly. "Dude."

"You black out?" he asked. "How long you been here?"

Willow looked at Kennedy, who had no answer to give.

"It's ok," the man said. "Listen, there's no reception here, but I live about six miles out. I can give you a ride to my place and we can get you warmed up. Don't want to take the time to call for help and wait for the ambulance to come if we don't got to. It's minus twenty-eight last I checked. Nothing broken that you can tell?"

Willow had already adjusted herself loose while he was talking. Kennedy tried to do the same, but her boot was still pinned.

"Here." The man handed her the flashlight, reached across Willow, and tried to set her free. After a minute of struggling, Kennedy finally had to slip her foot out of its boot and edge her leg loose that way. "You'll be cold, but at least my truck's heated. It's the best we can do. Want me to carry you, or do you think you can hop?"

Kennedy tried to wiggle her toes. How long did she have before she had to worry about frostbite? She didn't even know how much time had passed since the crash. Two minutes? Twenty?

When she was outside the car, she could see the damage. The entire hood was collapsed in on itself.

"I think you're far enough to the side of the road that we don't have to worry, but I've got a few flares I'll set out just in case. I'm Roger, by the way."

With Willow supporting her on one side, Kennedy hopped toward his truck. She turned around to get one last glimpse at the damage, but Willow grabbed her more tightly. "Don't look back there. It's not pretty."

Kennedy, still somewhat dazed, soon realized that Willow had been talking about the moose and not the car.

"Told you not to look," Willow said.

Kennedy shivered.

Roger's truck was just a small two-seater, so the two girls squished together, trying to conserve heat. "Here, bend your leg so I can sit on your foot." Willow's suggestion sounded odd, but soon Kennedy could feel the painful throbbing of her pulse in her toes. At least her blood was flowing again.

Willow wrapped both arms around Kennedy. "You ok? You're shaking."

Kennedy nodded, but her teeth were chattering so hard it was difficult to speak.

"All right." Roger hopped into the driver's side with an author-itative air. "My cabin's up this way. Hold on tight. It's a bumpy road."

Calling the path through the woods a road was quite an embell-ishment, as Kennedy was reminded each time they bounced over whatever boulders or tree roots or potholes lay underneath the snow. She was grateful for Willow's warmth next to her, thankful that the only pain she felt was in her joints, her neck, and her throbbing foot. Relief coursed through her, but she still couldn't stop shivering.

"It's all right," Willow whispered in her ear. "We'll be there soon."

"Yup," Roger confirmed. "Cabin's just up this way."

Declaring Roger's shelter a cabin, at least in Kennedy's opinion, was even more euphemistic. Willow, who apparently had seen plenty of hand-built lodgings that were hardly bigger than a bath-room stall, seemed quite at home.

"Sorry, ladies. I'm off the grid here," Roger explained as he shined the flashlight into the dark room. "Give me a few minutes to get the generator running."

"Right on." Willow nodded as if there was nothing out of the ordinary about a bearded man who lived miles off the highway without electricity or running water or even an indoor bathroom.

While Roger stepped out, Willow seated Kennedy on a wide stump in the middle of the room and knelt in front of her. She rubbed her socked foot until the friction made it burn and asked, "You doing all right?"

Kennedy nodded, convinced that normal people didn't live out here in the middle of the wilderness with nothing but a few stacked logs and a wood stove protecting them from the negative thirty- or forty-degree temperatures that were common to Alaskan winters.

"We're going to be all right," Willow told her. "The most important thing is to get you warmed up."

No, the most important thing was to call someone they knew and tell them where they were. She looked around the small room. "Think he's got a phone?"

"There's no reception out here." Willow was still rubbing her foot vigorously.

"I know, but we need to let someone know where we are. We can't spend the night here without cell coverage or electricity or anything."

If the thought that they were trapped in a cabin with a complete stranger bothered Willow, she didn't show it. "He's got a generator."

Willow could have said he had a thermonuclear reactor for all the difference it made. What did Kennedy know about generators? What did she know about surviving with nothing but a wood stove in the middle of the Arctic? She glanced at a pile of blankets on the floor. That couldn't be his bed, could it? He'd freeze right to the ground. There was a shelf in the corner with some canned goods, mostly spam and corn and hash. Not even enough to last a week. Who was Roger and what was he doing living way out here in the middle of nowhere? Off the grid? What did that even mean? Was he hiding from the government? Maybe he was a fugitive. They should have never gotten in the truck with him, especially in a no-coverage zone.

Roger stepped back into the cabin, and Kennedy studied him as earnestly as she'd prepared for the MCATs. She wasn't sure what she was looking for exactly, bloodstains on his flannel shirt, fangs instead of yellow teeth, something sinister behind the bushy, tangled beard that would make Nick's dreadlocks look well-groomed in comparison.

"Got the power up and running," he announced.

At this proclamation, Kennedy expected Roger to flip on a light switch, but after checking each wall, she realized there were none. She glanced over at Willow, hoping to steal a pinch of her roommate's calm.

Roger adjusted some dials on a small box tucked away in the corner. Kennedy tried to guess his age. Thirty-five? Sixty? There was no way to know with his entire face covered by that ridiculous beard. It was so ratted she couldn't tell if it was more gray or brown. He wasn't young or old, skinny or overweight, the kind of person she might have walked past in the airport or movie theater and never noticed. There was nothing to learn about him from his clothing either. Flannel and jeans in Alaska were about as common as premed students in the Harvard library.

Roger pushed a button, and Kennedy flinched at the sound. She hoped he hadn't noticed, but he straightened up and stared hard at her. "Space heater," he explained. "Nothing to worry about."

Great. *Nothing to worry about.* Isn't that about like a sleazy salesman crooning *you can trust me*?

Kennedy tried to dissolve her fears in the warmth from Roger's small heating unit. At least her foot felt better now, thanks to Willow's vigorous massage.

"Where you girls from?"

"We came in from Anchorage," Willow answered while Kennedy tried sending out telepathic messages to her roommate to keep her mouth shut. Maybe it was her dad and all his paranoia, or maybe she just couldn't trust a man who actually chose to live out here in the middle of winter in nothing but a hundred-square-foot shack, but she certainly didn't want to give Roger any more information than was absolutely vital. "My parents live out in Copper Lake," Willow added, "just past Glennallen."

So much for discretion.

Roger nodded. "Pretty place."

"Oh, I know. It's gorgeous. I'm getting married there the day after tomorrow." She sighed. "Actually, technically it's tomorrow already. Nick's going to be really worried about us. Frankenstein. I wish I could get a hold of him."

If Roger was surprised by her odd choice in exclamations, he didn't show it. "I took a look at that car of yours. Totally busted."

Kennedy waited for the part when he offered to drive them out toward Glennallen, but all he did was stare.

"You got any way to get in touch with my family?" Willow wound a strand of hair around her finger. "They're going to be wicked worried. You heard what happened earlier, didn't you?"

Roger nodded, then walked over by his small stash of food and slowly opened up a can of spam. Ignoring Willow's question, he held out the container. "I could heat it up for you, but it takes a while on the stovetop. You girls think you can handle it straight up?"

For the first time, Willow looked as terrified as Kennedy felt. "No thanks. I'm vegan."

"You're what?" Roger narrowed his eyebrows.

"Vegan," Willow repeated. "Kind of like vegetarian. I don't eat meat."

He frowned at her with suspicion then looked at Kennedy. "Do you?"

She nodded, and before she could tell him she wasn't all that hungry, he'd dumped the slab of spam into the palm of her hand. She'd never eaten it before and wasn't even sure what to do with it. She glanced at Willow, who scrunched up her face.

Roger was staring at her, so she forced herself to take the daintiest of bites. With all the salt and grease, she couldn't taste the meat itself, if it actually was meat. Kennedy wasn't sure, and Roger was still holding the can, so she couldn't read the label.

"How is it?" Willow was trying to hide a bemused smirk.

"It's ok." Kennedy forced herself to take one more taste and then looked for a place to put the rest down. Finally, Roger held out his palm. Kennedy handed him the cube of meat product, and he took a huge, noisy bite.

He pointed to the pile of blankets on the floor. "You two can curl up by the heater down there and get warm."

He didn't have any indoor plumbing or running water, and he didn't seem like the type to worry about carrying his dirty linen out to the lake every week. Besides, it would be frozen five or six months out of the year, and the closest laundromat was probably a hundred miles away. Just how dirty were those blankets? And was any amount of warmth worth risking fleas or ticks or heaven knew what else might be down here?

"Come on." Willow plopped down onto the pile and beckoned for Kennedy. "We may as well get comfortable while we wait for ..." She stopped and looked at Roger. "What exactly are we waiting for? What's the plan?"

"My buddy Buster," he answered with his mouth full of spam.

Kennedy hadn't realized there really were people named Buster in the world. She'd previously thought it was just a name you called someone you didn't like if you were a character in an old-fashioned cartoon episode.

Roger was still chewing on his canned meat. "Lives about fifteen miles down the road. Has a landline."

"Right on." Willow snuggled down in the corner of the cabin, completely unfazed.

Kennedy didn't bother to point out that even if this Buster guy had a landline phone, it did them precious little good if he was fifteen miles *down the road*, especially if Roger was referring to the little mountain trail they'd driven on to get here. Things didn't make much more sense when he took a large electronic box off the shelf.

"Buster?" He held it close to his mouth. "You hear me? Wake up, cranky."

The radio crackled, and an angry voice responded, "What you want?"

"Got me two girls here." Roger looked them both over. "Ran into some car trouble on the Glenn, and they have to get a message home."

More static, followed by, "Oh, yeah? They all right?"

Kennedy couldn't figure out why Roger was staring at her so intensely. "Yeah. Both fine. But there's a family around Glennallen they're trying to get a hold of. If I give you a phone number, could you call them for us?" He stared at Willow. "Ready?"

He brought the radio toward her, and Willow gave Buster her parents' phone number and a message that she and Kennedy were safe but the car was totaled.

"What about someone coming to pick us up?" Kennedy asked, still unwilling to sit down next to Willow on that dirty pile of tattered blankets. She tried to figure out how far away they were from Copper Lake, how long they'd have to stay here until they were rescued. At least she wasn't as cold anymore. The space heater and stove were far more efficient than she'd initially expected.

Roger overheard Kennedy's question and grabbed the radio back. "Buster, tell her folks to come get them tomorrow morning. I'll drop them off at Eureka Lodge."

A lodge? Kennedy's brain sprang to attention at the word. A lodge within driving distance? A lodge meant real walls, not logs piled up onto each other by hand. Heat that came out of floorboards, not a stove or space heater. Real beds, real sheets, and blankets that were at least occasionally washed by machine. Why weren't they already on their way?

"We could leave now," she suggested, but Roger was listening to his friend on the radio.

"You sure they're all right?" Buster had a wheeze in his voice. "Sound pretty young."

Roger glanced at them again. "Yeah, they're fine. Just make sure you pass their message on, got it?"

"Roger that, Roger."

"Hilarious," he grumbled. "All right, so we'll see you there."

Roger ended the call, and Kennedy wondered about his last words. *We'll see you there.* What did that mean? Did Buster live at this lodge? He had a landline, so he had to be a little closer to civilization. She still couldn't believe people voluntarily lived out here like this. Were there other mountain men, dozens of hermits like Roger, scattered through these woods?

Roger set the radio back on the top shelf and looked at Kennedy. "May as well get some rest," he told her. "I'll drive you up to Eureka in the morning."

Kennedy realized they hadn't set a time to tell Willow's parents to meet them at the lodge. What if Roger's idea of morning was 11:30, and the Winters showed up at six, frantic and worried? What if there was more than one lodge in Eureka, wherever that was? How would they find each other?

Willow motioned for Kennedy to sit down by her. "Come on," she coaxed, "you need some rest."

Kennedy couldn't argue with her. At least maybe the cold was enough to kill off bed bugs and ticks that might be living in the rags.

She hoped so as she sat down next to her roommate.

Willow started rubbing her back. "It's going to be fine," she whispered.

Kennedy scooted closer. "You think we can trust him?"

Willow smiled. "Yeah. Never mind what his home looks like. There are people like this all over the state. They're totally harmless. Don't worry about a thing."

CHAPTER 4

4:13 PM, THE DAY before the Winter Solstice

The plane landed with a jerk and then a roar that nearly deadened Kennedy's senses. Just a few minutes after four, but the sun had already set. She didn't know if her brain was playing tricks on her or not, but she shivered with cold when she looked out at the snow piled up on the sides of the runway.

She couldn't wait to get off this plane. She'd been either in the air or waiting in some terminal for the past fourteen hours.

"You have someone here to pick you up?" the woman sitting next to her asked. They hadn't talked much on the flight, only enough for Kennedy to know she was here visiting a new grandbaby.

Kennedy nodded. "My roommate's coming."

The grandmother smiled. "Well, tell her I hope it's a beautiful wedding."

"I will. And congrats on your daughter's baby. I hope you have a great visit."

It was almost heavenly standing up and stretching her legs once the slow deboarding process began. After traveling back and forth from China so often, Kennedy was still surprised at how much the simple four-hour time difference between Alaska and the East Coast could throw her off. Maybe the winter darkness had something to do with it. Her phone told her it was the middle of the afternoon, but her appetite was convinced it was past dinnertime and the sky was as dark as midnight.

She shifted her bookbag, which was lighter than normal since she was finally trying to get her eyes used to an e-reader. She could never fully give up on print, but it was convenient not having to lug around ten or twelve paperbacks whenever she traveled. In addition to studying up for her MCATs, she was reading as many books as she could about Alaska. Memoirs about kids who grew up in the homesteading generation like Willow's mom, photographs from the Klondike gold rush and Kennicott copper mines, collections of Native Alaskan mythology, historical fiction from the time of the Russian colonization.

Her legs were stiff from inactivity when she made her way down the tarmac and into the Anchorage airport. Or the Ted Stevens airport, as everyone here called it. Whoever he was. She'd have to ask Willow. Kennedy had only recently realized how much unique culture was packed into this arctic state. Willow teased her mercilessly about her general lack of Alaskan knowledge, which is why Kennedy was finally studying up on its people and history.

"Excuse me, Miss."

She turned around at the nasally voice. A tall young man, awkwardly skinny and long-limbed, rushed to catch up to her.

"Hi. I'm Melvin." He held out his hand. "I couldn't help but notice you reading on the plane. Do you like books?"

Kennedy was in no mood to enter into some random conversation with a stranger. She wanted to collect her suitcase, find Willow, and crash at their hotel.

He reached into his computer bag that was strapped across his shoulder. "I was thinking, if this is the kind of reading you enjoy, I've got an extra copy back home and wondered if maybe you wanted mine."

She glanced at the cover. *Why the World Will End on the Winter Solstice.* Not a very original title, but at least it made it quite clear what the short paperback was about.

"That's ok," she said. "You should keep it."

Melvin shoved the book into her hands. "No, take it. I mean it. You'll want to be prepared." He glanced at his watch. "It's all starting soon."

Kennedy took the book in hopes that it would get him to leave her alone.

Unfortunately, she was not so lucky.

"You know about the volcano, right?" he asked as they stopped in front of the baggage claim area.

"A little bit," she answered. As if her dad hadn't called her thirteen times in the past two days to warn her. Seismological reports suggested that one of the mountains on the opposite side of the Cook Inlet was about to blow. It wasn't in an inhabited area, but the ash was supposed to cover Anchorage within an hour or two of the eruption.

"Well, that's just the start." Melvin grabbed the book out of Kennedy's hands. After turning to the second chapter, he pointed to a constellation map as the suitcases began their descent down the conveyer belt. "See? It's got all you need to know. You ever read the book of Revelation?"

Kennedy nodded.

Melvin's eyes widened. "Really? Oh, well, ok then. You've heard all about it."

"All about what?" She was glad when her suitcase came into view. That was one perk of flying into an airport as small as this one.

"About the sign in the sky, the great wonder. Revelation 12. Here." He flipped ahead a few pages. "*A great sign appeared in heaven: a woman clothed with the sun, with the moon under her feet and a crown of twelve stars on her head.* You can read all about it. Where it talks about how these astrological symbols are lining up, just like the verse says, the crown of twelve stars, everything. And it all starts tomorrow on the solstice. That's what I mean when I said you've got to be prepared."

Kennedy did her best to fake a smile. "Well, thanks for sharing. That's really ..." She cleared her throat. "That's really interesting." Grabbing her phone from her pocket, she added in what she hoped sounded like a disappointed voice, "Oh, that's my friend. She's waiting for me outside. I don't want to be late."

Without waiting for a good-bye, she grabbed her suitcase, braced herself for the biting cold, and headed into the winter darkness.

CHAPTER 5

PAST MIDNIGHT, WINTER SOLSTICE

There was no way that Kennedy could manage to fall asleep, even as exhausted as she felt. She'd left her cell in the totaled car and there were no clocks anywhere, but it felt like she'd been at Roger's for hours by the time he mumbled something about stepping outside for a few minutes. Kennedy was relieved when he left. Maybe Willow had seen hermits like him her entire life, but Kennedy had no idea people still lived like this in America in the twenty-first century.

She nudged her roommate who lay beside her. "You still awake?"

Willow rolled over. "Yeah. What's going on?" She sat up and arched her back.

"Roger just stepped out. Didn't say where he was going."

"Probably to use the outhouse," she answered. "You should try to sleep. It's late."

"I don't like this place." Kennedy kept her voice low in case Roger was close by. "Gives me the creeps."

Willow shrugged. "Early days, everyone lived like this. Little cabins, you see them all over the place. My grandpa built one just like it. It's pretty standard for the homestead generation. You make yourself a quick cabin in the spring, clear the land and get your crops planted, and then after you get ahead a little you make yourself a proper home. My grandparents lived in a one-room like this until my mom was two or three. It's still there on the property. Remind me to show you."

Kennedy didn't reply. She was too busy trying to guess how much longer it'd be until morning. "Do you have your phone?" she asked Willow.

"Yeah, but there's no reception out here."

"I know. I was just wondering what time it was."

Willow glanced out the tiny window by Roger's cupboard. "Probably right after one." She pulled out her phone to check. "Yup. It's 1:13."

"How'd you do that?"

Willow shrugged. "Just looked at the angle of the moon. It's not neuroscience."

It was times like these that made Kennedy realize how ignorant she was about rural living. Even on their busy campus in Cambridge, Willow was always commenting about the lunar phases, telling Kennedy when a harvest moon was due or when a meteor shower was passing through.

"I wish it weren't so dark in here," Kennedy said.

Willow tapped her screen. "Hold on. I can turn this thing into a flashlight."

The cabin was no less creepy now than it had been in the dark.

"I can't wait until we get out of this place."

Willow reached over and offered a reassuring squeeze. "We'll be fine. If it weren't for me worrying about getting back home, I'd actually be enjoying our little adventure."

"What about that Eureka place?" Kennedy asked.

"It's not that far. Maybe twenty minutes' drive. Roger'll take us there in the morning. They've got decent food too. No more spam for breakfast."

Kennedy tried to match her smile.

"Don't worry," Willow said. "Just think about all we have to be thankful for. If your plane had come a few hours later, you might not have been able to land at all. We got out of Anchorage in plenty of time, and that moose could have done a lot more damage than it did. Honestly, it's a miracle Roger found us. We could have been lying in that car for hours before somebody drove by. This is all just part of being in Alaska, really. You have to learn to be flexible." She chuckled. "And you have to learn to watch the road for moose."

Kennedy let out her breath. "There's still something really off about this place."

"You're just not used to roughing it, City Girl."

Maybe Willow was right. Maybe Kennedy needed to be more flexible. More adventurous like her roommate.

Or maybe she just needed to be at that lodge in Eureka, sleeping in a real bed and not on a pile of rags.

"You want proof that there's nothing here to worry about?" Willow stood and shined her phone light around. "I'm telling you, I know all about these little homestead cabins. See, over here, this is where he keeps his two coffee mugs, two tin plates, fork, knife, and a spoon." She pulled open a drawer. "Oh, look. I was wrong. He actually has two spoons." She held them up.

"And over here, you've already seen his pantry. Spam, canned corn, and Ramen. Hey, just like Nick eats. And this ..." She picked up a shoebox. "I bet this is where he keeps every single personal item he owns." She paused with her hand on the lid. "Wait, let me guess. An expired driver's license, a postcard from his mom or grandma, and a third-grade report card." She opened the box with a grand gesture.

"We shouldn't be going through his stuff." Kennedy glanced nervously at the door. If Roger was just using the outhouse, he'd be back any second.

"I want to prove to you that this man is totally harmless. Like I said, he ..." Willow froze.

So did the blood in Kennedy's veins. "What? What is it?"

"Dude." Willow shook her head.

"What?" Kennedy repeated. "If this is your idea of a joke ..."

Headlights shined in through the window. Willow threw on the lid, shoved the box back on the shelf, and all but dove into Kennedy's lap.

"What's the matter?" Kennedy hissed.

"Just lie down," Willow whispered. "Lie down and pretend to be asleep." She thrust her cell phone into Kennedy's hand. "And the minute you get the chance, run."

CHAPTER 6

4:41 PM, THE DAY before the Winter Solstice

"Dude, you made it!" Willow wrapped both arms around Kennedy's neck and kissed her loudly on both cheeks.

Kennedy tried to muster up the energy to return her roommate's enthusiasm. Willow had been in Alaska for almost a week, making last-minute plans and getting everything ready for her wedding. Kennedy just wanted to grab some food and take a hot shower. She hoped that whatever hotel they were staying at for the night had good water pressure. She hated the feel of grime and sweat and germs on her skin after a full day of traveling.

Kennedy hefted her suitcase into the trunk of her roommate's car and only then noticed Willow's pout.

"Well?" Willow jutted out her hip and frowned. "Aren't you going to say anything?"

Kennedy hardly looked up. "About what?"

Willow stood silent and stared until Kennedy raised her eyes.

"Woah, your hair," she exclaimed once full realization set in. "It looks ... It's ..."

"Normal?" Willow finished for her. "Well, don't get your hopes up too high. I told Nick that as soon as we've taken the wedding pictures, the first thing I'm going to do on our honeymoon is dye it. I'm thinking of going black again. Black with gray streaks. What do you think?"

Kennedy was still staring. "So, is that your ... I mean ..."

Willow smiled. "Yeah, I'm a natural brunette. It's been so long since I've seen my real color I hardly recognize myself. At first, I was planning on doing it the same shade of red as the flowers, but then I started to think that maybe one day I'll be a respectable old church lady, and I might not want my wedding pictures to stand out so much. I don't know.

"Oh, speaking of wedding pictures, have I told you what my dad did yesterday? He surprised us, sent Nick and me on this helicopter glacier tour with a professional photographer. It was wicked cold, but I've seen one or two of the unedited pictures, and it was totally worth it. But look at you. You're freezing. Get into the car. I've kept it warming up while I waited."

Kennedy didn't argue. Classic rock music was blaring when she sank down into the passenger seat.

Willow sat beside her and smiled. "Hope you got a long nap on the plane. You're going to have to stay awake for a while."

No. Kennedy couldn't. "I thought we were going to head to the hotel and crash."

Willow snorted. "Well, there may be a few people who decide to crash, but I think everybody I know has already been invited."

Kennedy still wasn't following. "Invited to what?"

Willow raised her penciled eyebrows. "To my bachelorette party. Didn't you get my text? There'll be like forty of us, and we've got to go get ready because we only have five hours until they start showing up."

Kennedy was furiously scrolling through her phone messages.

Willow laughed. "I'm just kidding. Don't worry. There's no party."

It was a miracle that Kennedy's sigh of relief didn't blow the rainbow heart decals off Willow's dashboard.

Willow was still chuckling as they rolled away from the airport curb. "You should have seen your face!"

Kennedy did her best to share in the joke, but all she could think about was a steamy shower. Even with Willow's heater blaring full-power, it didn't penetrate her frozen core. She glanced out the window, surprised that there was actually traffic in a city this small. "So how far do we have to go to get to the hotel?"

Willow turned her head and yelled, "What? I can't hear you."

Kennedy repeated her question.

Willow turned down the radio. "Well, we could head over there right now. We're not too far, but if you don't mind, I'd like to make a quick stop downtown first. There's this cute little museum gift shop, and I still haven't found the right centerpieces for the reception. I thought I might get some ideas there."

Kennedy didn't mention that two days before her wedding was a little bit late to be shopping for décor. But as exhausted as she was, she still wanted to try to be a help to her roommate. "Sure, sounds interesting. I didn't even know Anchorage had a downtown."

Willow mumbled something about Kennedy being a greenhorn and continued driving.

As it turned out, downtown Anchorage was nothing more than a bunch of touristy shops lining congested streets. Willow spent a full twenty minutes driving in circles, hunting for a place to parallel park without traveling the wrong direction on a one-way street. Right when Kennedy figured she was going to fall asleep, Willow found a spot. "Well," she said cheerily, "at least we're close to the museum."

Kennedy didn't want to leave the relatively warm car, but she made herself get out and stamped her feet on the snowy sidewalk to try to stay warm. Willow grabbed her by the elbow. "Come on, rookie. We'll make a real Alaska girl out of you yet." She led Kennedy into a small storefront entrance with bells on the door that clanged and jingled when they entered.

An old man with spectacles about to fall off his nose smiled at them. "Welcome to the Alaska Historical Museum. I'm Jeb. You from out of town?" he asked, staring right at Kennedy.

She nodded. "Just flew in."

He scratched his cheek. "You look colder than a tourist in July." He turned to Willow. "What about you? Where you from?"

"Born and raised in Copper Lake." There was a hint of pride in Willow's voice.

Jeb let out a low whistle. "Yeah, how cold does it get out there this time of year?"

"It was thirty-eight below when I went out this morning to milk the goats."

"You have goats?" Jeb asked. "Any babies?"

"We have two pregnant does, but they won't kid until spring."

While Willow started browsing through the Alaska trinkets and souvenirs, Kennedy walked up and down the aisles of the small one-room museum.

"That there's about the Aleutian chain during World War II," Jeb told her. "Japanese came and took over two of our islands. Only US soil they managed to claim the entire war."

Kennedy didn't even know where the Aleutians were, but she wasn't about to flaunt her ignorance.

"And there," Jeb said, "those were supplies they gave the Washtub recruits in Seward during the Cold War."

Kennedy replayed that last sentence several times in her head and still failed to decipher any of it.

Willow, apparently forgetting that she was shopping for an Alaskan centerpiece, held up a pair of beaded earrings. "Dude, these are adorable. I have to get them."

Jeb seemed much more interested in giving Kennedy a crash course in Alaskan history than in making a sale. "You see our new '64 display?" He snaked his way out from behind the counter and led Kennedy to panels of large black-and-white photographs on the wall.

Kennedy squinted at pictures of collapsed houses, ruined railroad tracks, and massive cracks in roads and sidewalks. "What's this?"

"That's our '64 display. Didn't I just say that?"

Kennedy glanced at Willow for translation.

"The big Alaska earthquake," she explained.

Jeb looped his thumbs in his belt buckles and nodded approvingly. "Largest earthquake on record in North America."

"Were you here then?" Willow asked.

Jeb nodded. "Oh yeah. Wife and I just bought our first house in Turnagain. We had a bookshelf at the top of the hall. Darn thing chased me all the way down the stairs before crashing into the coffee table."

Kennedy had never felt an earthquake before, nor had she come across this part of Alaska's past in her reading on the airplane.

Jeb stared at the pictures on the wall. "Molly kept trying to run out the door to get to the kids. They were playing outside, but the ground was shaking so bad it just kept throwing her down. Like trying to run across a waterbed. We got out of the house as soon as it was over, and our front yard had turned into a cliff. Ten, maybe twenty-foot drop. Thankfully the kids were safe in the backyard." He cleared his throat. "You should've heard the sound. Thought the Soviets were finally bombing us. That's how loud it was."

Kennedy didn't know what to say. Thankfully, Jeb seemed lost in his own thoughts as he stared at the photographs.

Willow came over and plopped several items on the counter. "Found what I needed." She studied her painted fingernails while Jeb rang up several new pairs of earrings, beaded moccasins, a colorfully dyed scarf, and a pair of men's gloves. Kennedy didn't bother to ask her about that wedding centerpiece.

"You two girls heard about the volcano warning, haven't you?" Jeb asked as he ran Willow's credit card.

Willow nodded. "Yeah, wicked crazy, huh?"

He shrugged. "Some loonies came in trying earlier to tell me to close up shop and make for the hills. Saying the solstice marks the end of the world or some nonsense like that."

Kennedy ignored the flutter in her gut and wondered if she'd done the right thing by throwing away that book the man had given her at the airport.

"So I told them," Jeb went on, "the only thing the solstice marks the end of is each day getting darker, right?" He let out a wheezy laugh. "You two girls take it easy now. Stay safe."

His words followed them out the door, sending another shiver racing down Kennedy's spine. Or maybe that was just the cold.

"I didn't know about that big earthquake," Kennedy confessed as they headed back to Willow's car.

"Yeah, it's a big deal around here. Mom was seven or eight. She had relatives living in Valdez at the time. Got a big tidal wave there. Her uncle was working the docks and disappeared. Never found his body. It was wicked intense."

Kennedy couldn't even imagine. "Have there been any other earthquakes since?"

Willow shrugged as they got into her car. "They come and go. I've lived through dozens, but none that ever caused any damage or lasted more than a few seconds. Most of the time, you don't even know it's an earthquake until it's over. The one in '64 lasted something like five minutes, and if you talk to anybody who remembers, it was terrifying. Mom still gets a little spooked by any sort of loud rumbling noise."

Kennedy focused on buckling her seatbelt and was proud that her hands didn't shake. Two years ago, when her PTSD was at its worst, this kind of conversation might have triggered a full-on panic attack. But logically she knew she had very little to worry about. People had been living safely in Alaska for decades. Even with the weird seismological occurrences on the other side of the Cook Inlet, the kind of disaster Jeb was talking about was a once in a century kind of event at most. Even if another serious earthquake was doomed to hit Alaska in the next fifty or hundred years, there was no reason to think it would happen in the next few days.

What would be the chances?

CHAPTER 7

KENNEDY'S PHONE RANG A few seconds after they got back on the road.

She sighed and rolled her eyes before answering. "Hi, Dad."

"Hey, Princess. You made it in safely?"

"Yeah. Everything's fine." Could he take the hint and stop worrying about her? If it weren't for his constant paranoia, would she still struggle with anxiety as much as she did?

"Great." At least his voice was cheerful. "I've been keeping my eyes on the reports. Looks like that volcano's been pretty quiet the past ten hours or so."

Kennedy didn't know what to say in response.

"Well, just stay safe, all right?"

"I will."

Her roommate was chuckling when Kennedy ended the call. "What's so funny?"

"Your dad. Has he always been like that?"

"Yeah, but he means well."

"Oh, I know he does. That man would seriously do anything to keep you safe. It's wicked cute."

Cute isn't the word Kennedy would have chosen, but she decided not to argue.

"So what's he think about the whole winter solstice, end of the world thing? Does he buy into that?"

Kennedy shook her head. "No. I mean, there's been some weird stuff going on lately, those typhoons and tornados and things.

And obviously he's convinced that the volcano's going to erupt and bury us in ash. But more than anything, I think he's worried people might start acting crazy. Like riots are about to break out all over Anchorage." Kennedy chuckled, but surprisingly Willow didn't share her laugh.

"A lot of people are worried about that."

Kennedy glanced over to try to tell if she was joking.

"Anchorage might not be that big of a city, but crime is awful here. It's got one of the highest per capita murder rates in the nation. Same thing with rape. It's terrible."

Kennedy had no idea.

"Some of it has to do with the gangs in the Lower 48. The jails get so full they pay to relocate criminals up here. Just set them free in Anchorage. I would never want to live in a city like this."

"I wouldn't have guessed."

Willow shrugged. "Most people wouldn't. They think Alaska's all frontiersmen and fishing and igloos, but there's a major poverty and crime problem here. It's something Nick and I have talked about. We still aren't sure where God's calling us after we get married because there are so many needs everywhere. That's why we agreed for me to take the semester off, spend that time praying to find out what he wants us to do."

Kennedy wasn't ready to think about returning to college next semester without her roommate. "How long will you be with Nick's family in Washington?" she asked.

"Oh!" Willow swerved so fast that Kennedy thought they were about to crash.

"What was that?" Kennedy snapped her head back, checking the road for signs of danger.

"I just missed our turn." Crossing two more lanes of traffic, Willow backtracked down a somewhat shady-looking side street.

"This is where we're staying tonight?" Kennedy hoped her voice didn't give away her concern.

"No, silly." Willow pulled the car into a crowded lot. "This is where we're having dinner. Welcome to the Raven's Claw, home of the best pizza in Alaska. Or anywhere else for that matter."

Once inside the restaurant, Kennedy doubted that even the most delicious pizza in the universe could warrant a ninety-minute wait. After three and a half games of smart phone

Scrabble and another forty minutes from the time they ordered until their food arrived at the table, Kennedy would have been willing to eat roadkill moose or fried whale blubber.

Fortunately, the food was just as good as Willow had promised, even their vegan pizza made with cheese alternative. They finished dinner with nothing left over. "Come on." Willow grabbed Kennedy's hand after they'd paid the bill. "If we hurry, we'll make it on time."

"Make it where?" As far as Kennedy knew, the only thing she had to make tonight was her hotel room bed.

"There's that new movie out. Remember? The Christian flick about the end times. I haven't been to the theater in months, and I'm really curious about this one." Willow unlocked the car door and got in. "You know, I read all of Revelations. I even wrote down my questions to ask Pastor Carl, but he's so busy with church and still gets those bad headaches after his accident, and I hate to bother him. So what I was thinking was we can go see the movie tonight, and on the drive home tomorrow, we can go through the list because I know some of them are really basic. If you could answer those, then I wouldn't have to feel guilty for wasting Pastor Carl's time later on."

"It's getting pretty late," Kennedy began tentatively.

"Oh, don't worry about that. The theater's right around the corner."

"I'm not sure I'll be able to stay awake."

Willow smiled. "I know. I've heard it's super cheesy, and we'll probably get a lot of good laughs, but I'm still curious about it. Especially with what everyone's saying about the winter solstice and those constellations lining up like in that prophecy."

Kennedy had read the book the movie was based on years ago. It was an engaging story, but she wasn't sure how useful it would be for helping Willow understand Revelation, at least not without someone like Carl to help her make sense of what was biblical and what was fiction.

Thankfully, last fall Carl had astounded his doctors when he woke up from his coma, but he got tired more easily and sometimes suffered such debilitating migraines he had to take a day or two off work. Willow was right about one thing. If Kennedy could help get some of her questions answered, it would give Carl more time to rest and focus on his family and his preaching and his recovery.

The problem was Kennedy had no clue what she thought about the end times. The only solid opinion she had on the matter was that she hoped to be buried and dead long before any of the events in Revelation started to unfold.

"Why don't you ask Nick?" she asked.

Willow strummed her fingers on the steering wheel in time with the music on her radio. "Oh, you know Nick," she sighed. "I love that man to death, but when he starts talking theology, you better have a master's degree if you want to keep up with him. Which is probably why he and my dad get along so well."

Kennedy didn't have time to come up with any better plans before Willow pulled her car up alongside a miniature trailer in an empty parking lot. "Come on. I'll get you a coffee. That way you'll be able to stay awake."

"I'm really not sure ..."

Willow nudged Kennedy playfully. "Stop being so uptight. You don't have any classes to get up early for tomorrow. It will be fun."

CHAPTER 8

KENNEDY HAD NEVER SEEN a drive-up coffee hut like this before, but Willow told her they were all over the state. "I read online that if you took every stand in Alaska and stacked them from one point to the other, they would stretch all the way from Anchorage to Santa Barbara."

Kennedy wasn't so sure about that, but she could at least appreciate the convenience of grabbing a hot drink without having to get out of the car. Willow rolled down her window long enough to give her order then shut it again to keep out the cold.

Kennedy was surprised to see the girl inside was wearing nothing but tight shorts and a tank top. "She must be freezing."

"Don't worry, she's probably got a couple space heaters in there. I'm sure she's perfectly toasty."

Kennedy tried not to stare while the young girl mixed their drinks.

Willow raised her eyebrows at her. "Sheesh. Haven't you heard of a bikini barista before? They're all over Anchorage. That's why these coffee stands make such good money."

"So they get paid to look pretty in their swimsuits?"

"No, they get paid to make coffee. They get tips for looking pretty in their swimsuits."

Willow was joking, but Kennedy didn't think it was all that funny. "Isn't that dangerous? I mean, it's the middle of the night, totally dark. She's out here all alone ..."

Willow laughed. "First of all, that's a perfect example of rape culture right there. Second, she's an Alaska chick. Probably packs more heat than that police detective back in Boston. Don't be so uptight. In the past five years, there's only been one barista kidnapping."

"Only one?" Kennedy repeated sarcastically.

"Really sad story, actually. She grew up in Valdez, girl named Brandy. We knew each other from a few summer theater programs. Anyway, don't worry, she didn't even work at one of the bikini ones."

Willow rolled down her window to grab the two drinks. Kennedy kept her eyes on the dashboard.

"Oh, stop being all weird about it," Willow said as they drove off. "That barista's probably a straight-A student like you, working one or two late nights a week and earning enough in tips to pay for her entire college education."

They arrived at the theater two minutes before starting time. As they hurried through the parking lot, the air stung Kennedy's face, and she wondered how she'd handle Copper Lake, which was regularly thirty degrees colder or more than Anchorage.

Kennedy had never seen her roommate get so engrossed in a film before, especially not one with such canned dialogue and stiff acting as this one. Forty minutes into the movie, Kennedy found herself nodding off as many times as the camera changed its angle. She shouldn't have gotten a plain hot chocolate at the drive-up stand, not if her goal was to stay awake. She should either stop fighting her fatigue and squeeze in an hour-long nap or run out to the lobby and grab herself something more caffeinated. It didn't matter which she chose. Either option would be preferable to sitting here jerking herself awake every two or three minutes.

The main character was explaining the rapture to the perky love interest when Kennedy leaned over and whispered to Willow, "I'm going to grab a drink. Be right back."

Not surprisingly, the theater was almost empty. Kennedy didn't have to worry about stepping over anybody's legs or distracting any viewers behind her.

She stopped by the bathroom on the way to the concession stand and splashed cold water on her face. She could travel across twelve time zones a couple times a year and manage not to turn into a zombie. With a little gumption and a whole lot of caffeine, she could make it through the rest of this film.

She stared at her reflection, wondering what strangers thought when they saw her. She wasn't like Willow, never was one to stand out in a crowd. Not that she wanted to. She thought back to her first international flight by herself two and a half years ago. Straight out of high school, never suspecting the trials she'd have to walk through. She still didn't feel all that old, but she was definitely more mature than she'd been when she first stepped foot on the campus of Harvard University.

The same university that last semester had humiliated her, taken away her job as a teaching assistant, and threatened her medical school acceptance when all she'd done was write an article that certain people didn't like. She might have never gotten her offer reinstated if it hadn't been for her friend, Ian. The red-haired journalist had championed tirelessly for her before hopping on a plane to China to continue with his filming.

She hadn't heard from him since, which shouldn't disappoint her all that much. They'd only had a few breakfast dates together, not enough to know if there really was any spark or chemistry between them. Still, she'd thought he would at least text or email her from overseas, even just to let her know he was still safe.

She sighed as she made her way out of the bathroom. Standing in line to get a drink, she felt her pocket vibrate and realized she'd missed several texts from her dad during the first portion of the film.

Her mouth immediately went dry. She could taste the fear in the back of her throat. Her lungs constricted once. She did her best to swallow down her panic.

There wasn't time to write her dad back. Praying Willow had forgotten to turn her phone off before the start of the show, she steadied her hands enough to send a simple text.

Volcano erupted about twenty minutes ago. We've got to leave.

CHAPTER 9

PAST MIDNIGHT, WINTER SOLSTICE

Kennedy winced as Willow's fingernails dug into her arm. She wanted to ask what was going on, what Willow had found in the box that got her so freaked out, but she was paralyzed.

"Roger? You home?" The front door banged opened, bringing in with it a burst of cold and the foul smell of body odor.

Willow gave Kennedy's arm one last squeeze and asked sleepily, "Someone there?"

"I'm looking for Roger. Where is he?" The voice was gruff.

"He stepped out for just a sec. I'm sure he'll be back soon. Are you Buster, the guy with the radio?"

"Yeah, that's me. Who're you?"

"I'm Willow. Did you get hold of my parents?"

"Sure did. They were pretty worried, too."

"Oh, good. Thank you so much for getting that message to them. Hey, did my mom mention my goat?"

"Goat?"

Willow's voice was laced with concern. She sounded five years younger. "Yeah, she went into labor this morning, and I've been really worried about her. I thought for sure my mom would know how scared I'd be and give you a message to let me know how things went."

Buster cleared his throat. "Oh, that. Yeah, she said everything went just fine. No problems. Happy mama, healthy baby."

Willow let out her breath in a loud sigh. "I'm so glad. I've been worried sick."

Kennedy couldn't keep ahead of the conversation. What was Willow talking about?

Buster's voice softened a little. He scratched his massive belly. "Where's your friend? Roger said there were two of you here."

Willow let out an airy laugh that held no indication of how tightly she'd been squeezing Kennedy's arm just a minute earlier. "She's dead to the world. That's her way. She's like Cinderella. Turns into a pumpkin after midnight, or something like that." Another giggle.

Buster cleared his throat. "Roger say when he was coming back?"

"No. Should we sit and wait for him?" Something in Willow's voice had changed. She wasn't actually flirting with this mountain man, was she?

Buster lowered his weight onto the stump in the middle of the room. Now that he was closer to Kennedy's corner, she tried hard not to gag from the smell.

"Is it still pretty cold out?" Willow asked. What kind of question was that? It was the dead of winter, and they were stuck here freezing in the middle of nowhere.

"You could say that."

"I wonder if the stars are out. Want to step outside and see?" What was Willow thinking? Why would she go outside in the cold with this stranger? Kennedy thought about her roommate's directive to run when she got the chance, but she wasn't going anywhere by herself. Not without Willow, and not without a whole lot more answers.

What had Willow seen? What got her so scared? They were obviously in some kind of trouble, but until Kennedy knew what, until she found out what was in that box that spooked Willow so much, she had to be prepared for anything. What was lying around here that could make a decent weapon? There was a fire poker, wasn't there? Which side of the stove was it on? Kennedy reached out her hand slowly, terrified of making any noise that would alert Buster and let him know she was awake.

"Come on," Willow was coaxing playfully. "Take me outside so we can look at the sky. Don't you love the stars?" She sounded like an eight-year-old begging for a ride on the merry-go-round.

"You can see the sky and the stars from here. Just look right out the window. Don't even have to get cold."

"Yeah, but there's a spot right behind the house that I bet has an even better view. See that tree branch? It's blocking the view."

Buster made some sort of indecipherable grumble.

"Please?" Willow whined.

Think. Kennedy had to think. Figure out what she was supposed to do.

"Come on, let's go look. Just for a minute. We'll go behind the cabin, see if the view's better without the tree blocking it, and then we'll come right back in and warm up. Ok?"

Buster continued to speak in grunts and monosyllables, but since he was getting up off the log, Kennedy guessed he was assenting. Now was the time to make her decision.

Willow giggled. "Just behind the cabin," she repeated, glancing back once, "and then we'll come back real quick."

The door opened. The burst of searing cold nearly stole Kennedy's breath. As soon as she was alone she jumped up to grab the shoebox from the shelf. She had to understand what Willow was doing. Why she'd told Kennedy to run.

She shined the light from Willow's phone into the box. An old faded newspaper clipping lay on the top. *Anchorage Barista Still Missing: Police urge anyone with information to come forward.* Beneath the headline, a girl in a tank top smiled at Kennedy.

She moved the clipping aside. Beneath it were piles of photographs of a young woman in lingerie. Kennedy was certain that even from outside Buster and Willow could hear her pounding heart.

It was the same girl from the newspaper article.

She had to get Willow out of there. That was all there was to it. Even if Willow had made the sacrificial decision to distract Buster behind the cabin so Kennedy could make her escape, there was no way she was leaving here by herself.

She grabbed the fire poker then ran to the kitchen drawer, hoping to find something sharper than a butter knife. She shoved Willow's phone in her pocket. Stupid cell phone reception.

She eyed the radio. If she could figure out how it worked, would there be a way to signal for help? Would there be time?

"Buster? That you?"

Kennedy froze. It was Roger. She had no idea where he'd gone for so long, but his truck hadn't moved. Wherever he'd been, he'd gotten there by foot.

"It's me," Buster said. "Your cute little houseguest here wanted to see the stars."

Kennedy didn't have time to think about the girl in the pictures in Roger's shoebox. The front door opened, startling Kennedy so much she dropped the fire poker, which clattered on the hard floor, stinging her ears through the silence of the winter night.

"Everything ok?" Roger asked. Was he suspicious?

Kennedy wished she could absorb her roommate's acting abilities. She forced a smile. "Yeah, I don't know much about these wood stoves, but I was feeling a little cold in here, so I was ..."

Buster came in behind Roger, leading Willow who gave Kennedy a small shake of the head.

Kennedy stared at her feet. "I'm sorry. I probably should have left it alone."

Roger let out a laugh. He seemed far more jocular than he'd been earlier. Maybe the pack of beer he was holding with two cans missing explained why.

"Shut the door." Roger slammed the cans down. It took up his entire counter space. "I hope you girls got a little rest. Buster and me were thinking we'd treat you to an early Christmas party."

Kennedy was trying to find a way to politely decline when Willow sidled up beside her and grabbed her by the wrist. "Actually, I'm dying for a drink, but can you show us where the outhouse is first?" She shot her radiant smile. "We girls like to freshen up before a good party, right?"

Buster, all 250 stench-infested pounds of him, was leaning over Willow, grinning so widely Kennedy was surprised there wasn't already a puddle of drool on her roommate's shoulder.

Roger furrowed his brow. "I'll show you where it is, but there's not room for both of you at once."

Willow gave Kennedy a very obvious nudge. "Sounds good. You go first."

Kennedy understood what Willow was trying to do but refused to leave her roommate here alone. "That's ok. I can wait." She winced when Willow's fingernails dug into her wrist.

Willow sighed but kept her voice cheerful when she said, "All right, then. I guess we'll use the outhouse later. Who's ready to get this party started?

CHAPTER 10

IF KENNEDY HAD HER choice, the last thing she'd want to see would be these two men drunk, but Willow kept on giggling and popping lids off their beer. Kennedy held her full can close to her body as if it might ward off leering eyes, reminding herself to raise it to her lips every few minutes so it looked like she was taking a drink. Willow, by contrast, was already on her second can and was acting even more boisterous than she'd been back in her former partying days.

The twelve-pack was gone by the time Willow put her hand on Buster's shoulder and said, "You must be getting really tired. Think we should call it a night?" She glanced at Kennedy, who tried to guess what her roommate was thinking.

Trust me.

It wasn't Willow's voice she heard, even though she could sense that's what her gaze was meant to convey.

Trust me.

Her heart was pounding. She'd never been the type who "heard God" like some Christians she knew. Dominic, the chaplain of the police department back in Boston, had been incredibly gifted like that. Sometimes he had called Kennedy to say something like, "Hey, I was praying about you and just felt like God was telling me to give you some encouragement." Once, they'd been on their way to have dinner at Angelo's Pizza, but Dominic had said, "You know, this is going to sound crazy, but I really feel like the Lord's telling me we should go somewhere else tonight." So they grabbed clam chowder served in sourdough bread rolls from a walk-up stand, only to find out several hours later there'd been a gunfight right across the street from Angelo's.

Trust me.

Was that voice really God's? How could Kennedy be sure?

Roger's hand was on her shoulder. His breath stank and was hot on her neck. "You didn't drink much." He glanced at her beer, which Willow quickly grabbed.

"Let me take your empty can off your hands." She set it on the counter and smiled at Buster. "So, what happens now?"

Kennedy didn't understand why Willow was acting so friendly and eager, but she also couldn't shake that voice she'd heard.

Trust me.

Buster groaned as he plopped onto the tree log and pulled Willow onto his lap with a slurred, "Come here, you."

Willow giggled, but her serious eyes were fixed on Kennedy. What was she trying to say?

Trust me.

Kennedy took a deep breath. Tried not to shudder when Roger ran his hands up the back of her shirt and onto her bare skin. Kennedy was no actor. She wasn't like Willow. She couldn't pretend that any of this was right.

Willow was staring at her. What was she supposed to do?

Roger pressed his cheek against hers, the coarse hair from his beard bristling her skin and sending goosebumps up her spine.

She had to get him off. But how? Her entire body was frozen. She couldn't find her voice.

If that had really been God telling her to trust him, why wasn't he doing anything to stop Roger? Her body shivered.

"What's wrong, baby?" he asked. "You cold?"

Kennedy tried to swallow past the shameful lump in her throat. She hated the paralysis she felt, hated the helplessness that held her captive.

She didn't have to stand there like a statue and take this humiliation. She wouldn't. If she could just snap her brain out of its stupor, she could get him to stop. She'd force him to stop. When his hand started traveling around toward her chest, reflexes kicked in. She made her hand into a fist and slammed it into his groin. He doubled over, then reached out and grabbed her by the hair.

Willow yelled something, but Kennedy couldn't make out what was going on. It took all her focus to try to pry herself away from Roger's clutches.

"Get over here," he growled.

She lunged forward. He grabbed her by the waist. She brought her leg up, tried to kick, and missed. He was standing behind her now, taller than she was. Stronger, but she wasn't about to give up. Not without the fight of her life.

He wrapped his arms around her from behind. She snapped her head back and crashed her skull against him as hard as she could. She didn't know if she hit him in the chin or the cheek or the nose, but he swore and let go. She lunged toward the fire poker.

"I don't think so," he snarled.

There was no room to run. By the door, Willow was struggling with Buster. Even if Kennedy got herself free from Roger, there was nowhere to escape.

She thought about all that beer. Maybe they'd be too tired to fight for long. Maybe that had been Willow's plan all along. Kennedy recalled that still, small voice from just a minute earlier.

Trust me.

Ok, God, she answered back, *I'll start trusting you the minute you get us out of here.*

Roger grabbed her sweater and was trying to tear it off. Kennedy was using everything she could think of — fingernails, fists, feet. From somewhere behind her, Willow yelped in pain.

God, get us out of here.

A rumbling. It started low and came from the ground, as if something buried far beneath the cabin floor was awakening for the first time.

Angry.

It was the distraction she needed. She grabbed the poker and when Roger lunged toward her, she swung it at his head. She hadn't meant to hit so hard. Hadn't meant to do any real damage. She just wanted him to leave her alone. He crumpled to the ground. Kennedy stared and realized the fight had made her completely dizzy. She could hardly support her weight, as if the ground itself were rocking back and forth.

And what was that loud noise?

"Earthquake!" Willow grabbed the metal bar out of Kennedy's hands and whacked Buster in his massive gut. He doubled over, still conscious, and Willow grabbed Kennedy's hand. "Let's go."

Buster was so large and the cabin so small Kennedy practically had to climb over him. Willow gave him one last hit in the back with the poker, enough to give the two girls the head start they'd need to escape.

Once outside, Kennedy stumbled in the snow. She looked up. Trees were swaying. Over the angry roar from the earth beneath her, she could hear tree trunks snapping as easily as if they were twigs.

"Watch out!" Willow dove at Kennedy and covered her body as a great spruce landed on the roof. Kennedy shrieked as the cabin folded in on itself like a house of collapsing cards.

"This way."

Kennedy could hardly make out Willow's words. She felt her pulse surging through her ears but could only hear the deafening roar. How long had it been going on already? The earth couldn't sustain that kind of violence much longer. Every single tree would collapse before it was over.

Kennedy screamed again when the ground beneath her bulged up several feet, throwing her and Willow down. Kennedy landed with her stomach on a tree stump. Where was all the air? She couldn't inhale. She was going to faint.

No, there it was. Her breath returned to her lungs in pitiful spasms. When would it end?

She'd been following Willow blindly but realized that they were running behind the cabin now. They were going the wrong way. She reached out to grab Willow's hand, but the ground heaved and she fell again.

Willow yanked her to her feet. "Hurry."

Kennedy looked over her shoulder. "The road's back there."

Willow shook her head and pointed. In the distance was another shed, even smaller than Roger's. How had Willow known it was there, and why were they heading deeper into the woods?

A spruce tree that must have been twenty or thirty feet tall whipped down, its bare branches slapping her in the face. She tried to shield her eyes. They were almost to the shed. Willow surged ahead and threw the door open.

Kennedy recognized her immediately. The girl from the photos, the missing barista. What was she doing back here? How had Willow known? She was curled in the corner, shielding her face.

"Brandy, it's ok. We've got to get you out of here." Willow knelt down beside her.

"I can't leave," she answered in a panic. "He'll find me."

Willow was fumbling with something by her hands. Was Brandy cuffed to the wall?

"The man who trapped you is buried under his house. It collapsed on him. You don't have any reason to be afraid anymore," Willow said as the floor rolled like ocean waves during a storm.

"I can't go. He'll be too angry."

"He's dead," Willow snapped. "Dead or close to it. And we will be too if we don't find someplace safe. Now how do we get you free?"

With wide eyes, Brandy nodded toward the wall. Kennedy grabbed the key hanging by the door but had to try several times to get it into the lock.

The cuffs fell loose.

"We've got to get out of here," Willow said. "This place will collapse any minute."

"He's going to find me," Brandy protested.

"No, he's not."

The ground was still shaking, but the rolling heaves had stopped, and they could hear more than just the angry bellows of the earth. The cabin creaked and groaned.

"Come on." Kennedy took Brandy by the hand, but she couldn't pull her up.

"I can't. I'm not ..."

When Kennedy bent down to slide her arm around her waist, she realized Brandy was pregnant. Very pregnant. She propped her up on one side, and Willow took the other.

"Can you walk?" Willow asked.

"I have to stay here," Brandy insisted. "He'll be angry."

Willow and Kennedy led her toward the door. "Let's go."

Everything stopped in an instant. At first, Kennedy thought she might have blacked out. As fast as the noise came, it was now completely silent. She was dizzy from being tossed and heaved around like a bath toy in white water rapids, but now it was only her brain that thought she was still moving.

Still inside the cabin, she looked over at Willow. "Is it over?" she asked.

"Might be for now." Willow led Brandy toward the door. "But we're definitely not out of the woods yet."

CHAPTER 11

AFTER WILLOW TOOK HER sweater off and wrapped it around Brandy's shoulders, the rescued girl returned to her spot against the wall where she drew her legs up toward her pregnant belly and cowered. Willow led Kennedy to the opposite side of the cabin so they could talk about what they should do.

"I don't see how those two drunk buffoons could have survived the cabin crashing in on them, but we can't be too careful either. I'm not sure any of us are in a position to walk back to the highway in this cold, and we have to be prepared for aftershocks. It's a miracle this little shack is still standing. I wouldn't want to assume we'll be so lucky next time."

Next time? Kennedy wondered why she'd ever come to Alaska. Why hadn't she listened to her dad? "What about the radio?" she asked. "Maybe we could try to signal for help."

Willow paused. "It's not a bad idea unless either Roger or his fat, smelly partner are awake and feeling vengeful."

Kennedy thought back to the way the cabin had toppled in on itself when the tree fell on the roof. Had either Roger or Buster survived? Did they dare find out? "It may be worth trying."

"You're probably right. That radio might be our best shot. Even if we get to the highway, it's not like there's going to be a ton of traffic going in or out at this time of night. And if there were rock slides or anything along the Glenn, we could be totally cut off for weeks."

Kennedy wouldn't think about that right now. The biggest priority was to stay warm for the night.

And keep from starving.

"We can get some of the canned food, too," she suggested.

Willow nodded then looked back at Brandy in her corner. "I don't think she's fit to go anywhere. Not right now. When the aftershocks come, we'll have to get her out of the cabin though. At least in the open we'll have a chance to dodge the trees if they fall. But if the cabin goes down ..." She left the thought unfinished.

Kennedy took in a deep breath. "You stay here. I'll go back to see if I can dig out the radio and get some food. Anything else we might need?"

"Our coats, and blankets if you can find them. And batteries and flashlights. Who knows how long we'll be stuck here?"

Kennedy knew the answer to that at least. One night. Exactly one night. A night that was nearly over. All they had to do was survive the cold for a few more hours, and then when the sun came up, they'd make their way with Brandy back to the Glenn Highway and find the help they needed.

One night. That's all this nightmare was allowed to turn into. Just one night.

Willow took off her heeled boot. "You can't go out in nothing but a sock."

Kennedy had been so terrified during her run through the woods she hadn't even noticed the way her toes were burning with cold. She slipped on Willow's boot. There was something she still didn't understand. "How did you know about this cabin back here anyway?"

"I noticed it in the moonlight when I stepped outside with Buster. That's where Roger was coming from after he left the house. I'd already seen Brandy's pictures in that box and figured that if she were still alive, this is where he'd be keeping her. And I knew Buster was a phony with that message about my goat. He'd never called my family. All right. Do you still have my phone? You can use it as a flashlight." Willow frowned. "Or maybe we should go together."

Kennedy glanced at Brandy. "I don't think we better leave her alone. This is no big deal. I'll just get a few things and come right back." She forced confidence into her voice even though she felt none.

Willow reached out and wrapped her in a hug. "You be careful now, you hear? And if either of those men are still alive ..." Her voice trailed off.

As Kennedy stepped out again into the now silent moonlight, she tried not to ask herself what it was that Willow had been about to say.

CHAPTER 12

THE NIGHT WAS NOW eerily quiet. No breeze. No rustling of leaves. No indication that just minutes earlier, the entire woods had threatened to collapse in on itself like Roger's rickety log cabin.

Kennedy knew where to go. She told herself that each time she second-guessed her footing and wondered if she was following the right trail. It felt like she and Willow had run a mile during the earthquake, but if Willow had spotted the cabin from Roger's place, it couldn't be nearly that far.

She wouldn't get lost.

Shining Willow's cellphone flashlight in one direction and then another, Kennedy thought back to all the wild animals that might live out here in the Alaskan wilderness. Polar bears weren't this low beneath the arctic circle, were they? No, if this part of the state was known for its polar bears, Willow would have mentioned it sooner.

What about other kinds of bear, though? Hopefully anything out here would be deep in hibernation, but what creature could have slept through an earthquake like that? Kennedy was still dizzy, still trying to walk on shaky ground. It reminded her of the way she felt as a kid coming home after a full day at the waterslide park. She'd lie in bed, and her faulty proprioception would make her still feel like she was being tossed from side to side.

Faint moonlight shone on the debris from the cabin. Kennedy couldn't tell if she was trembling from cold or fear.

Get in, find the radio, get out. That's all she had to do. The radio, their coats, and a few cans of food. Hopefully something with a hint of nutrition. She could picture Willow starving before agreeing to taste spam.

After trying it earlier that night, Kennedy couldn't blame her.

She held her breath as she stepped onto the first creaky log of what used to be Roger's cabin. Half expecting his hand to reach out and grab her, she shined the flashlight all around, on the lookout for any sign of life. She wasn't sure which she was more terrified to discover — that the men who had attacked her and Willow were alive or that they weren't.

Beneath her, wood splintered loudly with each step she took. She scanned the debris. Where was the radio? She walked toward where she thought that shelf had been. What if the radio, their only connection to civilization, hadn't survive the quake?

No, she wouldn't panic. Not yet. It wasn't like they were in some remote island in a developing nation. This was the United States, with FEMA and all those other organizations meant to assist in situations like this. And wasn't the national guard involved too? Help would come. Kennedy would find their coats and the radio and anything else they'd need to make it through the night, and first thing tomorrow morning they'd be rescued.

They had to be.

CHAPTER 13

THERE. THANK GOD.

Buried beneath several cans of spam and layers of debris was the radio. Kennedy couldn't believe it was still intact. By the time she pried it out of the wreckage, the tops of both her hands were bleeding. She wasn't sure if that was from splinters in the wood or if her skin was just cracking away from the cold.

It didn't matter. They had their radio, their lifeline to rescue.

After finding their coats, she gave a little half-hearted hunt for spare batteries but soon gave up. Her hands hurt so much she realized she couldn't hold anything else in them anyway.

A bag. That's what she needed. Or some kind of blanket to use as a knapsack she could sling over her shoulder.

How cold was it out here? Negative what? And how long could she survive in this kind of temperature?

No, she couldn't be that pessimistic. She just had to keep moving. Keep moving and make it back to the little shed before her nose turned black and her fingers got frostbite. What if she needed her toes amputated?

Leave it to her overactive imagination to induce a major panic.

She wouldn't think this way. Her anxiety was behind her now. It was ...

She dropped to her knees at the sound of the first roar. She heard it before she felt any movement beneath her. Not again ...

It's just an aftershock, she told herself. *Just an aftershock ...*

She glanced up, hoping that if any trees decided to land here she'd be quick enough to move out of the way. Her limbs were rigid, nearly stiff with cold. She didn't try to stand up or run when the earth began to shake. She would have to ride it out.

Just an aftershock ...

There. It was over. That wasn't so bad. A person could get used to just about anything. Kennedy would get used to this too if she had to. But of course, this was only temporary. Just for the night. Maybe not even that long. Now that she had the radio, help was guaranteed.

Ok. She had her coat on. Before long, it'd start warming her up instead of stealing her body heat. She had the radio and some food. There was no way to carry everything, not with her hands balled up in her sleeves like they were. She shoved a few of the smaller cans into her pockets and figured she could come back for more if she really needed to.

Which she wouldn't because first thing in the morning — or sooner — they were getting rescued.

As much as she loved her roommate, she vowed to never visit Alaska again.

She was mustering the energy to start the cold journey back to Willow and Brandy when the second aftershock hit. This one was more intense. The ground didn't roll like it had in the initial quake, but it shook violently, like a dog thrashing its head from side to side while annihilating a chew toy.

The radio fell out of Kennedy's hands into a pile of rubble. She fell to her knees, praying it hadn't broken. The light caught on something. She screamed when she realized she was inches from Buster's fat, blotchy face. She scrambled back as the aftershock died down. Catching her breath, she kept her distance but shined the light toward him, looking for any signs of breath or life.

Nothing.

She wouldn't think about it. If she stopped to let reality sink in, she'd be too scared, too frozen to make it back to Willow and Brandy, who needed her. Brandy most of all. What had that poor thing lived through? And she was pregnant now. Kennedy didn't know much about childbirth, but she certainly could tell the difference between a baby bump and a swollen abdomen the size of a beach ball.

She had to get up. Had to forget about what she was leaving behind and return to Brandy with the food and the radio.

One step at a time. That's how she would get back. One faulty, unsteady step thanks to the uneven ground and Willow's ridiculous heel. She just had to ignore the fact that her feet were as cold as Buster's body beneath the rubble. Forget about the trauma she'd already endured. Survival meant pressing onward. There was no other way.

She just had to keep moving.

Couldn't stop ...

Why did it feel like the walk back to the cabin was taking so much longer? It's not like the radio was that heavy. The skin on the tops of her hands stung with cold and pain, but she wasn't so much of a wimp that a few cuts and scratches could slow her down.

Why was she so sluggish?

She wanted to rest, but knew she had to go on. It was too hard to hold Willow's cell phone while stumbling without exposing her hands to further cold, so she was relying on the light of the moon and nothing else. Maybe that's why it felt even creepier now.

Spookier.

Like the calm before a storm.

The only problem was Kennedy didn't know what disaster she was waiting for. Another aftershock? As long as they weren't any worse than the previous two, she'd be fine. They were terrifying reminders of the trauma of that first quake, but nothing that would put her in serious physical danger.

So why was she so nervous? Because she'd been attacked earlier? Because of what might have happened if she and Willow hadn't escaped those two drunk men? If that tree hadn't toppled down on Roger's cabin and freed them?

Wait a minute. That was it. Kennedy stopped.

Looked behind her.

Strained her ears in the nighttime silence.

She'd dug thoroughly around the wreckage hunting for that radio. She'd found Buster's body, but that was all.

So where was Roger?

CHAPTER 14

HER MIND WAS PLAYING tricks on her. That was it. Like kids who purposefully freak each other out telling ghost stories at summer camp until they can't go to sleep all night. It was all in her imagination. She was doing this to herself.

The reason she didn't find Roger was because he was buried so deeply in the debris. The reason he was buried so deeply was because he was a deplorable human being who had finally met God's judgment. Simple as that. She had no reason to be afraid. He was a nightmare, and that was all.

He didn't exist anymore.

Kennedy couldn't see the shed in the moonlight, but she knew she must be getting close. Just a few more minutes, and she'd be inside. Together again with Willow and Brandy, and before long, this entire vacation would be nothing but a terrible memory.

Just like Roger was.

Something sounded behind her. She refused to look. Refused to give in to her childish fears.

There it was again. A footstep?

No. It was nothing more harmful than a squirrel. Did they have squirrels in Alaska? Whatever it was, it couldn't hurt her. It wouldn't ...

"Get back here, girl."

Kennedy lunged ahead as if a few extra inches could save her from Roger's grasp.

His fingers grazed the back of her coat, but he couldn't hold on.

She surged forward, no longer aware of the cold but only of the burning in her lungs and the terror in her psyche.

A dream. A hallucination. She wished it were something that innocuous but knew from the pain as tree branches whipped across her face that she was stuck here in reality.

She had no other thought but to get to safety. Screaming now, as if the extra exertion could somehow lend her more energy.

Someone was standing in the doorway of the shed. Was Willow waiting for her?

She didn't know what else to do but run. That was her only plan. Into the shed. If Willow was there, if she saw what was happening, maybe they'd find a way to barricade themselves in.

Closer now. She was shouting warnings, at least she thought they were warnings. Her brain was so focused on escape she wasn't even sure what she was saying. She just had to trust that Willow ...

Except it wasn't Willow in the doorway. It was Brandy. Her huge swell of a belly protruded out in front of her. She stood with one hand behind her back looking peaceful and serene.

"Out of the way!" Kennedy tried to yell. Had the poor girl lost her mind? Had her imprisonment driven her insane?

Kennedy raced past the threshold of the cabin, nearly plowing into Willow, who was waiting for her with outspread arms. She tried to pull Brandy inside, but Willow held her back. "Wait."

Roger stopped a few paces away from Brandy. "What are you doing off your wall, girl? Did I tell you to come outside?"

"I got scared. I was waiting for you. I thought something bad might have happened."

"Something bad will happen all right if you don't get back on that wall," he snarled.

Kennedy sank into the shadows but kept her mind focused and alert in case Brandy needed her help. Roger was drunk and couldn't have gotten out of that wreckage uninjured. The three of them could fight him off. They would find a way.

"Come on." Roger's voice was calmer now. Steadier. He took Brandy by the hand and led her as if she were a child to her chains. "You know this is for your own protection," he crooned.

"Yeah," she answered submissively. "I know. But before I go back on the wall, will you hold me for a minute? I got really scared.

I thought you were hurt. Those two girls told me your cabin was destroyed."

He scoffed quietly. "They're just jealous. That's what. You don't pay them any mind, ok? You know I love you most. I always have, and I always will."

He wrapped his arms around her.

Kennedy glanced at Willow, wondering what they were doing waiting here in the shadows. If a pregnant girl wanted to allow herself to get chained back up on a wall in a shed that might collapse at the slightest hint of another aftershock, was there anything Kennedy or Willow could do?

"Hold me," Brandy pleaded. Her voice was so small, Kennedy thought she sounded more like a ten- or eleven-year-old than a grown woman. Pity gripped her soul and held her feet in place even while her brain begged her to run. She watched sadly while Roger held Brandy, murmuring kind words into her ear.

"You're so sweet," she said, but something in her voice had changed. Roger must have noticed it too. He pulled away as Brandy reached into his back pocket.

"This is for what you did to me." Brandy plunged his knife into his abdomen, pulled it back out, and hacked again.

CHAPTER 15

KENNEDY DIDN'T MOVE. JUST stood watching Roger's crumpled, bloody corpse and Brandy's expressionless face as she stared down at him.

Giving him a little nudge with her foot, Brandy asked, "Roger? You ok?" Her voice was sweet and childish again. "Roger?" She knelt down beside him. "I'm sorry. I didn't mean it."

Willow stepped forward and wrapped an arm around her.

Brandy jumped back. "Get away from me. You're the one who made me do this."

Willow didn't move. "It's all right, sweetie. You're safe now."

"I was safe with him," Brandy cried. "Look what you did." She stared at the body and recoiled as if she were seeing it for the first time. "Look what you did to him. You hurt him."

She pummeled Willow with her fists, but they landed soft. Willow wrapped her in a hug. "Don't worry. Everything's going to be all right. We're all safe now. We're all ..."

Another low grumble from the pit of the earth. Kennedy couldn't keep her balance and fell to her knees.

"We've got to get out of here," Willow called out.

"I'm not leaving him!" Brandy clung to Roger's dead body. Kennedy and Willow had to exert all their strength to pry her away from the bloody corpse.

Outside the shed, Kennedy hoped this would be another small tremor, but the back and forth motion of the earth quickly morphed into the familiar undulating. Brandy shrieked when a tree branch whipped in front of her. Willow kept her arms wrapped around her protectively. Kennedy just tried to keep her balance.

"How long is this going to last?" Brandy shrieked.

Willow stood there stroking her hair while Kennedy worried all the movement was going to make her sick.

Willow was running before Kennedy could realize what the danger was. "Move it!" she shouted. "Hurry."

Kennedy blindly obeyed as her ears were deafened by a new sound, no longer the low rumbling but a deadly, angry cracking.

Brandy shrieked as the snow in front of them shifted. "Hurry," Willow ordered, nearly dragging Brandy with her. The shed in front of them tossed from one side to the other as the snow around it collapsed in on itself.

"It's caving in," Willow shouted, still urging everyone further away from the crevice that was forming in front of their eyes.

"No! I can't leave him there!" Brandy turned around, and Willow and Kennedy both grabbed her arms before she toppled down the ravine that was swallowing trees and snow and everything else in its path.

"Roger!" Brandy shrieked as the cabin collapsed into darkness.

Kennedy and Willow dragged her away from the edge of what was now a cliff. It was too dark to tell how far down it went. Twenty feet? A hundred?

Brandy screamed and struggled free from Kennedy's arms. "I have to help him!"

"No, stay here," Kennedy shouted, but her voice was drowned out by the roaring earth. She lunged forward and grabbed Brandy's leg in time to stop her from jumping into the crevasse. Kennedy felt her own body starting to slip and knew she couldn't hold on for long. "Help!"

The earth gave one last defiant toss and then stopped. Kennedy's hands burned as she tried to keep her hold on Brandy. "Help!" she repeated.

Brandy wasn't struggling. Was she all right?

Willow knelt beside her and grabbed Brandy by the hips. Straining together, they brought her back to the surface. Willow shined her light down the fissure, shaking her head. "Dude."

The crack that had opened in the earth and swallowed the cabin was at least as deep as the tallest trees.

"Dude," Willow repeated.

Brandy was crying quietly. Willow wrapped her arms around her. "We've got to find her someplace warm."

Kennedy didn't want to be the one to point out that they were miles from the road and hours from daylight. Neither of Roger's cabins had survived the earthquake and aftershocks. Where was there to go?

"What about the truck?" Willow suggested. "If we can get it running, we can turn up the heater and make it until morning."

Kennedy was thankful for some kind of plan. "Good idea. Then we can radio for ..." She stopped herself and looked down at the gaping scar in the earth where the cabin, along with the radio, now lay in heaps of rubble. "Never mind."

Willow rubbed her back. "Don't worry. We just need to focus on warming up for a little longer. When the sun comes up, we'll make our way to the road. It's going to be just fine."

Kennedy nodded. They could do this.

Willow took Brandy by the arm. "Come on. Let's get you up out of the snow. Can you walk? We'll see if we can warm up in Roger's truck."

Brandy didn't respond. She had stopped weeping and was staring down at herself in wide-eyed bewilderment.

"What is it?" Willow's voice was full of compassion. "What's wrong?"

Brandy blinked once and continued to gaze at her lap.

"I think my water just broke."

CHAPTER 16

IT WAS OFFICIAL. KENNEDY was freaking out.

"We can't deliver a baby out here in the dark in the middle of nowhere!"

Willow tried to shush her. "Of course we can't. That's why we're going to take her to Roger's truck and get her warm."

"How do you expect to get her there? We can't carry her that far."

Willow raised her eyebrows. "You do know that women can walk while they're in labor, don't you? And that your water can break hours before you even start having contractions."

Kennedy didn't respond. When would she have ever learned that?

Willow wrapped her arm around Brandy. "Come on. The truck's not far. If we're lucky, we can drive you out of here. See how the roads are so we can get you some help. You're going to be just fine. Have you felt any contractions yet?"

"I'm not sure."

"It will be like cramps. Sometimes you only feel it in your back. And if you put your hand right here on your abdomen, it'll get hard. There, that's one now. Can you feel it?"

"A little."

"Good," Willow answered, although Kennedy couldn't dream up a single thing that was positive about their situation. Stuck in the middle of the woods, aftershocks destroying everything around them, and now they had a pregnant woman who was about to deliver a baby.

"We've got to get there fast," Willow was saying. "We don't want that amniotic fluid to freeze to your skin."

Kennedy didn't even want to know what that would look like and prayed they'd get to the truck on time. God had protected them this far. He'd just have to keep on watching out for them because Kennedy knew there was no way they could survive all the way until daybreak on their own.

By the time they got to Roger's vehicle, Brandy's pants were frozen stiff.

"I was afraid of that," Willow said and shined her flashlight around. A tree trunk had fallen across the back of the truck bed, and another one had flattened a four-wheeler that must have belonged to Buster. "Looks like we won't be driving out of here any time soon." She turned to Kennedy. "Can you look around for any blankets? I'll see if we can at least get the heater running."

"What about the keys?" Kennedy asked.

Willow chuckled. "This is the Alaska wilderness. Everybody leaves their keys in the ignition or on the dashboard. See?" She held up a single key on a chain and started up the truck.

Kennedy turned toward the cabin, feeling awkward on her uneven shoes. It wasn't until then she realized Willow was wearing nothing but her sock. "Your foot," she exclaimed. "I never gave you your boot back."

"Don't worry about it." Willow's face was drawn taut. "We were little busy back there."

"Yeah, but what about frostbite?"

Willow was coaxing Brandy out of her pants. "Worry about that later. Now go get some blankets. Please?" she added as an afterthought.

Kennedy remembered where Buster's body lay and made a wide circle to avoid him. She found the blankets without too much trouble and grabbed a few cans of spam, too.

"Any luck?" Willow asked when Kennedy returned.

"I got some blankets, but they're already frozen stiff. I don't know what good they'll do."

"Don't worry about that. Come in, and close the doors. I've got the heat running. Here. You sit on top of the blankets and get them warmed up for us."

It didn't seem like much, but Kennedy was thankful for something she could do to feel useful.

"Ok, the contractions aren't all that regular. It could be a while before anything starts to happen, and there's a good chance by then we'll have found some way to get help. Is this your first delivery?"

Brandy nodded. "Roger said he would take me to the hospital. He said everything would be ok."

"He's right. You're going to be fine," Willow assured her. "Kennedy, why don't you pray for us. Is that all right with you?" she asked Brandy.

Kennedy's rear end was freezing from sitting on top of the blankets, which could explain why she sounded so stubborn. "First, we need to look at your foot. You shouldn't have been running around in just your sock."

Willow shrugged. "Yeah, well, you don't always think things through when you're trying to stay alive."

Kennedy tried to think of something that might lighten the mood but couldn't. "Let's just take a look."

"I don't know what it is you're expecting to see." Willow stretched her leg across Brandy's lap and hoisted her foot onto Kennedy's knee. "Here it is. See? It's a foot."

Kennedy felt it. The sock was frozen stiff. "Should you take that off?"

"Go ahead. You're the one all worried."

Kennedy aimed the flashlight. "I don't know what I'm looking for," she confessed. Willow's toes were red, but other than that they looked just like toes. She wasn't sure what she was expecting. Tiny black stumps where the cold had already eaten away the flesh?

"See? I'm fine." Willow swung her leg back down and felt Brandy's midsection. "There comes another contraction. You tell me when they get real uncomfortable."

Kennedy still wasn't ready to ignore Willow. "Shouldn't you wrap it or something so it gets warm now?"

"Probably."

Kennedy took Willow's boot off her own foot.

"Here. Put this back on. I don't need it anymore."

Willow sighed. "Fine. But I'm only doing it so you stop worrying about me."

As if Kennedy would ever stop worrying at a time like this.

She hugged her arms around her, wondering how long it would take for the truck to heat up, wondering how long the night would last, wondering what they would do if Brandy's baby decided it was ready to be born before help arrived.

CHAPTER 17

"WHAT TIME IS IT?" Kennedy rubbed her eyes. She hadn't meant to doze off, but she soon came to realize that childbirth was nothing like the movies where your water breaks and in minutes you're screaming and writhing in agony. With nothing better to do, she had leaned up against the window and let exhaustion overtake her.

Willow swept some hair off Brandy's sweaty brow. "Almost eight. You were out forever. I'm glad you got that sleep. You really needed it."

Kennedy felt guilty for not being more useful. "How are things going? Is she doing ok?"

Willow smiled faintly. "You can ask yourself, you know. It's just labor. It's not like she can't talk."

Kennedy felt herself blush. "Ok, how are you feeling?"

Brandy winced. "Contractions are starting to hurt now."

"She's in the transition stage," Willow explained. "The good news is her body's figuring out what it needs to do just fine. I wouldn't be surprised if she'll start pushing soon."

"What? Don't we need to take her to the hospital?"

"First of all, the hospital wouldn't do anything for her but throw on a bunch of monitors and push an epidural that she doesn't need. But if we were in town and had access to a midwifery, then yes, we'd take her there, but did you see that tree? The entire back half of the truck is pinned down, and even if we found a way to lift it off, we wouldn't be able to get very far with the tail end dragging on the ground. Anyway, women have been delivering babies without men in white coats telling them how to do it for millennia. So what I need you to do is promise me that you won't freak out, and if I ask for your help, you just have to tell yourself to get over any nerves or squeamishness or anything else, buckle down, and do what I say. Got that?"

Kennedy swallowed down a wave of nausea and nodded.

Willow held her gaze. "I'm dead serious. You don't freak out on me, and you do exactly what I need you to do when I need you to do it. Have you ever seen a live birth before?"

Kennedy was sure that whatever blood she'd had left in her brain had rushed to her feet by now.

Willow shook her head. "Never mind. Just remember, when you're a doctor, you'll have to do all kinds of more stressful things than this. So here's your crash course. Ready? And you listen too, Brandy, because I think your time's coming up. When it feels like you need to push, that's your body telling you what to do. Kennedy and I are going to do our best to keep you squatting over the seat. You put your forearms here like this, and one leg on my knee and one leg on Kennedy's knee, and that way you'll have gravity on your side. When the urge comes, it'll feel like you're making a really big poop. I'm not going to try to put it in any nicer language than that. You're going to feel like you're forcing out a ten-pound piece of poop. You've probably seen in the movies where the mother screams and yells and thrashes around wasting all her energy, but that's not what you're going to do. You're going to stay nice and quiet and focus all your strength on bearing down. Not yet. Your body's not quite ready, but it will be soon, and when that happens, you just let us know, and Kennedy and I'll be here ready to help you. You can do this, right?"

Brandy's voice was choppy. "Do I have a choice?"

"No, you don't. But don't worry about that. Your body knows just what it needs to do. Kennedy, you ready? I want you to sit right there, and, Brandy, you put your knee on top of hers so it will sort of be like you're squatting. In between contractions, you just sit back down on the seat and try to get some rest. Are you doing ok? Are you warm enough?"

"I think I have to pee."

"That's totally normal," Willow said. "Here, Kennedy, hand me that coffee cup."

Kennedy was trying to convince herself that now would be no time to faint. Willow was right about one thing. As a doctor, she'd have to help people in all kinds of situations just like this, except she'd always planned to do it in a warm, sterile hospital room, with clean clothes, gloves, and plenty of nurses to assist.

"I think it's starting." Brandy's voice was tense.

"Just lean up here." Willow helped her rest her forearms on the dashboard. "Lean up here and when the contractions come, we're going to lift you up off the seat a little bit, and you follow your body's cues. This is going to be just fine. Kennedy, why don't you pray for us?"

It wasn't until then that Kennedy detected the hint of fear in Willow's voice. She would never get over how good of an actor her roommate could be.

Praying out loud would at least focus her attention on something besides the sweating, laboring woman squatting on her leg. "Dear God, thank you that you're always with us. Thank you that you've kept us safe so far."

Kennedy wondered what else to say. Her breath was choppy, and she hoped that it wasn't an indication that she was about to have a panic attack. She remembered what Willow said. She'd be in lots of situations even more stressful than this as a doctor, and she'd have to stay rational. Have to keep her brain from shutting down.

"Lord, please help Brandy's baby to be just fine. Help everything to go really smoothly. Help her to not be in too much pain."

Kennedy had to pause every few sentences and think about what she wanted to pray for next, but she always found something. After praying about everything she could think of for Brandy and the baby, she prayed for Willow and then for Nick and then for all of Willow's family in Copper Lake, and before she knew it she was praying for anybody who might have been injured in last night's earthquake.

She didn't stop there, either. She prayed for the whole state of Alaska. Right about the time she began praying for her parents and their ministry to North Korean refugees living in China, Willow interrupted with a loud, "This is it. Kennedy, get ready."

Kennedy didn't know exactly what she was supposed to be getting ready for, but she immediately stopped talking and held her breath.

"Come on, Brandy," Willow coaxed. "One or two more pushes and it will all be over."

Over? What was Willow saying? Was Brandy's baby really about to ...

Brandy let out a loud grunt, Willow reached her hands down between her legs, and just as Kennedy felt sure she was going to pass out, a sound like a cat meowing snapped her out of her near panic.

"Here she is," Willow crooned. "She's absolutely perfect." Her tone switched from gushing to demanding. "Kennedy, the blanket."

She handed Willow the blanket, thankful her brain was still in control of her body.

The baby cried faintly while Willow sang out, "Are you cold, little sweetie? Here. I'm just going to wrap you up like this, and then we'll let your mama keep you nice and warm. What a good baby. You did such a good job being born."

Kennedy wasn't sure if Willow had said something funny or if she was just disoriented from the stress, but she sensed now would not be an appropriate time to laugh and clenched her jaw shut.

"You did so well," Willow told Brandy. "Your baby is so proud of you. Look how she's watching you. Do you know what you're going to name her?"

"I was thinking something like Rylee."

"That's a pretty name." Willow leaned down and sang out in a high-pitched voice, "Hi, little Rylee. Hi, sweet baby." She looked again at Brandy. "You can go ahead and talk to her. She knows your voice."

"I don't know what to say."

"Tell her what a good baby she is. Tell her what a good job she did. Tell her anything that's on your mind."

Brandy leaned over her newborn, nuzzled her cheek, and whispered, "Your daddy will be so excited to meet you."

CHAPTER 18

BRANDY WAS EXHAUSTED AND fell asleep with Rylee on her chest almost immediately after delivering the placenta.

"What happens now?" Kennedy asked.

"When they wake up, it will be important to get Brandy nursing, but other than that, I think we're just fine."

"I was talking more about everything. The truck, the earthquake. How much longer before daylight?"

Willow chuckled. "Daylight's already here, Miss Observant. Sun came up about half an hour ago."

Kennedy looked out the truck window. "Oh."

"But in answer to your first question, I don't think Brandy can walk all the way to the highway after what she's gone through. That probably means one of us should stay here and one of us should head toward the Glenn to see if there's any way to get help."

"I can do that."

"I think you'll have to." Willow smiled. "Unless you've become an expert at breast-feeding and are ready to give Brandy and her baby a crash course."

"No, you stay here. But how do you know so much about all this anyway, delivering babies and nursing and everything else?"

Willow shrugged. "I've always been there when the goats and sheep are born. Usually, everything goes just fine, but sometimes you have to step in and help. Plus my mom's coached a few women around Glennallen who wanted to have home births. The clinic there won't deliver babies, so if you get pregnant, you either have to spend the last two or three weeks of pregnancy in town so you'll be close to medical care, or you plan on a home birth. Mom took me to a few of them when I was a teenager. Ninety percent of it is just keeping the moms from freaking out." She grinned. "And keeping your assistant from freaking out, too."

"Yeah, I'm sorry I wasn't better help."

"Don't say that. You did great. Who would have thought that a crazy, Type-A germaphobe like you could have handled a delivery in a truck without completely losing your head? You should be really proud of yourself."

Kennedy wasn't sure if she was being complimented or insulted and changed the subject. "How's your foot?"

Willow shrugged. "I'm fine. Here, you take the boot back. And take my coat on top of yours. You'll need it more than I do. I'll have to turn the truck off for now. We're running kind of low on gas. You know how to get back to the highway from here? You just follow the tire tracks in the snow."

Kennedy nodded. If her roommate could safely deliver a child in the middle of nowhere, Kennedy could walk a few miles without getting lost.

"So you sure you don't mind heading out alone?" Willow asked. "It will be kind of long you know. You should eat before you go."

"I'll grab something from the cabin, or at least what's left of it."

Willow shook her head. "All that will be frozen. Didn't you bring a few things back into the truck last night?"

"Yeah, I think there's a can of spam around here somewhere."

Willow grinned. "Bon appétit. And even if it's totally gross, you'll need the calories to stay warm. You probably don't have to worry about it, but you know the basics about hypothermia, right? You'll go from just shivering and cold to really exhausted. At that point, it messes with your brain. It will make you want to just sit down and sleep, and you'll tell yourself it will only be for a few minutes, but you've got to make yourself keep going, right?"

Kennedy couldn't believe she was actually getting a crash course in hypothermia in the middle of the Alaskan wilderness.

Willow gave her a reassuring smile. "Don't worry. You'll be fine. You can follow the tire tracks so you won't get lost, and you won't have to worry about going through the deep snow. Hey, you ok? You look like you're about to cry."

Kennedy shook her head. "This wasn't how I expected to be spending the day before your wedding."

Willow sighed. "Yeah, you and me both."

CHAPTER 19

KENNEDY TOOK A DEEP breath. She could do it. Her job was easy. Just follow the tire tracks to the Glenn Highway and signal for help. She didn't think about what she'd do if the roads were deserted. Maybe even impassable. God hadn't spared them from Roger's murderous rage and ensured Brandy's safe delivery in order to desert them now.

Help would be there.

It had to be.

The tire tracks made an easy path through the snow. Kennedy was glad she didn't have to wrestle her way through the two- or three-foot drifts. A few times, she came across a tree that had crashed along the path, but otherwise the woods appeared completely normal.

If you could call anything about watching the sun coming up at 10:45 in the morning normal.

She tried to remember how long they'd driven last night. After hitting the moose, she thought making it all the way to Roger's cabin would be the hard part. So much had happened since then. Was it really less than twelve hours ago?

She started to pray, thanking God for keeping them safe, but her thoughts were distracted. Wondering what would have happened to her and Willow if the earthquake hadn't saved them from their assailants. Remembering the way Brandy had rushed at Roger and then thrown herself on his corpse. Kennedy had never seen anyone sound so grief-stricken. So remorseful.

But if Brandy hadn't attacked Roger ...

It was silly to dwell on what hadn't happened. It wouldn't help her get to the Glenn more quickly.

She and Willow were supposed to be waking up in a nice heated Anchorage hotel and starting their five-hour drive to Copper Lake. Not battling insane attackers or delivering babies in negative temperatures.

She kept her fists balled up in her sleeves and cursed Willow's stupid boot. Did her roommate own any foot apparel with less than a three-inch heel?

Well, it was better than nothing. Besides, if it hadn't been for Willow stepping up last night and taking control, Kennedy didn't want to imagine what could have happened to her, Brandy, or the baby.

She wondered how badly the earthquake had hit the surrounding regions. With Anchorage reeling from the volcano, would the earthquake confirm people's fears that the world really was about to end? What about those riots her dad was so afraid of?

What would happen to Willow's wedding plans? Even if Kennedy found help, was the highway passable? What if they couldn't get back to the Winters' home? What about the wedding? With the earthquake as bad as it had been, was Copper Lake even standing anymore?

She wished she could check the news on her phone. She hadn't realized until now how accustomed she'd grown to having access to the internet all hours of the day. But even if she had her cell right now, there wouldn't be any reception. No way to signal for help or find out how badly the rest of the state was hit.

The only thing to do was go forward. Keep pressing on. She knew if she stopped to think, she could come up with one or two highly effective Bible verses. Metaphors comparing this trek of hers through the cold and the snow to the Christian walk of faith. But she didn't have time to stop and think.

She had to keep moving.

Her whole body was trembling. Even with Willow's extra coat, she wasn't prepared for a five-mile hike through the woods in temperatures like this.

How could Willow have grown up in this state and survived?

She thought about Brandy, wondered what she must have suffered from the time of her kidnapping until now. Would she ever recover from that trauma? There had been something so primal, so animalistic about the way she threw herself on Roger's body. It was easier to think of her as some nameless character, an animal in a cage, than a human being. A human being who'd once had dreams and joys and hopes for her life.

What had Roger done to her?

And what would it take to bring the real Brandy back up to the surface?

God, she's been through so much ... It wasn't fair. How could Kennedy try to wrap her mind around it? God could have kept Brandy from getting kidnapped. How hard could that have been? There would have been hundreds of opportunities. Let Brandy develop a cough. Make the coffee stand close down early that night because they ran out of espresso beans. Give a few other strong, hardy, and well-armed Alaskans the urge to get coffee or late-night snacks at the same time Roger was planning to abduct her.

Better yet, he could have thrown a moose in the path of Roger's car to keep him from getting to Brandy in the first place. Or stopped him a dozen other ways. Kept him off whatever trajectory turned him into the kind of psychopath who would go around kidnapping girls and handcuffing them to the walls of abandoned cabins out in the middle of the woods.

He could have made it so that Roger was never born.

An infinite number of possibilities — all of them preventing Brandy's abduction. Where would she be now? Preparing to marry the love of her life? About to graduate college? Working her way up the corporate ladder to land herself the career she'd always dreamed of?

It wasn't right. No matter how Kennedy looked at it, nothing was right. God could have stopped Roger. He was strong enough.

So why didn't he?

And what about Brandy's baby? Innocent little Rylee. What had she ever done to deserve being born in such squalid, terrifying conditions? If God loved all people equally — and who could read the Bible and come away believing anything else? — why did he

ALANA TERRY

allow some people to suffer such unthinkable trials and others to live relatively pain-free lives?

She was too cold to come to any real conclusions but figured the questions would still baffle her if she were relaxing in a steaming hot sauna. Some things would probably never make sense, but she wouldn't stop trying to figure them out nonetheless. Somewhere there had to be answers, and even if she never came up with a satisfactory explanation for life's injustices, at the very least she could work to try to alleviate them.

It was an overwhelming task to consider. How many other girls like Brandy were living victim to the whims of villains and sociopaths? How many were caught in the clutches of prostitution and sex slavery? It was so easy to think of things like that happening in other parts of the world, but here was an unforgettable reminder of the kind of suffering that happened regularly in her own country.

Was there any place safe left on the earth?

She thought about a conversation she'd listened to one morning around the dining room table with her pastor and his family. Sandy was reading from one of their devotional books and came across a quote. *The safest place you can be is in the center of God's will.*

Pastor Carl scoffed. "Yeah. Tell that to the Christians who are imprisoned in North Korea for their faith. Or the evangelists getting beheaded in the Middle East."

Sandy was quick to show her disappointment. "I think what it's saying, love, is that when we're doing what God has called us to do, we can trust him to watch out for us and protect us."

"Except for when he doesn't," Carl added dryly.

Sandy rolled her eyes and leaned over toward Kennedy. "You have to forgive him, sweetie. He's been getting mood swings ever since he had that accident."

"It's not a mood swing," Carl insisted. "It's the simple truth. *Everyone who wants to live a godly life in Christ Jesus will be persecuted.* Second Timothy 3:12. You don't get much more clear-cut than that."

Sandy frowned. "Well, of course there's persecution and suffering, but when a Christian is doing the will of the Lord ..."

"The Lord just might see fit to let them get fed to lions," Carl interrupted.

At that point, their son Woong, who previously had been absorbed in his food, jumped into the conversation. "Wow, fed to lions? Does that really happen, Dad? Do the lions eat them all up and then throw up their bones like an owl? Or do the bones go into the digestive tract and turn into poop? Do you think you could go to the zoo and look at lion poop and see if maybe they've fed a Christian to him or not?"

Carl and Sandy never finished their theological debate.

Kennedy still didn't know what to think of it. There were so many verses in the Bible that talked about God keeping his children safe, but nearly all of the original apostles and so many early Christians died in gruesome ways. Sawed in half, crucified upside down, burned at the stake ...

Kennedy shook her head. These certainly weren't the kinds of thoughts that made her trek through the woods any easier.

Find your happy place. That's what her counselor was always telling her to do to overcome her anxiety. Think about the things that made her feel truly safe and joyful. The problem was all her good memories from the past few years were tainted by the fear and trauma that went along with them.

Did Kennedy have a single happy memory that was untarnished by sadness or danger?

She thought about Willow's wedding. It was nearly all her roommate had talked about last semester. But what if something had happened to Nick? What if Willow's home had collapsed in the quake? No, she had to hold onto hope. It's what gave her strength to keep on putting one foot in front of the other. She reminded herself how deeply in love Willow and Nick were. How obvious it was that they were destined to marry.

And hoping that one day God would bring a soulmate into her life as well.

Preferably someone who wouldn't abandon her because he was HIV-positive or wouldn't die saving her from a crazy terrorist with a bomb.

Or a journalist who flew across to the other end of the world and didn't even think to send a text.

There she went again. She had probably kept happy images of Willow's wedding in her brain for all of twenty seconds before her mind wandered to her own unlucky love life. No wonder she was anxious all the time with that many negative thoughts.

So instead of trying to focus on joyful memories or hopeful dreams, she directed one foot in front of the other. That was the only way she'd keep from collapsing with cold and exhaustion.

She had to keep going.

Willow and Brandy and little baby Rylee were counting on her.

Time was passing, but the scenery looked exactly the same. She had to be getting closer to the highway now. There were no landmarks to back up her optimism, but she couldn't make it much farther. Not with her toes stinging like she'd stepped on fire and her gait still unsteady because of her roommate's stupid heeled boot. Even with her hands tucked up into the seams of her coat, the tops cracked open, and the blood froze immediately to her skin. Something rattled in her sinuses every time she inhaled so she wasn't sure if she was breathing through frozen boogers or if her snot had literally turned to ice.

Rest. Just a few minutes. Two or three at most. How long had she been out here anyway? The sun was so low on the horizon it was impossible to guess the time. It had been just after dawn when she started walking, but the sun was still so low it could be getting ready to set by now and she would have no way to tell the difference.

Keep walking. That's what she had to do. She couldn't stop.

She tried to think about what she'd do when she found warmth. There was a happy place. A hot shower — that was something she could imagine. That hope alone gave her strength to keep going.

And then came the shaking. Funny. She thought she had already been shivering, but it was nothing like this. She tried to wrap her coat more tightly against her, but her fingers had grown numb. She couldn't grasp anything.

The road turned right just a little bit ahead. She'd make it to that curve, and then she'd let herself rest.

But her legs wouldn't cooperate. How can you walk in uneven boots when your toes have lost their feeling? How can you keep pressing on when your body's shivering so hard you're panting from all the extra exertion? How can you force yourself into action when your brain's higher functions are shutting down with each passing step, each dropping degree?

And the road stretching so far ahead ...

Keep going, she told herself. *Don't stop moving.*

But her body wouldn't listen. She was still focusing on her happy place.

Hot showers. Steaming mugs of hot chocolate.

The snow was so soft. Soft and downy. A mattress and a pillow and a blanket all at the same time. Piles of blankets stacked three feet high.

That's what she needed.

She just had to stop and catch her breath.

Just a minute or two ...

CHAPTER 20

ROARING FIREPLACES.

Sandy's homemade cookies being pulled out of a piping-hot oven.

Electric blankets turned on high and piled on top of her.

Sunbathing on a Florida beach on vacation with her parents.

Hot. So hot.

Why was she wearing this coat? She had to get it off ...

"Kennedy!" She didn't want to wake up. Not yet. What was Willow doing here, ruining her perfect dream?

Come to think of it, what was Willow doing here at all?

"Kennedy," Willow snapped. She sounded mad. Kennedy should apologize. She hadn't meant to lie down in the snow.

Where were those cookies? The blankets?

"Wake up right now, and hold this baby while I try to get a fire going."

"There already is a fire," Kennedy mumbled. If she could just remember where she put it ...

"Come on, Sleeping Beauty. Snap yourself out of it and do it now. I'm not joking. I swear I'll slap you if you don't wake up and look at me. "

"I'm awake."

"Look at me," Willow demanded.

"Ok. Sheesh." Kennedy tried to say something about being bossy, but her words were garbled.

"I told you to open your eyes and look at me."

"I am looking at you."

"No you aren't. How many fingers am I holding up?"

"I don't know."

"Kennedy. Open your eyes. Wake up. You need to take the baby so I can make a fire."

"... Too hot for a fire."

Something bit her cheek. "Ow." Kennedy blinked.

Willow was staring, her hand still upraised. "You awake now?"

Kennedy nodded and rubbed her sore face. "I think so."

"You gonna be able to hold this baby?"

Every thought Kennedy tried to process had to make its way through a wall of Jell-O. "Why am I holding the baby?" She stared at the newborn Willow had placed in her arms. Rylee was wrapped in blankets so that only her nose and eyes were visible.

"Because if I don't make you a fire, you're going to want to go back to sleep, and no matter what happens, no matter how cold you feel, you've got to promise to stay awake. Promise?"

"I wasn't cold. I had blankets."

Willow ignored her and started making a pile of twigs and branches. "I found a box of matches back at the cabin. Just give me a minute or two and we'll get you warmed up, all right?"

Rylee yawned in her sleep. Kennedy started to giggle.

"What's so funny?" Willow sounded cross. Was she mad Kennedy hadn't made it to the highway?

"The baby made a face."

"Yeah, well just hold her tight. You guys need to warm each other up while I get this fire going."

Willow struck two or three different matches before the pile lit. "Here." She took Rylee, bundled up in all her blankets, and nudged Kennedy closer to the small flame.

"I don't feel it." Kennedy frowned.

"Yeah, you're probably already numb. It was stupid of me to send you out here by yourself."

"I never made it to the road. I'm sorry."

Willow shook her head. "Don't be. We'll get you warmed up, and then we'll go together."

Even though Kennedy's body couldn't feel the warmth from the fire, her brain began to slowly clear up, like a car's windshield with the defroster on. "Where's Brandy? Did you leave her back at the truck?"

Willow let out her breath. "A lot's happened while you were out here trying to nap in the snow. Brandy's dead."

CHAPTER 21

EVERY OUNCE OF MENTAL fog cleared away in an instant. Kennedy leaned in a little closer toward the flame. "Are you serious? What happened?"

Willow shifted Rylee over her shoulder. "She got freaked out by the last aftershock. I think something in her brain just snapped."

Kennedy frowned. "What aftershock?"

Willow stared at her. "You didn't feel it? How long were you asleep?"

"I don't know."

Willow shook her head. "You're really lucky I got here when I did. You know that, don't you?"

Kennedy wasn't thinking about her own health or safety. "So what happened with the aftershock?"

"Brandy jumped out of the truck. Set the baby down on the seat and made a run for the shed. You should have seen her go. I tried to stop her. I really thought I was going to get there soon enough, but she got to the edge of that cliff and just dove in. She was screaming for Roger the whole time." Willow shook her head. "I went after her. I know it was a stupid thing to do, leaving the baby alone in the truck like that, but I thought that maybe if I hurried I could get her to safety or something. But she was gone. Didn't survive the fall."

"How'd you get back out?" Kennedy asked.

I followed the fissure a little ways to where it wasn't so steep. Used the roots of a tree trunk to pull myself out."

Kennedy didn't know what to say.

"I would have gotten here sooner," Willow remarked, "but for as many times as I've seen my mom teach other women how to tie a sling, I couldn't for the life of me figure out how to make one for Rylee. Plus these shoes are huge."

Kennedy looked down and noticed Willow's boots for the first time. "Where'd you get those?"

Willow didn't meet her gaze. "They were Buster's. I know it's gross, but I needed something. Couldn't walk all the way down here in a sock."

Kennedy was ashamed that she hadn't even thought to ask about Willow. "I totally forgot about your foot. Are you ok? Should you take your shoe off so we can look at it?"

Willow shook her head. "I know what it's going to look like. You don't need to worry about me.

"But you might have ..."

"I'm fine. Hearty Alaskan chick, remember?" Willow smiled. "And I hate to say it, but we shouldn't stay here too long. We've used up over half of our daylight already, and I don't want to sound like I'm being melodramatic, but I don't think any of us are up to spending another night out here in the cold."

"I still say we should take a look at your foot to make sure that ..."

Willow shook her head. "We're getting really close to the Glenn. I still have some matches, so we can build ourselves another fire if we need to once we get there. Are you ready? No more naps?"

Kennedy tried to smile back. "No more naps."

Willow took in a deep breath and squared her shoulders. "All right. Let's get moving."

CHAPTER 22

KENNEDY WAS GRATEFUL TO have Willow by her side. Without her roommate's constant encouragement, she would have been tempted to lie down for another rest.

"How you doing?" Willow asked.

"Aside from freaking out about nearly dying in the cold, I'm great."

Willow smiled. "You don't need to worry. There's no way God's finished with you yet."

It was the same thing Pastor Carl said so many times about how certain he was that he wouldn't die until God had allowed him to complete the work he'd started here on earth. But how could anybody be so sure? How could you tell if God was finished with you or not? And where in the Bible did he promise not to allow people to die until they completed the tasks he had assigned them?

Kennedy didn't know. She was still trying to figure out how you could know what God's plan for your life actually was. Carl talked about certain mentors in his life suggesting that he had the gift of preaching. Willow and Nick spoke as if they'd known from nearly the first day they met that God wanted them to get married. They still hadn't solidified their post-wedding plans, but they were treating the next few months as a big adventure where God would lead them one step at a time.

Is that what he expected Kennedy to do, too? Was it possible that she'd wake up tomorrow morning and the Holy Spirit would tell her *I want you to be a missionary in Cambodia*, and all of a sudden she would be expected to drop out of school and forget everything she'd worked so hard to achieve?

Is that how God worked?

What about people who never received a clear calling from God in the first place? Was it just that they weren't listening? Was there one exact path every believer was supposed to take, and if they veered to the right or to the left just an inch, it would ruin their God-given destiny? If that were the case, how could any believer go forward with any life plans? Wouldn't you be constantly crippled with doubt? Paralyzed with fear that you might go the wrong direction?

Kennedy wished she knew. She hated not having a plan, which is why Harvard's early acceptance medical program had been such a good fit for her. She signed the papers the summer after her junior year of high school, and the next decade of her life was organized and arranged.

Then Harvard had rescinded their offer, only to reinstate it after threats of legal action. Months later, Kennedy still wasn't sure what she should do. After watching Willow deliver Rylee, recalling those waves of panic, she was beginning to wonder if she should go into medicine at all. What if the stress was too much to handle?

So much for her perfect laid-out future.

But maybe now wasn't the time to set out her ten-year plan. She was tired and cold and exhausted. Not to mention hungry. She was in no state to be thinking about anything clearly.

"I really hope Nick's ok," Willow said, breaking the silence. "I wish there was a way to jump online and find out how bad that earthquake was."

Kennedy didn't respond. If she wanted to keep up her strength and optimism, thinking about last night wasn't the way to do it.

"Kind of makes you wonder, doesn't it?" Willow asked.

"Wonder what?"

"You know. About all those end of the worlders and their pickets and pamphlets and things. Didn't they say earthquakes would be part of it?"

Kennedy shrugged. "I could run around naked on TV screaming that there's going to be a tornado in the Midwest, and at some point in the next year my prediction's going to come true, right?"

"Yeah, but why don't you prophesy with your clothes on like a normal nut-case?"

Kennedy let out a chuckle. "I'm just saying the whole thing's silly. Jesus says that when he comes back, nobody's going to be able to predict when it will happen."

"But he does say something about earthquakes, doesn't he?"

"Yeah, but there have been earthquakes at least since the time of Noah, right?"

"I don't know. Aren't you the Bible expert?"

"Hardly. But I do know that we're not supposed to get all freaked out when people tell us when or how the world's going to end. Only God knows that, and when it happens, there's nothing we can do to try to stop it."

"There's something that doesn't make sense though." Willow readjusted Rylee in her arms.

"What's that?"

"Well, Jesus says there's going to be wars and stuff, right? That it's going to get worse before it gets better."

Kennedy tried to remember if there was an actual verse about that. "Basically. That's what I've heard."

"So here's my question. Why do we bother at all? Why do we go on the mission field and risk our comfort and safety when things are destined to go to hell anyway, if you pardon the expression? Why do we work at ending slavery or pray for peace in the Middle East or march against poverty? If things have to get that bad before Jesus can come back, if they're going to get that bad no matter what, why don't we throw up our hands and stay in our safe little bubbles and hide our faces in the sand like good little fatalists? Nick's been talking about starting up a home for victims of sexual abuse and human trafficking, and after everything with Brandy, I could totally see myself jumping into that kind of ministry. But if the Bible tells us that the world's going to continue getting more and more wicked and violent anyway, why should we bother?"

Kennedy was embarrassed to admit that she'd never asked herself that question before. She had definitely grown more aware about the suffering and injustices around her than she'd been as a naïve little freshman, but had that information changed her? She always said she'd like to be involved in some kind of mission work when she became a doctor, even if it was only volunteering for short-term trips, but was that just a copout?

With so many people suffering right now, should she really wait another five and a half years or longer before she tried to help any of them?

She had the feeling that if her feet weren't so numb, if her hands weren't cracked open and bleeding from exposure, if her nose wasn't so cold that it felt like she was breathing through shaved ice, she might be able to offer Willow a more thoughtful response than, "That's a really good question."

Rylee let out a grunt in her sleep.

"Is she ok?" Kennedy had never been around a newborn before and had no idea what noises they were or weren't expected to make.

"The blankets are keeping her warm enough for now. I wish she'd wake up, though. I don't think it's a good sign that she hasn't acted the least bit hungry yet."

"How far do you think we are from the road?"

Willow sighed. "Let's just hope and pray we're close."

CHAPTER 23

KENNEDY WOULD HAVE NEVER guessed she could walk so fast given how exhausted and cold she was. Her lungs stung from panting, but all that exertion paid off. After rounding a corner, the Glenn Highway came into view.

"Thank you, God," Willow breathed.

Kennedy's sentiments exactly.

"We've got to find some place to warm Rylee up." Willow surged ahead.

Kennedy strained to keep up.

"Listen!" Willow called behind her. "There's a car coming. If we hurry, we'll make it."

Kennedy couldn't run. It wasn't possible. *Please God*, she prayed, *please tell the car to stop.*

"Hey!" Willow shouted at the passing vehicle. "Hey! Slow down. Wait!"

She reached the edge of the road as the sound died away. The car was gone before they'd even spotted it.

"Gobstoppers," Willow exclaimed.

Usually, Kennedy laughed at her roommate's creative choice in exclamations, but there was nothing humorous in this situation.

"Just a few seconds too late." Willow shook her head. "I've got to sit down."

Kennedy didn't argue. The girls plopped onto a snow drift on the side of the highway.

"Guess we should make another fire," Willow finally declared. "I swear I don't even have the energy. That car ..."

Kennedy let out her breath. She was still thinking about the speeding vehicle, too, their one chance of rescue.

"We can't stay here very long," Willow said. "It's too cold, and there's no telling when anyone else will make their way down here. We could go back down toward where we totaled the car, try to run the heater some, or we go the opposite direction and try to make our way to Eureka."

"How far away is that lodge they were talking about?" Kennedy asked. The idea of an actual heated room to sit down in, or a bed with blankets to pile on top of her, was almost too luxurious to fathom.

"From here? About fifteen miles. There's no way we'd get there by sundown, but maybe we'll run into someone on the way. Then again there's nothing to stop for between here and Eureka. Any cars coming or going that direction will come by here first anyway."

"So we wait?" Kennedy asked.

Willow frowned and felt Rylee's cheek. "We can't just sit here. I say we make a fire, get as warm as we can, then we go to where we crashed the car and pray the heater's working. I hate to say it, but that's probably our only option right now."

"Maybe someone else will come down this way," Kennedy added.

"You can always hope." Willow stood up. "All right. Can you hold her while I get another fire started? Just keep her as close to you as you can. And turn this way so your back's to the breeze. I'm not sure ..." She didn't finish her sentence. When Kennedy looked at Rylee's listless face, she was able to guess what Willow was thinking.

"A fire would be really good," Kennedy agreed.

Willow's voice fell flat. "It's our only hope.

CHAPTER 24

"Too bad we don't have any marshmallows," Willow chuckled once the fire was blazing.

Kennedy wondered how her roommate could keep up a cheerful attitude in spite of how cold and exhausted they felt.

"What else do you have to eat?" Willow asked.

Kennedy felt in her pockets. "I think there's still a can or two of spam."

"I swore I'd never touch this stuff." Willow grimaced. "If it weren't the last resort ..."

"Don't worry. It's probably all synthetic, right? Not even real meat at all?"

Willow laughed. "That's what I'll tell myself. So should we pray?"

"Should we what?"

"Pray. You know. Thank God for the food. If you could even call it that." She bowed her head and began without waiting for an invitation. "Dear God, thank you for keeping us safe to this point. Thank you that you know exactly where we're at and what we need. Please bless this food, even though it's full of nitrates and sodium and a whole lot of other ingredients that I don't even want to guess at right now. Please use it to strengthen us for the hours ahead. And watch over Rylee. Help her to ..."

Willow's voice caught. She adjusted the baby in her arms and tried again. "Help her to be ok, Lord. Please. In Jesus' name, amen."

Kennedy added a quick prayer of her own, and the girls each opened a can of spam.

Willow wrinkled her entire face as she took a sniff. "I really need the calories, don't I?"

Kennedy nodded. "Just pretend you're doing it for an acting class."

"Ha. There's a thought." Willow peeled a tiny bit of meat off and examined it between her fingers. The bite was no larger than a pea. "I guess I don't have any other choice. Well, didn't Jesus at one point say that all food was clean if you're thankful for it or something? Isn't that somewhere in the Bible?"

Kennedy shrugged. She hated to admit it, but her roommate was already more familiar with Scripture than she was.

"Well, thanks, God, for the spam." Willow brought the crumb slowly to her mouth but stopped. "Dude. Listen."

Kennedy strained her ears. She heard it too.

"Is that ..."

Both girls jumped to their feet.

"Another car!"

Kennedy stepped into the road and waved her hands frantically. There was no way they were going to let their chance at rescue pass them by again. "Wait!" she called out. "Help!"

Willow ran out behind her, holding Rylee in her arms. The car slowed to a stop. Willow was laughing so hard Kennedy worried she had gone hysterical.

"Look who it is!" Willow exclaimed and nearly tripped on some ice, rushing to the driver's side.

The door opened. Nick stepped out and threw his arms around his fiancé.

CHAPTER 25

"How did you find us?"

"Where have you been?"

"Whose baby is that?"

"Are my parents ok?"

"Are you hurt?"

Once they put out the fire and crawled into the heated car, Nick gave a quick run-down of how he'd discovered them. "The earthquake woke us up last night. Woke everybody up. I tried calling your cell but couldn't get through. I started hearing stories about riots in Anchorage. I guess those folks in the doomsday camp were really going crazy. I was afraid you'd get caught up in the middle of that, so I borrowed your parents' car and started driving.

"About five miles down the road, I saw the wreck. Talk about freaking out. So I stopped, thinking maybe you were in the woods somewhere and in trouble. I hunted around for a little bit, couldn't find you, but then I remembered passing a lodge a little bit earlier, so I thought I'd go up there. See if maybe you'd found your way to shelter. You have no idea how worried I've been."

Willow was sitting next to Nick, her legs curled up against her chest and her entire body burrowed into his. "Our story's a little longer than that." As they headed toward Eureka, she gave Nick the abbreviated rundown of their night, downplaying how much danger they'd been in before the earthquake hit.

Nick listened with wide eyes. He was so attentive even his dreadlocks held still. "I can't believe you delivered a baby all by yourself."

"I didn't." Willow turned around to smile at Kennedy, who was holding Rylee close in the backseat. "Kennedy was there to help."

It wasn't until they reached the Eureka Lodge that Kennedy's brain began to realize just how lucky she was to be alive. Moriah, a plump middle-aged woman who owned the establishment, brought in bowls of warm water for their hands and feet, set up three different space heaters, and covered everyone in blankets fresh out of the dryer.

Thankfully, within half an hour of their arrival, Rylee woke up and her fierce screams let everyone know she was ready for something to eat. After a couple phone calls, Moriah tracked down a local family who had baby formula as well as diapers.

"I can't believe I'm willingly bottle-feeding synthetic milk to a baby," Willow remarked.

Kennedy figured her roommate didn't want to be reminded about how close she'd come to eating spam either.

After her bottle and a change of clothes, Rylee was wrapped up again in even heavier blankets and went directly to sleep.

"You doing all right?" Willow asked Kennedy.

She nodded. Moriah had put salve on the cracked skin of her hands. Kennedy's fingers and toes burned as they thawed, but she was thankful for the chance to warm up.

It was Willow who had everybody the most concerned. "My feet are just mad at me for making them so cold," she remarked with a confident chuckle, but half an hour later after soaking in increasingly hot water, two of her toes remained black.

Moriah called the Glennallen clinic to ask what they should do.

"She's just being over-protective." Willow waved her hand dismissively. "It's what happens in Alaska when things like earthquakes hit. Everyone comes together, helps everyone else out whether they need it or not." Another chuckle, this one not so bold or self-assured.

While they warmed up with bowls of Moriah's hearty soup, Nick filled them in on what had happened in Copper Lake.

"Your mom ran out to check on the animals when the earthquake hit. I guess she was a little worried about the whole barn collapsing, but it was ok. You should have heard the chickens though. Even above the noise from the quake, I could hear your rooster crowing his head off."

Willow smiled. "That's Bach for you. He's such a drama queen. How did the goats do?"

It was good to hear Willow chatting about the farm animals she loved. Good to be wrapped up in blankets, surrounded by friends and strangers who were concerned for her well-being. Maybe too concerned, but Kennedy wouldn't worry about that right now.

When they were ready, Nick would drive them to the Glennallen clinic so the nurse could check out Willow's foot. There was a trooper station there too where they'd tell the officers what they knew about Brandy's kidnapping and figure out what they should do about her baby.

After Moriah filled their tank with gas and packed thermoses of soup for the road, they wrapped themselves up in extra winter gear donated by the generous folks of Eureka, piled into Nick's car once more, and made their way up the Glenn.

CHAPTER 26

"Yes, Mom. I'm sure I'm fine."

"Well, I've just been scared sick about you as soon as I heard about that earthquake. I told you that your dad and I had a bad feeling about this trip. All those weirdos claiming it's the end of the world. You've seen the news? They're rioting all over Anchorage."

Kennedy didn't bother to tell her mom that she'd been too busy running from attackers, dodging falling trees, and trying not to die of hypothermia to worry about what was going on in other parts of the state.

"I'm just glad you finally got hold of us. I called Willow's home yesterday. They said they hadn't heard from you either. Your dad and I have been so worried. You really need to call us or at least send your dad a text when things like this happen so we know if you're ok."

Kennedy guessed that if her mom had any idea how much of Alaska went without any cell coverage at all, she'd never consent to Kennedy visiting here again. "I'm sorry you were scared."

"But everybody's well now? You didn't catch a cold or anything?"

"Nothing like that." Kennedy was warm for perhaps the first time since she landed in Alaska, and her appetite had returned with a vengeance even after two bowls of Moriah's chicken noodle soup.

"And Willow? Is she with you right now? I hate the thought of you being out there all alone."

"She's in the exam room next door. She got some pretty bad frostbite on her toes. They may have to take her to Valdez."

"Why? What's in Valdez?"

Kennedy sighed. "The hospital."

"Oh, dear. And what about the wedding? What's going to happen?"

"I have no idea. Right now with her toes ..." Kennedy didn't finish her thought.

"Well," her mom said, "I'm glad you're all right. You should call Carl and Sandy too and let them know you're safe. You know they worry about you almost as much as your father and I do."

"I will. What's Dad doing, by the way?" Kennedy couldn't remember the last time she'd gotten herself out of an emergency situation and didn't have him there on the other line asking questions and giving directions about what to do next.

"Didn't I tell you? We have company." There was something teasing in her mom's tone.

"Oh, yeah?"

"Yes. A nice young man. He'd stand out in a crowd of a thousand because of his bright red hair, but I suppose you already know that about him."

Kennedy ignored the way her gut flapped and flopped like a landed fish. "Ian's there? At our house? What's he doing?"

"He's interviewing your father for a documentary he's making about North Korean refugees."

"Dad can't go on record with stuff like that."

"Don't worry, your friend's got a super high-tech camera, you know. He can blur the face, distort the voice. It will be perfectly safe."

Kennedy hoped so. She didn't like the thought of worrying over her parents' safety. Talk about role reversals.

"Anyway, your dad's just come out now and says that somebody wants to talk to you."

Kennedy took a deep breath to try to steady her nerves. She told herself that the only reason she was feeling anxious was because of all the danger and suspense she'd experienced since last night. "Hello?"

"Kennedy. It's me, Ian. Nice house you've got here."

She still couldn't picture Ian in her parents' home. "Thanks. Haven't heard from you in a while." Why was that the first thing she said? Would he think she was accusing him?

"Yeah. This trip's been quite a bit busier than I planned, but I've had a great time enjoying your mom's baking and sitting and visiting with your dad."

"Hi there, Kensie girl," her dad called out. Was she on speaker phone? "What's shaking over there in Alaska? Besides the tectonic plates, I mean."

Hearing her dad's voice made Kennedy realize how much she wished she were at home right now.

"Anyway," Ian said, "I was talking to your dad about a program I'm going to be part of this year. There's a group in South Korea involved in rescuing and resettling North Korean nationals, and they're holding their first-ever summer camp for some of the re-settled refugees in June. I'm going to go work on my documentary there, but like I mentioned to your dad, it would be really nice if I had someone who spoke Korean to serve as an interpreter."

"You're asking me to recommend somebody?"

"No. I'm asking you to come spend next summer with me in South Korea. What do you think?"

"It'd be a great opportunity, Kensie girl," added her dad.

Kennedy was glad there was no one around to see her blush. "Let me think about it, ok?"

"Sure. Take your time. And I know you've had your share of excitement, so I promised your dad that if you do agree to go, I'll make sure you have a perfectly safe, uneventful trip. Deal?"

She chuckled. "Sounds good to me."

"All right, princess," her dad cut in, "you've had a long day and need some rest now, but call us if anything else happens and keep us posted about everything over there. Tell Willow we're all praying for her. You know about aftershocks, right? And stay out of coastal areas. I don't know if they're expecting any tidal waves, but you don't go near the water."

"I'll be careful, Dad." For this time at least, Kennedy didn't mind all his unsolicited advice.

"I'm glad you called," he said. "You stay careful, all right? And tell Willow's parents hi. They sound like real nice folks each time we talk."

"They are. I'll be sure to pass the message on to them."

"Talk to you later."

"Ok. Bye."

Kennedy unwrapped her blankets and slipped on the pair of fur-lined boots one of Moriah's friends from Eureka had donated. She walked cautiously to the examining room next door and was surprised at how many people were inside.

Willow's parents, two nurses, a trooper, and a social worker in a professional business suit who was holding baby Rylee. Willow sat with her feet in a hot bath while Nick tightened the blankets around her shoulders.

"Thank you so much for answering all our questions," the trooper was saying. The conversation stopped when Kennedy entered.

"I'm sorry," she stammered. "I'll come back later."

"No, come on in." Mrs. Winters held out her arm and gave Kennedy a hug. "I'm so glad you're safe," she whispered, giving her cheek an air kiss.

The trooper put his notebook in his back pocket. "We'll probably have more questions for you before long. Just make sure to keep your cell with you so we can be in touch."

Willow nodded. "What's going to happen to Rylee now?"

"The baby?" the trooper asked and turned to the woman in the suit.

"We'll do our best to find some relatives. I don't believe there were any immediate members in the mother's family, but we'll do some research. Try to find someone."

"What about until then?" Willow asked.

"She'll be put in a temporary foster home that's equipped to handle infants this young. She'll be perfectly ..."

"What about us?" Mr. Winters interrupted.

"I beg your pardon?"

"My wife and I have taken in emergency foster placements in the past. You still have our records on file. Go ahead and look us up. Judson and Star Winters."

The social worker looked at Willow's mom. "And you'd be interested in the placement, then?"

Mrs. Winters nodded. "Absolutely. Unless my daughter's worried about how it will affect her wedding plans."

Willow smiled. "You know, I was always a little disappointed I never found a flower girl. You think Rylee's up for the job?"

CHAPTER 27

"THOSE BREAD ROLLS TURNED out delicious," Star told her husband.

It was Kennedy's second Christmas Eve dinner at the Winters' home in their Copper Lake homestead. She couldn't believe how fast time had flown since the earthquake.

Judson, who was holding baby Rylee on his lap, put his face close to hers and cooed, "It's too bad our sweet little baby girl can't eat the big yummy bread yet, but she can't because it would hurt her tummy wummy, wouldn't it?"

His wife let out a sigh. "I still think it's ridiculous that we have to give her bottled formula when we've got two perfectly healthy milk goats. Makes me remember why we don't foster full time."

He smiled and continued to talk in his baby voice. "No, but soon she'll grow big and strong and when she's a year, she'll be able to drink all the goat's milk she wants, won't she? Won't she?"

Star laid a hand on her husband's arm. "Just remember, there's a decent chance she won't be with us in a year. They haven't found any family members to take her in yet, but how hard do you really think they're looking with the earthquake causing as much damage as it did and it being the week before Christmas?"

He ignored her remark. "She'll stay with us because she wants to grow up on good, healthy goat's milk. Not the nasty stuff that comes in plastic containers from the store."

Nick cleared his throat. "This is a delicious dinner. Thank you so much."

Star turned to him and offered a smile just as dazzling as her daughter's. "Of course. You're our son now."

"Or will be," Judson added while glancing at his watch, "in about half an hour."

"What time's the pastor coming over?" Star asked.

"Right about six."

Willow smiled from her seat beside Nick. "I'm just glad everything worked out so well in the end. We had to wait a couple extra days, but I don't mind. I think the idea of a church ceremony was stressing me out anyway."

Kennedy doubted Willow had ever felt true stress for an hour out of her entire life, but she didn't say anything.

Nick stood up. "Well, if you'll excuse me, I'm going to carry my wife-to-be upstairs to her room so she can get ready."

"I can get upstairs by myself," Willow insisted. "They just cut off two toes, not my whole leg."

Nick grinned. "I'm especially glad about that tonight of all nights."

"Cut that out." Willow pushed him playfully away. "Kennedy, hand me my crutches, and then *you* can help me get ready. Nick's got to stay down here and pretend like he hasn't seen me all day."

"Oh, wait." Judson held up his hand. "Before you go, we have a new Christmas Eve tradition at our home, don't we? Isn't somebody supposed to read the Christmas story and then we'll sing a hymn? That's how we did it last year."

"You really want to do that, Daddy?" Willow asked.

"Of course. You're a Christian now, and so is my future son-in-law. What kind of dad would I be if we ignored something important like that?"

"I left my Bible in the guest room. I'll go grab it," Nick said.

Star leaned over and hugged Willow. "I'm so excited for you," she whispered. "He's such a good man."

"I know, Mom."

"You're going to be so happy together."

"You've got that right."

CHAPTER 28

AFTER NICK READ LUKE 2 and everyone sang *Silent Night*, Star began clearing the table while her husband asked Nick about the exact date of Jesus' birth.

"Come on," Willow whispered. "That's our cue to go upstairs and get ready."

"Sure you don't want me to carry you up?" Nick asked with a grin.

"After the wedding," Willow answered, her voice full of teasing.

Kennedy handed her the crutches, and they both went upstairs.

"How are you feeling?" Kennedy couldn't remember seeing her roommate look so peaceful and happy before.

Willow sank onto her bed. "I don't even know how to describe it. It's like I've been expecting Nick my entire life. Like I've known him forever and have just been waiting for God to bring us together. It's like living out a fairy tale."

Kennedy smiled and took down the dress Willow had picked from her closet. "You sure you don't want to go big and fancy?"

Willow smiled. "I'm sure. In fact, now that the big day's here, I almost regret letting my hair go natural again. I think I had this certain picture in my head that a bride had to look an exact way, but that's really just me being vain. Nick didn't fall in love with me because I could fit into an expensive white dress or revert back to plain old brown hair. I mean, if he'd shaved off his dreadlocks for this wedding, I might have called the whole thing off. Not really, but you know what I mean."

Kennedy smiled and helped Willow into her cotton tie-dyed dress that looked more appropriate for a summer fair than a Christmas Eve wedding.

The doorbell rang. "That must be Pastor Reggie," Willow said. "I'm so glad he agreed to come do this, especially with it being Christmas Eve and all. I guess the good news about having to postpone the wedding for a few days is that it's going to be wicked quick."

"How do you know that?" Kennedy asked.

"Because he's got two young kids, and he wants to get back home as soon as he can, I'm sure. And with as long as Nick and I have been waiting to do it right, I'm not interested in a two-hour ceremony before I'm able to take him to bed and make him mine forever."

Kennedy had been listening to Willow and Nick's innuendos for nearly a week. She wasn't even embarrassed anymore. She held out the pair of crutches. "You ready?"

Willow smiled. "Dude. Let's do this."

CHAPTER 29

THE WEDDING WAS AS unique and beautiful as Willow and Nick's love for each other.

Willow was a ray of colorful sunshine in her rainbow dress. Nick wore a T-shirt with a picture of Solomon proclaiming his love to one of his brides. Kennedy couldn't remember the exact quote from Song of Solomon, but it had something to do with comparing his beloved to a cow.

If the Copper Lake pastor was surprised by the unconventionality of the ceremony, he didn't show it. Kennedy figured that informality must somehow play into Alaskan culture, since even Pastor Reggie showed up in jeans and flannel. Baby Rylee was the most dressed up out of everybody in a white baby gown that had once belonged to Willow's grandmother. Unfortunately, she slept through the procession, and Willow never did get the flower girl she'd been hoping for.

Pastor Reggie kept the ceremony short and simple. Willow and Nick had written their own vows, and after they exchanged the rings, Pastor Reggie led them in a heartfelt prayer. After he asked God to bless their union, they signed the marriage license, and Pastor Reggie went home, taking several dishes full of leftovers to share with his family.

"Well, now," Willow's dad announced, "it's taken me twenty-one years to say this, but I finally have a son to call my own. Welcome to our family." He gave Nick an embrace large enough that it nearly swallowed him up.

Willow and her mom were both wiping tears off each other's faces, and Kennedy felt more than a little out of place.

Judson cleared his throat. "And now, a toast to the happy couple. Willow, I know that you're a grown woman, fully confident in your capabilities, fully assured of yourself, but there's a part of me that's always going to look on you as my Willow Willow Armadillo, the little girl who tried bungee-jumping off the chicken coop when she was seven and had to wear a leg cast for two months one summer. And now you're in a cast again, but you're not letting that slow you down. And I'm sure at some point you'll look at your feet and wish that you could get all ten toes manicured so you can show them off in those cute little sandals you like to buy, but instead of feeling sad or ashamed, I hope you'll always realize how proud we are to have a daughter who would sacrifice herself not only for her friend but for a perfect stranger who needed you. Little Rylee may not have survived if it weren't for you, and we have no idea how long she's going to be part of our family, but she's already made it so much richer. It's been over two decades since we had someone this little to share Christmas love with.

"As for you, Nick, I mean it when I say I couldn't wish for a better, more suitable spouse for my daughter. You and Willow complement each other so well, and I'm not ashamed to admit that you've taught this old dog a few new tricks. I had no idea there were Christians who were so committed to social justice and freedom. You put every single liberal who makes sweeping generalizations about how all Christ-followers are bigoted racists to shame, and I'm glad you proved them and me wrong.

"As for you, Willow Willow Armadillo, I'm speaking for your mother and me both when I tell you that we are so happy you've found a relationship with the divine that has obviously made you so happy and fulfilled and given your life a new purpose. And whatever crazy adventures the universe throws your way, I want you both to know you always have a home for you here in Copper Lake.

"Which is why we want to talk to you about your wedding present. You're down-to-earth, folksy kids. My guess is as long as you have food and shelter and Willow has a little pocket money to spend on her hair dyes and manicures, you won't have a care in the world. But your mother and I have talked it over, and we've decided it's time. We're splitting up the homestead. Willow, you're getting your grandpa's old cabin and half of the hay field, including the income it generates. Nick, I don't know how good you are with tools, but if you don't mind a little sweat and blisters, I guarantee you that over the summer we can make it not only livable but a place you can truly call home. But it's yours to do with whatever you like. Your mom and I mean that. You can sell it and go abroad for a few years, you can rent it out and finish up college, you can stay here and raise goats or chickens or grandbabies or whatever. It's entirely up to you. Our only stipulation is that you are both in perfect agreement with each other with whatever decision you make."

Willow wrapped her arms around her dad's neck and gave him and her mom noisy kisses on their cheeks, while Nick looked almost as shocked and woozy as if he'd just seen a needle coming straight at him.

"You guys are the best," Willow said and picked up her glass. "To the most wonderful family in the world."

"You sure you're supposed to be the one giving the toast?" Mr. Winters asked.

"Just drink with me," Willow laughed. Everybody obeyed.

CHAPTER 30

KENNEDY LOOKED OUTSIDE THE window of Willow's room while she waited for the call to go through. Star was outside, bringing eggs in from the coop.

"Merry Christmas. You've reached the Sterns."

She stared at her phone to make sure she dialed the right number. "Ian? Is that you?"

"Yeah. Don't sound so surprised. Knowing your mom, do you think she'd let a friend of yours spend Christmas all alone in a big, foreign country?"

"You're at my parents' again?" She still couldn't get the picture to settle in her mind.

"Yeah. Your dad's calling out merry Christmas in the background if you can't hear him, but he and your mom are stuffing sausages or something like that so they can't talk. Want me to put you on speaker phone?"

"No," she answered quickly. "I'll call back in a little bit. Or just tell them to call when they're free."

"How are things there?" Ian's voice was easy, like he had nothing better to do than hang out in Kennedy's parents' kitchen and talk to her from the other side of the world.

"Good. We just finished Christmas breakfast. Willow and Nick had to postpone their honeymoon plans until they fix the highway, so we're all here."

"You doing all right out there? Your dad and I were looking at a map last night. You're really cut off."

So he was there last night too? Had he moved in?

"It's ok. The Winters have a big pantry, and they grow or raise most of their own food, so it's not that bad for us, but it's causing a few problems for other folks around here, especially the ones who have to get into town for medical appointments."

"How are things in Anchorage?" he asked. "I haven't heard too much lately. Are the riots over?"

"Yeah, I don't think anyone had the heart to keep up the looting over Christmas, but the city's a pretty big mess. I think the last count was around fifty confirmed dead from the quake. Most of that was in Anchorage."

"Wow. I'm glad you're ok."

"Me, too."

"Well, your dad's cleaning up now, so I'm sure he'll want to talk to you, but before he does, have you thought any more about that summer camp in Seoul? I think it could be a really neat opportunity for us both."

Us both? She wasn't quite sure what he was saying but tried not to read too much into it.

Did she want to spend her summer in South Korea working at a camp for resettled refugees? It wouldn't build her premed resume. She still hadn't decided if she was going to stick with Harvard or apply to other med schools over the summer.

Or was medical school a dream of her own making? A dream that God was going to ask her to give up in exchange for something even better?

Did she dare take time off to volunteer at a camp for people she didn't even know and would never see again? Did she want to spend the summer away from her own family?

Kennedy took a deep breath. "You know what? I think I'll do it. I could use a change of scenery."

She could hear Ian's smile on the other end of the line. "Perfect. It's a date. I'll let you talk to your dad now."

"All right. Merry Christmas, Ian."

"Merry Christmas, Kennedy."

Captivated

Alana Terry

CHAPTER 1

"I HAD A GREAT summer." Ian reached out his hand and caressed Kennedy's cheek with the back of his finger.

She tried to pull her gaze away from him, knowing that what she had to say would come so much more easily if she weren't staring him in the face. If she didn't have to watch his expression change as he realized what she was doing.

She wanted to remember this moment exactly as it was now.

Not like it would be in another minute.

"I'm so glad you agreed to go to Seoul with me," he said. "I'll never forget these past few months."

"Neither will I," Kennedy answered truthfully. She tried to keep her sigh from sounding too melodramatic. After tonight, the memories of their summer together would be bittersweet for both of them.

Maybe it didn't have to happen now. The summer camp for North Korean refugees was over, and this was her last night at her parents' mission home in China. She could call him tomorrow when she landed in Boston, give him the news then. That way she wouldn't have to see his reaction at all.

There was a soft breeze in Yanji, and he wrapped his arm around her as if he were trying to ward off the cold. He didn't deserve to be crushed like this, but after she'd made up her mind, she couldn't change it any more than she could reverse the seasons. Keep the summer from turning into a cool, crisp fall.

"You aren't saying much," Ian observed. "What are you thinking about?"

What was she thinking? How frightened she'd been to spend her summer in Seoul working with people she'd never met. Thinking about what would happen when she hopped on that plane for Logan Airport tomorrow to begin her senior year at Harvard, wondering if deferring her med school admission for a year really was the right choice.

But most of all, she was thinking about Ian. About his shocking red hair that had served to open dozens of conversations with the North Korean refugees they met over the summer in Seoul. The way he'd always been so supportive of her academic goals. The way his skin felt when she ran her palm across his cheek. That exact moment when they'd gone from two acquaintances who occasionally shared breakfast together to a couple.

Most importantly, Kennedy was wondering how he'd react when she broke up with him.

She glanced up into his green eyes. How many late nights had they spent at summer camp, sitting by a bonfire or relaxing in lounge chairs at the conference center on the little island outside of Seoul? How many hours a day had they filled talking about their pasts — about Ian's childhood after his mother died, the eccentric granny who helped raise him and his sister, how he'd thrown off the confines of his religious upbringing in college but was willing to entertain the possibility that his spiritual old granny had been right.

They'd had so many deep discussions about faith, and even though Kennedy had watched Ian soften his views from diehard atheism to curious agnostic, he'd never taken the final step of embracing the truth of Scripture.

She'd been so convinced it would work, no matter how many times in the past her dad had warned her against the dangers of missionary dating. She'd jumped headfirst into a summer fling hoping that by the time she went back to college, God would have changed Ian's mind.

Which he hadn't. No matter how hard or fervently Kennedy wished it. No matter how many times she prayed with her best friend in Alaska. In spite of all of Willow's prayers and hers, Ian wouldn't accept the Jesus he'd grown up worshiping. He didn't tease Kennedy for her faith. In fact, he told her several times how deeply he admired her convictions. Kennedy spent her summer pretending that this budding romance would mean enough to Ian that he'd become a Christian just like her, but now she had to face the truth.

Summer was over. Tomorrow she was heading back to college, and if Ian was really the right man for her, he would have given his life to Christ by now.

She hadn't even told him that she'd emailed the dean to defer her med school admissions. He didn't know that in nine months, Kennedy would return to Seoul to work as an intern for Korea Freedom International, the group that had sponsored the summer camp where they worked.

He didn't know that this time together in the cooling Yanji air would be their very last.

She took a deep breath.

"What is it?" he asked.

He was so observant. Maybe that's why he was such a good photojournalist. Always looking. Perceiving intuitively what language alone could never capture.

She forced herself to meet his gaze, etched each detail of his features into her memory.

"What?" he repeated. Did he guess? Would he have any idea?

She had to follow through. She couldn't back out now. "I have something we need to talk about. Something important."

CHAPTER 2

"Do you hate me now?" Kennedy's voice was squeaky, but she dared to look up at her boyfriend.

No, make that her ex-boyfriend as of about ten seconds ago.

Ian shook his head. "You know I could never hate you."

She kept waiting for him to say something else. But what? What was left that hadn't already been said?

"This probably doesn't help," she offered, "but you know it has nothing to do with how much I like you."

Ian sighed. "I know."

They were sitting on a bench, watching the colorful lights in the busyness of Yanji's nightlife.

"Aren't you going to say anything else?"

He shrugged. "Like what? You've made up your mind. I knew from the beginning your faith was important to you. If I were to ask you to change your beliefs, I'd be asking you to fundamentally change who you are, and I don't want to do that. Because I love who you are."

She straightened an invisible wrinkle on her blouse. "Don't talk like that. It just makes it harder."

"You were honest with me. It's only fair for me to be honest with you." He turned to her with a look that was so poignant it felt as if he'd reached through her sternum and was squeezing her heart. "You know I respect your beliefs. I understand that this is the decision you feel is best for you, so I guess that's it."

"Unless ..." Kennedy bit her lip. She hadn't meant to let the word slip.

"Unless what?" He frowned. "Unless I get on my knees and say the sinner's prayer like I did with Grandma Lucy when I was six? Unless I find a pastor in Yanji and get baptized again just like I did when I was twelve?" He shook his head. "I've got my beliefs too. You know that. And one of the things I loved about our time together was that even though Christianity is such an important part of your life, you were okay with all my questions and doubts. Never tried to make me feel bad or as if I'm not as good or as righteous as you."

"You know I don't think about it that way," she began, but Ian cut her off.

"You don't have to explain anything. I get it. I'm sorry I'm not clapping my hands and jumping up and down because you're doing what you think is right. I realize this is your decision to make, but that doesn't mean it's easy."

Kennedy stared at her lap. "I know. I'm sorry."

"Don't be." He glanced over and offered a brief smile. "I knew what I was getting into when we started dating. Earlier in the summer I called my sister and told her that you'd either be the girl to bring the wayward son home like Grandma Lucy's always praying will happen, or you'd break up with me when you realized it went against your conscience to get involved with someone who didn't see God exactly the same way you do."

Kennedy opened her mouth to object, but Ian put his finger on her lips.

"You don't have to say anything, and you don't have to feel guilty. What I told my sister was that even if things didn't work out between us, if our differences in faith proved to be insurmountable like they have, I would still consider myself a better person for the time we spent together. For the chance to share a little bit of your heart and your life and your love. And when I look at it like that, I don't regret a thing."

A tear slipped down her cheek. He wiped it away with his thumb and kept his hand there, gently cupping her face.

His eyes were full of both joy and sadness. "We had a good summer, didn't we?"

She sniffed and tried to laugh. "Yeah, we did."

"Remember when Jin-Sun put on that wig and did his Sarah Palin impression?"

This time, Kennedy really did laugh. "Or when Mena sprained her ankle during the Gangnam Style dance off?"

His hand still caressed the side of her face. "Remember our first kiss?"

Kennedy tried to look away but couldn't.

"Remember how embarrassed you got when we realized we weren't quite as hidden as we thought we were?"

Kennedy put her hand on top of his, but she wasn't sure if she was holding it even closer against her cheek or trying to push him away.

"I never want to forget," she whispered.

"Me neither." He was leaning toward her now, the same intense gaze that she remembered right before their first kiss.

"One more for the road?" He was asking for her permission.

Maybe it was a dumb idea. Maybe she'd regret it. But she had piled up regrets over the summer like she used to collect antique books.

What could one more hurt?

She blinked back her tears and nodded.

"One more," she answered and anticipated the warmth of his lips.

CHAPTER 3

"You okay, Kensie girl?"

Kennedy glanced up from her half-filled suitcase as her dad stepped into her room. She couldn't quite remember when her parents' house in Yanji had stopped feeling like home. Nice as it was to spend this last week of her summer break with her parents, she was ready to head back to Boston.

"How's the packing going?" her dad asked.

Kennedy grabbed a pile of books and shoved them into her carry-on.

He picked one up. "You've been so busy with Ian all summer, we've hardly talked. I don't even know what you've been reading lately."

Kennedy glanced at the title. "That one's a collection of stories about Christian martyrs. Sandy recommended it."

Her dad flipped through the pages and frowned. "Not quite light reading, is it?"

Kennedy didn't respond.

Her dad sat on the edge of her bed. "How are you really doing, Princess?"

She shrugged. "I was hoping to be packed by now, but I'll have a little time in the morning before we leave for the airport."

Her dad sighed. "You know that's not what I'm talking about."

What did he expect her to say? That she'd spent every second during the past two hours remembering the exact feel of Ian's lips on hers, knowing that their goodbye kiss would be their last? That for all she told Ian about not regretting how close they'd grown this summer, she realized it was all a lie?

Better to have loved and lost? Not even close.

Her dad reached out to touch her cheek, but Kennedy pulled away. "I'm fine," she snapped then forced a smile to retroactively soften her response. "I'm just a little distracted with packing. That's all."

Her dad stood to leave. "Well, as hard as it was, and as much as your mother and I both liked Ian, I'm proud of you for making the right choice."

The right choice. Her parents must have used that phrase a dozen times since she came home with the news of her breakup, but if Kennedy had really made the right choice, she wouldn't have started dating an unbeliever in the first place.

What was it about that bonfire in Seoul? That unforgettable moment ...

A summer fling. Kennedy was far from experienced in the dating world, but there was no other name to call it. Still, the phrase certainly didn't do justice to the intensity of her emotions, either before or after she and Ian broke up.

"Got your passport?" her dad asked from the doorway.

"Yeah." She'd made this trip between Yanji and Boston over half a dozen times. She knew what she had to pack. It was just a matter of finding the mental energy to do it.

Her phone beeped. She reached over to look at the text, hating herself for hoping it might be from him.

There's something I want to tell you. Can we meet?

Kennedy knew Ian. Knew he wasn't the type to back her into a corner to get her to change her mind. He understood they were through. His goodbye kiss would have told her that much even if he hadn't said so in words.

She glanced at her clock. Her parents would whine about her going out so late, but they couldn't do much to stop her.

She stared down at her phone, her pulse still slightly elevated at the memory of their parting. She glanced at her suitcase, grabbed a sweater, and typed, *Where do you want to meet?*

CHAPTER 4

HER HEART GALLOPED IN her chest. Why did Ian want to meet with her? And what should she say when she saw him?

She glanced around at the surroundings. She knew the little café. It catered to English-speaking expats in Yanji, and she and her parents had met Ian here the first day of summer vacation.

Had that really only been just a few months ago?

So much had changed this year, perhaps more than any other she'd spent at Harvard. Her roommate, Willow, had gotten married over Christmas break and was now busy transforming her grandfather's homesteading cabin in Alaska into a foster home. Kennedy had spent the last half of her junior year of college without a roommate. By the time she finished studying for her MCAT in the spring, she had so much free time on her hands she started volunteering twice a week, one afternoon leading the Good News Club at a local elementary school and one afternoon giving English lessons for the Korean-speaking members at St. Margaret's sister church.

She had also spent some of her extra time praying.

Did God really want her to become a doctor? Or was that just a dream she'd latched onto?

Then came summer and the opportunity to work with North Korean refugees in Seoul, seeing Korea Freedom International's ministry firsthand. She'd been honored when the director asked her to come back to serve as an intern after graduation, but now that she'd actually made her medical school deferment official, she stayed awake nearly every night wondering if she'd done the wrong thing.

And of course, there was her relationship with Ian.

Who apparently was just one more thing God was asking her to give up.

She pulled out her phone and glanced at her cell. Her boyfriend was never late.

No, not her boyfriend. Not anymore. How long would it take her to stop using that word?

Then again, *ex* sounded so harsh. Like they both hated each other and had just gone through some sort of nasty breakup. Maybe it would be easier if they had. Easier to break up with someone she despised than someone she still loved.

She sighed. What was taking him so long?

"Kennedy?"

She glanced up as he hurried to her, breathless. "I need to talk to you."

"I assumed that when I got your text." Her joke fell flat, and she offered a small smile in apology.

"Can I sit down?"

What did he expect? That since they weren't officially dating anymore she'd refuse to let him pull up a chair? "Of course you can."

He let out his breath. "This isn't going to work."

She glanced around, hoping for some kind of visual clue that would give a hint as to what he might be talking about. "What isn't?"

"Never seeing you again."

She lowered her gaze. She didn't have the energy for this conversation. Not tonight, when she should already be in bed, resting up for her full day of travel tomorrow.

"Listen," she began, "you know I still really care for you, and this isn't easy for me either ..."

He shook his head to stop her. "You don't get it. I started thinking, and here's what I realized. The thing that makes us so good together is we don't try to change each other. We don't try to turn each other into little clones of ourselves. We can stay up until one or two in the morning talking about abortion or politics or free speech or feminism, and maybe we don't see eye to eye on every single issue, but that's what I love about you. That's what I love about us.

"You never once made me feel bad for not being a Christian. And I guess you were hoping that one day I might become one, but you never made a big deal about it until tonight. Even then, it wasn't like you came to me and said *you've got to convert or we're breaking up.* In fact, I doubt the thought even crossed your mind. You're too respectful for that, so you just called it off without even giving me a chance to think about it.

"Well, I have been thinking about it, and you're right about one thing. I'm not ready to convert. I'm not ready to throw away my textbooks and my scientific proofs and go out on a limb and say *Jesus is the only way to heaven* when that's not what I believe. You and I both know that I could just go through the motions to make you happy, but then our entire relationship would be based on a lie, and one of the greatest strengths I'd say we've got between us is how honest we are.

"So here's what I've decided. I don't want to give up on us. I don't think that's what either of us needs. You spent all of last semester after your roommate got married alone in your dorm room, and I wasn't there to take you out for breakfast or whisk you off campus to go on grand adventures. But I'm wrapping up my work here. I could be back in Cambridge in a week or two, and I don't want to spend all my free time in my studio staring at the walls any more than you want to be stuck in your dorm.

"Maybe we don't have the same religious beliefs yet, but our conversations have given me a lot to think about. Even that science book your dad loaned me about evolution and creation, it gave me a ton to digest and sit on. And what I really need at this point in my spiritual journey is someone who I can talk to about all these ideas, someone who isn't trying to change my mind and isn't afraid of my questions. I'm not even asking you to be my girlfriend again if the whole faith thing truly is a deal-breaker for you, but I'm not about to just let our friendship go extinct. Get what I'm saying?"

Kennedy blinked. Did she?

"What exactly are you proposing?" she asked.

"I wish I knew. Just something more than goodbye." For the first time, he cracked a small smile.

It would have felt so natural for her to reach out and take his hand, but she tightened her fist and kept it in her lap.

"Friends?" he asked.

A dozen different warnings whizzed through her head, telling her that she needed to think and pray through any major decision before she made up her mind. She bit her lip before she could say anything.

"You need more time, don't you?"

She nodded, thankful he could read her hesitation. Had she hurt his feelings?

He stood up. "Well, can I at least walk you back to your parents'?"

She glanced up at him and felt her face flush when she remembered the passion of his kiss just a few hours earlier. "Yeah," she answered. "That'd be nice."

CHAPTER 5

"IT's A QUIET NIGHT, isn't it?" Ian asked.

She nodded, wondering if he meant to take the roundabout way back to her parents' neighborhood or if he simply wasn't as familiar with Yanji as she was. She'd spent half her childhood and most of her teen years here. At certain points in her life, it had felt more like home than anywhere in the States.

In other ways, she still felt like a stranger here.

Their conversation had been strained during their entire walk. Maybe it was just because she was so tired. What had they spent all summer yakking about?

"How's the documentary coming?" she finally asked.

Ian could always talk about his work.

He sighed. "I wish I could head back into North Korea to shoot a little more footage." Several years earlier, he'd been invited to Pyongyang on a tourist visa but had gotten in trouble with government officials when they caught him trying to sneak unauthorized photographs out of the country.

"That boy you met made a big impact on you, didn't he?" Kennedy asked. Over the summer in Seoul, Ian had told her about one of the homeless children he'd photographed foraging for roots north of Pyongyang. Something in the boy's expression had branded itself onto Ian's soul. Every time he talked about the little flower swallow, Kennedy got the sense that she was getting to know a real child, not some nameless statistic.

"Have you tried getting another visa?" she asked.

He shook his head. "No. They know I'm a journalist now. They've probably seen some of my interviews with defectors in China. I'd be in huge trouble if I tried getting back in."

"Just promise me you won't try to sneak over the border then." She was trying to make a joke, but his silence was far from reassuring. She paused by an alleyway. "Wait a minute. You aren't seriously thinking about that, are you?"

He shook his head. "No. No, I wouldn't do anything that stupid."

"Good." She'd been preparing to tell him about all the Americans who'd been imprisoned in North Korea over the past five years — two journalists who tried to sneak across the border from China, a pastor who was on his way to make a prayer vigil to Pyongyang, even that poor college student who'd only wanted to see part of the world hardly anyone else in America had.

They resumed their walk. In ten minutes, they'd be back in front of her parents' home, and it would be time for one last goodbye. It was too bad they'd broken up. Even though it was August, the night air was chilly, and she could have used his warm arm tight around her.

Ian didn't talk. Was he thinking about that street kid? Tomorrow, she'd probably feel embarrassed at how she'd made him promise not to try to return to North Korea, but tonight, she was just glad he'd given her his word.

They weren't dating anymore, but that wouldn't stop her from worrying about him.

Maybe she'd always worry about him.

Her steps fell heavy on the sidewalk. Would the night ever end?

Her parents' house loomed into view. As a teenager, she hadn't thought twice about the mansion her parents owned in this upscale neighborhood for foreigners, but now that she'd seen how many people lived in poverty or suffered under the weight of injustice, she was ashamed at the grotesque opulence. At least her mom and dad put their home to good use. They almost always had a small live-in staff to help manage the gardening, the cooking, the cleaning, everything. Most of these were North Korean refugees, which is how Kennedy learned Korean growing up.

The Chinese police had gotten stricter about anyone, foreigner or not, aiding defectors, so her parents had to be extra careful with whom they hired, but thankfully God protected them for over ten years and allowed them to continue serving here in Yanji.

"Wait a minute." Ian grabbed her by the arm, but there was nothing inviting or romantic about his touch.

"What is that?" Kennedy had been so absorbed in her thoughts she didn't notice the police cars.

A flashlight shined toward them, and she was momentarily blinded.

"Get behind me," Ian ordered.

A policeman shouted something at them.

"Kennedy, run." Ian shoved her away, and she nearly tripped. A whistle blew in her ears, loud and shrill.

She only made it a few feet before someone tackled her from behind.

A blow to her head.

She couldn't see or hear anything.

CHAPTER 6

SOMEONE WAS HOLDING HER, keeping her steady. Protecting her from the cold.

She tried to open her eyes, but her head hurt too much to see anything. It was still dark. That much she knew.

Bumpy. Were they in a car? What was that on her wrists?

"Kennedy?" a kind voice whispered. "Are you awake?"

She tried to nod her head, but it rolled to the side again.

Sleep.

All she wanted to do was sleep, and in the morning, she'd wake up at the summer camp in Seoul and tell her boyfriend about the bizarre dream she'd had.

"Give me your name." The officer shouted at her in Korean but wore the uniform of the Chinese police.

"Give me your name," he repeated in a gruff voice.

"Kennedy." She licked her lips. How long had she gone without any water? "Kennedy Stern. I'm an American. I want to speak with someone from the US embassy." How many times had her dad made her recite those words since they moved to China? She could say them in three different languages but never thought she'd have to use them in a crisis situation.

She didn't like how many times in the past several years her dad's apparently outlandish fears and paranoid training had proven useful.

"The consulate," she demanded in English, in case he hadn't understood her Korean.

He shook his head. "First you will answer a few questions for us. Then we'll see about contacting the embassy." He picked up a glass of water that was just out of her reach. Kennedy had been handcuffed to a desk all night. Maybe longer. She'd dozed off several times before finally waking up for good, sore and disoriented.

"The American you're with. The one with the red hair. What's his name?"

Kennedy had lost track of how many dozens of times he'd asked her this or similar questions. She refused to tell him anything, just like her dad taught her, reminding the guard that she was an American and had every right to speak to her consul.

He shook his head. "You must be thirsty, no?" He held up his glass and made a noisy show of finishing the water off. Kennedy's throat nearly seized shut, and she licked her dry lips once more.

"What's the name of that redheaded American?"

She stared at the guard's polished boots, trying to figure out what it meant that he was far more concerned about Ian than he was about her or her parents.

"Let's make it simple," he said. "You tell me his name, I give you a drink. Who is he?"

Kennedy tried not to glance at Ian's picture on the desk.

"What if I told you that I already know who he is? Does that make it easier? Former film and journalism student from Harvard University. Grew up in the state of Washington. See? You won't be telling me anything that I don't already know." He cleared his throat and poured the water into the empty cup, holding it up to her. "What's his name?"

She tried her best to take in a deep breath. "Ian McAllister," she answered. "His name is Ian McAllister."

CHAPTER 7

SHE SHOULDN'T HAVE READ all those testimonies about Christian martyrs. For however long it'd been, for however long she'd been stuck here alone in this dark cell, her brain kept bringing to mind tales of torture and gruesome deaths from the time of the Roman Coliseum to the present day.

These stories of triumph in the face of suffering and persecution were encouraging and inspirational, but Kennedy didn't need inspiration at the moment. She needed the consulate.

She had answered several of the guard's questions about Ian, nothing that couldn't be found through a quick Google search. In so doing, she earned herself a full cup of water, a trip to the bathroom, and some hard, tasteless bread.

When the man started to ask her about the documentary Ian was producing about North Korean defectors, she reminded him again that he was obligated to get in touch with the American Embassy on her behalf.

That had been hours ago, although without windows, there was no objective way to mark the passing of time. She tried to doze. Her head still ached from when she'd been attacked.

And now she was sitting here in darkness, with no consul to speak to, no parents frantically trying to get hold of her on her cell, and no Ian.

Where was he? When she'd seen the police in front of her house, she'd been certain they were there to question her parents about their ministry to illegal North Korean refugees. But her interrogator hadn't asked a single question about them.

What was happening to Ian? She had vague memories of him holding her while they transported her here, wherever here was, but she'd been so out of it that could easily be some sort of dream or delusion. Was he safe?

Was she?

What a stupid question. Of course she was. She was an American citizen, and so was he. Maybe that didn't mean much in a country like North Korea, but here in China missionaries might get questioned. They might get pressed for bribes. In some scenarios, they might even get deported, but that was the worst thing that was allowed to happen to them.

And seeing as how Kennedy was scheduled to fly to Boston tomorrow to start her senior year, deportation was a perfectly acceptable punishment.

If only she could ensure Ian was safe. In the darkness, she ran through the script of her interrogation. Had she incriminated him somehow? Had she given any sort of information that might get him in more trouble than he already was? Ian was an American too, a world traveler with far more experience than she had with visas and diplomacy.

She'd be fine. Give the Chinese police a little bit longer to sort out their paperwork, and any minute someone from the embassy would come in, sign whatever forms were necessary, and escort Kennedy out of here.

Ian too.

She was no longer handcuffed, and she ran her fingers across the cinderblocks of her cell, wondering how soundproof they might be. If she called out to him, would he hear her?

And even if he could, what was there to say?

She leaned with her back against the cold wall, hugged her knees, and refused to give way to the tears that threatened to fall. There was no reason to cry, not when her American passport meant that the consul would come and walk her out of this cell if she could just hold on to hope a little bit longer.

Freedom was coming.

Any minute now...

CHAPTER 8

IT WAS SIMPLE KINDNESSES — like being able to use a real restroom instead of squatting over the pail in the corner of her cell — that convinced Kennedy everything would be fine.

A full day must have passed so far. Maybe more. At one point, she managed to sleep curled up on the floor of her dank cell. She woke up with a sore throat and stiff joints, but she encouraged herself with the thought that today she would be set free.

There was no way the Chinese were brazen enough to hold her here another twenty-four hours.

Hak-Kun, the young guard she'd been assigned after her interrogator was finished with her, asked all sorts of questions about her time on the East Coast. Apparently, he was obsessed with American baseball. It was hard to tell what made him more disappointed, that she'd never gone to a Red Sox game or that she couldn't answer questions about World Series played years before her birth.

Yet another sign that her freedom was imminent. Hak-Kun was as bored as she was, just counting down the minutes until this business got sorted out and they let her free. She didn't have any more information the police needed, except that which might satisfy her guard's curiosity. What were hotdogs made out of? Did every American family really own two cars? Wasn't she scared to go into malls or movie theatres with all those shooters running free with their dozens of guns and slings of ammunition?

He was also interested in improving his English and often asked Kennedy to explain certain idioms. Why would anyone say it was raining cats and dogs instead of fish and sharks? Why do Americans say *hit the sack* instead of *hit the mattress* or *hit the pillow?*

It was almost as if she were back at St. Margaret's Korean-speaking sister church, helping others improve their English conversational skills. Since Kennedy had no idea what time it really was, she decided that the food Hak-Kun most recently brought her was dinner. It was certainly the biggest meal she'd eaten so far, and she was thankful for a bowl of soup, whose broth was perfect for softening her hard-as-cinder-bricks piece of bread.

Hak-Kun sat across from her and watched her eat. If she hadn't been so hungry, she might have spent more energy wondering if it was rude not to share.

"So, your red-haired friend," Hak-Kun began as Kennedy swallowed down a bite of broth-soaked roll. "How long do you think he's been a spy?"

She was too absorbed with her food to let out a giggle.

Ian? A spy? "I think you're talking about the wrong guy."

Hak-Kun shook his head. "No, we have a record on him. That friend of yours is real trouble. Which makes my superiors curious to know how close the two of you are." He leaned forward and raised his eyebrows.

She'd heard all the time about good cop/bad cop routines, but she never thought one individual might try to play both roles in the same day. Wasn't this the same guard who only an hour or two earlier had asked her the difference between French fries and hash browns? What happened to all his English questions or useless baseball trivia?

"Ian's not a spy." She wasn't sure why she was wasting her words. Did she think that simply telling Hak-Kun the truth enough times would make him believe it?

"Then what's he doing making all these videos?"

"He just wants to show people how hard it is for North Koreans living in China. That's all."

Hak-Kun scoffed. "It's hard because they're not supposed to be here in the first place. You understand. You Americans hate your illegal immigrants too."

Kennedy didn't feel qualified to dive into a political debate with anybody, American or not. "I don't know about Ian's documentary, but I do know that you have absolutely nothing to worry about. He's a journalist. Not a spy."

Hak-Kun drummed his fingers on the tabletop. "Did you say he's making a documentary?"

Did she? Wasn't that one of the things he had already known about Ian anyway? Why couldn't she remember?

She took another bite of her bread. "Did you get in touch with the embassy yet?" she demanded.

He nodded. Was that a grin on his face? "Yes. They're eager to talk to you, as I'm sure you can imagine."

She had no idea what he meant by that last part, but at least she'd be leaving here. And none too soon. How had the Chinese managed to keep her locked up like this without a major international catastrophe breaking out?

Or maybe it had. Would she be met by dozens of press members when she stepped into the blinding light of day? Maybe she should have a few words prepared. She'd have to ask the consul about that.

"I've cooperated," she reminded Hak-Kun. "You can't keep me here any longer."

This time the grin on his face was unmistakable. "Oh, don't worry. Let's see. How do you Americans put it? *I wouldn't dream of it.*"

CHAPTER 9

"HAK-KUN?" KENNEDY CALLED INTO the darkness. Her ears were still ringing with the sound of her own scream that had woken her up when something scurried across her leg. "Hak-Kun?"

Was it night now? How could he have left her in here? Wasn't she supposed to meet with someone from the Embassy?

Maybe it was just all the time alone without any windows or outside light. Maybe she'd really only been here a few hours total. She tried to count the meals she'd eaten but couldn't remember.

"Hak-Kun?" she called again, straining her eyes to try to detect the rodent that had woken her up.

Tears leaked down her cheeks. This wasn't fair. She'd kept her composure, promised herself that the embassy would get her out of this cell. How many hours, how many days had she been telling herself the exact same thing?

But no consul.

"Hak-Kun?" Her cry echoed off the cinder blocks surrounding her, holding her captive? "Hak-Kun? Anybody?"

Her voice died down along with any hope of rescue. What was the point? She'd been lying to herself for as many hours or days as she'd been trapped down here. Help wasn't coming. These people wanted to know something about Ian, and they weren't going to release her until they got it.

They probably hadn't even contacted the embassy. No, there wasn't even a probably about it. If the embassy knew she was here, they would force the Chinese to free her. Which meant they didn't know where she was, which meant her parents were frantic with worry. She was so nauseated she felt like she was about to throw up whatever contents were left in her stomach from dinner.

"Hak-Kun." She whispered her guard's name. He wasn't here. He'd deserted her. She was alone.

She thought back to that book of martyrs, how glorious their suffering had sounded. Many of them sang hymns in jail or shared the gospel with their captors. All Kennedy had told Hak-Kun was that *Jingle Bells* was a more popular Christmas song than Mariah Carey's *All I Want for Christmas is You.*

And there was certainly nothing glorious about the darkness, the fear, or the hunger.

She screamed again when some creature ran over her shin. How big was that thing?

Her scream turned to sobs. She didn't even try to keep her volume down anymore. What did it matter? She was the only one here.

"Kennedy?"

She sniffed in the darkness, trying to calm down her breathing so she could hear more clearly.

"Kennedy? Is that you? It's me. It's Ian."

The Chinese prison that held her captive was certainly an inappropriate place for laughter, but she let out a chuckle that mingled with her tears. "Ian?" she choked on his name, uncertain if she was laughing or crying.

"Can you hear me? Where are you?" he asked.

"Over here." She waved her hand as if that would do any good in this darkness.

"Are you all right?" he asked. "How long have you been here?"

"I don't know. Two days? I've lost track. Have you been here this whole time?"

"No, they just transferred me here. I was ..." His voice trailed off, and then he started again. "I was somewhere else. Thank God you're all right. I've been so worried about you."

"What's going on? What are we doing here?"

"Did they question you?" he asked at the same time. "What did you say?"

She didn't want to talk about her interrogation sessions. She wanted Ian to say something to help make sense of this chaos.

"Nothing. I hardly mentioned anything." Her voice was hoarse from speaking so loudly. Screaming at a rat and then crying over her misfortunes certainly hadn't helped. "Do my parents know where we are?"

"I don't have any more information than you do," he admitted. Not at all what Kennedy had been hoping to hear. "But we're going to be all right."

"What makes you so sure?" She hadn't meant to sound testy, but that was a bold promise coming from someone trapped with her in a Chinese jail cell.

"Because we're together. Trust me. It's all going to turn out just fine."

CHAPTER 10

KENNEDY HAD BEEN RIGHT. It was nighttime when she and Ian found each other. By morning, when Hak-Kun turned on the lights, she strained her neck as far as she could, pressing her face against her bars, but she still couldn't make out any other cells. She knew from the sound of his voice last night that Ian was somewhere to her left, at least some distance apart judging by how loudly they had to speak.

She hadn't heard from him since the lights turned on. They'd already decided it wouldn't be safe to communicate if anyone was around.

And so she waited. Thinking about Ian, about the summer they spent together.

Seoul was a considerably bigger city than Yanji, but ironically it felt less congested. She'd spent her first weeks getting to know the people in the Korea Freedom International home office. Mena, the director, was a young newlywed working with her husband, a defector from North Korea. Jin-Sun had spent some time in a North Korean jail before his escape and was missing a few fingers, but he never explained what happened.

While Ian spent his days interviewing the workers at the non-profit and editing his documents, Kennedy volunteered her services in a number of different ways. Proof-reading emails, setting up an English-speaking social media account, and double-checking some English translations of Korea Freedom's flyers and brochures.

Then they all traveled to a small island just outside of Seoul, with locusts so loud she'd get a headache any time she went out before sunset. Thankfully, the camp was held at a retreat center, with most of the daily activities taking place inside the air-conditioned reception rooms.

But the nights were spent outdoors, with bonfires, laughter, music, and games.

And, of course, Ian.

It was at a bonfire the second week when he'd leaned over and kissed her. She hadn't been ready for it, was terrified that her breath must stink like the fish stew she'd eaten for dinner, but he didn't seem to mind, and she quickly forgot her concerns.

At another bonfire, they stayed up until two in the morning talking about creation science, followed by a lively debate about whether or not Jesus was the only way to heaven. The next night they discussed Washington's response to illegal immigration until one, right after they finished arguing about American education reforms.

But they didn't just talk about religion and politics.

One morning, Ian woke her up early so they could watch the sun rise before the heat and bugs became unbearable, and they spent their time cuddling together and talking about their favorite Charles Dickens novels. Ian told her about his travels. His film work had taken him to a dozen different countries in Asia, and he'd studied abroad in both Greece and Iceland during his time as an undergrad.

He had a little old granny in Washington State he spoke of adoringly, even though he freely admitted she was a religious fanatic, a right-wing Christian fundamentalist who saw it as her life's duty to see every one of her dozens or hundreds of grandchildren and great-grandchildren living moral Christian lives. It seemed there wasn't anything Kennedy and Ian hadn't talked about over the summer.

Except, of course, what might happen if they got in trouble with the Chinese police who refused to grant them access to the American embassy. But she was glad they were together, glad she didn't have to worry about where he was or how badly he was being treated.

Now she'd just have to wait. At some point after dinner, Hak-Kun would turn off the lights before heading home, and they'd be free to talk again.

Nighttime couldn't come quickly enough.

CHAPTER 11

"COME ON. GET UP."

Kennedy didn't recognize the voice. Where was Hak-Kun? What time was it?

She blinked her eyes open. How long had she been asleep? She'd been talking with Ian after the lights went off. He was telling her about how his grandma had suffered two separate heart attacks, how he was worried that if she found out he was imprisoned she wouldn't be able to handle the shock.

Had Kennedy fallen asleep in the middle of their conversation?

The overhead lights blinded her, and she tried to shield her face when someone entered the cell. Rough hands yanked her to her feet.

"Let's go. Get moving."

She was even thirstier than normal and could barely ask, "Where are we going?"

"Come on."

What about Ian? Was he coming too?

She called his name. No answer. It wasn't until then that her heart started thudding loud enough to hear.

"Where are we going?" she asked again. "Where's Ian?" She dug her heels into the ground, but her impractical fashion boots just slipped right over the concrete floor as the guard dragged her toward a flight of stairs.

"You can't do this." She forced as much confidence as she could into her tone, just like her father had taught her. "I demand to speak with the US consulate. You have no right to take me anywhere."

The man scoffed. "You want to speak with the consulate? Fine. That's where we're going. Hurry up. His Excellency's waiting."

The chuckle he let out chilled the blood in her veins. Her legs nearly collapsed beneath her. The man swore, and all Kennedy could do was manage a faint, whispered prayer.

"Dear Jesus, please get me out of here."

CHAPTER 12

"SO THAT'S IT? I'M free to go?" Kennedy stared at the round-faced consul who had secured her rescue.

"Yup. Unless you'd care for more coffee or tea before we get you to your parents."

She shook her head, hardly able to believe she was free or that her entire captivity had only lasted three days.

She stood up, grasping her chair for support. She'd eaten a hearty egg and pancake breakfast with the man from the embassy but still felt somewhat nauseated. "And you'll let me know as soon as you hear anything about Ian?"

He nodded. "Unfortunately, as I already explained, now that the Chinese have involved the DPRK government, it's going to be a lot trickier to handle." They'd gone over this countless times already, but Kennedy still didn't understand. How could an American in China get in trouble with the North Korean government for some photos he'd taken years earlier? The consul was sympathetic, but since the US had no diplomatic relationship with North Korea, he told her all she could do now was wait.

"Be thankful you're free," he added, "and trust the official processes to work themselves out as far as your friend is concerned." He hadn't been able to look her in the eye with that last bit.

Well, there was no use pitching a fit here. Her parents were just outside. She couldn't talk to them until getting this last debriefing out of the way, but after a few apologies for how long it had taken them to locate and free her in the first place, coupled with a few more boilerplate assurances that Ian's safety was their top concern, she was led into a small sitting room where her parents were waiting.

Her mom immediately started to cry. After hugging Kennedy, she ran her hands over every part of her body, checking for injuries and asking dozens of questions. "Did they hurt you? Is anything broken? Have you eaten? Why do you look so skinny? Did you get any sleep at all?"

Her father was mostly silent, his drooping eyelids as certain a tell-tale sign of his sleepless nights as the black smudges under his eyes. He hugged her as soon as her mom let go but didn't say anything other than, "I heard about Ian. I'm sorry."

What had he heard? The consul wasn't exactly a reservoir of information. All he'd told Kennedy was that Ian had been on some sort of North Korean watch list because of his photographs a few years earlier, and it was possible that the Chinese were planning to hand him over to Pyongyang. Even though they'd managed to get Kennedy out, thanks in large part to her father's relentless lobbying on her behalf, the US Embassy hadn't even received official admission from the Chinese that they were holding Ian at all.

She clung to her parents, let her mother fawn over her, and thanked God that she was finally safe. Still, she knew that until she saw Ian standing in front of her in the flesh, the nightmare was far from over.

CHAPTER 13

TWO AND A HALF weeks later

Kennedy pulled her phone out of her backpack. Any time it rang, her heart would start pounding in hopes that it would finally be someone who could give her an update on Ian.

"Hello?"

"Hi, sweetie. It's Mom. Did I interrupt something? Are you in the middle of a lecture?"

Kennedy let out her breath. She had been so excited and nervous when the phone rang, she'd answered it before even checking the caller ID.

"No, I'm finished with my classes for the day." She was two weeks into her senior year at Harvard and more behind than she'd been in her entire academic career. The campus counselor she'd been seeing for years thought Kennedy had unresolved trauma from her three-day vacation in a Chinese jail, but she hardly thought about that anymore. All of her mental energy was tied up worrying about Ian. If she'd known that their conversation in the dark would be the last she might ever hear from him, she would have made it a point to stay awake the entire night. Maybe she would have heard something. Some sort of clue regarding his current whereabouts.

"Well," her mom continued, "if you don't have anywhere else to be, I'm going to do a little furniture shopping and wondered if you wanted to tag along."

Kennedy glanced at the time. Her parents had returned to the States the week after she did, having been warned by the consul that now might not be the best time for them to continue their clandestine mission work in Yanji. Her dad was still operating on China time, spending every evening and night on the phone with the manager of his printing business, which meant her mom was left to herself to set up and furnish the little Medford townhouse they were renting.

Kennedy glanced out the window at the students scurrying to and from their afternoon classes. She longed for the days when all she had to get stressed out over were lab reports or her upcoming science tests. "I'm sorry," she answered. "I've got a paper to write for my Dickens class, and I'm still fighting that sore throat. Could we spend some time together tomorrow instead?"

Her mom's voice was full of forced cheer. "That's fine. Maybe I'll call Sandy and see if she's busy. Seems like ever since we got back to town, she and I have only seen each other in passing. You drink lots of tea and get some extra sleep and take good care of yourself. You hear that?"

Kennedy wasn't sure how she felt about having her parents live a twenty-minute drive away instead of a twenty-hour plane flight. It definitely had its advantages, but the new arrangement would take some time to adjust to.

"Oh, before I go," her mom added, "I got another phone call from Ian's grandma. She's a fine Christian woman, you know, and we even prayed together over the phone. Grandma Lucy thinks Ian is going to be just fine, and she's praying for you too. We all are, but I'm sure you know that by now."

Kennedy was ready for the phone call to end. She mumbled her thanks, said goodbye, and stared at the books and folders on her desk. When had she gotten so disorganized? Maybe it was nothing more than a bad case of senioritis. After all, she'd aced her MCAT entrance exams last spring and had already deferred her med school acceptance. She'd planned to spend that year after graduation in Seoul working with Korea Freedom International, but she wasn't even going to think about that right now, not when she could only guess where Ian was.

The Chinese government denied ever holding him in the first place. Kennedy's detainment by contrast had made a very tiny ripple in certain Christian publications as an example of American underground missionaries suffering persecution, but since she'd only been held for a few days and had no real injuries to show for it, and since her parents still needed to downplay their involvement in missions, the story never took off. Which was fine with her. She'd spent enough of her college career in the public eye.

She sank her elbows on her desk and cradled her head in her hands. It was days like this that she missed Willow the most. Why did Alaska have to be so far away?

She never would get her paper written if she kept procrastinating like this, but her mind was too heavy with worry to think through anything clearly. She went to the Korea Freedom International webpage, a deep ache in her soul as she scrolled through pictures of the staff she'd worked with last summer. Why was she torturing herself like this? What did she think it would accomplish? If she wasn't going to write her paper, she should be doing something productive. Petitioning the US government — for the twentieth or thirtieth time — to look more closely into Ian's case. To respond to one of his grandmother's plentiful emails and voice messages. Kennedy had met Grandma Lucy on an airplane, but it wasn't until Ian showed her a picture on his phone she realized the tiny old spitfire of a Christian was related to her boyfriend.

Or ex-boyfriend.

And did it really matter what she called him if he was being held in some jail cell until he died?

She chided herself for her pessimism and rummaged through the folders on her desk until she found the lecture notes from her Dickens class. She had been staring at the instructions for her paper for at least ten minutes when her phone rang again. This time she remembered to check the caller ID.

"Hey, Willow."

After her wedding, Willow and Kennedy had talked on the phone nearly every day, but they'd both had such busy summers that sometimes weeks would go by when all they could do was text.

"Have you seen what's on the news?"

Kennedy's stomach felt as if it were in free fall. She clicked off her screensaver and jumped onto Channel 2's website.

"I didn't know if you'd heard yet," Willow was saying, "but I thought maybe you could use someone to talk to or pray with. We've got a little extra money set aside from last summer's haying, and I could fly out to be with you if you wanted. Kennedy?"

Kennedy had stopped listening and was staring at the screen. *Boston-based journalist imprisoned in North Korea.*

CHAPTER 14

"IT'S GOING TO BE all right, honey," her mom said as she stroked Kennedy's hair. "You just wait and see."

Kennedy buried her face in her parents' pillows. Did her mom seriously think that platitudes would help?

Her dad stood in the doorway of the bedroom and cleared his throat. "Sometimes news reports are wrong, Princess," he began. "One could always hope ..."

Sandy, a longtime friend of the family and Kennedy's pastor's wife, clucked her tongue. "Now, you listen to me, pumpkin. What's happening to Ian, if these reports are true, is a real tragedy, and I'm not going to pretend to have the words to say to make you feel better about any of it. None of it's right, nothing at all, but somehow, in the midst of all this confusion and turmoil and sadness, we know that there is a God who loves Ian more than any of us ever could, and he doesn't sleep or faint or grow weary. So you cry all the tears you want. You tell God just how you're feeling, and don't sugarcoat it or pretend or put on your best face or none of that nonsense now. You just remember that when all is said and done, when those tears run dry, that God loves this young man more than you or I could even imagine." She leaned over the bed and rubbed Kennedy's back, the gentle, soothing touch, producing a fresh round of heaving sobs.

"Do you think we should call the doctor?" Kennedy heard her mom ask.

"You just leave her be," Sandy answered, "because it's perfectly natural, this kind of reaction. Sometimes I think that if we really understood how much terrible suffering is going on right in our own backyards, none of us would be able to get out of bed at all."

Her mom started to talk, but Sandy gave a loud shush. "Now, I've got to pick up Woong from his science co-op, but Kennedy knows she can call me any time, night or day. I've got a big pot of chili heating up at home in the crockpot. Should I bring you some a little later this evening?"

Kennedy didn't pay attention to the rest of the conversation. She didn't know if her body was in shock or if it had physically revolted against what she read about in that news article. While her mom walked Sandy out, Kennedy's dad sat beside her on the bed.

"How you holding up, Princess?"

She didn't bother to answer.

"I just checked Channel 2," he said. "No updates yet."

It figured.

"Do you think he's really there?" Her dad was asking her? How should she have any idea? All she knew was the news report was full of lies. They said that Ian had been caught sneaking into North Korea. Kennedy hadn't even started to cry until she read the comments at the bottom of the article.

What's he expect if he goes spying around in a commie country like that?

North Korea's crazy. Why would anybody want to go there in the first place?

And that's why smart people don't try running across borders. If you ask me, the reporter got what's coming to him. Let's just hope they don't send him home in a coma like they did that college kid.

For the past two weeks she'd been telling herself and God that it would be so much easier if she just knew where Ian was. Now she realized having at least some hope was better than this. She didn't need a Google search to find all the stories about how North Korea treated its prisoners. She'd met enough defectors and heard their accounts firsthand.

Still, something had always made it feel foreign. Removed. These things happened to people inside the Hermit Kingdom. Not to Americans.

Not to Ian.

Kennedy's mom came back in, looking tired and somewhat sheepish. "Sweetheart, your phone was ringing." She held out Kennedy's cell. "It's Ian's grandma. Do you feel like talking?"

No, she didn't, but her mom thrust her phone into Kennedy's hand without waiting for an answer.

Kennedy didn't have any choice. "Hi, Grandma Lucy."

"Oh, thank the good Lord I got hold of you. You've heard the news by now, I'm sure." Grandma Lucy's voice was full of cracks and warbles but also a spiritual intensity that could put even the most ardent of believers to shame.

"Yeah, I heard." She sat up in bed and motioned for her parents to leave. "How are you? Does the rest of the family know?"

"We've been calling around since we got the news. A nice young man from the embassy got in touch with us earlier this afternoon, so we heard just a little bit before the press. The whole time I've been praying for my grandson, but the Holy Spirit's been impressing on me to be praying just as hard for you too. How are you? I was so happy when your mom picked up. I didn't like the thought of you being in that dorm room all sad and scared and by yourself."

"I'm all right. Both my parents are here, and my pastor's wife just left."

"Well, good. I can't tell you how much it means to me knowing people are praying for my Ian. I told the Lord just a few minutes ago, I said, *God, thank you that the truth has finally come to light,* because it's the truth that sets us free. You know that, don't you?"

"Yeah. I know." As tired and mentally exhausted as she was, Kennedy still realized that this was a completely backwards conversation. She should be the one offering Ian's grandma comfort. Not the other way around.

"I've been praying for that boy his whole life," Grandma Lucy went on, "and somewhere in my spirit, I said to myself, *Lucy Jean, do you really think you should be praying so hard? Because you know he's the kind of boy that's going to need his world shaken up before he finally gets on his knees and repents of his sins.*"

Kennedy didn't reply. Out of everyone in the entire world, it was possible that she and Grandma Lucy wanted Ian to come to

Christ more than anyone else, but that still didn't mean Kennedy would wish any catastrophe like this on him.

"Well, it sounds like you're doing okay," Kennedy said, trying to find the most polite way to move the conversation toward goodbye. "It was nice of you to call."

"Oh, I'm not finished, you know. I have a Bible verse I wanted to pass along. I came across it this morning in my quiet time. There I was, sitting in my prayer chair, just rocking away and about to doze off for my mid-morning nap, when all of a sudden, the Holy Spirit just took me by the shoulders and said, *The truth will set you free.* I'm still praying, asking God for more wisdom to know exactly what he was trying to reveal to me, but I know it has something to do with Ian and the way that boy was blinded by so many lies. He knew the truth once. Back when he was a little boy, he loved Jesus with his whole heart, with that innocent and simple faith of a child. But something happened when he went off to college, and I've been praying ever since that God would take hold of him once more and show him it's only in Jesus the real truth can be found. So I wanted to call and share with you what God had told me earlier, and now I figure since we're on the phone, we may as well pray together. I can guarantee you the devil's going to be doing everything in his power to keep Ian from ever finding the truth. And how could he be free then?"

Without waiting, Grandma Lucy began to pray. Kennedy listened, feeling more like a voyeur than a participant. Even after Grandma Lucy said goodbye, Kennedy mulled over what the old woman had said.

The truth will set you free.

Maybe there was something to her words. At least now that she knew where Ian was, she could pray for him more specifically. That should count for something, right?

She thought back to her time on the phone with Grandma Lucy and decided that if a little old lady who'd already survived two massive heart attacks could devote so much power and energy into her prayers, Kennedy may as well try to do the same.

CHAPTER 15

THREE MONTHS LATER

"Dude." Willow's voice from thousands of miles away in Alaska still sounded just as if she was standing behind Kennedy, staring over her shoulder. "What are you going to do?"

Kennedy studied the notebook in her hand, surprised that it looked so normal. For what it contained, she would have expected something entirely different. Something of this magnitude shouldn't feel like plain paper, should it?

"And that's all she said?" Willow asked. "She just said you should read it and left it at that?"

Kennedy didn't have time for this. Her first final was in ten days. She still hadn't completed her *Hard Times* paper, which had been due before Thanksgiving. It was the first time she ever needed to ask a professor for an extension.

In some ways, it was miraculous she was still in college and hadn't failed every single one of her classes. Some of her motivation came from a few not-so-peppy pep talks with Professor Adell, her former chemistry professor and academic advisor, who made it very clear that if Kennedy couldn't manage to work her way through what should theoretically be an easy sixteen-credits semester, she had no business presuming to belong at Harvard.

And some of her motivation came from the fact that there was simply nothing else she could do.

Ian was still in North Korea. The headlines had made a field day out of his arrest, and then the publicity died down until it could be three weeks or longer before any of the news stories would contain any updates, and the ones that did simply restated what they'd already written so many other times. *Ongoing story ... details as they come in ... blah, blah, blah.* In short, nothing that would help Ian and nothing that would give Kennedy any clue as to how he was being treated or mistreated in North Korea.

She'd grown so emotionally numb she could hardly pray for him except for during Grandma Lucy's weekly calls. Kennedy just had to hope that Ian's grandmother and the thousands of people praying for him around the world — or at least who claimed to be praying for him — would make up for whatever she couldn't offer God right now.

Willow had come out earlier in the fall for a three-day girls' weekend, which helped get Kennedy's mind off her own sorrows for a little bit. Over vegan pizza, Willow told her about the first two foster daughters she and Nick had taken in. While they sat getting their hair done, Willow prattled on about the little baby girl her parents had adopted. They even took Carl and Sandy's son Woong to a Red Sox game, where Willow gave Kennedy a rundown on all the plans she and her husband Nick had for their new home in the middle of nowhere, Alaska.

"Once we finish the second story next summer, we can get approved for eight kids total. Then I think we'll be done adding on."

Somehow, it was nice to hear that in certain parts of the world — even places as far away as Copper Lake, Alaska — people were working in their own quiet spheres to help others. Willow and Nick would probably never win an award for the foster care they provided, would probably never get their names plastered all over the news, but Kennedy knew they were living out God's call to love their neighbors as themselves.

Now Willow was back in Copper Lake, where the sun set at three in the afternoon and everything was blanketed in several feet of snow. This would be Kennedy's first Christmas break in several years without spending at least a little bit of time in Alaska. It would also be the first Christmas with her parents here in the States, so she shouldn't complain. Besides, with Ian celebrating in some North Korean labor camp or jail cell, she couldn't picture it turning into any sort of festive holiday. Grandma Lucy and her friends from church had planned an all-night prayer vigil for Ian in Seattle, and several other churches in other cities across the country were joining forces. Grandma Lucy had invited Kennedy to fly out to Washington after finals were over, and her parents had offered to buy the ticket if she wanted to go and participate.

She told them all she'd think about it. Really, she just couldn't face the fact that she was almost done with an entire semester of school and God hadn't done anything for Ian.

"You still there?" Willow said, interrupting Kennedy's thoughts. "I asked if you want me to stay on the line while you open it or what."

Kennedy didn't know what to do with the package from Grandma Lucy. The Swedish ambassador who had taken on the role of intermediary between the North Koreans and the US government in Ian's case had delivered a private bundle of letters that Ian had written his grandmother. She spent two afternoons making copies so Kennedy could read them too. Nothing could make its way into the press, but Kennedy was ready to stay out of the spotlight for the rest of her life and didn't need the extra reminders about the importance of privacy.

"I'm not sure," she told Willow, who was still waiting for her answer. "I think maybe I'll take some time off tonight to read them."

If she could bring herself to open to the first page.

"Or maybe I'll wait until I'm ready." Whatever that meant.

Their phone conversation was interrupted by babbling noise in the background. "Listen," Willow said, "I've got to go. I'm watching Rylee while my parents go pick up a new goat in town, and she's determined to dump everything out of the pantry. But call me if you want to talk after you read them, okay? Or if you'd rather they stay personal, that's fine too. Just know that you can call me any time. Seriously."

"I know." Kennedy was thankful to have such a strong and supportive friend. She wished Willow could live a little closer than four time zones away.

She hung up the phone and sat Grandma Lucy's binder on her lap. Maybe it was because these were photocopies. Maybe that's why she didn't feel any magical connection to Ian while fingering the pages.

Or maybe she was scared to read whatever might come out, terrified that what Ian was suffering was even worse than the torment her own mind conjured up.

She turned to the first page. Uncertainty was worse than anything, wasn't it?

Maybe. Maybe not.

Either way, she was about to find out.

CHAPTER 16

Dear Grandma Lucy, Remember when I first told you I wanted to travel the world? I must have been, what, thirteen? Thirteen going on fifty, like the little twerp I was back in the day.

Well, I told you I wanted to travel the world, and you said God could use me as a missionary. Hey, it sounded good at the time. And you agreed to pray that God would open doors for me to travel.

You and I both know my life took quite a different turn than what you expected, but I've got to hand it to you, Grandma, maybe you prayed too hard on this one for a change.

So I'm sure the Swedish guy's told you by now. I'm here in the good old DPRK. Maybe you've heard it from the news that the North Koreans caught me trying to cross the border ...

Here, several lines were blacked out, and when Kennedy could start reading again, Ian had moved on to an entirely different thought.

Well, say hi to everyone for me, give them my love, all that stuff. And please try not to worry. I mean, compared to what it could be, it's really not that bad. And no, I'm not just saying that because I know this letter's going to get censored. I haven't been too hurt or anything. In fact, I'm starting to feel pretty lazy. Just wish I had my camera here so I could document everything going on.

If you talk to Kennedy, maybe you could pass a message on for me. The Swedish guy (I'm assuming you've met him if you're reading this, but I'm not supposed to include his name here) said she's back in the States now, and you have no idea how much weight that took off my shoulders to hear that.

Anyway, I'm sure you won't mind if I take a few lines here and give them to her. Kennedy, I know this isn't the time or the place for a really deep Define the Relationship talk or anything like that, but I just want you to know that I've been spending all this extra free time I've gotten (thanks to our dear friends in the DPRK) to think long and hard about everything we talked about.

And maybe when I get out of here and find my way back to Cambridge we can pick up where we left off. Or maybe have that Define the Relationship talk. Or maybe just go out for pizza. You have no idea how much I've missed pizza. And clam chowder, of course, in sourdough bread bowls.

Oh. You and Grandma Lucy will both get a kick out of this. I have a dog here. Serious. His name's Rusty. At least that's what I call him. I don't know if he's a stray or what. People around here don't really keep dogs for pets the same way Americans do. Sometimes they have guard dogs, but that's about it. Anyway, Rusty's started hanging around, and when they let me spend time outdoors, he's right there by my side. Good dog. Ugly as you can imagine, but he's ticklish on the right side of his tummy, and his tongue is spotted black. Hope that's a breed issue and not some sign of disease or anything!

Anyway, just thought the two of you would like to know that even way over here on the other end of the world, I've managed to make a friend.

I'll be talking to you soon. Not sure if Mr. Swedish Courier is going to manage to get this to you before Christmas or not, but don't let my being here spoil your holiday fun, all right? And, Grandma, I want you to know that even though I may have ended up on a different faith trajectory than you hoped or expected I would, I'll still remember to sing a few verses of Silent Night *and imagine I'm back at Orchard Grove's candlelight service. And maybe you guys will think of me when you light the candles. Remember how fleeting life is, all that sentimental junk.*

Okay, that's enough soliloquy for now. Warm hugs to you both.

Yours,

Ian

CHAPTER 17

KENNEDY WASN'T SURE WHY she'd torture herself. The more of Ian's letters she read, the more certain she was that he was telling her goodbye.

How could God be so unfair? Why would he allow Ian to go through so much horror? If anything, it should have been Kennedy left to suffer in jail. Isn't that how all the martyr stories turned out? With the Christians in prison, singing hymns to God and sharing the gospel with their captors. Not that Kennedy had done either of those things. But still, if God wanted Ian to be saved, why didn't he intervene? Wouldn't a miraculous deliverance from captivity prove to him once and for all that Jesus was real?

Why did God tarry?

And why did she torment herself devouring these letters? Why couldn't she leave them alone? No matter how upset she got picturing Ian in jail, even though he tried to put a positive spin on nearly everything he talked about, she couldn't stop reading. It was past dinnertime now, and she hadn't eaten since her bowl of dry Cheerios at breakfast, but still she read on.

Hey, Grandma, guess what? I have another friend here, and this one's not a canine.

So I'm in a hospital for the time being, which I know sounds like it's all big and bad and serious, but hey, that's one thing you got to hand to the North Koreans. Free health care for all, right? Haha.

Anyway, I'm in this hospital, and one of the doctors speaks a little English, and it's hilarious to hear his questions. One day, he came in and asked why we have such big grocery stores since we all eat at McDonald's anyway.

So yeah, Doc and I are good pals now, and I thought maybe I should say thanks. You know, if you're the one who's been praying for me. Solitary confinement's about as boring as it sounds, and you know how much I like some time to myself every now and then, but I'll take Doc and his questions for the time being.

And, Kennedy, since I assume I can trust Grandma to pass this letter on to you as well, guess who I've been thinking about most lately? I mean, besides you and Grandma Lucy and everyone back home? I find myself thinking about our two-fingered friend more and more. I know there were tons of things about his past he couldn't talk about, but I guess it gives me comfort knowing that if he can come out of a place like this and go on to lead a well-rounded life, hey, maybe there's hope for me.

You and I talked a lot about PTSD and all that stuff, and I guess it's possible I'll have issues like that when I get out of here too, but with your interest in medicine, maybe you could go on to become the cutting-edge doctor in post-traumatic injuries, and then you can earn tons of money and hire me to go around and make a documentary about you and all your research. Hey, a guy's got to have some future plans to look forward to, right? So think about it.

I bet we'd make a pretty decent team.

Doc's standing at the door of my room frowning, which I think means he wants me to put this pen down and answer his questions about America.

Anyway, hugs to you both. And thanks for sending me all those prayers. God knows I need them.

Yours,

Ian

CHAPTER 18

"HOW MANY TIMES HAVE you read those by now?" Willow asked Kennedy a few days later when they were catching up on a video chat.

"I don't know," Kennedy answered.

Willow ran her fingers through her fire-red hair, which she'd gotten done while visiting Kennedy in Boston that fall. "Seriously. You can tell me. I won't judge."

"I don't know," she had to repeat.

Willow huffed. "Fine. Then take a guess."

Kennedy shrugged. "Twenty?"

"Dude." Willow turned around to talk to someone off-screen. Kennedy wasn't sure if she was talking to one of her foster kids or her husband.

"Okay," Willow resumed, "so what can you tell me? I mean, I know it's all hush hush and all that stuff, and I don't want you to betray confidentiality or anything, but you know me. I'm the last person to go blabbing to the press. How does he sound? Is he all right? Do you think they're torturing him?"

Kennedy shook her head. "It doesn't sound that bad, but he did mention he's in the hospital."

"Really? For what?"

"Wouldn't say." One of the reasons she'd studied Ian's letters so many times was because she kept trying to read between the lines. Were things far worse than he was letting on? Would he be allowed to write about them if they were? What if he managed to sneak some hidden message into his notes? It was probably a stupid, juvenile thought, but Ian was one of the most intelligent people Kennedy knew. If anyone could manage to slip in some kind of code that would get past the North Korean censors, he could. She'd studied every single dot of every *i*, practically holding a microscope up to each little period and comma to see if there might be any patterns or trends.

She could probably recite half of his letters by heart but still hadn't come up with anything other than what was on the surface.

"Well, can you summarize or read me a little bit of one or anything like that?" Willow asked. "Seriously. I know you've had enough excitement to last you an entire lifetime, but I'm going crazy here. The power was off for the past two days, and our generator decided to stop working. We just got internet up again, and I literally haven't done anything in the past forty-eight hours except feed kids, take care of the animals, and clean up messes. I'm dying of boredom. You've got to help me."

Kennedy glanced at her stack of letters, which were never far from her. Even when she went from class to class, she carried the binder with her. She told herself it was because the contents were confidential and she didn't want them falling into the wrong hands, but really, she clung to them because they were all she had to remind her of Ian.

She'd prayed far more in the past few days than she had all month. Having his letters, seeing his handwriting somehow made his imprisonment feel that much more terrible. And the fact that he wasn't able to tell her how truly awful it was made things even worse. What if his legs were broken? What if they were giving him psychotropic drugs?

That was one of the stories in her martyrs book that bothered her the most. Some pastor in Communist-led Romania had been sent to a psych hospital when he wouldn't give up his faith. The line of reasoning was that anyone who believed in an invisible God must be crazy. While he was there, they pumped him so full of mind-altering drugs he didn't even know who his wife was after he was released.

Well, at least Ian knew who he was. No matter how bad things really were over there, she had his letters to prove that much. Except most of them were several months old. The most recent was from early November. What else had happened to him in the meantime? And when would Grandma Lucy hear from that Swedish guy with more news?

Kennedy had written Ian some letters herself and forwarded them on in case Ian's grandmother found a way to pass them on. She tried to match his positive tone but ended up printing her words out on the computer when her tears kept splashing onto the paper.

Someone started crying in the background, and Willow frowned. "Sorry, but I've got to go. We're having a couple *bona fide* meltdowns here. But we'll catch up soon, I promise. Talk to you later!"

Kennedy sat blinking at the blank screen, thinking about how much had changed. This time last year, she and her roommate were busy giggling about Willow's upcoming wedding. Kennedy and Ian had gone out on a few breakfast dates off campus, but nothing serious had developed between them. Now Willow was raising a house full of foster kids as well as watching over her small herd of goats and other barnyard critters. Kennedy was behind in just about every class with finals only a week away, and Ian was trapped in some North Korean jail cell or hospital or labor camp.

If he was even still alive.

She squeezed her eyes shut and ignored the lump in her throat, wondering how much she'd be willing to give up for a chance to go back to last year when everyone was happy, content, and free.

CHAPTER 19

DEAR KENNEDY, I'M SURE Grandma Lucy doesn't mind sharing her letters, but every once in a while I thought it might be nice to write directly to you. Thankfully, Doc here at the hospital is more than happy to keep me supplied with paper, although you'll have to excuse the sloppy handwriting, as I'm trying to write with an IV in my arm. No, don't get alarmed. I'll let you know if things take a turn for the worse. Promise. I think Doc is just paranoid. Doesn't want to lose the only American patient he's ever had.

You should see how people react seeing my hair for the first time. It's hilarious. I've travelled enough to know it's a pretty uncommon sight, so you'd think I'd be used to it, but the people in North Korea, man. Maybe it's because they're even more cut off ... No, scratch that. I'm sure if I were to go on with my train of thought it would never make it past the censors.

Anyway, Kennedy, I've been dreaming up this letter for you for a couple days now, which sounds a little pathetic, like I don't have anything better to do with myself, but I don't. Doc's not the most lenient of physicians either. Doesn't like to see his patients up and about. It's so bad that now Rusty, you know that old mangy mutt I've befriended, just sits outside my window whining. I think it's been a full week since he's gotten a tummy rub. But the good news is I've had a lot of time to think about what I want to tell you.

Knowing you, you've probably spent the entire fall semester freaking out about me, and I'm not going to blame you for that. If the roles were reversed, you can be certain that I'd be just as worried about you. But seriously, Kennedy, you're almost done with your senior year. Don't let this little plot twist get you too far off track, okay? You're a perfectionist if there ever was one, and you'd never forgive yourself if you didn't finish your last year of undergrad on a high note. Got that?

Of course you do.

It's funny. Now that I've got this paper and I've started this letter, I'm not sure what to say. I mean, I guess there's all the expected, trite stuff like you'll always know how much I care about you, I miss you so much, blah, blah, blah, but that's probably not what you need to hear right now even if it's true (every word). So I guess I'll start talking about what we were always so good talking about in Seoul.

God.

I've been thinking. (Did I mention I have a lot of spare time these days?) And maybe you're worried that I'll take this whole situation and get really mad at God and blame him for letting this happen to me or whatnot, and I can guarantee you that those types of thoughts sometimes cross my mind.

But then I think about other things too. Like what if it had been you detained, and I was the one set free, and how hard would that be for me? And maybe this sounds strange and New Agey and a little spacey and woo-woo for you, but sometimes I'm convinced I can literally feel your prayers. I had this best friend in elementary school. Gabe was his name. Did everything together, and then one summer his family moved away to Seattle. It's pretty typical. I mean, who doesn't move at some point in their growing-up years, right? But this was different. I mean, Gabe and I did everything together. He lived catty-corner to us, and his family had a swimming pool (I nearly drowned in there once, but that's a story for another day), and we rode our bikes all over Orchard Grove, and literally we were closer than brothers.

So he moved away one summer, and of course I was devastated, but whenever we went over to Seattle for anything, my dad would make it a point to let me stop and see him. The first few times it was great. Then after school started we went again, only Gabe had a new Nintendo and was totally distracted, and he kept talking about these kids on his brand-new soccer team that I didn't even know, and I realized he'd moved on.

I was ticked, and it's a super long, drawn-out story that I don't really have the time to get into right now, but it was Grandma Lucy who came in one night when I threw this major temper tantrum. She took me into her prayer room and told me that it's often hardest for the people who are left behind.

And I have no idea why, but I've thought about that story dozens of times, and it always makes me wonder what it would be like if I were the one back in the States and you were the one here.

Honestly, I don't think I'd be able to do it. I'm just fine here. Literally all I have to do is lie down and sleep a lot and eat what they give me and let Doc give me whatever it is he thinks I need. That's it.

But you ... I mean, I picture you back in Cambridge, and you've got your classes to go to and your grades to keep up, and I'm sure your parents have been freaking out about what happened to you over the summer, so they're probably breathing down your neck, and this whole time you're worrying about me. (Now that I write that, I realize how totally arrogant and full of myself I sound, so you're welcome to save a slap for me if I'm crossing any lines.) But what I'm saying is I don't think I could handle it if our roles were reversed, and I think prayer has a huge part to play in that.

So I've been praying too. And yes, Grandma Lucy, I know this is going to make it to you first since that's what the Swedish guy says, but please don't get your holy-rolling bloomers all in a wad. Yes, I'm trying to pray more (who wouldn't in a place like this?), but that doesn't mean I believe exactly what I used to believe as a little kid. I just don't want to give you any false hopes.

Anyway, back to you, Kennedy. I mean, you never talked a whole lot about prayer and stuff, but I know you do it, and I know it means a lot to you. Heck, you and Grandma Lucy are probably BFFs by now, right? Correct me if I'm wrong, but I'm guessing if she hasn't sent you one of her famous prayer shawls yet, she's making you one for Christmas. Mark my words. (You read that, Grandma? Better get on it if you haven't yet!)

I guess I've been rambling, but that whole story about Gabe and everything else really boils down to my feeling grateful to you (both of you) for the way you've kept me in your prayers. Last year, I probably wouldn't have thought prayer could seriously do any good whatsoever. Now I'm not as sure, and I'm definitely not going

to risk it by asking you to stop. So keep praying for me (and don't fall too behind in your schoolwork no matter how worried you get. I'm fine. Really, I am.)
   Yours,
   Ian

CHAPTER 20

"Hey, you're late!"

Kennedy glanced down at Woong, her pastor's son.

"Good to see you too," she joked.

He shrugged. "We were supposed to start practice five minutes ago, but Mom's in the prayer room with someone. Again."

Kennedy hadn't planned to help out with St. Margaret's Christmas pageant, but after a recent stomach bug hit town, Sandy lost several of her other volunteers and begged Kennedy to step in.

It was probably for the best. Kennedy had hardly set foot off campus in weeks. She tightened her hold on her backpack, where all of Ian's letters were stored in his grandma's binder. She glanced around the sanctuary. "Are all the kids here?"

Woong shrugged again. "Becky's sick. She's home throwing up, and Brian's got the stomach flu, and Grant has a fever."

Good thing Kennedy had brought her Germ-X. She squeezed some onto her hands and did a quick head count. They were short by at least a third of their cast.

"How long you think my mom's gonna be in there?" Woong whined.

"You'd know that better than I would."

He let out a melodramatic sigh. "I can't stand it when she makes us all wait like this. It's an *abomination*." He rolled his eyes dramatically.

Kennedy thought about saying something responsible like *it's not polite to talk about your mother that way*, but she was too tired. "How was school today?"

"I'm homeschooled, remember?"

"I know that. So how was homeschool?"

He shoved his hands in his pockets and stared at the floor. "Mom got all grumpy because I'd been doodling in my language arts workbook, and she told me to do five pages, but I thought she was joking, so I only did two, and she says if I don't catch up, I'll have to work straight through Christmas. Have you ever heard of such a breach in justice?"

Kennedy was thankful for Woong, thankful for the reminder that for some people, having to do a little extra homework over Christmas break was the most they had to worry about.

Just then Sandy bustled in from the side door. "I'm so sorry to keep you all waiting." She clapped her hands together to get everyone's attention. "All right, kids. Come on. You've had enough free time. I hope you used it to warm up your voices."

Woong beckoned Kennedy to come closer, and she leaned down toward him.

"Don't tell Mom she's an abomination, okay? Then she'd get even more grumpy at me."

Kennedy smiled and agreed to his terms even though her mind was thousands of miles away.

Like always.

CHAPTER 21

"THANKS FOR GIVING ME a few extra days to hand this in." Kennedy was still breathless from her run to her lit professor's office.

"Perhaps next semester you might think of reading the syllabus ahead of time so you'll know what assignments are coming up." Dr. Penn had a thick British accent, which made her sound even more stern and intimidating than she might have otherwise.

Kennedy held out her paper, finally setting it on the desk when her lit professor didn't take it out of her hands.

"I'm sorry. It won't happen again."

Dr. Penn frowned. "Of course it won't. This is the last paper of the semester, and you're not enrolled in any of my classes in the spring."

Kennedy didn't know what else to say. If she hurried back to her dorm, she might be able to finish her research paper for her cellular biology class that was due tomorrow. It wouldn't be the best assignment she'd ever handed in, but at least it wouldn't count as an incomplete.

When her professor didn't say anything else, Kennedy prepared to leave.

"Miss Stern?"

She turned around. "Yes?"

"I'm aware you are on friendly terms with the journalist being held in North Korea, and I wanted to let you know that I hope he's released safe and unharmed."

Kennedy stared at her professor's feet. "Thank you."

"Perhaps focusing more on your assignments instead of worrying about things you cannot control or change will help you find your way through this uncertain time."

Kennedy wasn't entirely sure if she was being given a lecture or a pep talk. She repeated her thanks and hurried outside. Winter had tarried in New England this year, as if time were standing still until Ian's release.

If only.

She glanced at her clock. Kennedy was officially done now with three of her four classes, and if she finished that cell bio paper tonight, she could call it a semester. She'd tried. Even though it had taken nearly daily phone calls from Willow, she'd managed to complete her assignments.

By this time tomorrow, she should be enjoying Christmas break.

Not that there was anything to enjoy with Ian still imprisoned. But at least she had his letters. She tried to imagine how much harder it would be if she hadn't heard from him at all, if they never even confirmed where he was being held. Somehow she knew it was always best to know the truth. Isn't that why she promised herself that once she became a doctor, she'd never lie to her patients?

The truth will set you free.

Grandma Lucy's words still ran through her head months after she and the old woman had started praying together on the phone. Grandma Lucy still wanted Kennedy to fly out to Washington. The candlelight vigil was in three days, and Kennedy hadn't given her answer, citing her upcoming finals as her reason to hesitate. Really, she'd been hoping for some sort of miracle, that Ian would be released before she had to make a decision.

His case was still garnering national attention, even if the new sites didn't find his story to be quite as worthy clickbait as it was when updates were first coming in. Kennedy heard from Grandma Lucy regularly about different politicians who promised to look into Ian's case. One of the biggest roadblocks was that there was no direct relationship between the US and North Korea. Every diplomatic decision had to go through the Swedish embassy who promised to represent Ian's case as best as they could.

Several US Senators, and even the President himself, had made public statements urging the North Koreans to release Ian, but what good were words? With no incentive, why would anyone in Pyongyang listen to them? It was like a mouse walking up to a tiger and ordering it to share its meal.

Even worse were all the people who would get on Ian's social media page and say things like *sending thoughts and positive wishes your way* or *praying that you come home soon.* Telling someone you would pray for them was all fine and good, but first of all, Ian wouldn't see their posts until he was already free. Second of all, anybody could say a quick prayer or promise to send *positive thoughts*, whatever that meant, but how did it help? Why weren't these people taking the same thirty seconds out of their day to write their senators or email the embassy or find some other way to pressure the right people, people who actually had the clout they needed to get Ian released?

It's not like the US was powerless. Kennedy was no politics expert, but she knew that if Ian had been a senator's kid or related to some high-up military general, he would have been home within a few days of his news story first breaking. It wasn't that the US was helpless to get him out of there. It was just that they didn't think he was worth the effort it would take. Kennedy knew there were probably political nuances she wasn't considering, but that didn't matter. To all the senators and policymakers and embassy workers, Ian was just some random American who happened to get himself in trouble. Most of the public still believed the initial propaganda reports Pyongyang circulated claiming he had illegally crossed their border.

She finally had to get her dad to post a block on some of the worst news websites because the comments were so upsetting.

What did he expect, sneaking into a country that backwards appeared to be the general consensus of the ill-informed American population.

He should have never gone there in the first place. How many times had she cried over comments like that? It was a smoke-screen argument if she ever saw one. Instead of asking why a country like North Korea would hold one innocent journalist in solitary confinement or worse, people just remembered the initial headlines and wondered why Ian would have traveled to a country as volatile as North Korea in the first place.

The wind was howling when she reached her dorm, and she hoped that wherever Ian was right now he was warm. She'd grown so tired praying for his release with no apparent impact that instead she was focusing more on his day-to-day comforts. *May he have enough food. May he sleep well at night. May he not feel too lonely. May he be healed of whatever complication landed him in the hospital in the first place.*

Somehow, it was easier to pray for these simple things than to ask God to send Ian home, which would take a miracle. And as the night continued to darken and the temperature continued to drop, it was getting harder and harder for Kennedy to put her hope in miracles.

CHAPTER 22

"Pass me more cornbread, would you, my dear?" Carl said.

Sandy spun the Lazy Susan. "You know, hon, all those carbs aren't the best for your blood sugar levels. Can I get you more salad instead?"

Carl scowled. "The day I want a second helping of salad is the day I'll trade my Charles Spurgeon collection for one of those mega-church prosperity preachers.'" He turned to Kennedy. "Could you do me the kindness of passing the cornbread, please?"

From his side of the table, Woong took a noisy gulp of milk.

"Smaller sips, son," Sandy chided. "It's rude to drink that loudly when we have company over."

"Aww," Woong whined. "It's just Kennedy. She's not real company."

Kennedy had to laugh. It was nice of the Lindgrens to invite her over for dinner to celebrate her end of the semester, but if they meant to get her mind off of Ian, their plans so far hadn't turned out all that successfully. She could hardly taste the food Sandy prepared without wondering what Ian was eating and whether he had enough.

"Well, I'm right grateful to you, Kennedy, for stepping in and helping me with those last-minute rehearsals. I think it's turning into a great pageant."

"Yeah," Woong muttered, "except Chuckie Mansfield is refusing to learn his lines on account of him saying that church is for sissies, and anyone who believes the son of God could've come born as a baby is full of ..."

"Woong," Sandy interrupted, "would you please pass Kennedy some more of the cornbread?"

Woong pouted and spun the Lazy Susan so haphazardly it was a wonder the centrifugal force didn't send the dishes flying off.

"So," Carl said, leaning back in his chair, "any word about your reporter friend?"

Sandy widened her eyes and nudged him, not very subtly, but he waved his hand in the air. "Oh, come on now. We all know that's who she's thinking about, so let's stop pretending everything is hunky-dory and actually talk about all the reasons Kennedy has to be worried."

"I'm really not sure now is the best time," Sandy whispered, but Kennedy jumped in before their bickering could grow too out of hand.

"I talked to his grandma earlier today. She says there's now at least twenty-five different cities that are going to participate in the prayer vigil on Thursday."

"That's wonderful news," Sandy breathed.

"Yeah," Carl grumbled, "if you think that somehow holding a candle in your hand like you're a hippie at Woodstock makes God more likely to answer your prayers."

"It's the principle of the thing that matters," Sandy declared at the same time Woong asked, "Dad, what's a hippie? Is it one of those little yappy dogs? Can they really hold candles? Won't they burn their fur off?"

"All I'm saying," Carl insisted, ignoring his son, "is that more often than not these prayer vigils are just big publicity stunts. So let's say five thousand people come together. Or make it ten thousand across the whole nation. I don't care. They light their candles and say a few words, and then they go home to their nice warm houses. Then what? How's any of this helping Kennedy's friend?"

Sandy shot Kennedy an apologetic glance. "It helps, love, because any time people pray, God answers."

"What's stopping people from praying in their own homes?" he retorted.

"I'm sure they're doing that too," Sandy replied. "But really, sugar, I wonder if maybe we better have this discussion later when ..."

"And that's another thing that bugs me," Carl interrupted. "How many of the people going to these prayer vigils or love-ins or whatever you want to call them are actual Christians, and how many are showing up because it's the cool, progressive thing to do?"

"Prayer is prayer no matter who you are," Sandy insisted.

"Unless you're praying to the devil," Carl replied dryly.

Woong, who had appeared somewhat bored at the conversational turn, sat up in his seat. "Wow, Dad. Do people really pray to the devil? Does that mean if I ask God for something and he doesn't answer, I could turn around and ask ..."

"Woong, honey," Sandy interrupted, "you left your glass right on the edge of the table. You're about to spill and make a mess all over. See what I mean? Too late now. Pass Kennedy some napkins and tell her you're sorry for spilling on her jeans."

"Sorry," Woong mumbled, apparently forgetting the part about passing the napkins.

"I think it's great so many people will be praying for your friend." Sandy handed Kennedy a towel. "The way I see it, that poor boy needs all the prayer he can get." She shot her husband a glance as if daring him to contradict her.

Carl shrugged. "I don't disagree, at least not in principle. But I'm also not into turning prayer into a big flashy event. What does Jesus say? He tells us to go into our closet, shut the door, and pray to our Father who is unseen. Now, if people want to show up to these prayer vigils and truly ask God's blessing and protection to bring Ian home, well, then I think it's great and time well spent. But if they're just going there because it's the hip thing to do, then I'd just as soon save the energy." He shook his head and muttered, "I still can't see what candles have to do with any of this."

Sandy reached over and grasped Kennedy's hand. "I think it's wonderful, and of course you know that our family is lifting him up every day. Are you still thinking about flying to Washington to be with Ian's family?"

Kennedy was embarrassed that she still didn't have an answer. Her dad thought she should go, but her mom didn't want Kennedy traveling anywhere. Kennedy had been so focused on finishing her schoolwork she wasn't even sure what she wanted.

"And what about diplomacy?" Carl asked, apparently not finished with his rant against public prayer vigils. "Can you imagine how much more progress could be made if every single one of these candle wavers took the time to petition the government instead of dripping wax all over public streets and holding up traffic?"

Sandy reached out and touched him gently on the forearm. "I think, dear, that some people might be called to take their petitions to the government, but that doesn't mean we should stop taking our petitions to God in the meantime."

Carl let out a loud sigh. "I suppose you're right. And I'm sorry, Kennedy, if I turned your friend's misfortunes into a personal soapbox. I suppose when things look the most desperate, sometimes all we can do is pray."

Sandy straightened up in her chair. "Now, hold on one minute. You're my husband and you're my pastor and you're the head of this family, but you're also dead wrong. Prayer is never a last resort. At least it shouldn't be."

"Of course. That's not what I meant," Carl said, "but I certainly agree with your point. And that, my love" — he leaned over and kissed her noisily on the cheek while Woong grimaced — "is why we make such a good team."

Sandy nodded her head appreciatively and scooted back her chair. "All right then. Who's ready for dessert?"

CHAPTER 23

IT TOOK KENNEDY SEVERAL seconds to realize that she was awake at six in the morning because her phone was ringing.

She picked it up. "Dad?"

"Hi, Princess. You awake? Good. There's news about Ian."

She sat up in bed. "There is? What?"

"Good news, we hope. They're sending Hamilton to Pyongyang." He waited as if he expected Kennedy to start squealing and jumping up and down.

"Who?"

"You've got to pay more attention to the news. I'm talking about Barbara Hamilton. The Secretary of State. Apparently, the trip's been planned for quite some time now, but the media's just confirmed that Ian's case is going to be one of the major points of discussion."

"Does that mean he's coming home?"

"Don't get your hopes up too high yet, Kensie girl. You know how these things work. These diplomatic relations are far more complicated than anything you or I could wrap our minds around, but I'll go so far as to say it's certainly a step in the right direction."

"Yeah. It is."

"So, you're all done with finals and all set for us to come pick you up this afternoon? Will you need any help packing up your dorm?"

She shook her head, trying to wake herself up fully. "No, I don't have all that much to bring with me."

"Well, all those prayers you and Ian's grandma are praying, you keep them up, all right? Like I said, I don't want you to set yourself up for disappointment, and I don't want to speculate about anything too prematurely, but I really think this is the big step forward we've all been waiting for."

Kennedy wondered why she didn't feel more excitement. Was her mind still half asleep? Would it just take a little bit more time for her dad's words to sink in?

"One more thing," he added. "I've been up looking at plane tickets, and if we order in the next forty-five minutes, we can get you to Seattle and back for just $249. I really think that's the cheapest we're going to see this time of year."

Kennedy thought over what Carl and Sandy had talked about over dinner last night. Prayer should never be the last resort. They had both agreed on that much at least. The truth was she could pray for Ian anywhere, and she would. But she also liked the idea of gathering with others who were also asking God for the exact same thing. Usually when Kennedy prayed, even for something as serious as Ian's release, her mind wandered after the first few minutes. Maybe this vigil would help her stay focused long enough for it to make a difference.

Maybe God really would bring Ian home.

She swung her legs over the side of her bed, reaching for her socks so she wouldn't have to put her bare feet on the cold floor.

"Yeah, if the tickets are a good deal, let's do it. I'll give Grandma Lucy a call in a little bit and let her know the details."

CHAPTER 24

"Excuse me! Excuse me!"

Kennedy turned around at the sound of footsteps rushing toward her. "Yes?" She glanced at the wiry man with his thick-rimmed glasses and tattered notebook in his shirt pocket.

"Are you Kennedy Stern?"

She nodded tentatively, trying to recall if she was supposed to recognize him or not. He looked too old to be one of her classmates. "Have we met?"

He held out his hand. "No, I'm Eugene from Channel 2. I understand you were close with Ian McAllister and wondered if you had a moment to give me a short statement about Secretary Hamilton's trip to Pyongyang."

A short statement? Well, what could it hurt? "I hope he's brought home safe and sound very soon." There. Was that short enough for him? She kept on walking.

He didn't bother writing anything in his notebook. "Are you going somewhere? You look like you're in a hurry. Can I offer you a lift?"

She shook her head. "I'm just grabbing some breakfast off campus before I head home for Christmas break."

He stepped in front of her so she'd either have to go around him or stop. "And what would you say, Miss Stern, about all the other tens of thousands of political prisoners presumed to be held captive in North Korea? Do you think that just because they

ALANA TERRY

aren't American citizens they shouldn't receive the same degree of publicity that Mr. McAllister's case has garnered?"

"I really don't feel qualified to give a statement about that."

He thumbed through some pages on his notebook. "That's odd. It says here your parents worked for years in China and were active in aiding North Korean refugees, so I assumed that you'd have an opinion on the matter."

How had he found that out about her parents? Up until the day they left China, they'd been more than careful to keep their mission work under everyone's radar. Had Kennedy somehow let it slip at any point?

"Well, I can see you're very busy." Eugene's voice was polite, but he looked like the words tasted sour as they came out. "I'm writing a piece on the way Americans get so up in arms about human-rights abuses when they happen to one of our own citizens. But how many people praying or petitioning for Ian McCallister's release have ever spent more than ten seconds worrying about the other political prisoners in North Korea, I wonder? And do high-profile cases like this promote the cause of freedom or just force us to become even more self-centered as a nation? There's a question I'd love to hear your response to."

He pulled out a card. "Give me a text or send me an email if you decide you want to talk about this further. I can't wait to learn what you have to say."

He yanked some keys out of his pocket and took off in the opposite direction, leaving Kennedy alone on the curb and suddenly without any appetite for breakfast whatsoever.

CHAPTER 25

"No, I'm not upset he asked for my opinion," Kennedy tried to explain. "I'm upset because he kind of has a point." She was backstage helping Sandy set up before all the kids arrived for their pageant rehearsal.

Kennedy had spent the day at her parents' new home in Medford, lounging around, reading books for pleasure again instead of for class, and trying hard to stay calm even with the news about the secretary of state's upcoming trip to Pyongyang. Still, it was different than when she'd usually spent her school breaks at the Lindgrens'. She hadn't realized that having her parents in town would also mean seeing less of her pastor and his family.

Sandy propped the manger on the stage. "So, tell me again exactly what it is that you've been thinking over. Because I hate to admit it, sweetie, I'm not sure I understand."

That was probably Kennedy's fault. She'd been flustered by the journalist's remarks all day but hadn't found anyone to talk to until now. "Okay, so his basic question was why is it that when something bad happens to an American, everyone gets so upset, but those same things happen to people from other countries on a regular basis, and people don't seem to really care."

"Well, I can certainly understand his point on one level," Sandy reflected. "It's just like when a little kid gets kidnapped, and terrible as it is when that happens to anyone's family, it does make you wonder why some cases receive more publicity than others."

Kennedy had listened to Willow and Nick talk extensively about this very issue and how children of color who were abducted were far less likely to even get an Amber Alert sent out. At first, Kennedy assumed they were overreacting until Nick jumped online and showed her the statistics.

"But still," Sandy went on, "I don't think it's necessarily something to get worked up over. Maybe just something to be aware of. Here's an example. You remember that Christian woman from the Middle East who was given a life sentence for breaking her country's blasphemy laws?"

Kennedy nodded. Carl had mentioned the case several times from the pulpit.

"Well, as it turns out, there are more than two dozen Christians in that same country with that same sentence. But she's the only one most of us have heard about. Does that sound fair to you?"

Kennedy glanced around, as if she might find the answer on the walls of St. Margaret's sanctuary. "I guess not."

"Why?" Sandy asked pointedly.

"Because there are so many others too." Kennedy realized how immature the words sounded as soon as they left her mouth.

Sandy pulled out some shepherd staffs. "Well, here's how I see it. Let's say I read a news report about fifty Christians imprisoned for serving Christ in some specific nation, let's say somewhere in the Middle East. And that story reminds me to pray for them, so I do. But then the next day, I might not think about it so much. Sure, if that news article comes to mind again or I read something else similar, I'll remember to pray, but that's probably about all that would happen.

"Now, let's say I read a story with a picture of a woman who's at least in the ballpark range of my age (give or take), and it talks about the difficult time her kids are having with her in jail, and her husband is begging everyone to pray for her release. I hear about it in the news, I know her name, and I know thousands or tens of thousands or hundreds of thousands of believers are joining with me in prayer for that specific woman. How does that sound?"

"It sounds unfair to the other Christians who don't have that kind of support."

Sandy frowned. "I suppose that's one way to look at it. But now let's think. Let's say we've got fifty thousand people all praying for this one woman. And let's say ten percent, or if you want to be even more conservative let's say that five percent, of them go on to pray for that country in general. Or maybe they pray for the entire Middle East or the whole Muslim world. Is that going to make a difference?"

"I suppose so."

"So here's how I see it, hon. You and me, we're made to be in relationships, right? For example, I'm called to be a friend and an encouragement to the folks at St. Margaret's Church. That doesn't mean I'm supposed to find every single hurting person on the East Coast and reach out to them, because that just wouldn't be possible, would it? So instead of feeling guilty that I can only focus on a few individuals when there are so many others out there in need of God's comfort and encouragement, I just tell God I'm ready to serve who he puts in my way today.

"It's the same with praying for others, least as far as I see it. I may spend ten minutes a day praying for that poor woman imprisoned for her faith because I've seen her face. I know her name. I remember her story. But while I'm praying for her, I can also pray for her entire country to open up to the gospel, can't I? And I can pray for those in jail with her even if I don't know all their stories as well. I guess what I'm saying is that humans will often make any excuse they can for not praying like they should. Some of them will say things like *it's not right for me to only pray about this one person when so many other people are going through terrible things.*

"Let me give you an example. Back when Woong was so sick, remember? I can guarantee you I was praying for my son to be healed more than anything. Now, would it make sense for you or someone else to come up to me and try to make me feel guilty for praying for Woong when thousands of other kids across the globe were suffering from his illness or something even worse?"

"But you're his mom," Kennedy insisted. "That makes it different because it's personal."

"That's what I'm saying. Prayer should be personal. The way I see it, the more personal it is, the better. Let me tell you a story. Back when I was about your age, I would get this newsletter that shared stories of Christians being persecuted around the world. I'd gotten this publication for years and did my best to pray for each and every Christian I read about who was suffering for their faith. But it's like I said earlier. I prayed about them when I read their stories, and then most of the time I just forgot.

"Well, then one day I read a story about a young woman who was my age. And she had a little nursing daughter who was the same age as my baby, too. And her husband kicked her out of the house when he found out she was a Christian, and that's not the end of it. He was so mad, he took that baby, and ... Well, I don't want to depress you with the horrible details. But this little baby, who hadn't done anything other than be born to a woman who happened to believe that Jesus is the Way, the Truth, and the Life, ended up suffering some pretty severe brain damage and died because the hospital doctor refused to provide assistance when he heard about the circumstances of the injuries. And let me tell you, that's the first time I've cried over a story about someone I never met. And the reason I cried was because I had a baby that same age, and I knew that could have been me left to forgive my husband for doing something so terrible. And I prayed for that mother by name every day for years because her story stayed with me. Now, that wouldn't have happened if I'd just read some general report about how wives in such and such a country are sometimes kicked out of their homes when they convert. Understand?"

"I suppose. But don't you think it's sometimes manipulative?"

Sandy stared as if she didn't understand the word. "Is what manipulative, sugar?"

"The way they tell these stories just to make you feel bad."

"Feel bad?" Sandy let out a chuckle. "Honey, we're members of the body of Christ, remember? When one part suffers, all the other parts are supposed to suffer with it. I don't see that as manipulation. I see that as us fulfilling our call to remember those in prison as if we ourselves were suffering with them like it tells us to do in the book of Hebrews."

Just then Woong ran up. "Mom! Mom! You've gotta come quick. Becky and me were in the little kids' room even though I know we're way too old to play in there. I didn't mean to but I got Play-Doh stuck in her hair, so I went to help her clean up in the sink, but one of them springy curls of hers got stuck in the drain."

"Oh, my," Sandy breathed. "Is she hurt?"

"No, but she's wicked mad and says she never wants to play with me no more. Can you come help?"

"Of course I can." She stood up and looked at Kennedy. "Well, I suppose it's time to get ready for rehearsal, isn't it?"

CHAPTER 26

THE PAGEANT PRACTICE THAT night was like a scene out of a bad family sitcom. Woong's friend Becky spent the first half of the rehearsal crying because her hair had gotten so tangled Sandy had to cut some of it off. Woong was sulking because she refused to tell him she forgave him.

Finally the night was over, and Kennedy was waiting for Sandy to finish locking the church up before heading back to her parents'. Usually, she looked forward to Christmas break as a chance to relax, but between packing up her dorm room, shopping with her mom for new furniture for the guest bedroom, and helping Sandy tonight at the rehearsal, she hadn't had a moment to herself. And tomorrow she'd fly out first thing to Washington to meet Ian's grandmother for the prayer vigil.

"Hello?"

Kennedy glanced up at the familiar voice. It was Hannah, one of the North Korean refugees Kennedy's parents had taken in years ago in China. She and her husband were now in Cambridge, where he was the pastor of St. Margaret's Korean-speaking sister church.

Kennedy gave Hannah a hug. She felt guilty for not having spent more time with her. Hannah and Simon had adopted a little girl earlier in the year, and Kennedy hadn't even met her yet.

"So this is little Emily?" Kennedy had never been all that good with children, let alone ones this little. She didn't want to insult the child by speaking in that silly, high-pitched baby voice, but she did her best to smile at the bundled-up infant.

Hannah was beaming. "Yes, isn't she perfect? I still thank God every single day for completing our family like this."

Kennedy didn't know how to respond. She thought she remembered her parents mentioning something about how Hannah struggled to conceive but couldn't recall any details.

"Is Sandy still here?" Hannah asked. "She told me to stop by to pick up some tablecloths we could use for our church's craft bazaar, but I've been running late."

"She's here somewhere." Kennedy glanced around. "I'm not sure what she's doing. But I can show you where they keep the tablecloths."

"That would be wonderful."

Kennedy still couldn't explain why she felt so uncomfortable. Maybe because when they'd lived together in Yanji, Hannah was such a super-saint. Kennedy had certainly grown in her walk with the Lord over the past three and a half years at Harvard, but she would never measure up to someone like Hannah.

"I hear you're leaving for Washington soon. Is that right?" Hannah asked as she followed Kennedy down the stairs to St. Margaret's kitchen.

"Yeah, I fly out tomorrow."

"I heard Pastor Carl mention something about an update. Did you hear anything about your friend?"

Kennedy nodded. "The Secretary of State's scheduled to visit Pyongyang. Some people think it ..." She stopped herself. There was nothing more painful than shattered hopes. "It might mean progress, but there's really no way to know for sure," she concluded with a shrug.

"I hope you know Simon and I and our whole church family are praying for your friend and his safe return."

Kennedy ignored the way her throat tightened and instead mumbled her thanks.

"It must be hard for you, not knowing if he's okay," Hannah remarked.

Kennedy sighed. "Yeah, it's hard." If anyone could understand what she was going through, it was Hannah. She and Simon had been imprisoned in North Korea before escaping to Kennedy's parents' in Yanji.

Hannah reached out and touched her shoulder. "The promising news is God is watching out for him, right? Just like he did for Simon and me so many years ago. If he could help us find healing and peace after everything we went through, I know he can do the same for your friend."

Kennedy opened the door to the linen closet and stared at the stacks of tablecloths, all organized by size and color. "Yeah, but you two were Christians."

Hannah nodded. "That's true. But suffering is suffering no matter what you believe."

Kennedy wondered if she hadn't expressed herself clearly enough. "That's not quite it. I mean, you and Simon had a lot to endure, but God helped you through it, so it couldn't be all that bad."

Hannah stared at her, and Kennedy felt the need to rush ahead into a lengthier explanation. "I'm not trying to make light of what you went through, but with God shielding you from the worst of the pain ..."

"What did you say?" A flicker of fire lit Hannah's eyes, an intensity Kennedy had never known in her.

"I'm sorry. I didn't mean it like that," she stammered. "But wasn't it sort of like that? In a way?"

"Like what?" Hannah repositioned the pacifier that had fallen out of her daughter's mouth. She didn't look angry, but Kennedy thought her hand trembled slightly.

Kennedy realized she had absolutely no idea what she was talking about, but she still couldn't stop herself from trying to cover over whatever blunders or mistakes she had already made. "I guess, it's just that I've been reading this book about persecution, and all the believers talk about how when they're being interrogated or beat up or things like that, they describe this Holy Spirit bubble that kept them protected from it all."

Whatever anger or intensity had passed over Hannah, it was gone now and she let out a bright, musical laugh.

Kennedy shut her mouth before she tried to make an even more convoluted explanation.

"I'm sorry for laughing," Hannah finally breathed, "and I certainly don't mean to be rude to you or the author of that book, but honestly, that's one of the silliest things I've ever heard."

Kennedy blinked, uncertain what she was supposed to say or do next. "I don't see what's so funny," she finally confessed. After hearing even a fraction of what Hannah and Simon had gone through before making it to the States, she couldn't understand how anything about that time could induce such a jocular reaction.

"Okay." Hannah wiped her cheeks and tried to make her expression look more serious. "I can't pretend to speak for other believers who have endured persecution, but I can assure you that suffering is quite real."

"I know that," Kennedy was quick to assure her. "But I just thought ..."

"That maybe because we were suffering for God he would make it a little less painful?" Hannah finished for her.

Kennedy tried not to grimace while Hannah wiped some snot off her daughter's nose with her sleeve.

"I'm sure he can do that, and I'm sure he sometimes does," Hannah went on, "but when I was in jail, when I was suffering, it was just as real and just as painful as it would have been for any other prisoner in my situation. And like I said, I know God sometimes does protect his children so they don't feel the pain, but supernatural protection isn't promised or guaranteed. I know the kind of books you're talking about, by the way. And although I'm glad they exist to bring awareness about persecution worldwide, I think they can also be dangerous if they're teaching others that believers are immune from pain just because they're being persecuted for Christ. In fact, it's the opposite that's true, which is why they need our prayers so desperately."

Kennedy pretended to be busy pulling out some tablecloths even though she had no idea what size or color or quantity Hannah needed.

"Oh, there you are," Sandy called out as she bustled down the stairs. "Hannah, I'm so glad you came. I nearly forgot you were on your way over. Are you finding everything?"

Hannah glanced at Kennedy with a smile that clearly told her whatever blunders or false assumptions she'd made were forgiven. Sandy bustled around the linen closet pulling just about everything out, and Kennedy waited patiently for the two women to finish up so she could catch a ride with Sandy back home to her parents' house.

CHAPTER 27

"ALL RIGHT, KENSIE GIRL. You've got your ID on you, right? And you have your phone charger? I don't want your batteries dying on you while you're in Washington."

Kennedy leaned her head against the car window. Five o'clock was too early for anyone to be awake, let alone on the road.

"We're making good time." Her dad, who hadn't worn a watch in years, still glanced at his wrist out of habit. "Do you have some cash to buy breakfast at the airport, or did you grab something from home?"

"I have a granola bar and some trail mix, but I've got my wallet in case I get hungry."

He frowned. "Well, you know airport food is a racket. I can stop by a drive-through on the way if you want."

"I'll be fine." As long as she didn't have to engage in any deep or meaningful discussion while she waited for her brain to wake up.

"I want you to call me when you land in Seattle, all right? And then send me a text when you get to Ian's grandma's house. Where'd you say she lives?"

"Orchard Grove."

"Never heard of it," her dad remarked.

Kennedy remained silent.

He reached over and patted her knee like he had when she was seven years old. "You ready, kiddo?"

She turned to look out her window so he couldn't see her roll her eyes. "I'm fine."

"Been a tough few months for you, hasn't it?"

"You could put it that way," she mumbled. What did he think? That five in the morning was a good time for a heavy heart-to-heart?

"I'm glad you'll be with Ian's family. I think it will be good for you. And I'm sure you'll be checking the news, but I'll let you know if I hear any updates about Secretary Hamilton's trip. I just want you to remember ..." He sighed and didn't complete his thought.

"Remember what?" What was this? A guessing game where she had to try to read his mind and fill in the blanks?

"Oh, it's probably nothing. I was just thinking about Ian. If he comes home, you know he's probably not going to be the same person."

"What's that supposed to mean?" she demanded, even though she knew exactly what her dad was trying to tell her.

"What I'm saying is that as difficult as these past few months have been for him, trauma like that's not something you just jump back from overnight."

What did he think? That Kennedy hadn't experienced her share of trauma since she first arrived at Harvard? Getting kidnapped, being stalked, standing fifteen feet away from a lunatic who blew himself up with a homemade bomb ... Should she start listing out all that she'd gone through? Sure, she was different. She was changed. But at her core, she was still the same Kennedy who first arrived at Harvard University three and a half years ago.

It would be the same with Ian. Yes, he'd gone through some unimaginable suffering. But if he was set free — no, *once* he was set free — he would still be the same person.

Wouldn't he?

"Some people who suffer trauma become withdrawn. Depressed. They might lash out at the people closest to them ..."

"All right, I get it," she snapped. What was he thinking? Did he seriously believe that now was the appropriate time for one of his WebMD recitations?

What was he trying to scare her away from? From ever wanting to see Ian again? Insinuating that even if he ever did return to the States, he'd be a completely different man than the one she'd fallen in love with last summer?

Prey on her worst fears by telling her things she already worried about?

He cleared his throat. "I just don't want to see you get hurt, Princess."

Yeah, Kennedy thought to herself. *You and me both.*

CHAPTER 28

"I HAVEN'T STOPPED PRAYING for you since the moment you got on your plane this morning."

Kennedy accepted the old woman's hug and figured that Grandma Lucy was probably being more literal than figurative.

"My niece Connie is waiting to drive us home. You ready to visit Orchard Grove?"

Kennedy nodded. She had forgotten how short Grandma Lucy was. "It's so good to see you."

Two Christmases ago, both Kennedy and Grandma Lucy had been passengers aboard the same flight. At the time, she never would have guessed that she'd one day end up dating the woman's grandson.

"You have no idea what it means to have you here joining us for the prayer vigil." Grandma Lucy led Kennedy out of the Seattle airport. "I'm so thankful the Lord gave you peace in your heart about coming all the way out here. I was praying about that, you know."

Kennedy was certain she had. Based on her own interactions with Grandma Lucy and coupled with everything Ian told her, Kennedy had the feeling she was walking beside the most prayerful woman she'd ever met or ever would.

"You'll like the farm," Grandma Lucy was saying as she led her to a red car parked by the curb. "We have goats and the cutest little gift shop with soaps and lotions and I'm just so pleased you came out here. I was telling Connie the other day how blessed I feel in my spirit about your visit. I truly sense God's favor." She reached out and gave Kennedy's hand a squeeze. Her skin was surprisingly soft for someone that old and wrinkly.

"Now, listen to me," she sighed, "prattling on while you must be so tired. She released Kennedy's hand and instead put her palm flat against Kennedy's forehead and started to pray right there on the curb. "God, precious Redeemer, merciful Savior, comforting Friend, you are the healer of all our sorrows. You neither grow faint nor weary, and you call us to cast all our cares upon you, which is what we're here to do. Thank you for bringing my sweet little friend to come and be a ray of sunshine to me for these next few days. May we be a mutual blessing to one another, Lord, and may your word dwell in us richly in all our conversations. May everything we do and think and say bring glory and honor to your name, mighty Lord of hosts, King of the universe.

"I'm so thankful, Jesus, yes so thankful. First of all, we give you praise that the Secretary of State herself is going to meet with the leaders in Pyongyang. And I know it's no coincidence that her visit is at the exact same time as our prayer vigil. You yourself have told us that where two or three are gathered in your name, there you are in our midst. Just like you did in the days of Peter and Paul, may you open prison doors and set the captives free in the powerful name of Jesus, who forgives all our sins and heals all our diseases and shows us the way we should go and redeems us from sin, hell, and the grave.

"We come before you, two daughters of the King who both love my grandson very much, who are both waiting with eager expectation and hope for the day when you bring about his release, and not just release from his physical captivity, dear Jesus, but release from all the sin and ignorance that have held him captive for so long. Open up his eyes. Show him that you are the Way, the Truth, and the Life and that no one comes to the Father except by the powerful name of Jesus Christ of Nazareth, for there is no other name under heaven given to men by which we must be saved. And so we trust you, dear Lord, to be the author and finisher of my grandson's faith, to complete the good work you began in him so many years ago when he was just a small boy with the simple faith of a child. You promise that nothing can snatch us out of your hands, dear Lord, so that's what we pray for him today. Take his heart of stone and give him instead a heart of flesh. Let these dry bones rise up and praise you because you alone are the King of kings and the Lord of lords, and you alone are worthy of all of our honor and glory and praise."

Grandma Lucy took her hand off Kennedy's forehead, opened the back door of the car, and without so much as an *amen* or any other indication that she'd just spent the past several minutes praying loudly outside the Seattle airport, she leaned into the car and said, "Kennedy, I'd like to introduce you to my niece Connie. She's going to drive us back to Orchard Grove, so you just find room for you and your bags and make yourself comfortable. We've got a long trip ahead of us, so go ahead and nap if you want. Heaven knows that's what I'm planning to do."

CHAPTER 29

KENNEDY HAD NEVER BEEN to Washington before except for some layovers in the Seattle Airport. True to her prediction, Grandma Lucy slept for nearly the entire drive with a handkerchief draped over her face. Ian's aunt was cheerful and talkative, but Kennedy spent most of the trip staring out the window in silence. She had no idea it was so mountainous out here. Light snow fell on the pass, and she drifted in and out of sleep from the hypnotic sight of the snowflakes falling outside.

"Well," Connie breathed after they turned down what at first seemed to be a never-ending driveway, "we're here. Welcome to Safe Anchorage Farm."

While Connie nudged Grandma Lucy awake, Kennedy opened the car door and was immediately greeted by the sound of bleating.

"You just ignore that," Connie told her. "It's our goat Peaches, the drama queen of the herd. I'm sure she thinks she's dying, but the truth is she's old and ornery and pregnant, so you don't pay her no mind." She nudged Grandma Lucy again until the old woman woke up mid-snore.

"We here?"

Connie smiled and nodded. "We're here."

"Thank the Lord." Grandma Lucy stretched her legs when she got out of the car. "Sweet Jesus, you've given me this one body, and I've done what I can to take care of it all these decades, but Lord, I pray that you'd reach down and heal this stiffness in my bones because you know how grumpy I can get when I'm aching, and I know that's not what you want for me."

Kennedy glanced over at Connie in hopes of finding some sort of clue as to what to do next, but Connie just went around and shut Grandma Lucy's door as if the old woman talked to God out loud any minute of the day.

Actually, she probably did. It was something Kennedy would have to get used to.

The goat Peaches bleated again, and if it hadn't been for Connie's reassurances earlier, Kennedy might have thought the animal was getting slaughtered.

"Come on," Connie said, pulling Kennedy's arm and leading her toward a large farm house. "We're so excited to have one of Ian's friends as a guest. I can't wait to show you around."

CHAPTER 30

KENNEDY HAD NEVER MET a woman like Connie, who could turn a tour of a two-story farmhouse into a ninety-minute rundown of a century's worth of family history, starting with Grandma Lucy's parents and their ministry in China before the Communist takeover.

When Kennedy mentioned her parents had also served in Asia, Connie clasped her hands together. "Oh, I just knew the two of you would be kindred spirits. She mentions you all the time, you know. Whenever I pass by the prayer room, if it's not Ian I hear her talking about, I can be pretty sure it'll be you."

Kennedy wasn't exactly sure why Grandma Lucy would spend that much time in prayer for her. They hardly knew each other.

"Oh," Connie continued, her voice as animated as the perkiest of flight attendants, "speaking of the prayer room, I've saved the best for last. Are you ready?"

She led Kennedy to a screen door. Putting her finger to her lips, she beckoned Kennedy forward.

"She's still praying there, so I don't want to bother her," Connie whispered, "but this is where Grandma Lucy spends most of her time."

Kennedy glanced in. Grandma Lucy sat in a rocker. Her back was to the screen so Kennedy couldn't see her face, but her arms were raised heavenward and her voice rang out loudly and clearly.

"Dear Father, King of the ages, the Prince of Peace and the Lord of lords, you are the one who calms my troubled heart. You are the one who comforts me in all my distress. You are the balm of Gilead, the one who tells me that your yoke is easy and your burden is light. Today I confess my fears to you, Lord, and how distressed I'll remain until my grandson acknowledges you as his Lord and Savior."

Kennedy leaned forward. She'd never been great at long or lengthy prayers, but something in her wanted to stay and listen to Grandma Lucy all evening.

"She'll be a while." Connie took Kennedy's hand and led her away.

Kennedy followed reluctantly, and while Connie showed her the antique tea sets in the dining room, Kennedy's ears still strained to catch the echoes of Ian's grandmother as she poured out her heart to God.

CHAPTER 31

"You're a skinny little thing, aren't you?" Connie piled another massive scoop of shepherd's pie onto Kennedy's plate. "Is that how bad dorm food is these days?" She let out a chuckle. "No wonder my pa wouldn't let me go to one of those co-ed schools."

Kennedy wasn't sure if Connie was making a joke or being serious. What she did know was that if she ate another bite of anything, she'd probably burst her stomach.

Connie sat beaming and elbowed her husband, Dennis. "Isn't she a skinny thing?"

Dennis, who had been reading at the table, looked over the top of his newspaper and scowled. "Guess so."

Connie nudged him again. "Remember when I was that petite?" She exploded into chuckles.

Kennedy wasn't exactly sure what was supposed to happen next. She glanced at Grandma Lucy, who looked as if she were about to fall asleep in her chair.

Connie stood up to pour more lemonade into Kennedy's glass. "Now, don't be shy. You eat everything you want, but be sure to save room because we have some of our famous cinnamon rolls that will be out of the oven soon."

So that's what Kennedy smelled when she came downstairs from the guest room. "This has all been delicious, but I really can't eat another bite."

Connie waved her hand in the air. "Of course you can. You just have to wash it down with more water to make room for it all."

Kennedy moved her food around her plate with her fork. Her head was swimming with the names of Ian's dozens of cousins that Connie had spent the afternoon rattling off. Hopefully there wouldn't be any pop quiz.

Connie hadn't taken her eyes off Kennedy since she refilled her glass. Kennedy brought a forkful of shepherd's pie to her lips.

"Do you like it?" Connie leaned forward in her chair.

"It's wonderful," Kennedy assured her just like she had after the previous two servings.

"Well, you know, my shepherd's pie is one of Ian's favorites. Isn't that right?" Connie nodded toward Grandma Lucy, who still looked more asleep than awake, but Connie didn't seem deterred. "I'm so glad you liked it. I just had to guess. In fact, I kept meaning to ask Ian what foods you ate after we got one of his electronic pieces of mail where he told us he'd met a nice girl in Seoul. You know, we all assumed you were Asian, didn't we, Dennis?" Connie asked her husband, who continued to read. "And then he sent us your picture, and Grandma Lucy was the first to recognize you from that terrible plane trip you both took, isn't that right?" She nudged Grandma Lucy. "And I had to laugh and tell him, *Ian, when you tell us you found a girl in South Korea, you know you've got to spell out that she's white, or we're all going to assume otherwise, know what I mean?*" This time, her question wasn't directed at anyone in particular, and Kennedy kept her focus on her plate.

"And boy, we could tell after those first few pieces of electronic mail that he was really taken with you, couldn't we, Dennis? I remember telling Grandma Lucy, I said, *I think that boy's finally found a woman who'll make him want to settle down once and for all.* Isn't that what I said? Well, of course Ian didn't get into too many details, and I never could make heads or tails of it. Did you two actually meet over there on the other side of the world? Or did you know each other before that?"

Kennedy wished Connie's husband would put down his newspaper or Grandma Lucy would wake up so she wouldn't have to carry on this conversation alone, but since neither one changed their position at the table, she took a deep breath and tried to decide where to start.

"We knew each other in Cambridge, at least a little bit."

A smile lit up Connie's face. It was the same expression Kennedy's mom would get when she was watching one of the cowboys on her sappy farm romance movies telling the heroine how madly in love with her he was.

"So he was your beau before you went over to Asia, is that right?"

Kennedy tried to recall if she had ever heard anyone called a *beau* outside of a historical fiction novel or a centuries-old classic. "Well, we didn't date all that seriously. I mean, we went out a couple times my junior year, but it really wasn't all that much."

Connie shook her head. "You know, dating was so simple when I was a kid. Isn't that right, Dennis? If a boy was interested in you, he made his intentions known, and by the time you'd been out four or five times, you could both assume things were serious, and that was that. Now with Dennis and me, we knew right from the start, didn't we? We knew we had something special between us. That spark, as I guess you young kids might call it today. I don't quite remember if we had a word for it back then. I'm sure we did, but it's probably so outdated by now. But that's how it was for us."

"So how did you meet?" Kennedy asked.

Connie's eyes grew even wider, although a few seconds earlier Kennedy wouldn't have guessed it was possible. She crossed her arms and let out a laugh. "Ours is a story of love at first sight a year delayed. See, Dennis and I were employed in difference sections for the same company, and we just so happened to work right across the hall from each other. Our bosses were friends, and once they took each of their staffs out to a mixed lunch. Dennis's car was closer than mine, so I asked if I could ride with him to the restaurant. Well, it happened to be payday or else I'm not sure our story would have ever turned out the way it did, but I needed to cash my check. So after our luncheon at the restaurant, I asked him if he could make a quick stop at the bank so that I could go and turn my paycheck in. You know, that's how we had to do it in those days. None of this computer banking nonsense.

"And, Dennis, you'll have to correct me if I'm getting the facts wrong, but he said something like, *Oh, that's no problem. I have to drop my check off too.* Well, I happened to find out much later that he didn't even have a checking account, so you can imagine what was on his mind this whole time, except of course I didn't know it back then. I didn't suspect a thing. So we stopped by the bank, and on the way back to the office, he said — and you'll never believe the cheek — he said, *Oh, by the way, it was my birthday last week, and I didn't get a single birthday kiss*. What a line! Right?" She took her cloth napkin and hit her husband's newspaper with it. He turned the page and kept on reading.

"So that's what he said to me, and then, talk about nerve, he asked if I would give him one. I said yes, expecting a nice, sweet, chaste kiss, but nope, that's not what he had in mind, the scoundrel. He really laid one on me. Then he asked me to go to the movies with him that night. We did, and that was that. When I got back home I told these two other guys that I had been dating — nothing too serious since back then it wasn't uncommon to have a couple of beaus at once — I had met the man that I wanted to marry, so thank you very much, but I didn't need to be seeing anyone else. Six weeks later we went to the little chapel and got ourselves hitched. Isn't that right, Dennis? Isn't that how it happened?"

Dennis grunted from behind his paper, and Connie stood up to clear the table.

CHAPTER 32

GIVEN HOW EARLY KENNEDY had woken up coupled with the full day of travel, there was no reason why she shouldn't be sound asleep.

Except for the way that old goat's yelling carried all the way to her room.

She glanced at the clock. Half past ten, which meant one- thirty in East Coast time. She sighed and rolled over. The attic guest room gave her some privacy, but it was drafty and faced the barn, which probably didn't help the noise level from that silly goat. In the morning, Connie planned to take Kennedy milking. Unfortunately, if Kennedy didn't get to sleep soon, she'd be no better than a coma patient when the sun rose and the time came for barn chores.

The bathroom was all the way on the lower level, so Kennedy threw off the crocheted quilts on the bed — Grandma Lucy's prayer blankets — and made her way down the uneven steps to the ground level. Passing by the prayer room, she saw a faint light and peered in.

Grandma Lucy was on the floor, with her forehead resting on the seat of her rocking chair. Kennedy didn't know a whole lot about growing old, but she didn't guess there were too many people Grandma Lucy's age who could still kneel while they prayed.

Sensing this was something of a private moment, she continued walking past on her way to the bathroom, but Grandma Lucy's warbly voice carried through the screen door.

"I want you to know how much I love him, Father God. I want you to know that even though he's a grown man now, he's still that same scared little boy I cared for all those years ago when his poor mama died. And that's how I'll always see him, Lord, and I know you understand, you being the Father of us all. I confess, sweet Jesus, that I worry more for him than a Christian should, but the truth is, sweet Savior, part of me feels guilty, like I should have been praying more fervently for him to be kept safe on all his travels. Like if I'd been faithful, he wouldn't be in this mess he's in. But even the trials he's suffering right now pale in comparison to the torment and the torture that you went through when you died for him on that cross. And so I'm praying Lord, even if you don't save my grandson's body, even if the Secretary isn't able to secure his release, even if he ends up dying battered and scared and all alone, I can accept that, Lord. But don't let him die without knowing you as his Savior and Redeemer. Preserve his life until just like the thief on the cross he admits that you alone are the Son of God and that you alone hold the key to eternal life. I might never see my grandson again on earth, and if that's the way it's going to be, well, I know that not even a sparrow falls to the ground apart from your will. But if you're asking me to spend an eternity separated from this boy I love, well, Lord, you know I'm not one to tell you how to run your universe, but I won't stand for any of that. Not a chance."

Kennedy had heard enough. Too much, really. She felt guilty for eavesdropping and closed herself in the bathroom. Splashing water on her face, she studied her reflection in the mirror. She looked so tired. They say that worry and stress can age you far more effectively than time. If that were the case, she was probably two or three decades older now than she'd been when she started out as a first-year student at Harvard. Yes, her trials had shaped her and matured her and developed her faith, but if she were given the chance, would she willingly walk through any of them again?

It was one of those times where she knew what answer she was supposed to give, which was different than the answer she would give if she were being truly honest with herself.

It was the same thing with Ian, in a way. At first, she had only been asking herself if going out with him was worth the pain of their breakup, but now it was so much more complicated than that. If Kennedy had known how difficult the semester would be with her worrying about Ian, if she had been given the choice to never go with him to South Korea over the summer in the first place, if they had never gotten serious about their relationship and had ended things with those few quick breakfast get-togethers last year, would it be better? Or was it worth the worry? If she had the choice to spare herself all this anxiety and all she had to do was to never start dating Ian in the first place, never develop these feelings she had for him, feelings that had grown even stronger since his imprisonment, what would she have chosen?

And in the end, what did it really matter?

The past couldn't be changed. Neither could her emotions. She splashed water on her face one more time and turned off the bathroom lights.

CHAPTER 33

KENNEDY EXPECTED TO SNEAK past the prayer room and make her way upstairs undetected, but when she came out of the bathroom, there was Grandma Lucy in the hallway, staring at her.

"I thought you might have a hard time sleeping. Won't you come and sit with me for a spell?" Without another word, she took Kennedy's hand and led her into her private sanctuary, some sort of converted greenhouse with glass walls on all three sides overlooking a perfectly clear night sky. She never saw stars like this in Cambridge.

"Have a seat." Grandma Lucy plunked Kennedy down in an overstuffed loveseat that looked like it must be Connie's age or older. Grandma Lucy pulled up her rocking chair and sat so close to Kennedy that their knees touched.

"Now, child, here we are." Grandma Lucy spoke in an authoritative voice. "Tell me what's troubling you so we can take your burdens and offer them to the Lord as a sweet sacrifice to the one who bears our sorrows."

Kennedy wondered if she would ever get used to the way Grandma Lucy spoke, as if she were some sort of walking Bible concordance.

Talk about what was troubling her? Where should she begin?

"I hear that you and my grandson broke up before your arrest."

Kennedy nodded.

"Let's start there," Grandma Lucy said. "When did God tell you it was time to break up, and how did that act of selfless obedience feel?"

Kennedy stared at her lap. "I don't know that there was any exact moment or anything like that," she began. "We spent the summer together in Seoul, and we had a lot of good discussions about faith. It sounded like he was at least curious enough to question what he'd believed, so I thought if I gave him enough time, he might ... We might end up on the same page. But then the fall came, and I was about to go back to campus, and I realized he still didn't believe in God, and I knew it wouldn't be wise to keep on dating anymore."

Funny how she had broken up with him nearly half a year ago, and this was the first conversation she'd had with anyone about Ian that didn't revolve around his imprisonment.

"The Lord promises to be gracious to us and to pour out his blessings on us when we follow him, even if the way is painful. Just like Abraham sacrificing Isaac on the altar, you sacrificed this relationship that meant a great deal to you and offered it to the Lord, and I'm convinced that he has smiled on your act of submission and will grant you his mercy and favor."

Well, that sounded fine if you were a walking Bible encyclopedia, but Kennedy couldn't figure out how spending three nights in the Chinese jail and an entire semester worrying sick about someone she cared so deeply for meant that she had somehow earned her way into God's good graces.

"Honestly," she confessed, "it feels more like he's been punishing me for dating an unbeliever to begin with."

Grandma Lucy frowned. "Well, did you have peace in your spirit about it before you agreed to date him?"

Kennedy thought back to that night of their first kiss. They had been talking about Russian literature, and then before she knew what was happening, his lips were on hers, and they spent the rest of their summer as a couple. "Actually, I'm not really sure I knew what I was getting into. It happened sort of fast, you know ..." She stared at Grandma Lucy's slippered feet, hoping the old woman wouldn't think less of her after the admission.

"Well, you won't get a lecture from me. I know how the heart can lead you astray, and I'm the last one to judge based on my own experience."

Kennedy must have looked incredulous, because Grandma Lucy insisted, "It's true. You can ask Connie to tell you the story in the morning if you want. Or better yet," she added with a chuckle, "I better tell you now so you can stick to the short version."

She adjusted the blanket on her lap, which Kennedy assumed was another one of the prayer quilts she had crocheted, and sighed deeply. "My husband and I divorced after the kids were grown. I'm not proud of that fact, but it's there in my past, and Floyd has moved on to glory now anyway, so it's not like I could seek to be reconciled at this point. Although, in the end, I did try. Well, after he was gone, I found myself communicating with a pen pal in Australia, an elderly gentleman who sometimes wrote articles for Prayer Warriors International. Do you know that magazine?"

Kennedy shook her head, although she figured a publication like that would be perfect for Grandma Lucy.

"Well," Grandma Lucy continued, "I took a difference with something he said in one of his articles. He wrote that since God already knows the future, prayer isn't so much meant to change any predetermined event but to draw us into a closer relationship with the Lord. So I wrote back to tell him what a load of hogwash that was. Think about Hezekiah. The king is sick and the prophet Isaiah himself tells him he's about to die, but Hezekiah prays so fervently and so passionately that God changes his mind and adds fifteen years to his life. Now I'm not making that up or putting words in God's mouth. That's exactly what the Scriptures say. So I went back to Harold and asked how dare you imply that our prayers are only meant to give us some sort of do-good award with the Almighty and not a tool God uses to shape all of history? Because I had already determined that if I weren't completely convinced my prayers were going to change the world, well, why bother? And I don't say so flippantly. That's truly the way I thought about it then and the way I still think about it now.

"Before you know it, Harold and I are writing each other letters every week, and next thing he's booked a cruise that's going to be in the Seattle port for a few days and wants to take me out to dinner. Naïve and unsuspecting as I was, I imagined we'd find ourselves facing off across the table from one another, continuing on in our debate. Because he never did manage to change my mind, but I have to admit that he had some pretty solid scriptural basis for his point of view, fatalistic and pessimistic as it may be.

"So imagine my surprise when he shows up at the restaurant with a dozen roses and a pearl necklace he tells me belonged to his late wife. And something I suppose you'll eventually learn about me is I'm a woman of prayer, and I don't typically do anything without taking it before the Lord and getting his opinion on the matter, but it's not like I thought to excuse myself at that restaurant and lock myself in the bathroom stall until God told me whether I should except his flowers and his dead wife's necklace or not.

"Long story short — and here's where Connie can fill you in if you really want all the details and have a couple hours to spare — Harold became my beau."

Kennedy wondered if talking like you were a character in a turn-of-the-century novel was a requirement for living at the Safe Anchorage farmhouse or if she'd pick up the habit by the time she headed back to the East Coast.

"And in the end," Grandma Lucy concluded, "it became clear in a matter of weeks that Harold and I simply weren't meant for one another, and even now I wish I had had the foresight to get up and go into that bathroom and pray before I accepted his little tokens. All that to say I understand that when the heart is concerned, no matter what your age, you might not make the wisest of choices. And I know my grandson. He can be quite a charmer." She fingered her blanket and chuckled. "When he was just a tiny thing, we took him to see the Little Mermaid movie. Then he came home and swore that when he grew up, he was going to make that little redhead his wife. I shouldn't tell you this, but all through high school he had a slew of girls vying for his attention, but he never got too serious with anyone until he and Abby got engaged."

Grandma Lucy looked at Kennedy with so much certainty and familiarity that Kennedy was slightly embarrassed to find herself asking, "Who's Abby?"

Grandma Lucy started fidgeting furiously with her crocheted prayer blanket. "Now, listen to me. Getting my stories all mixed up so I can't remember what I've already told you and what I haven't." She let out an unconvincing laugh. "That's what happens when your brain gets as old as mine. I'm just thankful the dear Lord allows me to keep my head on straight most days."

"Who's Abby?" Kennedy repeated.

Grandma Lucy sighed. "Well, now, I thought since you and Ian were together he would have mentioned her, but I suppose that's not my story to tell. It's his."

How fair was that? Ian might never get out of North Korea, and then what was Kennedy supposed to do?

She thought about pressing the issue but then wondered if she really wanted to know. If Ian thought it was important to tell her something about his past, he would have, right?

She stood up. "Well, it's late. I should probably head back to bed."

Grandma Lucy made no move as if she were ready to leave her rocking chair. She took Kennedy's hand in hers. "Goodnight, sweet child of the Most High King."

Kennedy smiled at her, wondering if she'd always been this eccentric or if the change had come with age. It was nice to think about something besides Ian and some fiancée he'd never bothered telling her about.

She offered Grandma Lucy one more goodnight, reminding herself that just because Ian had been engaged at some point in the past, it didn't change anything about those wonderful months they'd spent together.

By the time she reached the guest room in the attic, she still wasn't convinced.

CHAPTER 34

OUT OF ALL THE things she might be upset about, this really should be pretty low on her list.

So her boyfriend had been engaged to another woman and hadn't told her. That just meant it wasn't all that serious.

But how can you be engaged and have that count as *not serious*?

Was it her business? She and Ian weren't even dating anymore. But if he'd been keeping something this big from her that whole time ...

It was stupid to get herself so worked up. She was probably overly tired and wasn't thinking straight. That's all there was to it. So Kennedy wasn't Ian's first girlfriend. Big deal. At his age, she would have seriously wondered what was wrong with him if he hadn't dated other women in the past.

And it wasn't like Kennedy told him about every single guy she'd dated. Well, actually, she had, but that was because she could count all her serious relationships on one finger.

She rolled over in bed. It made sense for her to lose sleep worrying if Ian was being starved or tortured.

It didn't make sense to be anxious over something this tiny.

So Ian had a past.

Who didn't?

She'd been moving around so much the sheets were tangled up with the blankets. Kennedy had never heard of prayer quilts before. What made a prayer quilt different than any other handmade blanket?

She rubbed her hands over the wool, finding some soothing comfort in the feel of the numerous bumps.

She was overreacting. That was all. If she were talking to her therapist, he'd probably make some suggestion like it was easier for her brain to worry about something relatively common to relationships — a past love that made her feel threatened or vulnerable — than to fixate on something as unfathomable as a man she'd been so close to suffering unthinkable torment in some prison camp or jail cell.

Yeah, that's what it was. Her brain could handle something as petty and universal as jealousy.

Why had she come to Orchard Grove in the first place?

Why couldn't she pray for Ian back home?

She tried thinking over everything she and Grandma Lucy had talked about in the prayer room but had a hard time focusing on anything that came before the mention of some woman named Abby. Didn't they talk about prayer?

And dating?

Grandma Lucy didn't make Kennedy feel bad for seeing Ian in the first place, but the guilt and regrets had been creeping up on her for some time now. Maybe she should have prayed, just like Grandma Lucy said she should have done with that Aussie gentleman who gave her the pearl necklace. It was strange to think of someone Grandma Lucy's age struggling with romance and unruly emotions just like Kennedy did.

And tonight her emotions were especially chaotic.

Okay, Lord, she started to pray. *Maybe I didn't make the wisest of choices by dating Ian in the first place, and if I did something that wasn't pleasing to you, I'm sorry. But now I don't know what to do. I seriously don't know how I can handle another week, let alone another semester, with all this stress about Ian. I worry so much about him I don't sleep, I'm not eating well, and I barely passed my classes last semester. I just can't do this much longer.*

I thought he'd be home by now. I expected you to hear all these prayers from around the world and act. Do something. How hard can it be? You're God. You can do anything.

Don't you want Ian to come home?

Kennedy paused, ruminating over that last thought. Did she want Ian to come home?

Of course she did.

But somewhere in the back of her mind she recalled her dad's warnings.

Some people who suffer trauma become withdrawn. Depressed. They might lash out at the people closest to them.

If he comes home, you know he's probably not going to be the same person.

Well, no surprise there. Who would go through something that awful and then jump back into day-to-day life as if nothing had ever happened?

But was she ready for the changes?

And since she technically wasn't dating him anymore, did it really matter? Maybe he'd come home and wouldn't want anything to do with her. Who knew? Maybe he'd go find that Abby girl and get back together with her.

It shouldn't matter.

But it did.

And she would continue to be stressed and tired and scarcely functional until she learned how to truly surrender her emotions and anxiety and any thoughts or plans about both her future and Ian's to the Lord.

If only she knew how.

CHAPTER 35

"Now, Peaches is a special goat," Connie explained, "and you've got to be real careful when you're milking her because she likes to make a game out of spilling the pail. And you never want to stand directly behind her either, because let me tell you, I've never had a heart attack, thank the good Lord, but I can't imagine it being much more painful than a goat hoof straight to your chest."

She chuckled while cleaning Peaches' udders.

"Is it just the light in here, or is this goat pink?" Kennedy asked.

Connie didn't slow down. "Nope, it's not the light. She's a special one, all right. That's how she got her name. Now you get your hands clean and hand me that bucket."

Kennedy had watched Connie work on two of the other goats already. A few summers earlier, on one of her trips to Alaska, Willow had tried to teach Kennedy how to milk, but she never got the hang of it. So far, today's lesson wasn't shaping up to be any more promising.

"Careful not to squeeze all at once," Connie said. "It's got to be a fluid motion." She reached out her fist and drew milk from an imaginary teat. "There you go," she exclaimed when Peaches produced a small trickle. "Now just watch your aim and see if you can get it in the bucket this time. We'll make a farm girl out of you yet."

Kennedy finally got into her rhythm right as her hand cramped up. Unfortunately, she didn't have nearly as good luck with her left hand, so Connie took over and Kennedy made herself useful helping to get the goats in and out of the milking stand and keeping their grain trough full.

"Did you sleep well last night?" Connie asked while milking a black and white doe. It came no higher than Kennedy's knee but had just as much milk or even more than the animals twice its size.

"It was all right," Kennedy answered tentatively. She was still deciding how to broach a certain subject. Or if it should be broached at all.

"I got up to use the bathroom and ended up spending a little time with Grandma Lucy."

"I bet she took you into her prayer room, didn't she?" Connie asked with a smile.

"Yeah."

"Did you have a good time?"

It was the opening Kennedy had been waiting for. "Yeah, it was all right. We talked and prayed and had some interesting discussions. She told me about her beau from Australia."

Kennedy glanced at Connie's face to make sure she'd pronounced the word right.

Connie broke into a smile. "Oh, is that a story for you."

Kennedy rushed ahead before Connie decided to give her all the details. It wasn't Grandma Lucy's love life she was interested in learning more about.

"She mentioned something else, too, but I was so tired we didn't talk about it much. I was wondering what you could tell me about Ian's old girlfriend Abby, the one he used to be engaged to."

CHAPTER 36

WHEREAS GRANDMA LUCY SEEMED reluctant to talk to Kennedy about something as private as Ian's former love-life, Connie showed no such hesitation.

"Ian was something of a ladies' man in high school," she began. "Always had some girl or other hanging around and at least half a dozen more nursing major crushes on him. I'm not saying he was stringing them along or doing anything untoward. I think he was so bright and charming and intelligent that the girls just fell over themselves around him. But even though he had his fair share of girlfriends, nothing ever got real serious until he went to college. It was at Harvard that he met a girl named Abby. She was pre-law, and he was going into film and journalism, and for as casually as he dated in high school, with him and Abby it was hot and heavy from the get go. Maybe I shouldn't put it that way, since I truly don't know all those details, but he was quite taken with her. Brought her home for Christmas break their very first semester. I told Dennis, he can tell you this too if you ask, but I told Dennis that I thought she'd be the one he was going to settle down with, and everyone else in the family assumed the same. Everyone except Grandma Lucy. And maybe I should have paid more attention then because one thing you learn about Grandma Lucy is she has an uncanny sense of discernment. Once a friend called her up who Grandma Lucy hadn't talked to in years, and the first words out of Grandma Lucy's mouth were, *So you're finally going to become a grandma.* And she was right. Not only that, but this friend of hers only had one child, a daughter that doctors had said for years wouldn't ever be able to conceive, and Grandma Lucy knew from the minute she picked up that phone, or at the very least had a very strong premonition, that this daughter the doctor had declared infertile was now pregnant, and that's exactly what her friend called to tell her. So maybe we all should have paid more attention when Grandma Lucy declared that Abby wasn't the one for Ian."

Connie cocked her head to the side with an expression that made her look like a curious puppy dog. "Come to think of it, I would have thought Ian would have told you this himself."

"No," Kennedy admitted. "He never mentioned it."

Connie shook her head and mumbled, "Men. It's like pulling teeth getting them to tell you anything."

Kennedy didn't think the comment warranted a response, so she kept quiet and waited for Connie to continue.

"Well, things were going great from what we could tell. In the summer between their junior and senior year, if I remember right, Ian called to tell us that he and Abby were engaged. Cute story too, by the way. People nowadays are so creative in their proposals. Have you noticed that? Back when I was seeing Dennis, there weren't much more to it than a ring, but now it seems like every beau's trying to surprise his girlfriend and then you get the whole thing on video, which was exactly what Ian did. I can dig it out if you want me to. We have it somewhere on DVD." Connie stopped herself. "Well, never mind," she added quickly. "It's been a while since I've gone through those old boxes, and you know DVDs are far less durable than the old videotapes were, so let's just forget about that." She cleared her throat.

"So where was I again?" Connie frowned and stared at her full pail of milk.

"You were talking about the engagement," Kennedy reminded her.

"Oh, that's right. Well, you don't need the details, I'm sure, but anyway, they got engaged and set the date. You know, I never did understand how real long engagements got to be popular with the young crowd these days. When Dennis and I were seeing each other, all you needed time for was to make your dress and fill out all the invitations, but today people are getting engaged and then waiting two or three years before the wedding itself, and I just don't see the point in that at all, but maybe I'm just an old fuddy-duddy who needs to get with the times." She chuckled and picked up the last pail of milk, and they started heading back toward the house.

"Speaking of engagements," she went on, "I have a girlfriend whose daughter was engaged to be married, and they were going to have their wedding six or seven months later — a nice, reasonable amount of time if you ask me —even though like I told you yesterday Dennis and me did it a lot quicker than that, but this friend of mine, her daughter had her heart set on getting married at some fancy chalet or however you say that. I think it's a French word, but I'm not sure. Anyway, the place they wanted was booked for the whole summer, so do you want to guess what they did? They didn't find some other chalet that would have worked just as well, although you don't even want to get me started on my opinion about young folks who choose to get married outdoors instead of in a church and all the guests have to hike to get to the location, which is what this couple was planning. Since they couldn't get the place they wanted that summer, well, they just push the wedding back a whole year. A whole year. Well, now I've gotten myself all sidetracked. Did I finish the story about Ian and Abby? Isn't that what you asked about first of all?"

She stopped on the back porch and wiped her boots on a mat before stepping into the house.

"All you told me was that they got engaged." A small part of Kennedy wasn't sure she should be hearing this story, but if the past few months had taught her anything, it was that the only thing worse than receiving difficult news was not getting any news at all.

Connie carried the pails into the kitchen and pulled out some clean jars and a funnel. "Well, Ian was engaged, and we were all happy for him. Of course this Abby, she was the sweetest thing and smart as a whip, and she and Ian seemed like a perfect match for each other."

"What happened?"

Connie washed her hands and started pouring the goat milk through a filter. "Well, the way Ian explains it is that Abby's mom was none too happy about their relationship. Abby was a lovely Japanese girl, or at least part Japanese, I don't remember if her father was Asian too or just her mother. Well, I don't know if it was prejudice, or maybe she looked down on Ian because he didn't come from a family with any fancy credentials or extra money, but somehow that woman managed to poison her daughter against him so completely that they had a really nasty, messy breakup, and as far as I know, they haven't spoken to each other since." Connie pointed toward the cupboard. "Can you be a dear and pass me down a couple of lids for these jars?"

Kennedy did as she was asked and tried to decide how she felt now that the great mystery was solved. In reality, the whole story seemed a much smaller deal than it had sounded last night. So Ian had been engaged to someone else, it didn't work out, and that was that. On the one hand, she was relieved that she didn't have to worry anymore or make up stories about why Ian wouldn't have told her about this part of his past, but on the other hand, she felt guilty for prying into what wasn't her business and didn't change anything. Whatever had passed between Ian and Abby, it happened years before he and Kennedy met, and now if she ever did see him again, she'd have this awkward burden of knowing something about his past that he hadn't been the one to tell her.

Then again, maybe it didn't matter.

The chances of Ian's ever coming home felt like they were growing asymptotically smaller with every passing day.

CHAPTER 37

"DO YOU LIKE THE meatloaf, dear?" Connie asked at lunch the next day.

Kennedy nodded, even though her appetite had completely deserted her after her dad sent her such a depressing news link. Secretary Hamilton was unable to meet with North Korea's top leadership like she'd been promised. Instead, she'd been driven around Pyongyang with petty officers who lacked the authority to do anything but serve as glorified tour guides.

"You really should eat more," Connie insisted.

The food wasn't bad, although it might have been more palatable if Grandma Lucy hadn't taken such a long time praying before their meal that everything went cold. Oh, well. Kennedy's appetite had been poor all semester. She hated going to the school cafeteria, seeing all the leftover waste and excess that only reminded her of Ian, who must be close to starving if he weren't already.

She tried to force down Connie's meal, which was actually quite tasty, but her stomach wasn't used to much besides dry Cheerios and Craisins, her dorm room staple.

"I just can't believe how quickly the time has gone," Connie stated, elbowing her husband in the ribs. "Don't you think, Dennis?"

"Huh?" He glanced up from a fishing magazine.

"I said, 'don't you think the time's gone quickly?' Kennedy's going to have to pack soon."

Dennis didn't reply, but Connie was right. In just a few hours, one of the men from Orchard Grove Bible Church would come by to drive Kennedy and Grandma Lucy to Seattle for the prayer vigil. Connie had to stay home with the goats, and since Kennedy was flying out the following morning, it made more sense to spend the night in Seattle rather than drive all the way back out here just to catch a few hours of sleep.

"Do you need an extra suitcase, dear?" Connie asked.

Kennedy shook her head. Even though she was returning to Boston with one of Grandma Lucy's prayer blankets and several trinkets Connie gave her from the farm's little gift shop, she had plenty of space.

Connie let out a contented sigh. "I do declare, it's been so nice having a friend of Ian's with us, hasn't it?" She scooted back her chair. "Well, I suppose I need to get these dishes cleaned up, and then I'll help pack Grandma Lucy a few things for her big trip to Seattle. I'm just so tickled you'll be there praying tonight for Ian, that poor boy."

Connie clasped her hands together by her chest and looked up toward the sky. Kennedy wondered what she had to be so excited about.

Ever since she heard about Secretary Hamilton's failed mission to North Korea, Kennedy got the sickening feeling that tonight's gathering would be less like a prayer vigil for someone who had hope of rescue and more like a memorial service for a man who'd already died.

CHAPTER 38

"COME IN, COME IN." Connie swung open the farmhouse door and embraced the young man with a giant hug. "Scott, this is Ian's good friend Kennedy. Kennedy, I'd like to introduce you to Scott Phillips, who just moved to Orchard Grove from your neck of the woods."

"Actually, I've been here a year," the tall man said, stepping into the farmhouse. He gave Kennedy a smile. "Nice to meet you."

Connie had already given Kennedy the abbreviated version of Scott's entire life story. He'd spent years on the mission field before moving to Orchard Grove and marrying a local girl, and Kennedy figured they could find quite a bit to talk about on the way to Seattle.

"Grandma Lucy!" Connie called out. "Scott's here. Are you ready?"

Grandma Lucy emerged from her prayer room, groaning slightly as she leaned against the wall.

Connie bustled over to help her. "You tired today?" she asked.

Grandma Lucy paused before making her way down the hall. "No more so than usual, praise the good Lord. And Scott, I hope you don't mind if I just rest my eyes on the drive over. I'm afraid I won't be much company to you on the road."

Scott smiled. "Don't worry about it. Can I help you to the car?" He offered his arm.

Kennedy carried her suitcase and set it in Scott's trunk then turned to say goodbye to Connie. "Thanks for everything. It was really nice getting to know you."

"Well, you take care of yourself now." Connie wiped her cheeks and smiled. "I hope you know that even though I can't make it to Seattle tonight, I'll be praying for Ian more than ever." She leaned in for one last hug that smelled like cinnamon rolls and goat milk and old-lady hair spray all at once.

Kennedy glanced behind Connie's shoulder. "Where's your husband?"

Connie waved her hand in the air. "Don't worry about him. He's probably in the den reading or something, but I'll tell him you said goodbye." She wiped her cheeks again. "Be safe. God bless you." She hurried over to help Grandma Lucy get situated in the back seat, and the old woman was asleep even before Scott made it halfway down the long, winding driveway.

"What'd you think of the goat farm?" he asked as he turned onto the road.

"It was great," Kennedy replied automatically, although she knew she'd need more time than thirty seconds to process everything she'd experienced in the past couple days. For some reason, she'd come out here thinking she would find some sort of connection to Ian. As much as she admired his family, even with their little oddities, she realized now more than ever just how far away from her he really was.

Ian wasn't in Washington.

He was in some jail in North Korea, suffering for crimes he never committed, at the mercy of one of the most horrific, oppressive regimes in recent history.

She thought about the conversation she'd had with Hannah. *When I was in jail, when I was suffering, it was just as real and just as painful as it would have been for any other prisoner in my situation.*

It was a new way of looking at suffering and persecution for sure. Up until she started to really think through it, Kennedy had bought into the whole idea that Christians who were persecuted for their faith were guaranteed some sort of special grace or miraculous power to rejoice in their trials. It seemed like a biblical concept. After all, God did promise to work everything together for good.

But what Kennedy hadn't ever thought about before was that the suffering of persecuted believers was just as real as any other form of suffering on earth.

She thought about her own experiences in college, how many times she'd been forced to walk through terrifying circumstances or come face to face with grief or terror or anxiety. Yes, at certain points she'd been aware of God's presence. She'd experienced the supernatural peace that believers talked about.

But just as often, she'd experienced the despair and fear and darkness. Just because she was a Christian didn't mean she didn't feel the pain or the sorrow as poignantly as anyone else would.

Still, she'd feel better if Ian were a Christian, if she could at least picture him finding some sense of comfort from the Holy Spirit. His collection of letters, which she continued to carry with her nearly everywhere she went, were cheerful, but how much of that was a show so she and Grandma Lucy wouldn't worry so much?

And how selfless did he have to be, Christian or not, to put his own suffering aside in order to make the people he loved feel better?

Kennedy let out her breath.

"You must be tired from traveling so much," Scott commented from the driver's seat.

"Yeah." She chuckled. "I should be used to it, though. My parents were missionaries in China for years, and we traveled all the time."

"I remember Connie saying that." He turned onto Orchard Grove's Main Street and let out a chuckle. "You'll have to forgive me. Or maybe it's her you'll have to forgive, but I already got the rundown of your life story when she made the arrangements for us all to drive together."

Kennedy laughed. "Don't feel bad. I know all about you too."

"Really? What'd she say?"

Kennedy wasn't sure how much she should divulge.

"Come on," he prodded. "Connie's a talker, but she's a perfectly harmless old soul. What did she tell you?"

"Well, I didn't get all the details, but there was something about you meeting a girl online, then moving out and marrying her right away and causing some sort of scandal around town."

He laughed. "Guilty as charged." He pulled his phone out of his pocket. "Here. Go to my home screen and you can see her and our daughter."

Kennedy swiped the screen. "Oh, my goodness. What a tiny baby!"

"That's little Gloria." He was beaming even though his eyes were on the road.

"Connie didn't even mention a baby."

Another laugh. "Yeah, well, Susannah had the unfortunate luck of getting pregnant on our honeymoon and delivering three weeks early, so you can guess what a stir that made in a town like this."

"I bet." Kennedy wasn't exactly sure how she felt about discussing conception dates with a married man she'd just met, so she tried to change the subject. "So you were a missionary? Where did you work?"

"All over. I'm with a group called Kingdom Builders, and we have field offices on six continents. Basically, we're the missionaries to missionaries. We provide encouragement and counseling services to other workers on the field, run quite a few programs for missionary kids ..."

"Really?" Kennedy interrupted. "Like what?"

"Well, we have summer camps set up in various countries. We take kids all the way from K through 12, basically give them what you'd think of as a typical summer camp experience for the week. But in addition to cabins and canoe races and mosquitoes and campfires, we have special discussion groups about some of the unique difficulties you confront as a TCK."

A sense of warmth rushed over Kennedy's whole body. Finally, someone was speaking her language.

Scott glanced over. "You know all about it, I'm sure. You were a third-culture kid yourself."

"Yeah." She let out a chuckle. "It was really hard coming back to the States for college. All through high school, I kept telling myself that once I was back in America, I'd finally feel like I belonged, but I wasn't American enough to fit in here just like I wasn't Chinese enough to fit in there."

"Typical third-culture kid dilemma," Scott remarked. "So tell me. Connie says you've had quite a few close-calls and things since you first came to college. I know she can sometimes tend to exaggerate, but most of the stories sounded really serious. What's up with all that?"

Kennedy glanced at the clock. "How much time have we got?"

CHAPTER 39

THEY WERE ALREADY HALFWAY up the North Cascades pass when Kennedy finished telling Scott about each of her close calls over the past three and a half years.

He let out a low whistle. "What are the chances of all those things happening to one college student?"

"I know what you mean." How many times had she asked herself that same question?

"You should write a book or something," Scott said. "You could turn it into a whole series. I think readers would love that."

She rolled her eyes. As difficult and dangerous as her life had been, she still couldn't picture anyone wanting to sit down and read about it. "They'd probably get too depressed," she joked. "Or decide it's way too implausible."

He shrugged. "Yeah, maybe. But how are you doing? I mean, you sort of glossed over that time you spent in the Chinese jail."

"It was only three days." Why did her core start trembling now of all times?

"Three days or three years, that sort of thing is really hard to go through."

"I guess I've been so worried about Ian, I don't really think my time in China was all that bad. Know what I mean?"

He nodded. "For what it's worth, I'm sorry you had to go through that, and I'm sorry for Ian too. I haven't met him, but Grandma Lucy talks about him all the time."

She let out her breath and glanced in the backseat where Grandma Lucy snoozed with a cowboy handkerchief covering her face.

"What is it you do now?" Kennedy asked. "I mean, do you still travel a lot for your mission work and stuff like that?"

"Most of what I do is telecommuting at this point. Home office support. You know, a couple years ago I hated the thought of staying put anywhere, but now that I'm married, and especially now that we have little baby Gloria, there's not anywhere else I'd rather be. I'm glad I'm able to keep working for Kingdom Builders and still support my family."

Kennedy was years away from settling down, but Scott's young bride in the photo hadn't looked any older than she was. She thought about her best friend Willow, married now and helping raise foster kids out in Alaska ...

When had everyone around her become an adult?

"Hey," Scott said, "here's something you might be interested in, with your connections in both China and North Korea. I've been asked to prepare a TIM talk for the World Missions Digest podcast."

"What's a TIM talk?"

"*Teaching in Missions*. It's all topical stuff, ways to encourage missionaries and sending churches and basically the global church in general when it comes to the ways we think about and go about and fund world missions. My topic is on persecution myths. I've been working on it for a few weeks now, every night when I'm up late on baby duty."

"What kind of myths are you talking about?"

"Oh, the typical. How we tend to over-glamorize persecution, so we get this sense that anyone suffering for their faith must be some sort of super-Christian. I want to talk about not only the problems with that sort of thinking but how I think it's really stunted church growth. Want to hear my rough outline and give me some feedback?"

Kennedy glanced at the time. They were still at least an hour from Seattle. "Sure."

"All right. One thing I want to bring up is the way people glorify suffering to the point that they'll say things like the American church needs to be persecuted if we want to become purified. And they'll cite China as if it's some big Christian utopia, but as I'm sure you and your parents already know, persecution has made it so hard to obtain Bibles in China that there might be only one copy of Scripture in a city of a million. Most folks in the west have no idea of all the heresy that can come when people don't have access to God's word.

"My other big problem with that sort of thinking is when we treat persecuted believers like super-Christians, we sort of get this feeling like they're so spiritual and so lucky to be suffering for their faith they don't even need our prayers. Right? Because we want to assume any Christian who suffers for the gospel is automatically going to be protected, so it's not really suffering. But here's how I look at it. Let's say, heaven forbid, you or I get diagnosed with some fatal illness. Now, for some believers, they're going to have a ton of peace and be completely faithful and trust that whatever God has in store for them, it's part of his perfect will. And some of us are going to handle it a lot differently. Same thing with persecution.

"And then there's one other major problem I see with glorifying believers who suffer for their faith, and this is the one I'll focus on most in my TIM talk. We get so enamored with the idea of suffering for the gospel that we've got this horrible persecution complex. I mean, all you have to do is go to one of those watchdog websites that talk about religious freedom in the US, and you'll see it all over the place.

"Someone's not allowed to wear their cross necklace, and all of a sudden we're acting like evangelical Christians are the most hated, marginalized population in the country. Sure, if I were the one making up all the laws, I'd say let them wear their crosses. But then you've got to be prepared to let the Muslims wear their hijabs and the Jews their kippahs and the Sikhs their turbans, and as long as that's not offensive to you, then yeah, let's keep promoting religious freedom.

"But just because someone's not allowed to read their Bible on company time, I don't see how the kingdom of God is going to be advanced when we take these cases to court or we plaster all these fear-mongering headlines meant solely to convince people that Christianity is the most despised religion in the country. That's what I meant when I say we've got a persecution complex, and I think that's dangerous for two reasons. First, it diminishes the very real persecution that Christians around the world do face. Trust me, it's not cute or pretty or glamorous. I've sat in the same room while our India field director told a mother of four that her husband was killed by Hindu extremists. I've visited a ten-year-old boy in North Sudan who was the only surviving member of his family but who suffered so many machete injuries he's going to be permanently disabled. After you see a few dozen instances like this, you tend to not have much sympathy for American Christians who have never seen the inside of a jail cell but who are a little upset because some store decides to say *Happy Holidays* instead of *Merry Christmas*. Not to mention how it makes all Christians sound whiney and petty."

He let out his breath. "Sorry. I get kind of worked up about this."

Kennedy didn't know what to say. How could she argue when he had seen so many things she couldn't even imagine? "It does make the suffering we've got here in the States sound pretty minor in comparison," she admitted.

"Oh, I'm not denying the fact that Christians suffer. It's universal," Scott went on. "Think about your life, for example. Just because someone else on the other side of the world is experiencing a different kind of suffering, that doesn't diminish what you've gone through. I can only imagine how hard it must be for you with your boyfriend in North Korea right now."

"Actually, we broke up right before the arrest."

"Really? Connie didn't mention that part."

"Yeah, it got muddled in all the other news."

"I'm sorry. What happened?"

She let out a heavy sigh. "Well, you know he's not really a Christian even though he was raised in the church, and ..."

"And you gave up your relationship because you knew that's what God wanted you to do?" he finished for her.

"Pretty much."

"That's hard."

"Yeah."

"I'm assuming you probably still have strong feelings for him, all that?"

"Pretty much."

"So things would probably be fairly complicated and confusing even if he weren't in jail."

"Pretty much," she repeated.

Scott glanced in the rear-view mirror. "Well, Grandma Lucy's out like a light, and I certainly can't promise to be nearly as eloquent as she would be, but I'd love the opportunity to pray for you if that's something that wouldn't make you too uncomfortable."

"Sure," she replied, although with all the people who'd been praying for her and Ian over the past several months, she wasn't sure how much faith she had that one more prayer was going to change anything.

CHAPTER 40

IT WAS DINNERTIME WHEN they arrived in Seattle. Scott stopped to grab everyone sub sandwiches and then went to gather on Capitol Hill where Ian's prayer vigil would start in about half an hour.

Kennedy didn't love the idea of being in such a huge crowd. She'd never really gotten over her germaphobia, and getting stuck in that hospital during an epidemic a few years back only exacerbated the issue. She was glad it was winter, so she could wear mittens and cover her mouth and nose with a scarf.

For a short time, she'd considered giving up her plans to become a doctor altogether. In addition to her fear of germs and her hatred of hospitals, she'd kind of flipped out last winter when she had to help Willow deliver a baby in the middle of nowhere. Going to South Korea last summer and seeing the work that Freedom Korea did to help refugees made her rethink her plans even more, especially once the director asked her to intern after graduation.

She had prayed about her decision, and even though she felt called to work in Seoul, she still couldn't give up her dreams of med school altogether, which is why she'd requested the deferment.

It was funny how she'd spent so long worrying over her future, getting anxious about choices she wouldn't have to make for years, but over the past semester, she didn't have the mental energy to worry about anything other than Ian's release. Maybe that was one blessing that came out of this entire ordeal. But couldn't God have taught her to worry less some other way without throwing Ian in a North Korean jail?

Scott helped Grandma Lucy to a podium in front of the growing crowd, where she could sit for the vigil and not have to worry about getting jostled or thrown off balance. He told Kennedy there was room for her on stage too, but she wasn't sure which she feared more — all the germs she'd come into contact with once the crowd numbers swelled or all the eyes that would be staring at her if she took her place up front. She decided to hang out near the stage where she could always make a quick escape if the crowds got too overwhelming, but she wasn't right up there in front of the microphone for everyone to see.

"You doing okay?" Scott asked her after he made sure Grandma Lucy was comfortable and warm.

"Yeah. It's already quite a turnout, isn't it?"

Scott smiled at her and nodded. "It is. I have a good feeling about tonight. I really think we're about to see God move."

It was a comforting sentiment, but Kennedy's soul was too tired to put much hope in his words.

CHAPTER 41

KENNEDY WASN'T GREAT AT estimating numbers, but Scott said there were at least a thousand or more people by the time the prayer vigil started. Christian leaders from around the Seattle area took turns at the microphone, and in between their prayers a hipster-looking guitar player in skinny jeans led the crowd in a few songs Kennedy hardly knew.

Scott was one of the ones scheduled to speak, and he gave what Kennedy figured must be some sort of dress rehearsal for his upcoming TIM talk on missions and persecution. Kennedy wasn't sure how appropriate it was to talk about Christian martyrs at an event like this, especially since as far as everyone knew, Ian was still alive, and it's hard to become a martyr for a faith you'd rejected years ago.

She sighed. Maybe she shouldn't be so pessimistic, but she'd been hoping for something more than this. Something deeper. For God to reach into her heart and speak to her personally, to promise her that she'd see Ian again or give her some other sign or comfort to hold onto. All the prayers and songs were nice, but they didn't change the fact that Ian was still so far from home.

What had he already gone through? Was he still in the hospital? What were they treating him for anyway? Was he in one of the infamous prison camps now? Or what about solitary confinement? Kennedy had only been in that Chinese jail for three days, and she had an inquisitive guard to talk to by day and Ian at night. Even then the darkness and fear and oppression had nearly driven her to despair. How much worse would it be for Ian, stuck there for so many months, without even the hope in Christ that Kennedy had?

In one of his letters, he mentioned feeling her prayers for him, but in the past few weeks, she'd grown so tired and discouraged most of her prayers were nothing more than complaining to God about the situation. What did that mean for Ian? Did he sense the change when Kennedy stopped praying for him so fervently? She had always believed in the supernatural power of prayer, but as a biology student she also figured there was some scientific basis for a lot of it as well.

Praying — no matter what your religion — had been shown to reduce stress, optimize health, and decrease anxiety. In her mind, that just gave scientific backing for what she already knew from the Bible to be true.

It made perfect sense when you were talking about praying for yourself. But what about praying for someone else? What about praying for people who didn't even know they were being prayed for?

Would the results be as beneficial?

Could researchers propose some sort of scientific explanation, or was it all supernatural?

And in the end, did it matter? If prayer worked, prayer worked, right?

But she still felt guilty for the way her petitions for Ian had tapered off lately. Thankfully he still had his grandma to pray for him. That woman would never waver in her faith. Grandma Lucy's body swayed during Scott's closing prayer, then she stood up and shuffled toward him. Kennedy was afraid she might fall and was about to jump on the stage to support her, but Grandma Lucy reached Scott in time and told him, "I'd like to say a few words if I may."

Scott smiled. "Of course. Shall I introduce you?" After she nodded, he spoke directly to the crowd. "This is Ian's grandmother."

The introduction was met by soft murmurs and muffled clapping. Grandma Lucy took the mic.

"Thank you. Thank you all for being here. I can't tell you just how pleased I am to see so many of you coming out here to honor my grandson with your prayers and support, and I'd like to remind you of the passage from Scripture that says if anyone agrees anything in the powerful name of Jesus, it will be granted to us. There is power in agreement, power when we come together and with one spirit raise up our voices and petition the King of the universe to hear our prayers and work justice on behalf of the oppressed.

"My grandson is suffering tonight in a country where thousands have lost their lives. This is a country of darkness, both literal and spiritual, but tonight, I want to ask you to do something special. I don't want you to just focus on my grandson. Heaven knows he needs our prayers, and there will be plenty of time for that. But let's not lose sight of the grand scheme, either. The grand scheme is that not just one American but tens of thousands and maybe more prisoners are languishing behind North Korea's closed gates. They are torn from their families. They are tortured and starved. Some of them are our brothers and sisters in Christ but others have never heard the name of Jesus.

"Now, I'm not going to pretend that these months worrying for my grandson have been easy, but I do want to stand here today and tell you that the time of fellowship I've had with the Lord while praying for my grandson has been sweet and refreshing to this old weary soul of mine. Before his arrest, my mind was weak. Doctors said it was dementia. But learning to pray so steadfastly for my grandson has proven to be all the cure I need. My mind is sharp, and I know this is God's gift to me and nothing medical science can explain. Not only that, but God has used this terrible situation to teach me to pray more deeply for the people in North Korea. It would be selfish of me to spend all my time praying for Ian when so many thousands of others are suffering with no one to pray for them, with no one in the free world who even knows their names. I admit that at first it felt overwhelming. How could I pray for an entire nation of people when my heart was so riddled with terror and anxiety on behalf of my own flesh and blood? But then I told the Lord that if he wants to use my grandson's imprisonment to teach this old dog one last trick, to teach me to pray for the people of North Korea in a way that I've never prayed for anybody or anything before, well who was I to argue with the Almighty?

"And so I prayed. Each time I prayed for my grandson, I remembered to pray for his guards too. And then I got to thinking that those guards have families, and many of them are just doing what they're doing because if they don't, their families could starve, and I felt compassion growing in my heart for this entire people group because even those who aren't in prisons like my grandson are still held in captivity, slaves to a dictator, slaves to darkness. And so I prayed. Dear Lord, I prayed, open those floodgates of heaven and pour your light onto the people of North Korea. Shower your grace upon them so they can see you are the one true God and with you there is salvation for their souls and forgiveness of their sins. Tear through the veil that holds them captive, Father God, for you see them, these sheep without a shepherd, these orphan souls who have never known the truth about their divine Father. Reach down, Lord, and see their misery. Mark their tears on your scroll, and heal them from their darkness and their pain and their despair. Heal them from their ignorance, and shatter those chains."

Grandma Lucy emphasized each individual word.

"Let them be free," she continued, "and let them know that with you there is hope. With you there is salvation for their souls. And with you there is a reason to live and exist. You created these children to worship you, so show them who you are. Break down the walls that hold this entire nation in captivity. Rip off those blinders that have kept generations in darkness. Father God, I believe that you are doing something new in the nation of North Korea. I believe that the day is coming when every single prisoner will be set free from their chains, and I'm not just talking about the ones like my grandson, Lord. There's a spiritual bondage that's an even crueler fate than what Ian suffers today. But I believe and I declare that you are the God of North Korea, that you will reign in that nation once more. That the darkness will have to give way to the glorious light of the one true King. That whatever idolatry has been set up will be shattered, that whatever demonic influence is holding this people captive will be slaughtered and destroyed in the name of Jesus. It's a war, Father God, which is why we declare you as the conqueror. This isn't a battle we can fight with politics or diplomacy. This is a war that can only be won by the blood of Jesus Christ, the blood that was shed on the cross so that the people living in North Korea today would know the truth that you are their Savior and their healer, their creator and their king.

"And so I speak to the darkness tonight, sweet merciful Savior. I speak to the darkness that is hovering over North Korea, and I tell it to be gone. It has no place anymore. I speak to the forces of evil that have their talons entrenched in the ruling class of North Korea, and I command them to flee before Jesus Christ, who conquered death, hell, and the grave and who has already declared victory in North Korea."

A low grumble rose from the crowd, Christians breaking into applause or murmurs of agreement, but Grandma Lucy only raised her voice and spoke even more boldly into the microphone, her words carrying above the rumble of the masses.

"The devil thinks that North Korea is his little playground, and that's what it's been, but no longer. From this moment on, we declare victory. We set up Jesus as the high and sovereign King over North Korea, over every law, over every politician, over every government official, from the lowly schoolteacher to the Supreme Leader himself, and we proclaim that there is no authority under heaven that has not been established by God and that the same God who sets up kings and deposes them will have his way in North Korea. We declare that freedom will reign, and the blood that flowed down from Jesus's nail-pierced hands when he hung and died on that cross is the same blood that right now covers North Korea and washes away the sins of its past. All the massacres, all the purges, all the murder and strife and starvation and sickness and despair, we proclaim these healed by the blood of Jesus, and not only that, but we speak redemption. We don't ask simply for a North Korea where oppression is ceased. We ask for a North Korea where every single individual will encounter the one true God, will acknowledge him the Savior of their lives, to repent, to be forgiven of their sins. We pray for the land itself, the land of North Korea that is flowing with so much blood, to be cleansed so that the ground itself will become a haven, not simply of political freedom, but of spiritual worship, that the men and women and children there, yes Lord even those alive today, will one day bow down and worship you and exalt you as King."

Grandma Lucy reached out and took Scott's arm, and he led her on wobbly legs back to her seat. Kennedy wasn't sure what had just happened. She'd need time to think about it before she could articulate her thoughts even to herself, but she realized Grandma

Lucy's prayer had done more than just inspire the crowd to pray for North Korea.

It had healed something in her soul, a woundedness Kennedy hadn't even known existed. It was like having a sore throat for weeks until she scarcely noticed it anymore, but then one day she woke up and it was gone, and she realized how much better she felt.

She didn't know what it was, but something had changed in her spirit. Something had been fixed, and now that she knew what it felt like to no longer be so broken, she prayed that she would never have to go back to that fear and anxiety she had lived with until now.

After helping her back to her seat, Scott returned to the podium, holding his cell phone and smiling broadly. "I don't know how many of you have kept up with Secretary Hamilton's visit to North Korea. At first, it looked like after she travelled all the way, the top leadership in Pyongyang refused to see her, but look." He held up his screen as if the hundreds in the crowd could read the news headline. "*Secretary Hamilton Secures Meeting with North Korea's Top General*," he read.

Hope swelled in Kennedy's chest, the same hope that just an hour earlier felt like it had died within her. As the crowd's cheers rose to a crescendo, Scott summarized the bullet points of the article. "They say it was confirmed that she was able to speak with the general about Ian's release, and she's scheduled to fly back to the States tomorrow."

CHAPTER 42

"THAT WAS SOME PRAYER service, wasn't it?" Scott held the car door open and helped Grandma Lucy into the backseat. "And I have to say it seems like pretty opportune timing with Secretary Hamilton just about to fly home from Pyongyang."

Grandma Lucy didn't respond. Kennedy turned around from the passenger seat to look at her. "I was really encouraged by your prayer," she said. "Thank you for that." She wondered if it was premature to make a connection between such a powerful prayer vigil and the Secretary of State's last day in Pyongyang.

Grandma Lucy smiled faintly, and Kennedy couldn't be quite sure if she'd heard or understood.

"Come on." Scott sat down on the driver side. "Let me take you two ladies to your hotel. It's been a long night, hasn't it, Grandma Lucy?"

Grandma Lucy didn't respond.

"Do you think she's all right?" Kennedy whispered. She hated talking about Grandma Lucy like that when she was right there, but she hadn't been acting like herself since she finished praying.

"My guess is she's just tired," Scott said. "Connie says it's hard for her to stay up late. I'll take you two straight to your room, then I've made plans to crash tonight with my buddy who lives out this way."

Kennedy was tired too, but that didn't stop her from worrying on the short drive to the hotel. Scott helped them check in, and with Grandma Lucy leaning on his arm, they all walked to the elevator.

"I think your prayers tonight made a huge difference," Scott told Grandma Lucy on the ride up, "not just for Ian but for the thousands of people living in North Korea."

She gave a faint nod, and the elevator doors opened.

Grandma Lucy had suffered a few heart attacks over the years. What if something happened while they were alone at the hotel? Kennedy pulled her cell phone out of her pocket, thankful and slightly surprised to find the battery fully charged. Well, at least if they needed anything, she'd have a way to call for help.

When Scott left, Kennedy asked Grandma Lucy if she needed any assistance getting ready for bed. Grandma Lucy shook her head. "I think I'll just lie down for a while if that's all right with you."

Kennedy felt silly pulling down the sheet and blankets, but Grandma Lucy didn't seem to mind. She reached out and took Kennedy's hand. "I believe the truth will set him free."

Kennedy leaned over and tucked Grandma Lucy in as if she were a little girl.

Ignoring the absurd urge to kiss the old woman good night, she patted her on the shoulder and simply whispered, "I sure hope you're right."

CHAPTER 43

KENNEDY WOKE UP EARLY the next morning, still not having adjusted fully to Pacific time. She spent twenty minutes scanning news reports, and when Scott drove her to the airport, they listened to a talk-show host making speculations about the Secretary of State's visit to Pyongyang. Even though it was encouraging to hear Hamilton had finally managed to secure an audience with the North Korean general, nobody could confirm if she'd made any progress with Ian's case. There wouldn't be any more updates until the Secretary landed in DC later today.

More waiting.

"Thanks again for the ride and the good conversations and everything else," Kennedy said as Scott heaved her suitcase out of the trunk of his car.

"No prob. And hey, thanks for giving me an excuse to come out here and join your prayer vigil and hang out with my buddy last night. It was great."

"I'm glad to hear that." Kennedy opened the passenger side door while airline announcements sounded in the background. "Bye, Grandma Lucy. I'm really glad we got to spend some time together." It was too hard to try to explain how encouraged Kennedy had felt after Grandma Lucy's prayer last night. She just hoped she could give her the smallest idea of how blessed she'd been. Even if the only reason Kennedy came to Seattle was to hear that one prayer, it was enough.

And even though nobody knew what Hamilton and the North Korean general had talked about in Pyongyang, there was always the chance the mission had been a success.

The chance Ian would be coming home.

How could Kennedy survive half a day on a plane not knowing anything?

Grandma Lucy smiled, looking much more rested than she had last night. Clasping Kennedy's hand in hers, she sang out in her rich voice, "May God bless you and keep you and make his glorious face to shine upon you. I don't know when we'll see each other again. I suppose it's here, there, or in the air, right?"

This time Kennedy did bend over to plant a small kiss on Grandma Lucy's wrinkled cheek. "Take care of yourself." She refused to think of what might happen to Ian if Grandma Lucy were to die while he was still imprisoned. Who would pray for him then?

"Have a safe flight home," Scott told her, leaving her and her suitcase on the airport curb.

It was the longest flight of her life. Kennedy turned on her cell phone as soon as her plane landed and jumped onto Channel 2's website. Secretary Hamilton should have arrived in DC by now. She had to find out what the Secretary had to say about her trip. Ian wasn't mentioned in any of the top headlines, but that could mean anything.

Her fingers shook while she typed his name into the search bar. *Hamilton returns Stateside without American reporter.*

It would be all right, she told herself. As long as her lungs remembered how to breathe, it would be all right.

Inhale and exhale. Just like that.

So the Secretary's trip to Pyongyang wasn't the immediate success she'd hoped for. That was okay.

There would be other trips.

Diplomacy took time.

Time she wasn't sure Ian could spare.

All right, God. I have no idea what you're doing in this situation, but I'm going to trust that you have a plan for it all.

When she got off the plane, her breaths were even, her legs were steady, but her soul felt heavier than it ever had.

CHAPTER 44

"KENNEDY!" WOONG SHOUTED IN his shrill voice. "Kennedy!"

She stopped in the church hallway and turned around. "What's wrong?"

"I can't get this beard to stay on. I'm gonna be the only shepherd out there without any facial hair. It's an abomination!"

Kennedy tried to get the fake beard to stick with no success. "Your skin's just too soft."

He pouted, and then his eyes lit up. "Wait a minute. I got an idea." He reached into his pocket, pulled out a stick of gum, and shoved it into his mouth. Guessing his intentions and not necessarily wanting to find herself implicated in his plot, Kennedy walked downstairs, where Sandy had asked her to look for more candles.

They had to be down here someplace. Where did Sandy tell her to look?

"Kennedy?"

The voice startled her. "Oh, hi, Hannah. How's the baby?"

"She's perfect. She finally fell asleep, so I brought her down here where it's quiet."

"That's a good idea." The Christmas pageant would start in less than fifteen minutes, and the entire upper half of St. Margaret's church building was as chaotic as a Manhattan subway station, only with far more kids.

"I was sorry to hear the Secretary came back without your friend Ian," Hannah said.

"Thanks." Kennedy had been meaning to ask Hannah something about that and figured now might be as good a time as any. If only she could find those candles.

Oh, there they were.

"Kennedy!" Woong plodded down the stairs. "Mom wants to know if you found the candles yet and when you're gonna bring them up."

Kennedy passed the box to Woong and told him to hurry upstairs, then she pulled up a chair beside Hannah. "I know you want to keep it quiet for the baby, but can I ask you something?"

"Of course." Hannah had always been so calm and serene. Maybe that's why they had never spent much time together in Yanji even though they weren't far apart in age.

Kennedy stared at her hands, trying to figure out how to formulate the question she'd been mulling over since she returned to the East Coast.

"I know you don't talk much about what happened to you in North Korea, and I don't need to know any details," she hurried to add. "But I never actually heard the story of how you escaped."

She glanced at Hannah to make sure she hadn't asked anything inappropriate.

Hannah's face melted into a gentle smile. "Oh, it was Korea Freedom and their underground railroad. That's why I was so happy when your mom told me you were working for them last summer."

Kennedy shook her head. "That's not quite what I mean. I mean, before you got connected to Korea Freedom, before you even knew about the underground railroad. When you were still ..." She hesitated to use the word. "When you were still in prison," she finally managed to get out.

Hannah nodded, but her smile had faded.

"It was the Lord," she answered. "We were all outside, there was a distraction, and I managed to get away."

"Was it dangerous?" What kind of stupid question was that? Of course it was dangerous.

Hannah nodded.

"But I mean, after ..." Why couldn't she think of the words she wanted to say? "When you got out, even after all the bad things that happened to you there, was it ... Did it make it hard for things to go back to normal after all that? After all you went through?"

She stared at Hannah's baby sleeping peacefully in her arms.

Hannah kept her voice low as if she were reciting nursery rhymes to her daughter. "Are you asking me if I was the same person after my time in prison?"

Kennedy nodded. Yes. That was exactly what she wanted to know.

Hannah sighed. "I wish I could give you a more hopeful response. And I know you're thinking about Ian and wondering what things will be like if he ever makes it home, but to be quite honest with you, the answer would be no." She shook her head and repeated the word. "No. I was never the same after that."

Kennedy let out her breath. That's what she had been afraid of.

CHAPTER 45

NINE DAYS LATER

"Five. Four. Three. Two. One."

Kennedy forced herself to join the countdown while the small crowd in Carl and Sandy's living room watched the ball dropping on the television screen.

"Happy New Year!" everyone shouted, and Kennedy was hugged at least a dozen times, her ears ringing with the sound of the party horns Woong seemed particularly eager to use to welcome in the New Year.

Kennedy's mom handed her a glass of sparkling cider. "Drink up, honey. You know, New Year's a time for fresh starts." She lowered her voice. "And you know we all want you to be happy now, right?"

No, it was Kennedy who was trying to make her mom happy. That's why she suffered through a noisy pageant and an over-crowded Christmas Eve dinner and a plethora of presents at her parents' house and now this night of joy and festivities. The most important goal in Kennedy's life was to make it through the day without her mom sitting down and asking her if she needed to schedule extra counseling appointments or visit the doctor to see if her antidepressants needed to be adjusted.

It was for her mom that Kennedy smiled and drank the sparkling cider that stung her nose and clinked glasses with everyone in the Lindgrens' tiny house and put up with Woong throwing confetti all over her hair.

If Kennedy had her way, she would have locked herself in her bedroom and fallen asleep by nine. The last thing she needed was a reminder of how many months had passed with no word from Ian, no news about his case.

Kennedy's mom frowned at her. "Honey, are you sure you're all right? You don't look like you're having a very good time."

Her dad came up beside her. "Come on, Baby Cakes. Our Kensie girl's doing the best she can, isn't that right, kiddo?"

Her mom let out a melodramatic sigh. "Well, maybe we should tell her now. What do you think?"

Her dad lowered his voice. "I thought we were going to wait until tomorrow."

"I know, but she's miserable already. I don't see how it could get much worse, honestly."

"Will you two please stop talking about me as if I weren't even here?" Kennedy didn't mind if her foul mood was ruining her parents' New Year's celebration. She couldn't stand the thought of one or both of them keeping secrets from her.

"What is it?" she demanded, staring at her parents both in turn.

It was her father who broke down first. "Princess, we got a letter from Connie, Ian's aunt back in Orchard Grove. It appears Ian managed to write one last letter ..."

"What do you mean last?" Her throat went dry.

"I knew we should have waited," her mom moaned.

"What do you mean last?" Kennedy demanded again, becoming aware by degrees that the guests around her had all stopped talking.

Her dad reached into his pocket. "This came in the mail two days ago. Connie warned us. Said maybe we should wait until after the holidays to let you ..."

"Give me that." Kennedy snatched the envelope out of his hands. "You mean you already opened it?"

"No, honey," her mom insisted. "That was just so we could read the note Connie wrote to us. We haven't seen the rest of it, but we do know what it ..." She stopped short when Kennedy's dad cleared his throat.

"I'm sorry if you're mad at us, Kensie girl. Your mom and I thought it was best to wait, and Connie seemed to think so too." He shook his head. "It's not ... It's not the greatest of news."

Kennedy ignored his words. How had they received a letter and not given it to her right away? Who cared about what holiday the calendar claimed it was?

She turned her back to her parents and stared at the envelope. Sandy came up and wrapped her arm around her from the side. "You can go into the guest room if you'd like some time to yourself," she whispered.

Kennedy swallowed past the lump in her throat and nodded.

Her legs grew heavier with each step she took down the Lindgrens' hall. Her throat was parched even after a full glass of cider.

She walked into the guest room, turned on the light, and locked the door behind her.

Anything's better than not knowing, she told herself as she unfolded Ian's letter.

CHAPTER 46

Sweet, precious Kennedy, I'm so sorry to be writing you like this, and you'll have to forgive my atrocious handwriting too. I'm back at the hospital again. Doc doesn't think I'm going to make it. And that's not because he hasn't tried. I swear that man would give me one of his own lungs if he thought it could help.

I've got pneumonia. Funny, right? Strong, healthy man like me. I'm glad you can't see me like this. Wasting away wouldn't do it justice. And it's not just the pneumonia either. Doc says everything's shutting down one system at a time. There's nothing left to be done.

He's risking a lot letting me write you this one last letter, but I told him how important it was to me. He promised to find a way to slip it to the Swedish ambassador when he visits on Tuesday.

By then this letter may be all that's left of me.

There, how's that for melodrama?

I want you to know I've fought this disease. I've fought as much as I can. And it's probably because of you that I'm still alive at this point. I keep remembering our summer together, all those long talks. How much I want to see you again. And that's what I'm fighting for.

The chance to tell you face to face how much I love you.

But you should see me now. No, scratch that. I'm glad you won't see me. This way you can remember me as I was then. Hehe, there's some more good melodrama for you.

I don't want you to be sad. I actually have good news for you. All those prayers Grandma Lucy's been praying for me (and I'm sure you have too) they've finally managed to work. It's a really long story, and I can't give you any details because if this letter gets intercepted I don't want to get anyone in trouble, but I understand now.

I've made my peace with God.

I'm ready to go home.

I have fought the good fight, right? Isn't that one of those Bible verses? I remember something about that at least.

I know someone literary like you is bound to pick up on the irony. You broke up with me because I wasn't a Christian. And now I am, but I'm on my deathbed (quite literally).

Maybe one day you can find it in your heart to share a little laugh with me.

I guess some things were only meant to be in heaven. But don't worry. I don't expect you to die an old maid just so we can hook up when you join me there. I don't think it works like that. (I'm trying to be funny, by the way. Sorry if it comes across as morbid.)

We had a great time together, didn't we? And I'm not just talking about last summer. I still remember the day I saw you on the Red Line your first semester at Harvard. There was something in your eyes, something so sweet and innocent and trusting, something that reminded me that in spite of all the injustice I'd already seen around the world by that point, there were still things loving and beautiful. Things worth fighting for.

I love you, Kennedy. If it hadn't been for you, I probably would have died here and gone to an even more miserable fate, but now I know that I'm releasing my soul to Jesus, who has opened my eyes to show me how great a love he has even for a silly old blockhead like me.

I hope by now you and Grandma Lucy have grown close. It makes me happy to think of the two of you as friends.

And I thank God for the chance to tell you this one last goodbye.

I dream every night that I'm holding you in my arms, and for those short moments of bliss, I'm not cold or hungry or afraid.

You've done more for me than I could ever find words to thank you for even if I had the time (and the strength). Now go on and keep on doing great things for the kingdom of God. Maybe you don't see it, but he has used you already to advance his kingdom and fight against injustice and oppression in so many ways, and I'm so lucky to have known you and had you in my life.

All my love (and this time I'm not just being melodramatic),

Ian

CHAPTER 47

THERE WAS A KNOCK on the door. "Kennedy? Kennedy?" It was her mother.

She opened her eyes enough to glance at the clock. Quarter after one.

"Kennedy?"

"Maybe we should just let her rest." She recognized her dad's muffled voice.

"What if she's hurt?"

"Here, I can unlock the door for you both."

Kennedy squeezed her eyes shut and held perfectly still while Sandy stepped in. She ran her hand across Kennedy's forehead and clucked her tongue. "Poor little lamb. She's fallen asleep."

"Should we wake her up?" her mom asked.

"What for?"

"That's right," Sandy agreed with her dad. "Why don't you two go on home whenever you're ready, and in the morning, I'll take her to your house or let you know when you can pick her up."

"I just hate the thought of her sad and all alone," her mom protested.

"She's asleep," her dad remarked. "The most merciful thing to do is let her rest."

The light turned off.

The door closed.

And Kennedy was once more completely alone.

CHAPTER 48

MID FEBRUARY

Kennedy was glad this was her last semester. Even at a school like Harvard, professors were known to be lenient when grading the spring-semester seniors. She'd made her way through her last twelve credits in a mental haze that no amount of counseling sessions or anti-depressants could change. Finally, she told her therapist and her doctor and her parents that there was no reason for them to keep trying to make her happy. It wasn't like her brain was misfiring, telling her to act sad when life was perfectly fine.

She had every reason to mourn.

She refused to let anyone take that away from her.

It was mid-afternoon, and she trudged her way back toward her dorm where she would spend the evening munching on dry Cheerios, staring at her uncompleted syllabi and counting down the days to graduation. There was nothing more she could do for Ian. Even though the news outlets had never uncovered any more updates about his condition, she knew in her soul he was gone.

Now she had to find a way to say goodbye.

To move on.

She was even more determined to return to Seoul after graduation. By working with refugees at Korea Freedom's headquarters, she could honor Ian's memory.

It was the least she could do.

I love you, Kennedy. If it hadn't been for you, I may have died here and gone to an even more miserable fate, but now I know that I'm releasing my soul to Jesus, who has opened my eyes to show me how great a love he has even for a silly old blockhead like me.

She had memorized those lines from his parting letter. Actually, she had memorized the whole thing. Not an easy feat, seeing as how half of it was tear-stained after that awful New Year's Eve party.

Thankfully, her college classes gave her a reason to pretend to be busy. No more parents breathing down her neck like they had during Christmas break. Kennedy was having a hard enough time handling her own grief. She couldn't try to assuage her parents' guilt on top of her own.

She hadn't even tried to get in touch with Connie or Grandma Lucy. What would be the point? It was time to move on or at least try to. Things would be easier once the US embassy was able to confirm Ian's death. Maybe if they held a memorial service for him at Orchard Grove, she'd return one last time.

For now, it was simply a matter of existing through one day and into another. She'd grown so despondent she only returned about one out of every three or four of Willow's calls. Willow and Nick were even busier now, making plans to add on to their cabin to make room for all the extra foster kids they wanted to take in.

Everyone else was living their lives, but Kennedy was stuck in some timeless, emotionless existence. Yet another reason why she looked forward to graduation. Maybe Seoul would be the change in scenery she needed. And working with Korea Freedom, she wouldn't have as much time to sit around and mope, an art she'd perfected over the last few months.

She made her way into the dorm. It was only four, but she was thankful to be in for the night. No reason to run around campus when there was nowhere to go.

She walked toward her door and heard two familiar voices as she got closer to her room.

"Sandy? Carl? What are you doing here?"

Sandy jumped up from Kennedy's bed and dried her eyes. "I'm sorry, dear. We didn't mean to startle you like this."

"How'd you get in my room?"

"Your RA let us in," she answered. "We explained we had some important news to share with you, and ..." Her face broke, and she buried herself behind a tissue.

Kennedy glanced to Carl. What was going on?

Sandy blew her nose loudly. "Have you eaten anything, dear? Are you hungry?"

What kind of question was that?

Sandy cleared her throat. "We got a call from Ian's aunt Connie. She said she's been trying to get hold of you and couldn't."

Kennedy didn't answer.

Sandy wiped her face again. "It's the kind of news we wanted to tell you in person, honey. We want you to know we'll always be here for you, Carl and me both ..."

"Oh, will you spit it out, woman?" Carl interrupted. "I know you said that you wanted to be the one to tell her, and I went along with it, but look at the poor girl's face. It's like you're about to tell her the family dog's been run over by the dump truck."

"Poor Snoopy," Sandy murmured.

"Huh?"

"Will you just tell her?" Carl bellowed.

"Okay, you're absolutely right." Sandy reached out for her husband's hand. "What Carl and I came over here to say, it's about Ian. I think I told you that already, and his aunt wanted you to hear before it made the evening news ..."

"Oh, let me do it." Carl put both hands on Kennedy's shoulders. "Congratulations, Kennedy. Your boyfriend's alive, and Secretary Hamilton is flying him home as we speak."

CHAPTER 49

KENNEDY HAD NEVER BEEN more thankful to be tired and jetlagged. She hadn't bothered to carry anything besides what would fit in her backpack so she could take a cab directly from the airport to the hospital in Seattle where Ian was being treated.

The details of his release were still coming in, but Kennedy didn't care who had gotten him home or how. All she wanted was assurance that he really was alive and that he was going to survive.

Connie had told her by phone, and her parents had both issued dire warnings as well, that she needed to be prepared for the worst. When she saw him, he was going to look awful (*think Holocaust survivor,* her dad had said, planting a very helpful image in her mind), and his recovery would probably have to be measured in months and not weeks or days.

It didn't matter.

He was here.

Nothing else was important, not even her schoolwork, which is why she had insisted her parents get her just a one-way ticket. They were reluctant until she got emails from two out of her three professors stating she could turn in her assignments by email so she wouldn't fall too behind. Her only other class just had one more final paper and test, and even if Kennedy failed, she had taken enough credits early on in her college career she could still graduate in May.

She had memorized his room number and already looked up directions by the time she arrived at the hospital. She sprinted nearly the whole way and ended up taking three flights of stairs instead of standing around waiting for an elevator.

She was going to see Ian.

Hurrying past nurses in scrubs and orderlies with their clipboards, she scanned the room numbers, which turned out to be an unnecessary practice. Of course his room would be the one guarded by Feds.

Funny. Just like in the movies. Two men in black suits, walkie talkies, the works. She'd have to tell Ian he'd turned into a walking cliché.

"I'm Kennedy Stern," she told the first official. "Ian's expecting me."

He shook his head. "No visitors."

"I've been talking with his aunt. She knows I'm coming."

"No visitors," he repeated.

"Oh, Kennedy!" Connie called out from down the hallway.

Kennedy hurried toward her. "Is he okay?" she asked. "The men said I couldn't go in ..."

Connie frowned. "I'm sorry, sweetie. It turns out, well ..." She bit her lip and looked over one of Kennedy's shoulders and then the other before lowering her voice. "He's in a mood today. Doctor says it's totally normal, but he, um ..." She cleared her throat. "He doesn't want to see anyone."

What?

"I just flew in," Kennedy argued, as if that should change everyone's mind. "I ... Is he all right?"

Connie frowned. "He's self-conscious, sweetie. I'm sure that's it. He's lost a lot of weight, and, well ... Here. You let me go in and talk some sense into that boy. No nephew of mine is going to turn away his girlfriend who's come all this way just to see him, no matter how he looks. You just wait here, and I hate to say it, but you better start preparing yourself."

As if Kennedy hadn't spent the past nine hours of travel doing exactly that.

Connie bustled past the two guards and slipped into the room. A minute later, she nudged the door open and beckoned Kennedy over.

"Come on. He's asleep. Let her in," she told the officers in an authoritative voice. "This is his girlfriend."

It wasn't until she stepped into the room that Kennedy finally understood what Connie and her parents and everyone else had been trying to warn her about. He looked like a corpse. Not Ian, not the man she loved and had grieved over. His hair was thin and hung in clumps against his pale face. The sunken cheekbones were hard enough to take in, but even with his hospital robe on, Kennedy could see his ribs sticking out. Watched the way his collarbone pulled with each breath he took.

"Come on." Connie took her hand and led her to the bedside.

It was confirmed.

She hated hospitals.

Tears stung her eyes. She had to look away.

"It's all right," Connie assured her. "In fact, he's looking stronger than he did when they first brought him in."

Kennedy couldn't imagine anyone looking closer to death. She shook her head. "Maybe I should have waited to come."

"No," Connie argued. "He wants to see you. Really he does. He just doesn't know it yet."

Small comfort, seeing as how Kennedy had rushed all the way over from Boston just to be with him.

Connie's phone beeped. "Oh, that's Grandma Lucy. You wait here. I'll just be a minute." Without giving Kennedy the chance to protest, Connie slipped out of the room, leaving Kennedy alone with this ghost of the man she had once known and loved.

CHAPTER 50

YES, SHE HAD DEFINITELY made a mistake coming to Seattle.

What did she expect? For Ian to be sitting in his hospital bed, smiling at her and ready to play a few rounds of Scrabble?

Tears streaked down her cheeks. Hot and angry tears.

Why, God? You brought him home, but like this?

Maybe she was no better than the Israelites in the desert, grumbling for meat when God had so recently fed them manna, but she didn't care.

She didn't want to leave him alone, but she didn't want to stay. How long was Connie going to take?

"You sure you want to go now, Kensie girl?" her dad had asked. "It might make more sense to let him recover some of his strength first."

He'd tried to warn her, and she had ignored him. Like some silly girl with a Florence Nightingale complex, she had it in her head that being here would bring Ian the peace and healing he needed.

Stupid, stupid, stupid.

Shouldn't she have learned by now that her dad was always right?

Good thing she'd bought a one-way ticket. That way she could go home immediately. Back to Cambridge, back to her cold, lonely dorm, back to her Cheerios and Craisins ...

"Kennedy?"

Oh, no. He was awake. What was she supposed to do? He wasn't supposed to see her here.

Why had she come?"

"Kennedy?"

"I'm sorry. I was just leaving." She turned so he couldn't see her tears, even though her voice made it obvious she was crying.

His next few words were garbled. "... missed you so much."

She couldn't do this. Every word he spoke was raspy, the rattling in his lungs so pronounced she felt vicariously lightheaded.

"I'm going to see where Connie is." She still couldn't bring herself to turn around. What had she done? Injuries like his, illnesses like his, trauma like his needed time to heal. She was never meant to see him this way. No wonder he told the guards not to let in any visitors.

"... don't want you to leave."

"I can't ..." she started to stammer and then stopped. Beneath the rattling lungs, beneath the unbearable wheezing, she heard something she recognized.

She forced her body to turn around, demanded herself to stop crying.

Their eyes met.

"You came."

At first, she was afraid he'd be mad to see her here, but the look in his eyes, hollow as they were, wasn't anger.

She stepped forward. "I came. I needed to see you. I thought you ..." She stopped herself when the tears started leaking down once more. "I thought you were gone."

Why had he done this to her? Why had he written her that letter from the hospital? Why had he forced her to go through these months of mourning all alone?

Emotionally, she was as much of a ghost as he was.

How could he have been so cruel?

"Don't be sad." His face was so emaciated it reminded her of the grimace on a Halloween skull. "Please don't be sad." His chest heaved. Was this how skeletons cried?

He reached out his hand, bony with red and black lesions on the skin. Bruises. What had happened to him?

"I missed you," he repeated. "So much."

She took his hand, surprised that it felt warm. She'd been prepared for the tepid temperature of a cadaver.

"I missed you too." She bathed the sores on his hand with her tears. "I stopped praying for you. I'm so sorry. I thought you were dead."

"Shh." He was the one comforting her now. "Shh," he repeated. "That's all over. It's all in the past. We're together now. Nothing else matters."

For a fleeting moment, Kennedy forgot about his raspy breath, about whatever physical and emotional wounds he bore and how long it would take for him to heal.

She forgot about the assignments she'd have to complete if she wanted to graduate in May. She forgot about her obligations back in Cambridge, forgot about how eager she'd so recently been to run back to her dorm.

For a fleeting moment, all those details disappeared.

Ian was alive.

He would survive.

God would heal each and every one of his wounds, both those she could see and those she couldn't.

And she would be there to pray for him and encourage him while he regained his strength, no matter what it cost her.

In that moment, she knew she loved him and he loved her.

In that moment, nothing else mattered.

CHAPTER 51

FEBRUARY 18 — "THAT'S great!"

Even though Ian had asked her not to make a big deal about it, Kennedy couldn't contain her excitement. "You're doing great," she squealed. "Keep it up."

He landed back in bed after walking three laps with his nurse around the room and collapsed, breathless, on his pillow.

"You really enjoy watching me suffer, don't you?" he asked.

"Just keep getting stronger," she said, and he promised he would try.

February 22 — "I swear if I have to eat one more hospital meal, I'm going throw my mashed potatoes against the wall, just like a VeggieTale."

"So I guess it's a good sign you're getting sassy."

"I'm not sassy. I'm hungry."

"Well, that's a good sign too. You're getting your appetite back."

He grinned at her. "Yeah, easy for you to say since you can walk yourself down to that cafeteria any time you want. And what about me? I'm wasting away here!" He laughed, still excited about the four pounds he'd gained since he arrived in Seattle.

February 24 — "Hey, no fair. You promised me you wouldn't cry."

Kennedy sniffed and tried to look cheerful. "I'm sorry. It's just going to be so hard not to see you every day."

He pulled her face close toward him and pressed her forehead against his. "Look at it this way. If you don't go back to campus now, you're not going to graduate. If you don't graduate, you're not going to med school. And if you don't make it to med school, how are you going to nurse me back to health?"

She laughed. "I certainly hope you don't expect me to wait on you like this once they discharge you from the hospital."

He stroked her hair, his eyes gleaming. "Of course I do. Why do you think I allowed myself to get so sick in the first place?"

Their smiles faded. The laughter ceased.

He cleared his throat and lowered his voice. "Go back to campus now. I'll be fine. You heard the doctor say so himself. And to be quite honest, I think you being here so much has made Connie jealous. Seriously, you'll be doing her a favor. Once you're gone, she can do nothing but take care of me all day long."

"You're so spoiled," Kennedy teased even though her heart was heavy.

"One more kiss before you go?" he asked.

"Of course."

March 3 — "Hey, you ready for our big date?"

She smiled. "Some date with you lying in bed three thousand miles away."

"Oh, great," he joked. "Way to spoil the romance. Come on. What movie are we watching tonight?"

"Well, I figured I'd give you two choices." She did her best to match his playful tone. "We could do *Mr. Smith Goes to Washington*, or if you're feeling particularly adventurous, we can watch *To Kill a Mockingbird*."

The video image of his smile on her laptop warmed her almost as much as if they'd been in the same room together.

"I could use me a good old-fashioned filibuster."

She pressed a few buttons on her computer. "Mr. Smith it is."

March 14 — "How's your appetite? Are you still gaining weight?"

"Sheesh," he whined. "You're as bad as my aunt. I swear if I don't eat three helpings of everything she's made she'll sit and literally start to cry, just like a little baby."

"Oh, she's probably just crying tears of joy that she doesn't have to hire someone else to take care of all her beloved goats while she nurses you in Seattle anymore. Are you managing the stairs to the attic okay?"

"Hey, I'm a recovering pneumonia patient with a flaming case of PTSD that gives me terrible flashbacks, but that doesn't make me a gimp."

"Really?" she teased. "Because the last time I was out there, you needed an entire cheerleading section just to make it to the toilet and back."

"Well, I always did think you'd look good in one of those short little cheerleading skirts."

"Stop it or your aunt will hear."

"Oh, she's listening right now. Say hi to Connie."

"What? Are you serious?"

His laugh rang out and echoed in her dorm room. "No, I'm joking. Now, are we going to do that Bible study or what? Or do I need to wait until next week when you come visit? Because I was planning for things to be real serious then too, but I'm not necessarily talking about the studying."

March 17 — "This has been the longest semester of my life." She leaned her head against his chest, and he ran his fingers through her hair.

"You two want some popcorn?" Connie poked her head into the living room.

"We're fine," he answered somewhat tersely.

"Well, don't forget that Kennedy's been in the air all day. Poor thing's probably starving."

"Trust me," he said, "I know what starving is, and she's not even close. Actually, wait, I better check to make sure." He tickled her ribs. "Nope. Not starving yet. But I'll let you know if that changes."

March 19 — He was laughing so hard he doubled over. "I'll never forget your face when you saw that goat just pop out. For a minute, I thought I was going to have to drop the kid and come catch you before you fainted."

"It wasn't that bad," she insisted while the newborn goat tried to suckle her finger.

"How in the world are you going to be a doctor if you get woozy at the sight of blood? Oh, never mind. You can do anything you set your mind to. I know that much about you at least."

"I wasn't woozy," she insisted. "You just didn't tell me there'd be so much blood."

"This is childbirth," he replied. "What'd you expect?"

"Something a little more sterile and a lot less messy," she answered honestly.

March 23 — It was so nice to feel the strength in his arms when he hugged her goodbye.

"I'm going to miss you," he said, speaking into the top of her head.

"I'm going to miss you too."

"Just another month, though. Then finals, and then bam. You'll be a college graduate, and we'll all be there together celebrating your bachelor's. Have I told you lately that I'm proud of you?"

"Yeah, I think I've heard that once or twice before."

He kissed her forehead. "It's true. You are the most amazing woman I've ever met. You know that, don't you?"

"More amazing than a certain Miss Abby?" she teased.

He shook his head. "I still can't believe Connie told you that whole story. But you're joking, right? You're not seriously jealous or anything are you?"

She wrapped her arms around him. "Why would I be jealous when I have you all to myself?"

He nuzzled his nose against hers. "Don't you forget it. Now go catch that plane, study hard, and I'll see you at graduation, all right?"

"All right."

She picked up her suitcase and turned to go.

"Oh, and Kennedy?"

"Yeah?"

"I love you. Have I told you that?"

"I've heard that once or twice before."

CHAPTER 52

GRADUATION DAY

"I've just got to hug you one more time." Sandy reached over and swallowed Kennedy in her embrace.

"Thanks." She glanced at the Lindgrens' clock. What was taking Ian and his grandma so long? Had they gotten lost on the way to the house?

"You looked darling in that cap and gown," Sandy said. "Feels like just yesterday you were in Cambridge on your own for the very first time. And now look at you, a real college graduate with a diploma and everything."

Kennedy didn't have the heart to tell her that the piece of paper the dean handed to her on the stage was just for show. The real thing would be mailed out to her parents' address sometime over the summer.

She glanced again at the clock.

"Where is that boy of yours?" Sandy asked.

"He'll be here soon." Carl came out from the bedroom, where he'd changed out of his collared shirt and tie, and wrapped Kennedy up in a hug just as big as his wife's had been. "We are so happy and honored that we get to share this special day with you."

"Thanks." Besides her parents, who were out picking up the cake, and Ian, who was on his way over with Grandma Lucy, Kennedy couldn't think of anyone else she'd be happier to share today with.

Woong ran out from his bedroom holding a Lego spaceship. "Pew! Pew! Pew!" he shouted. "Destroy the evil scientist!" He aimed the guns at Kennedy.

"Watch where you're pointing that thing, son," Sandy chided.

The doorbell rang. Sandy grinned at her. "That's probably your man. Go on. Open it. You look stunning, by the way, an absolute jewel."

Kennedy threw open the door. Ian and Grandma Lucy had flown in late last night. Other than a quick chat while she and her dad drove them from the airport to their hotel, she'd hardly had the chance to see him.

He squeezed her tight and lifted her off the floor. "Not bad for a man who was halfway starved just a few months ago, right?"

Kennedy giggled. When he set her down, Grandma Lucy took her hands in hers. "I am so very blessed to be here. So very blessed. I couldn't think of a more beautiful day to celebrate all your accomplishments or a more wondrous God who's brought us all together again."

CHAPTER 53

THE SUN HAD SET, and Woong was in bed by the time Sandy filled all the glasses with sparkling cider. It was almost ten, but Kennedy's whole body was reacting to the excitement of the day. She could probably go a full week without sleep.

Her dad cleared his throat and raised his glass. "To my daughter Kennedy. I know you probably hate hearing this story, but I'll never forget the day your mother and I brought you home to our tiny little apartment during the biggest blizzard on record. You were such a tiny little thing, and when I stopped at a red light, I started crying. Your mom thought it was because I was scared of being a dad, but I was overwhelmed by how beautiful and perfect you were, and I can't begin to express the way God completed my life the day you were born.

"Kensie girl, I've watched you change and grow from wanting nothing more than to become a horse trainer, to a bomb squad technician, to the first woman to travel to Mars. And I've watched the way you've handled yourself through every difficult situation God has brought your way, and believe me, it wasn't easy, especially with your mother and me on the other side of the world, only able to watch and pray."

He let out a sound that was a half laugh, half cough. "You probably won't understand this until you have kids of your own one day, but your mother and I have prayed for you so much, and today it feels like every single one of those blessings we've asked God to grant you has been fulfilled. You're a college graduate. You have a wonderful year ahead of you in Seoul before you go on to finish your training as a doctor. And as if that weren't enough, you have a strong, godly boyfriend ..."

Her mother nudged him in the side. Kennedy laughed and held up her left hand while her dad cleared his throat. "Excuse me. You have a strong, godly *fiancé* as of" — he checked his wrist — "about twenty minutes ago, and I couldn't be happier for you or prouder of the woman you are, the woman God is creating you to be."

He leaned over and gave her a hug. "Now, you and Ian probably haven't had time to formulate all your plans, but Ian, I hope you know how grateful my wife and I are to have you in Kennedy's life, and when you're not traveling the world doing your documentaries or spending time in Seoul with my daughter planning your wedding, I hope you know our home is always open to you. I've never had a son, and I have no idea what it's like to be a father-in-law either, but I'm excited for this chance to learn."

He raised his glass. "To Kennedy, with congratulations for graduating *summa cum laude*, with prayers for a safe trip to Seoul and a wonderful year serving the Lord with Korea Freedom International. And to the happy couple, may God bless you, lead you, and bring you both all the encouragement and love and wisdom you need to please him in all you do."

The guests raised their glasses and murmured their agreement.

Kennedy looked up to kiss her fiancé, and out of the corner of her eye, she saw Grandma Lucy standing in the background, arms outstretched, eyes raised toward heaven, lips forming silent prayers that seemed to surround the entire gathering before floating up to heaven, where she was certain they found their audience in the throne room of God.

Printed in the USA
CPSIA information can be obtained
at www.ICGtesting.com
LVHW092026070624
782622LV00004B/609

9 781951 834166